Seven Point Eight
The First Chronicle

Marie Harbon

ISBN 13: 978-1461072485
ISBN 10: 1461072484

© Marie Harbon 2007 – 2011 All Rights Reserved

The right of Marie Harbon to be identified as the author of this work has been asserted by her in accordance with the Copyright, Designs and Patents Act, 1988.

This book is sold subject to the condition that it shall not, by way of trade or otherwise be lent, resold, hired out, or otherwise circulated without the author's prior consent in any form of binding or cover other than that in which it is published and without a similar condition, including this condition, being imposed on a subsequent purchaser.

A copy of this work is registered with the UK Copyright Service.

Typesetting by Satori Creative
Cover by Richard Crookes
Photography by Gryphon's Egg Productions
Model: Monique Candelaria

www.satoricreative.co.uk
www.richardcrookes.co.uk
www.gryphonseggproductions.com

About The Author

Marie Harbon has worked in both the retail and fitness industry. She has a degree in sport and fitness and taught group exercise for several years before settling into a post delivering BTEC Sport courses for two years. Since then, she has instructed dance with children and has decided to focus on writing as her main career.

She wrote her first novel length story at the age of twelve and has written on and off subsequently, evolving her style and literary maturity. 'Seven Point Eight' began life as a short story in the early nineties and was later developed into a full five part series of books. Work on 'The Second Chronicle' has already begun.

Marie has two children and lives with her son and four guitars in the town of Eastwood, Nottinghamshire, which is in England. She divides her time between writing, making clothes, teaching and being a mum.

Acknowledgments

While it takes one solitary writer to actualise the initial inspiration, a polished and complete piece of work can only be attributed to a supportive team. I'd like to thank Quentin Thorpe, my first reader for without his enthusiasm and encouragement, this book would still be lurking in the files of my laptop. I'm also indebted to Chris Parkin for providing some constructive and positive feedback that has enabled me to publish a perfected piece of work.

Furthermore, I'd like to thank Richard Crookes for creating such a beautiful and stunning cover that is truly a work of art. I also extend my appreciation to Monique Candelaria for agreeing to model for the character of Tahra and to Shawn Darling of Gryphon's Egg Productions for the necessary photography. Finally, I would like to thank Sarah Holder of Satori Creative for the typesetting.

I would also like to thank all of those who have shown interest in my project each step of the way, it is much appreciated and I look forward to sharing the fruits of my labours with you.

This book could also not be complete without the research of others and I have drawn from a variety of published books. These are listed in the bibliography.

Contents

Prelude to Odyssey – Sign of the Times 11

Part One: Genesis of Genius 21
   1 Room 104 23
   2 The Establishment 30
   3 Key to the Door 64
   4 The Institute 77
   5 The Waking Dream 105
   6 The New Recruit 111
   7 Forlorn Genius 126

Part Two: Kismet 133
   8 The Nadir 135
   9 The Golden Girl 143
   10 Blood 190
   11 Pandora's Box 205
   12 The Egg 224
   13 To See the Truth 240
   14 OOBE's Birth 249

Part Three: OOBE 281
   15 A Year's Work 283
   16 Satus 291
   17 The First Time 310
   18 Long Way From Home 338
   19 Personal Experiences 358
   20 Now Recruiting 394
   21 Seventy Five 432

It is said that a long time ago, our ancestors lived in a very different world from the one we inhabit today. We understood the language of the Earth, the stars, the sky people and we knew of the Number. Life was sacred and we lived in harmony with nature.

But over time, we forgot all of this and began to feel separate from the Earth and the stars. We became lost souls, without direction and harmony was replaced with fear and distrust. The wisdom of the number was lost.

Our love of material possessions now reflect our hollow satisfaction with ourselves and the world we inhabit. We built technology to enable us to remain connected to each other, made institutions of our most sacred beliefs and manufactured chemicals to heal our bodies and grow our crops. However, the further we wandered from our true selves and nature, the more unhappy we actually became.

Yet, we retain a deep and hidden memory of everything that we ever were. There lies within us the hope that one day, we can remember that sense of harmony and connection with the Earth, the stars and the sky people.

Life is a cycle, and that which is lost will one day be found…

Prelude to Odyssey
Sign of the Times

Deep down everyone wants to be someone else, a person who is admired and perhaps respected such as Cary Grant, Winston Churchill, Mae West even or Stanley Matthews. But Dr Paul Eldridge wanted to be Albert Einstein. Or, at least be another cast from the same mould, a great scientist who would go down in history for an outstanding contribution to science. Paul wanted to make such a contribution, to see his name preserved for all posterity, to see his work published and acclaimed. He had the doctorate, the ultimate educational accolade and had devoted his life to the study of the quantum world, devouring contemporary theoretical physics as a connoisseur would consume fine food or wine. But still, recognition dangled before his eyes like crown jewels behind glass casing.

In many ways maybe he was already like Einstein, who was in fact very much a loner and considered himself to be an interesting curiosity. Very few people in the scientific community had the gall to stand out, Paul concluded. Einstein was a philosophical, almost spiritual pacifist whereas although Paul didn't truly believe in God, he wanted to. Some of what he truly believed was suppressed by his need to remain logical and rational, contradicting his Christian upbringing but he was passionate about his work and sought nothing but technological and educational advancement. He was eager and impatient to break boundaries and stretch frontiers, perhaps more of a seeker of the limelight than Einstein although no less a genius or an advocate of idiosyncrasies.

This strength of character was reflected in his proud, dignified features. He conveyed a natural sense of authority and although not particularly handsome, he was a charismatic and fascinating individual. His blue eyes were quite small with a suggestion of both wisdom and curiosity, exemplifying the ardour of his scientific interest and his willingness to communicate that. They possessed a warmth and humour but also a special intensity, as if they were the doorway to some great cosmic knowledge. His fair hair curled in an anarchistic fashion, so he kept it short to ensure absolute follicular rule. He dressed conservatively when necessary and casual when that rule didn't hold, this particular day wearing a cream shirt with neutral coloured belted chino-style trousers, acceptably smart.

Paul had been delivering a series of lectures on recent scientific discoveries at the quantum level to a small selection of universities throughout England since he had completed his doctorate in 1947, just last year in fact. They were designed to serve as an introduction to physics but mainly to propound the new theories concerning the quantum world, in the hope of enticing further students into studying the subject. Paul believed fervently that this was the future of science and that it held the clues to the many mysteries of the universe. All the lectures had been full of potential students, accompanying parents, past alumni and curious adults, dressed in a typical array of post war fashions; casual and smart suits, pencil skirts, full pleated skirts, tailored dresses, trilbies, pill box hats and real stockings. The audience usually sat and listened politely and asked sensible questions, except this lecture would become the black sheep. He was certainly filling the seats; maybe word was getting around about his colourful presentations where he would dress up as a Greek, or take an oratory ride on a photon. His delivery had been well received so far and he proceeded to reflect upon what he had lectured.

"We began our journey in Greece, fourth century B.C. when Democritis first speculated on the existence of indivisible elementary particles, which he named 'atoms'. This view prevailed and atoms were finally found in the nineteenth century. They are so small that if an apple was magnified to the size of the Earth, then the atoms in the apple would be approximately the size of the original apple. However, as we journeyed through the twentieth century, it became clear that atoms were not, in fact, unbreakable.

"We have explored the world of classical, Newtonian physics, where there is a clear and certain differentiation between matter and space, the fullness of form and the empty void, a universe which accommodated God, for He created the particles and the forces between them. But what of the more recent scientific discoveries in the realm of physics; is there still a place for God?

"Newtonian physics is perfectly adequate when we need to explain why an apple drops out of a tree, or why planets orbit the sun, but it simply cannot explain the universe at a fundamental quantum level or apply itself to the peculiar qualities of the fabric of space. The classical foundations of physics were shattered in the early part of the twentieth century, firstly by Einstein's Special Theory of Relativity and then by quantum theory. We began to accept space, not as a three but as a four dimensional fabric. What Einstein postulated in his E=MC squared hypothesis, that enormous amounts of energy are latent in all matter has been actualised in the atomic bomb.

"Today you have ridden a photon, where we discovered that time is only relative to the speed of the observer and that as we travel closer to the speed of light, time slows down. If we were to journey to the star, Sirius which is eight light years away at close to 186,000 miles per second, we would return home to find everyone much older than ourselves. Einstein also attempted to draw together space, time, matter, gravitation and electromagnetism into one unified theory but this eludes him and it remains incomplete.

"We are now able to use machines which smash apart atoms, freeing a host of new quantum characters with the discovery of new particles, the electron, proton and neutron with the latter two making up the atomic nucleus and the electron in surrounding orbits. There is also the lepton; a type of particle residing outside the atomic nucleus that demonstrates a weak interaction, the electron is an example and then we have the strongly interacting particles, such as the meson which has just been discovered this year, these reside within the nucleus. Many of these are transient beings, who once freed, decay.

"The strangest thing about looking into an atom is that its solidity is, in fact an illusion. The nucleus within the atom compares to a fly in a cathedral, and that leaves us with an awful lot of empty space. Over ninety percent of an atom is missing and over ninety percent of the universe is empty space too. We are now beginning to peel away and penetrate the bottom layers of our reality; will we yet discover smaller and smaller particles?

"We have also revealed that particles appear to have twins; for each quantum character, there is an anti-particle. This anti-matter, when it collides with our matter is capable of producing an enormous explosion. Perhaps one day we will be able to generate and contain anti-matter, or we may discover even stranger particles, such as the theoretical tachyon which travels faster than light and potentially, backwards in time.

"This brings us to the world of quantum weirdness; where the universe exists as an infinite number of possibilities within a quantum soup, having no precise location or being until something happens to lock one of those possibilities into place. This is known as Heisenberg's Uncertainty Principle and was postulated in 1927. When a photon is fired at a plate with two slits, a striped pattern emerges, suggesting that it is wave-like and has passed through both slits simultaneously. But if we observe and measure which slit the photon passes through, it chooses a definite pathway and behaves like a particle. When we observe something, we turn quantum possibilities into reality; we see the version that we have focused on. It suggests too that we can, in fact be in two places at once!

"And finally, I introduced electro-magnetism, which holds atoms together, gives us sunlight and fires synapses in the brain so that we may think, feel and move. It is conveyed by photons, better known as light and the exchange of photons generates the electro-magnetic force. Quantum Electrodynamics links quantum theory with electro-magnetism and our particle cast of characters plays a key role.

"I conclude this session with a question; where is quantum theory taking us? Will our reality be further shattered, will our quantum experiences break the bottom of the proverbial pail, is the world changing beyond recognition? What applications will we find for this new knowledge? And where, if any place whatsoever, is there room for God? Any questions?"

The audience was briefly silent, most had just drifted off into their own universe, either parallel, quantum or classical. A flashbulb fired, the camera of which was pointed at Paul but was also capturing the audience for posterity. It was an audience that seemed reluctant to part with any of their deepest thoughts and queries, creating an almost embarrassing silence. Most lectures were never short of those willing to attempt the opening of Pandora's Box, to be oppositional or controversial, to challenge the contemporary notions of science.

Then finally someone spoke up, a fairly unassuming man in his early twenties who appeared to be bamboozled by the lecture.

"You said that atoms are full of empty space. Explain to me why things look and feel solid."

Paul smiled, it was a difficult concept to comprehend.

"Okay," he began. "The nucleus and electrons inside the atom jiggle about in a state of excitation, they vibrate. It's this vibration that gives the appearance of solidity."

"I still don't understand," the man responded.

"Well, think of a bicycle wheel... inside are spokes which represent the solid matter, with space in between, right?" The man nodded so Paul continued. "When the wheel spins fast, the spokes blur and look solid and if you touch it, it repels your fingers and feels completely solid as you couldn't pass your hand right through it, yes? When the wheel isn't spinning, it is solid no more."

The man nodded, indicating he was no longer as bamboozled.

"So, if the nucleus and electrons stopped jiggling, we can walk through walls?"

"Theoretically!" Paul exclaimed.

The audience laughed.

"But," the man added, "What's in the empty space?"

Now that was a question without a satisfactory answer.

"It simply appears to be empty space," he replied. "We don't know what it contains, if anything at all."

"Isn't it full of the ether?" the man countered.

Paul smiled.

"Science considers the ether to be an archaic concept, akin to hogwash. It originated with the Greeks and referred to a universal field of energy that connects everything, it was the air breathed by the Gods. Pythagoras and Aristotle saw it as the fifth element of creation, along with air, fire, water and Earth. Many of the greatest minds in history believed in the ether, saying it was necessary for the laws of physics to work. Einstein stated that without ether there would be no propagation of light and no possibility of standards of space and time."

"Well, if so many great minds believed in it, why isn't it an accepted part of science?" the man questioned.

"Because science requires proof, not faith. In 1887, two gentlemen set up an experiment to prove the existence of ether. Just we're able to detect a breeze blowing a field of corn, they proposed that it was possible to detect the ether in a similar way. They shot two rays of light simultaneously in different directions, thinking that one ray would experience resistance in the way that when we say, cycle into the wind, our progress is slowed. However, no ether wind was detected and the hypothesis was disproved. This result has hindered the concept of ether in its quest to be taken seriously."

The audience looked fascinated and the man nodded appreciatively, listening attentively.

"Do you believe in the ether, Dr Eldridge?"

Paul looked thoughtful then replied, "I would have to concur with Konrad Finagle; if we took the empty space away from the universe, everything would crunch together into a volume no larger than a speck of dust. Whatever lies in that empty space stops everything happening in the same place."

Then someone else stepped forward, a woman who he could have sworn was never in the audience but nonetheless spoke as if she had listened intently to the whole lecture. She was tall and rather striking with hair as black as ebony swept up in an elegant 40s chignon and, oddly, she wore a pair of large sunglasses. Her clothing was typical of the war years and around her neck was tied an exquisite red, silk scarf. Strangely for the period and her manner of dress, she was also rather Mediterranean skinned, ethnicity uncertain.

"Doctor Eldridge, why didn't Einstein finish his Unified Field Theory?"

The audience looked uncomfortable as the question was spoken with an unaccustomed authority and confidence, for a woman so many thought.

Paul stood staring at her momentarily, her directness made him feel a combination of discomfort and admiration.

"I think maybe he realised what an enormous undertaking it was, to develop a single theory that explains not only the electromagnetic, gravitational and nuclear forces, but incorporates relativity in addition." He chose to address her as a scientist and not just merely as a woman. "Possibly the mathematical equations were not adding up, so to speak, I believe he simply wasn't satisfied with his theory and abandoned it. He may yet complete it, wouldn't it be wonderful, a theory to explain everything, that allows everything we know to suddenly fall into place?"

"I see what you're saying, but do you think he thought the world wasn't ready?"

Paul had never contemplated the sociological pitfalls.

"In what way? I think physicists are already accepting the new reality, we are very open-minded. Our perceptions of what we believe to be real and illusory are altering rapidly."

"Perceptions of reality… there are many, many levels of reality… I mean ready to use the knowledge wisely."

The latter implications of that statement were overlooked in favour of her first comment, she actually mentioned multiple levels of reality. His mind almost drifted then he re-aligned himself with her intended train of enquiry. Paul had never really thought of anything other than philosophical or scientific applications for quantum theory, or electro-magnetic research. The ethical, psychological and sociological considerations had received little thought. Had any of this knowledge ever fallen into the wrong hands? What would happen if that was the case? Most of his peers simply wanted to comprehend creation, the universe, its structure, its alpha and omega.

"Have you heard of the Philadelphia Experiment?" she continued.

Paul didn't want to admit in front of his audience that he hadn't so he replied, "Please, enlighten us."

"A few years ago, the American Navy conducted an experiment, to make a destroyer class ship radar invisible. It not only made the ship invisible to radar, it made the ship invisible to the human eye. The ship vanished and some say it re-appeared in Chesapeake Bay, others say it briefly visited another reality."

The audience began to react with incredulity but Paul tried to remain open minded. It was hard to believe though.

"How was this achieved? If this is true, why is this not more widely applied, or to that matter, why hasn't the study been published?"

"Something went wrong, although the experiment was a success, the men were failures and their minds couldn't cope with the experience. The study was never published as it was a top secret experiment."

Paul sincerely wanted to ask her whether this was indeed true but also how she claimed to have gained access to knowledge of top secret information. Instead, he asked another question because he was genuinely curious but also to attempt to debunk the claims.

"How was invisibility achieved?"

"By means of a powerful electro-magnetic field," she answered.

Now that came under his jurisdiction, so to speak. Could it be possible?

"Could you explain in more detail?" Paul queried, hoping to blow her ruse.

"The experiment was based upon Einstein's Unified Field Theory and involved the use of naval type magnetic generators called degaussers. They pulsed at resonant frequencies to create a tremendous magnetic field on and around the ship. As there are three planes of space, there were three fields; the first two created at right angles to each other and the third produced by the magnetic pulses, through resonance. The use of powerful magnetic resonance is equivalent to obliteration in our dimension while the field is in operation and our delicate human minds are not ready for this."

Paul was speechless at her technical competence. Where did this information come from? Now he desperately wanted to know.

"We should be very careful how we use new knowledge," she added. "There are consequences."

"Just look at the atomic bomb!" a middle aged man interjected. "I'm sure Einstein doesn't sleep well at night anymore, if he hadn't written E=MC squared on a blackboard at the turn of the century, think of the thousands of people who would still be alive today. And not to mention Pierre Curie tried to warn the world of the effects of radiation!"

An Indian man, who had so far remained quiet now spoke

up. "When Oppenheimer watched the first atomic blast at Alamogordo, he said *'if the radiance of a thousand suns were to burst at once in the sky that would be like the splendour of the Mighty One... I am become Death, the Destroyer of Worlds.'*"

"The Mahabharata..." Paul mused.

Another man now spoke out loudly, clearly and confidently. The Mediterranean skinned woman who had discussed the invisibility experiment turned to look and appeared to recognise the new speaker, although he did not acknowledge her. He had listened intently to Paul throughout the lecture and remained thoughtful during the open question session but now he had a burning question to ask.

"Dr Eldridge, I find your lecture and quantum physics fascinating. May I pose a philosophical question?"

"I'm open to any question a person may wish to ask," Paul replied, watching the woman who had just disclosed a top secret project to him begin to walk towards the door.

"These electromagnetic fields and quantum particles you spoke of," the questioner continued, "and even the ether... could they form the basis of the human soul?"

Now that was the question of the millennium. How could he reply to that? Yet it was not that query that aroused his curiosity, it was the tantalising possibility of an improbable experiment that could potentially reveal another layer of reality. He briefly answered the philosophical question to the best of the ability then he excused himself so he could follow the woman. But when he ran through the door, she was nowhere in sight. It was as if she had disappeared into thin air.

Part One
The Genesis of Genius

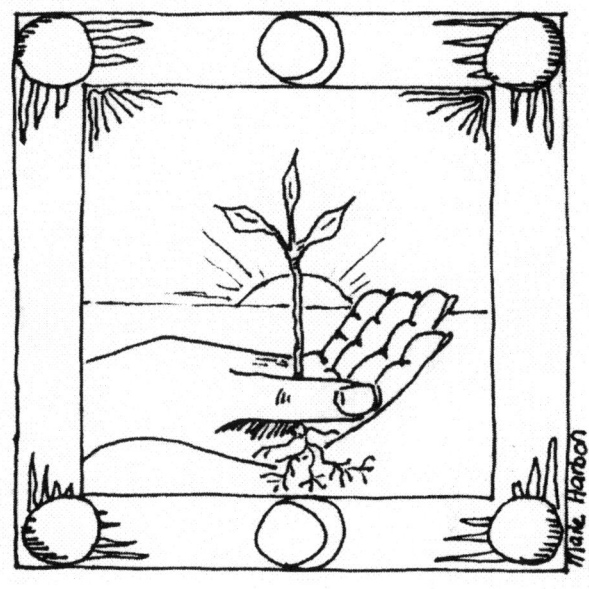

I cannot but regard the ether, which can be the seat of an electromagnetic field with its energy and vibrations, as endowed with a certain degree of substantiality, however different it may be from all ordinary matter.

Hendrik Lorentz, physicist, 1906

1
Room 104

The London underground was a sinister place to be when you knew you were being followed, even more so for a woman travelling alone. It wasn't the first time this had happened, this expedition being the third of its kind but the situation was becoming more and more disturbing each time. Whoever was following her always seemed ambiguous and at times almost inhuman, often fading into shadow but mostly amorphous.

She jumped on a train on the Victoria Line and instantly felt safer, being surrounded by a heady concoction of commuters, tourists and Londoners going about their daily business, accompanied by the smell of sweat and perfume. It was easy to hide amongst them, especially during busy times, to cling to a rail or challenge your balance by relying on muscular strength to resist the rapid acceleration and deceleration of the train. However it was not as straightforward trying to avoid being jammed against the men with formidable body odour, or to resist the temptation to read someone else's newspaper or book. Before long she arrived at her stop and jumped off, ever aware of whatever it was in pursuit.

Often she caught the scent of flowers at this point in the journey; a classical looking matriarch with long dark hair was watering hanging baskets at the front of her house. She always smiled, which was comforting especially when being pursued. Each time she passed, the matriarch was performing some chore, or chatting to a neighbour. Once or twice there had been children at the door too, a few in their teens and a younger boy who would hide behind the matriarch, unsure what to think.

As she walked through a park, the next stage of the journey, she encountered the black man playing football with his two teenage boys. They were often involved in a vociferous tackle or simply dribbled the ball towards two trees which were the goal posts. In the same park was the elderly gentleman walking a multitude of dogs, who would always tip his hat to her. Finally, the same forty-something man sat on a bench, watching her intently, contemplating whether to approach and perhaps afraid to initiate. He was always curious and either partially hid behind a book or sipped tea in a polystyrene cup. Vague memories plagued her, suggesting she had encountered this man before but she could not recollect where, when or why.

He appraised her, this lithe young woman who often looked troubled. She carried about her a quiet dignity with an introspective demeanour, internally preoccupied with some great secret or purpose. Yet she had an interest in people and a deep curiosity regarding others, she was intrigued rather than afraid; that the man could see. She had a sensuality that was inviting and not threatening, coupled with a compassionate aura. Somewhat untamed, golden hair shone in the late summer sun and curled down past her shoulders. She had an olive tint to her skin, as if she originated from the Mediterranean and her face had a soft, oval shape. A young student with spiked hair gave her a second glance as she walked past but she paid no attention to him, she was too preoccupied with the purpose of her journey. She locked eyes with the man on the park bench for a moment and there was a hint of affection in his eyes, but, she thought, 'he's too old for me'.

Was it a comfort or just plain spooky that she encountered the same people on each journey? The big question was: were all these people actually acknowledging her or was it just her imagination? She didn't want to be extraordinary, or to stand out; she merely wanted to contribute something extraordinary, something that stood out, there was a difference. That was probably the reason she chose to be a scientist, her particular specialism had the potential to understand what it was to be human and how to become a more effective being. Could it be her work that attracted this undeserved interest from these unknown faces? She would soon become involved in a critical project that was unprecedented in contemporary science, but how would these people know that? They wouldn't. It was her imagination, had to be, unless her pursuer knew.

As she drew closer to her destination an overall disheartened emotion took over. She arrived at an austere building which had that effect on her, akin to an architectural vampire and it bled the energy of other people too. Even the design resembled fangs and it exemplified sobriety, bearing down upon the miniscule human ants that swarmed around its base. It was an institution specifically for people with severe psychological problems, who had been sectioned because they were a danger to themselves and to others. Furthermore, it housed a number of inmates who were certified criminally insane. The thing that disturbed her the most was the fact that one of her relatives was a permanent resident here.

The place amplified her feelings of being watched and every fissure, every crack in its stone structure seemed to haunt her, harbouring some presence or aftershock of a catastrophe. Walls appeared to have faces which were stark and non-human, corridors felt active with people passing through as if it were a busy high street, even though no bodies could be seen and the corridors were in fact, empty. Light seemed to have a life of its own, it danced a cosmic waltz in a sinuous fashion and intertwined with the dark shadows. Was it the people here or the place itself that was insane? Did its aura drive sane people crazy in insane places?

This was the most difficult thing she had to do in her life, it broke her heart to see her sister in that catatonic state but she was compelled to be here. At the outset of each journey she swore it would be the last time. Each time she would brush her sister's hair and talk about events in the world, something funny that had happened or what she had been doing all week but the conversation was always one-sided. Each visit she wished something would change, or that there would be a cure. She never let herself cry until she left because she wanted the time with her sister to be a happy experience but when she did finally release the tears, she was not only weeping for her sister, but also for herself. Her recent feelings of being watched, faces in the walls and aberrant lights made her fear for her own sanity. The fear was of becoming her sister.

She reached the reception where a rather matronly woman recognised her. Despite this, the woman announced herself and the name of her sister.

"Hi, it's Ava Kavanagh and I've come to see Maria Martinez."

She signed into the visitors' book, which was then replaced behind the desk where it belonged and she was escorted to the low security wing. It sat at the end of a long corridor, which was not well-lit but even so, the light twisted acrobatically across the walls, as if projected by car headlights. Ava behaved as if the situation was normal, as not to attract undue attention to her erstwhile grasp of reality.

The route to Maria's room passed some rather unusual residents and each time, Ava had glanced through the window in their door, very inquisitive as to what their story was. The first curiosity was a dark haired man who was always surrounded by reams of paper and this time, the woman felt a strong desire to enquire about him.

"Is he a writer or something?" she asked.

Her escort smiled.

"We call him The Scribbler, as the only way we can manage his behaviour is to give him access to paper and a pen. He writes constantly, but it's all gibberish, rows and rows of symbols."

Ava gave him a lingering glance, feeling a sense of sadness

regarding his predicament. It was such a waste of human life.

They passed another character, a blonde haired woman with an intense and seething look on her face. This time she wasn't restrained although she crouched on her bed with a menacing expression on her face and when she saw Ava, she snarled.

"What's wrong with her, if you don't mind me asking?"

Her escort acquiesced to her questioning.

"Schizophrenia, she hears voices which she claims instruct her to do evil. She enjoys inflicting pain on others, so we have to isolate her."

Ava made eye contact with her, which sent a chill down her spine.

"She reminds me of the girl from The Exorcist," she said.

They turned the corridor and there were two more people that Ava felt drawn to; a black man and woman who resided in the same room. They appeared to be actors in a play of their own making.

"Lost in their own little world, aren't they?" she commented.

"We call them The Time Travellers, as they always insist they've travelled to the past and future. Most of the time they're locked in an imagery scenario, living some other reality. We keep them together, as their behaviour is much more manageable if we do so."

The final curiosity that Ava had to ask about was a man with fair hair who could often be seen punching at the walls, or shouting for books. He was oblivious to their presence and Ava's gaze and on this day, he was stood in front of a wall and was reaching out to touch it with his fingers.

"What is he doing?" Ava asked.

"He believes he can walk through walls," her escort explained. "My, we've had some bruises over the years. I don't know what's worse, his wall or his book obsession."

They passed through some double doors, which required a security code to gain entry into the next corridor. There, they soon found room 104 and the escort opened the door for Ava.

"You're Maria's second visitor today. In fact, she's been very popular just lately."

Ava found it quite strange that Maria had received other visitors, just who exactly would want to put themselves through the torment, suffer the intense and foreboding, unforgiving atmosphere of this austere prison? In the back of her mind, she wondered if some blood relatives had made contact or perhaps their biological father, they surely must be the only people interested in the sad figure in room 104 who now existed in a persistent vegetative state. She looked like once a fire had burned within her but was long extinguished. Ava wished more than ever to see their real family.

She entered the room and her catatonic sister sat in a chair. One could only wonder, just what had driven her sister to be incarcerated in the low security wing of a psychiatric institution? No one had ever told her the reason, the events that signed her death sentence and cemented the course of her life. What had caused the persistent vegetative state and was this the reason she was here or had something criminal happened to place her here and the institution had literally destroyed her mind? Ava had noticed on the first visit that Maria bore scars on her wrists, what had compelled her to do this to herself?

But there was another pressing issue for Ava, her own perceptions and misgivings about what was real and what was a hallucination. Were her own new, disturbing experiences the beginning of a progression into the same never-never land? Was this how Maria's descent into hell began?

Ava spent an hour in room 104, today just holding her sister out of despair for both her relative and herself. There were so many questions to ask, a number of burning issues but all the solutions lay within Maria, who would never be in a position to tell. She had asked the staff of the institution a few times but they knew little as Maria had been transferred from another facility, who revealed only the fact that she was a danger to herself and to others. That fact seemed hard to believe in light of the vegetative state she now sat in, and Maria had been in this institution for at least three years. During all that time, as told by the staff, she had never responded to any external stimuli. What transpired before would remain a mystery, as the records were sadly, mislaid. Ava felt deeply frustrated at the lack of history of Maria, it was as if someone did not want her background to be known.

Once the hour had passed, she left feeling even more angry and upset. To know that there had been other visitors aroused her curiosity but to be told that the identity of these visitors was confidential incensed her more. As Maria's only relative, she had the right to know. As she left, someone watched her go, a person who lurked in the corridor, unhindered and unquestioned by the staff.

She now retraced her steps via the Victoria Line and was relieved to find that whoever had previously followed her was thankfully absent. Her journey to the institution failed to unhinge her so maybe the pursuer had given up, or found a more vulnerable target. It was still a relief to turn the key in her front door and collapse on the sofa in her flat. She closed her eyes and tried to dissolve today's frustration through positive thinking but didn't totally succeed. Rather than cook a meal, she decided to grab a takeaway. Only when she opened her handbag did she notice something that certainly didn't belong to her, or any of her flatmates. In fact, she was certain it had not been in her bag before she left the flat. She was staring at a red, silk scarf. How had it found its way into her bag and why did she feel it held some personal meaning for her? This innocent little object disturbed her greatly.

2
The Establishment

Writing my memoirs is a bizarre thing to do, I am not famous, no one would recognise either my face or my name yet I have led a full, enriched and most peculiar life. I would hardly believe it myself and these memoirs may read like a work of science fiction yet I feel compelled to put pen to paper, or finger to typewriter to record the absurdities of my life. Maybe this will help me put things into perspective and understand why events progressed as they did, why everything I cared about was lost and what the future may hold for me.

I was born in St Albans on the 21st February 1921 at 11.30 a.m. Greenwich Mean Time. It was a year that was not particularly memorable, although in the space of my first 12 months of life, the Communist Party was formed in China, the first flight was made in a helicopter and the Irish Free State was formed. The movie industry was a fledgling one and dominated by stars such as Charlie Chaplin, Rudolph Valentino, Douglas Fairbanks and Mary Pickford, although at that stage in its journey, the movies were silent of course.

I weighed about seven and a half pounds from what I've been told. As a baby I apparently appeared to be very alert and active, with white blonde hair and a mischievous aura. My father was Peter Eldridge, for many years he was headmaster of a local grammar school and eventually died of lung cancer, most likely as a result of excessive pipe tobacco. That forms one of my strongest memories of early childhood, I would stand in the sitting room doorway, and from beyond the back of his favourite armchair I would see the smoke puffing, twisting and writhing in the air. The house always smelt strongly of pipe tobacco. A cup of Earl Grey tea would always accompany the pipe, they were like an old married couple in themselves. He was an excellent parent though, I wouldn't have attained all I have without his influence and drive. I inherited his fair hair, enthusiasm for learning and his piercing blue eyes. My mother was Margaret Eldridge, nee Roberts, a proud and honourable woman and a conspicuous red-head. She outlived my father by several years and died quite simply from heart failure. I inherited her compassion, humour and strong constitution. She was a very religious woman and inherently charitable, active in the community and a church regular. My spiritual leanings are a direct result of her influence.

Childhood was a happy experience as we were a closely knit family. I was not the only child, being the youngest of three. Patricia was the oldest, auburn haired and bossy; Philip was the second, quiet and thoughtful; and then there was me, Paul Alexander Eldridge. I stood out, not in my appearance or dress, or anything like that but I was unusually bright, almost a child prodigy. This did not make me popular with my peers at school, except for a boy called Rupert who wore glasses and always had a runny nose; he was my friend, perhaps because I helped him with his homework. Therefore, my siblings were extremely important to me. They accepted me, even though I received more attention than they, perhaps because they knew they were all I had and mother instilled in all of us a sense of Christian charity.

We moved to London very early in my life so that my father could take up the position of headmaster at the Grammar School where he worked until his retirement. Therefore this great city provides many of my formative memories: I vaguely recall the Thames flooding in 1928 and people wading in dirty water up to their knees in the streets, not a pleasant experience in winter. The water reached the downstairs windowsills, lapped around the wheels of the Austin 7 family cars that were sparsely parked and broke embankment walls in places. The floodwater had an eerie stillness at night, illuminated by gas street lamps in places.

I also clearly remember the excitement of our first rotary dial telephone, as I would frequently get into trouble accidentally on purpose calling the operator on the manual switchboard as I would play with the dial a little too often. They were a very polite bunch of women, those operators and my first experience of chatting up the female of the species.

It was an era where home comforts were very basic indeed. You would sleep in your jumpers and big socks and your bed would be layered with blankets because there was no heating in your room and in the winter, there'd be a layer of ice on the inside of your window. The covers and clothes created such cosiness that you were extremely reluctant to throw the blankets off in the morning and place your feet on the cold lino which covered the floor. You did everything in the kitchen; ate, drank, chatted, washed in a tin bath in front of the open fire and listened to the wireless. Toilets were outside and incredibly draughty places in the winter. No one locked their doors, children played outside in the street, babies were parked outside the front door in their perambulators and children were rigorously disciplined at home and school. If you got into trouble with the teacher, your parents would find out and you'd get another dose of discipline at home too. At Christmas, you would find an orange, some nuts and a small piece of chocolate in the stocking at the foot of the bed.

I was fortunate to grow up in a decade that had a great buzz and vibe about it too. My mother loved jazz music, which signalled more hopeful times after the conclusion of the First World War and it was then the dance halls became popular. She was fascinated with the wireless, otherwise known as the radio and it would play often in the kitchen, where she would attempt to encourage my father to dance with her. I recall him having two left feet, much to her consternation. She loved the movies too and sometimes, Patricia would look after my brother and I while my parents would catch the latest talkie.

As a child I had an aptitude for science and mathematics, not jazz music or dance and father was quick to seize upon this. There was never a shortage of books and scientific toys, my father also used to provide additional education for me at home then finally, he saved enough money to send me to an outstanding school which could offer me the opportunities I required. Mother was always at odds with science, she could never accept evidence no matter how strong a case it put forward. She had instilled in me the importance of God as a foundation to life, ethical issues always returned to God whenever I questioned them, like some moral boomerang so consequently, I always found it difficult to reconcile my scientific and mathematical knowledge with the concept of God. Initially, I could believe that some intelligent being created the people, trees, animals, the land and the sea, which is a fine and simplistic concept for a young child but soon, almost too soon I questioned how this was possible in six days. It wasn't long before atoms entered my life and I could accept that maybe God controlled them, despite the infinite quantity that must inhabit the universe. But then I had to question where God was located, in the great void of space, a paradise in the sky? Indeed, was He a He after all? I'm still looking for Him in my own way but since my childhood I have come to accept that the universe is not as ordered as Einstein hoped. There is chaos and uncertainty, and these discoveries led me to simply search for any kind of intelligence, or cosmic presence at all in the seething froth of quantum life.

Anyway, it was inevitable that I graduated with a first class honours degree in physics, in 1942, in the midst of World War Two, more specifically during the Battle of Midway. America was by now embroiled in the war and their troops were arriving in Europe, yet to liberate it. I achieved part of my destiny to the sounds of 'We'll Meet Again' and films such as 'Casablanca', 'Bambi' and 'Yankee Doodle Dandy'. It was also inevitable that I met the love of my life while at university. She was, to me, a classic English rose, tall, with long blonde hair and porcelain skin. Her name was Madeleine and she was smart, funny, sensitive, compassionate and caring. I knew, on our first date that I would marry her and only shortly after, we were engaged. Her family were wonderful and lived in Kent, they adored me. We were to marry as soon as I completed my degree and she wished to start a family. But that did not come to pass, those plans were scuppered long before the completion of my studies as she became a casualty of the war and was killed during an air raid attack. Air raids began on 'Black Saturday', which was the 7th September 1940 and they continued for around 2 months. Madeleine died on the 10th October 1940 on her way to the underground to take shelter while I was already safe in my parents' Anderson Shelter, listening to the shrieking roar of the blitz get closer and closer, the thumping of the bombs, with the possibility of being blown to bits at any moment. So far in my life there had been a *semblance of order, absolute order with everything being so predictable it was actually unreal. Despite the war, my destiny had been clear. Perhaps it was inevitable that chaos would rear its ugly head, ironic for a scientist who studied the very nature of uncertainty and quantum probabilities.*

But I didn't know how to grieve, I am a male after all, even at the funeral I felt unable to show any emotion and even in my private life, I would just sit quietly with our favourite songs playing in the background. We had enjoyed Glenn Miller, Duke Ellington and the songs of Cole Porter, to name a few. Contemplation was my drug, I would spend hours reflecting and evaluating the course of my life so far and how my destiny had changed in one fell swoop. Just what would I do with the rest of my life with no wife or children to provide for? I needed a purpose so although I was devastated, I immersed myself in the completion of my degree and endeavoured to undertake a PhD scholarship in quantum mechanics. At the time, this seemed heartless and disrespectful to her memory but the truth of the matter was that I needed a reason to continue with my life. If it wasn't for the study I probably would have drowned myself in the Thames and I couldn't put my family through that torment. So as Londoners became more defiant and strengthened their resolve in the war effort, I made intellectual pursuits my purpose in life while they aerially bombarded Germany.

My research began in 1943, which was a monumental step for me and the zenith of intellectualism. That same year, there was synchronous research of iconic status; in Auschwitz Josef Mengele was torturing twins in grotesque investigations into heredity; Erwin Schrodinger was lecturing at Trinity College, attempting to understand chromosomes and life and DNA was also being identified as the manifestation of heredity. Of course, no one then could conceive of DNA's structure, remember, it was infantile research as of then. My research focused on electro-magnetic fields, others had a passion for biological life whereas I was more interested in cosmic life, the building blocks and forces of the universe.

Aside from my scholarship, love did not figure in my life, I did not develop a close relationship with another woman. Of course, I dated a number of women albeit briefly, but they weren't Madeleine and I couldn't bring myself to fall in love again. It didn't matter to me, my peers would ask me, 'don't you crave a woman, don't you want a wife and a family?' No, I didn't, if anything I was in love with my work. Quantum mechanics filled my life with meaning; I felt closer to understanding the universe and even thought I may find some faint whisper of spiritual life within the cosmos. That didn't actually happen, that would have been too good to be true. However, during this period in my life, the war in Europe and then Japan was over and there was much celebration in the land. I became part of the real world again and joined in the singing and dancing, the relief of the finality of the conflict, but grief for the thousands and thousands of Jews who were exterminated in the Nazi death camps and the destruction of two Japanese cities by atomic bomb. The sense of hope that Germany was defeated and all was right with the world was tinged by the fear that we were developing fearsome weapons with the capacity to wipe out mankind.

I completed my PhD in 1947 shortly before the pilot Chuck Yeager broke the sound barrier in flight, attaining a speed of 670mph, just over Mach 1 that is. Along with my research I began to feel like many boundaries were soon to be exceeded. In retrospect, my thinking was correct but at the time, I had no idea to what extent this would be true.

Soon after my doctorate, I fell into lecturing, as teachers often do, 'just fall' into the profession. 1948 was a key year for me in many ways, I'd finally started a real job at the ripe old age of twenty eight and it was also an important year historically; over in India Ghandi was shot, the new state of Israel came into being, the Soviet Union's blockade of Berlin began, the Kinsey Report into the Sexual Behaviour of the Human Male was published and London staged the Olympic Games, as no other city wanted to or could afford to act as host. Not surprisingly, Germany and Japan were banned from competing in this post-war era.

But 1948 was an important indicator in signifying the path that my life would take in the future. The science faculty wished to recruit more students and asked me to promote new developments in quantum theory as a way to increase their roll. This was a fantastic opportunity, one I did not refuse. It was at the last lecture that a significant person entered my life. He sat quietly throughout the lecture, a dark-haired, well dressed man. His question was the last: 'Could atomic particles form the basis of the human soul?' That was the basic gist of it. Now science had never contemplated the existence of this archaic concept, or, to be more precise, ever taken the idea seriously. My reply was not a conclusive one, 'I don't recall any studies concerning a human soul.' To which he pressed, 'But isn't it possible?' I had never contemplated searching for the human soul. 'How could it be observed, measured?' I responded. 'Our reality has always been gauged by the things around us we can see and touch or observe, matter comprised of atoms, of neutrons and electrons. The soul is neither. However, quantum physics is taking us into a new dimension entirely, it is feasible science will find a solution to the perpetual problem of the human soul.' I thought very little of this interaction at the time, more concerned with a mysterious woman who divulged the details of a top secret experiment but the questioner continued to ponder as I concluded the lecture.

Following the snapshot lectures, I became completely engrossed in my teaching job. It was a fulfilling role and I was able to devote my full attention to the position, especially as I had no spouse to consider or support. A year into my teaching post, I received a visit, one I would see in retrospect as being life changing, the kind we ultimately realise as harbingers of destiny.

The students were leaving the lecture theatre when a man Paul vaguely recognised entered the room. He had dark hair that had a smidgeon of wave; it gave the appearance of being tended by an expensive stylist despite being a typical 40s cut. His eyes were quite small and brown, they seemed quite placid and gentle in some ways but also hard and pragmatic. Overall he was actually a very handsome man with an intriguing sexual charisma. He had a suggestion about him of charm and good, albeit luxurious taste and he wore a typical 1940s suit, which concealed a naturally muscular torso. He sat down at the back of the theatre and waited patiently for Paul to collate his notes, when Paul began to head towards the exit, he spoke.

"Do you remember me?"

Paul hesitated, trying to place him. "Yes, I believe you attended one of my lectures over a year ago."

"My name's Max Richardson," he introduced himself and they shook hands, his was a firm grip. "Do you remember the question I asked you?" he added.

Unfortunately Paul didn't at that particular moment in time, perhaps at the time it didn't stand out or fire his interest, either that or it made him feel uncomfortable.

"I wanted to understand the complexities of the human soul, define it, measure it, prove it exists," Max continued. "And you never really answered my question."

He remembered finding that comment amusing. "I may be a genius, but I don't know the physics of the human soul. Applications of quantum theory for the purpose of scientific advancement, more up my street."

"And you think that's not my line of pursuit?"

"Why are you here?" Usually Paul warmed to people easily but this particular person had an odd aura about him that was difficult to place.

"To offer you an opportunity," he ventured.

One part of him was content teaching undergraduates and infecting others with his scientific enthusiasm, the other part of him was ambitious and keen to be challenged. He had always found it difficult to refuse an opportunity, if anything he admitted his impetuousness could be a liability but so far, he had made the right decisions.

"You have a religious background," Max stated, confident of his facts. "I can tell by the way you spoke of the cosmos, it is tinged by childhood ideologies of God impressed upon you by, most likely your family. In your lecture, you have expressed a desire to find God in the cosmological equation, so to speak. But yet, you profess the advancement of science is the single most important quest for mankind. How do you reconcile these... antitheses?"

The answer was clear and simple. "I don't."

"Have you ever had the opportunity to discover something deeply spiritual in your research, your work?"

Paul replied quite cynically. "Science does everything it can to disprove that there is anything beyond the material world."

Max continued, with a tinge of regret in his voice. "I have been involved in scientific research that has placed me in a wealthy position, not the sort of work that I'm proud of. War creates the need to experiment, to bring about destruction of the enemy, to defend your country using whatever measures necessary. But it has also placed me in a position to divert some funding to posing some much needed spiritual questioning. I think you're the man to undertake this. You have spiritual desire, enthusiasm but also a scientific, enquiring mind that cries out for evidence. I'm the businessman, the shrewd investor. You're the genius, the child prodigy, the anathema to this sterile, reductionist world. I agree, science would like to destroy God but I believe it is possible to prove the existence of the human soul, to comprehend consciousness, to unite quantum reality with the realm of mysticism."

Paul was stunned. Max didn't portray himself as some kind of philanthropist at first and he wasn't entirely convinced of his motives but he had allied himself with Paul's frustrations and aspirations. He had tempted him with the correct bait and he was ready to be reeled in.

"Would this role be as a research fellow?" Paul tried to ascertain how profitable this venture would be, as spiritual as he wished to be, he had his dreams of scientific glory.

"You will only have me to answer to. Regard yourself as autonomous, I have a set fund and you can prioritise the research, within the boundaries of my objectives"

Paul laughed, but not mockingly. "This sounds too good to

be true."

"Maybe this is something you were always meant to do."

This was too good an opportunity but Paul also felt a certain responsibility towards his students.

"I'm halfway through the last semester. Let me see out the end of the academic year then count me in."

Max respected his loyalties. "Here's my telephone number. I'll be expecting to hear from you soon."

Paul handed in his resignation not too long after; it was not an opportunity to be passed over.

Paul's first day at Max Richardson's research facility was on a fine day at the end of August 1950. It was synonymous with a new decade, there was definitely a fresh path waiting to be trod. Technology was picking up in pace with the first live broadcast by the BBC of pictures across the Channel, although the world was not at peace; British troops were arriving in Korea, America was filled with Communist paranoia in the McCarthy witch-hunts and disaster struck in Penmaenmawr when 6 were killed in a train collision. Nevertheless, Paul Eldridge was hopeful.

The journey took him through several sleepy Surrey villages, where early in the journey, he saw the paperboys performing their daily duties and the postmen out on their first delivery, in their shirt and tie and flat peaked caps. As the morning progressed, the milkmen were making deliveries from a hand pulled cart, cheerful in the late summer sunshine and horse-drawn drays transported coal to homes, men with black hands and faces lugging sacks of coal and emptying them down the coal holes into the cellars below. By now, people either rode their bicycles to work or walked their children to the shops, wearing their smart summer coats, flat caps and short trousers. The bakers and butchers were opening their shops, ready for the day's business and the first housewives were waiting to secure their daily requirement of bread and meat; times were austere, war time restrictions were still in place and these things were still rationed even though the war had concluded five years ago.

He arrived a little later that morning at a location in Surrey, having been picked up from his home as the first ray of dawn tickled his retinas. The facility was a manor house but it didn't appear homely, quite stately in fact and very private, deadly silent apart from the crunch made on the gravel by the tyres of the Daimler Consort Paul rode in. Trees surrounded the house, which enhanced its aura of privacy and suggested a closed shop. Max met him at the imposing front door and his personal assistant, John Eames, took Paul's suitcases. The hallway was as formidable as the entrance portal, with a grand staircase, high ceilings, oak panelling, illustrious reds and crimsons adorning the walls and extravagant statues and paintings. It suggested the owner sought to impress others with a first impression of incredible wealth.

"Welcome to The Establishment, Paul," Max said it like it was a real honour, not only to be here but to have him research there. "Do you wish John to show you to your room, or would you like a tour of the facility?"

"I'm keen for you to give me a guided tour," Paul replied, "far too early in the day to retire."

John disappeared with the suitcases while Max led the way forward. Downstairs to the left was a generous sitting room, currently empty, furnished in green leather sofas and William Morris wallpaper. This was adjoined to a dining area, with one large oak table and chairs and then a kitchen.

"This is a communal living area for research seniors and fellows, plus any volunteers, read lab rats who may be participating in any of our studies. Feel free to make yourself at home, there's a radio and a phonograph in the corner of the sitting room. I employ a cook so everyone based here can sit and enjoy an evening meal together."

Paul reflected briefly, it would be strange living here. He had relinquished his accommodation in Oxford to pursue behind the scenes research, in effect, he would be AWOL from the scientific community for a time, this opportunity could potentially alienate him from that circle or it could propel him towards the ultimate accolade.

Max walked back through the sitting room, across the hallway to its right hand side, where there were a number of offices, complete with filing cabinets, oak desks, mahogany and leather armchairs and doors with individual nameplates. One had *Dr. Paul Eldridge* engraved on it.

They ascended the stairs and again, on the left hand side were a number of rooms for staff and guests, with a communal bathroom then on the right hand side were three laboratories and a storeroom.

"Any equipment you don't find in the labs will be located in the storeroom. Specific equipment can be custom built, you may wish to call upon the services of our supplier, I will give you their telephone number."

Finally, Max showed him his room, surprisingly spacious and suitably ostentatious. He had a four poster bed that was apparently Victorian, oil paintings of former residents on the wall, oak floorboards with an old, red patterned rug in front of a small, black, cast iron fireplace and there was an armchair in the corner, plus a small desk.

"This is the finest room," Max said, "suitable for the finest of my staff."

Paul felt honoured.

"Come, let us discuss research in my office."

Max led Paul into his office, where they sat in leather armchairs, appraising each other across the solid oak desk. The walls had dark blue wallpaper and a huge sash window overlooking the garden, which itself was worthy of a tour. Max lit a cigar and offered one to Paul, who accepted.

"You're still wondering why exactly I brought you here," Max postulated.

"It's not the research facility I envisioned," Paul offered.

Max shrugged nonchalantly. "It's one of many."

"Well, I hope your proposals are as enticing as the bait you caught me with," Paul laughed, belying the nervousness he suddenly felt.

Max blew out cigar smoke with a cool demeanour, psychologically masticating what he was about to volunteer.

"Do you think the human soul is in fact an electro-magnetic field?" he boldly questioned. "And composed of quantum particles?"

Paul was taken by surprise. "Does this mean you have a fledgling hypothesis? I'm beginning to see my connection in all of this."

"I don't make queries lightly."

"Are there any intended applications for this, or is it purely philosophical?" Paul was thoughtful.

"I wish to follow this research with the effects of an electro-magnetic field on the human body."

"That's assuming I make a significant discovery." Max had high expectations. "I could spend the rest of my life working on this."

"Well," Max persuaded with an anomalous confidence, "I have faith that you will produce results in a shorter time frame than that."

Paul wasn't sure if the remark was an attempt to diffuse the overwhelming enormity of the task, or true faith in the project. But what concerned him were Max's motives, if anything, he seemed to be hiding something.

Paul asked. "Do you wish to use this knowledge for benign purposes?"

Max thought carefully about his answer. "I would like to understand. One day you will see the research in perspective, to see how it slots into the bigger picture. For now, let me assure you your discovery will be of immense importance."

"Why search for a human EM field?" Paul was curious to hear Max's real intentions. "Of all the subjects you could choose...."

Max looked at Paul with an expression that queried why Paul should need to ask.

"It could be, not only the manifestation of the human soul but also the energy of existence, surely this is something you seek."

Maybe he was trying to find ulterior motives where there were none, no sense in looking a gift horse in the mouth, as the cliché went. He had handed in his resignation, expressed a desire for more out of life and had taken a leap of faith, driven by some impetuous notion of grandeur.

Paul agreed. "When do we start?"

It's funny how you spend your life desiring and searching for something precious and elusive, but when you finally get what you want, you experience a nadir, an apathy. Actually being in possession of that thing that you sought so vociferously changes the entire impetus of your life and your raison d'être. That's how I felt on my first day at The Establishment. I had everything my heart desired in the palm of my hand, yet I didn't feel satisfied. The world had suddenly become uncertain and I was unsure what answers I would find, they could explode my faith in one fell swoop or completely vindicate what I and millions of other people round the world believed.

I spent the first week ambling, minutes at my desk pondering the incredible resources I had at the tip of my fingers, which rapidly turned to hours, trying to make the transition from wanting to having. Occasionally I would pick up a photograph of Madeleine, wondering if she was actually watching from some form of alternative quantum state. I contemplated contacting my family, but what would I say? This wasn't the type of research you openly discussed with members of the general public.

Finally, a spark ignited my momentum, namely the presence of Max Richardson with a face of expectation. I began constructing a double proposal and spent the next week wrapping my brain around the necessary equipment to attempt to measure a magnetic field emanating from the human body. Unintentionally, my mind raced ahead and made assumptions, pre-judgements about the existence of a human electromagnetic field. One of the questions that played on my mind was whether the field, if found I tried to remind myself, was a direct product of matter, that is, the physical tissue of the body or whether matter was a product of energy, the field itself. Which was the by product? This was a new chicken and egg for me.

The measuring device took four months to design and build then another three to test it intensively, so from my arrival at The Establishment to actually undertaking EM field measurements, it was a period of 9 months, allowing for recruitment of volunteers. I remember the first day of testing quite clearly, twenty volunteers arrived at the Establishment looking very nervous. Personally, my own trepidation was tantamount in my mind, that inner fear of disproving there was anything other than physical tissue to the human organism. But I had come so far, too far to get cold feet.

What surprised me was the monotony of taking the measurements. Although I got a tingle of excitement in anticipation of discovery, the actual nitty-gritty was rather dull and unfortunately, there was no one to assist. A conversation with Max and a week of intensive training afforded me the luxury of a research assistant, who was content to measure while I languished in discovery. This arrangement suited me fine and it did facilitate the speed of the process. Before long I found myself typing out an extensive and exhausting report, all that remained was to present it to Max.

Between his first arrival and the final presentation of his findings, two and a half years elapsed. His own personal perception of the world remained static in the mean time, while the Korean War played out. As Paul was ignited with a spark of inspiration, UN forces were crossing the 38th parallel into North Korea and as he drafted his proposal, the North Korean capital was captured. By the time truce talks began in the summer of 1951, Paul had built and tested the necessary equipment for his research. The Chinese invasion of Tibet also surpassed him, as did Winston Churchill becoming Prime Minister again, the gaining of independence by Libya and the defection of two British spies to Russia. To Paul the world had stood still. Music filtered through; he listened to Maria Callas on the radio, Gene Kelly 'Singing in the Rain' and he acquired a taste for Billie Holiday. Movie stars flared into recognition or burned brightly in his absence from the world, films went without viewing, he would have to catch up on 'The African Queen' with Bogart and Hepburn, a classic piece of early science fiction called 'The Day the Earth Stood Still', 'High Noon' and 'Singing in the Rain' at a later date. None of that mattered while he was chasing and fulfilling his dream to completion.

On 2nd April 1953, some six weeks after his 32nd birthday Paul was ready to present his findings to Max. Only the month before, James Watson and Francis Crick had suggested the double helix model of DNA structure in the scientific journal 'Nature', a publishing accolade Paul could only dream about at the moment as his research was too unorthodox. In the United States, a secret project known as MK ULTRA was initiated, testing the power of hypnosis to induce anxiety, the beginning of a whole host of mind control experiments.

Paul attended the board meeting for The Establishment's committee, a conglomerate of funding bodies, directors and executives with vested interests in the findings. The dining room was used as a makeshift meeting room and the whole Establishment was locked down to exclude any irrelevant members of staff. Ten people, 9 men and just one woman were seated at the table. Max Richardson was obviously one of the committee but Paul didn't recognise any of the other people, they represented a faceless but powerful, behind the scenes body. Everyone wore suits but nothing to distinguish who they were or their motives for attending this presentation.

Max Richardson was the chair of the committee and gestured for Paul to stand at the foot of the table.

"We'd like to thank you for your persistence in this endeavour, Paul, your contribution is much valued by the committee. I see you have brought along your thesis based on the last two and a half years of research. Could you enlighten us with an executive summary?"

Paul felt slightly intimidated by the faceless, staring people but proceeded. "We have tested and measured seven hundred people over a period of two years, ordinary people from many walks of life. Obviously, I removed any items of jewellery, etc that may interfere with the measurements. In all seven hundred people I collated measurements of an electro-magnetic field and in all cases I found the presence of a weak field. The precise readings are contained in this thesis." Paul gestured to a thick wad of paper, the contents of which he had laboriously typed. "The human electro-magnetic field is generally a weak one, extending on average three to four inches from the skin but in 25% of the sample, I found evidence of a much stronger field, giving higher readings and extending some six to ten inches from the skin."

Some of the committee discussed the findings inaudibly amongst themselves, while Max simply smiled to himself.

Paul continued. "At present I am unable to ascertain the origin of the human electro-magnetic field. The logical assumption would be that it emanates from the brain tissue itself but to draw a definitive conclusion, I would need to study living brain tissue. I believe such a study would be unethical."

Max smiled to himself, as if ethics should really be an issue where the advancement of scientific knowledge was concerned. He reached across the table and picked up Paul's thesis, flicked through it and set it down.

"I'm very impressed with your findings and your dedication to The Establishment. Before you commence with your next project, I believe you should take a month off, have a holiday… relax. I also have a surprise for you, a reward for your loyalty".

Paul was almost taken aback by the sudden generosity. He left his thesis with the committee, curious as to what would happen to it, would it be published? His uneasiness accompanied him back to his room, where he lay on his four-poster bed, aware of the committee chattering in the dining room below. Unfortunately, he couldn't pick out anything coherent from their conversation. He put his concerns to the back of his mind, what right did he have to complain? After all, this research was turning Paul into a rich man. While he was here, he had very little to pay out and the money was stacking up in the bank. He was removed from city life here, being surrounded by fields where he could take country walks, ride a horse or go fishing. His social life was not entirely negligible, there was a small number of research fellows with which he could share his leisure time. Women were lacking from his life but research consumed his time, unlike his peers, finding a wife was not cause for concern.

A knock at the door surprised him and cautiously, he opened it to find Max standing there.

"I didn't want to say this in front of the committee, but I'd like to invite you to a night of wine, women and song at my house. God knows, you need it, although don't take that the wrong way. I'm just concerned at the lack of… female companionship in your life. John will collect you tonight, 7.30; the dress code is quite formal."

Max left, presumably to prepare for the evening to come. Paul stood, stunned. How could he refuse such a direct offer?

Max's personal assistant, John, picked Paul up at 7.30 that evening and drove him in the Daimler to the secret residence that was never spoken about. It always seemed as if Max had no place to call home, but that misconception was ready to be shattered. Max's home was as grand as expected, a three-bedroom coach house located within the grounds of The Establishment. Ivy swathed the exterior of the house and it had grand sash windows. To the right of the house was an attached garage for his cars, which were currently out of sight. The garden was well tended and had an inordinately pretty symmetry about it, with shrubs and flowers placed in a design of absolute order. However, it was unlikely to be Max who dealt with the practicalities of horticulture, even if he did have a say in the layout.

The front door was imposing; a huge oak panelled leviathan with two columns stood either side like sentries, supporting a classical looking porch. Inside, it was surprisingly tasteful in furnishings and not quite as ostentatious as Paul thought it would be, perhaps reflecting the quieter, inner sanctum of Max's personality. The hallway was a room unto itself; it had a flagstone floor, walls of aqua green and several antique pictures were hung in strategic places, depicting unknown personages and landscapes. They looked like they were collectable as opposed to personal items. A huge oak staircase with a carpet runner gave an open invitation to go upstairs, it curved in a gentle semi-circle. Three coat stands stood to attention in the corner under the stairs, loaded with outdoor clothing and hats, suggesting guests were a regular thing.

The main living area was accessed through an open archway with wooden architrave. It was huge and dominated by a decorative plaster ceiling, complete with chandelier and contained furniture that was simple and functional; Chesterfield sofas and armchairs plus free standing items made of oak. There was a beautiful cast iron and tiled fireplace on the chimney breast, although no flames burned in there tonight and above it, there was an ornate mirror. The walls were plain red and again, there were antique pictures hung there.

Adjoining this room was a dining room which was accessed through oak double doors. It had a simplicity about it with stone coloured walls and a few pictures although the huge oak table had been pushed aside to make more space. Off this room, there was a study full of oak panelling, a heavy desk, some filing cabinets and bookcases. There was a connecting passage between the dining room and a huge kitchen with oak cabinets, breakfast table and Aga stove. The study had originally been the kitchen and Max had contracted builders to create a huge garage and kitchen extension onto the side of the house. Overall, his house had traditional overtones, although there were no family portraits to be seen anywhere which gave it a strangely impersonal feel.

Questions often crossed Paul's mind concerning how Max Richardson had acquired his wealth, he never wanted to talk about it, maybe it was none of Paul's business but there never appeared to be a shortage of money. Max spent half of his time away from The Establishment on business, sometimes Paul caught a glimpse of unnamed men entering and leaving the facility late at night, which was somewhat disconcerting. But Paul knew he hadn't made an erroneous decision coming to work here, the material benefits outweighed the ethical doubts in the back of his mind.

Paul arrived at the same time as a number of other guests, a mixture of men and women, none of which appeared to be married to each other. Max had never mentioned a wife on one single occasion and Paul assumed it was because he didn't want to share his wealth by having to provide for a woman. Although he was soon to learn that Max's life wasn't entirely devoid of female companionship. Max led Paul into the fold.

"Paul, I'd like to introduce you to Roslyn, Margaret and Eve, the longest serving members of the circle."

They all smiled, revealing shiny white teeth. Roslyn had mahogany hair set in the classic 1940s wave, while Margaret, a brunette favoured the long and straight look. Eve had peroxide hair and modelled herself like Marilyn Monroe, the new star of Hollywood. They were all large breasted with hour glass figures and eager to please.

"Take your pick," said Max, "I highly recommend all three."

Paul watched as Max rejoined a group of four peroxide blondes.

Max had hired a group of musicians for the night, they were squeezed into the corner of the main living area and played big band music typical of the mid and late 1940s, plus a selection of jazz tunes. Vintage wine and quality champagne was served. The food was exquisite, although many of the women ate very little of it. A group of wealthy looking men formed an intellectual clique, standing near Paul and creating great clouds of tobacco smoke. He cocked his ear in their direction to listen to the conversation, which was politically driven.

"Well, at least Stalin got his just desserts," he heard one man comment, who had a pencil thin moustache and wore black and white spats straight from the 1920s.

"Why do you draw that conclusion?" another questioned him, a slightly younger man with immaculate brown hair and a staid suit. "Where was the legal and moral punishment for his crimes, his purges, all those deaths..?"

"My dear fellow," came the response, "he made doctors the victims of his latest purge, so that when his soldiers finally managed to send for medical help, it turned out the best doctors were in prison, by his own hand. Quite possibility the ones not already imprisoned they too delayed his treatment, wanting him to die, then they would not be the victims of a continuation of his purges if he survived. You see, your actions in life have a nasty habit of coming back to bite you on the backside."

There were murmurs of agreement and Paul diverted his attention to the group of four peroxide women, now engaged in their own discussion as Max had moved on.

"I can't wait for Queen Elizabeth's coronation," one woman said, "it is going to be such a street party, with bunting, and tables of food."

"I think it's going to be on the television," added another, "so it will be like we're actually there. How wonderful."

"My family doesn't have a television," the first woman said, "we all crowd in the sitting room of our neighbours. We've always managed perfectly well with the wireless."

Paul really didn't know what to do with himself, how long had it been since he attended a party? Socialising had started to become a distant memory, he had gotten so used to discussing research, methodologies, results and conclusions that the art of normal conversation eluded him. Plus, he didn't know any of these people. He drifted around, listening to other people's conversations and finding some surprisingly liberal and intellectual.

"I do concur," a dark haired man in his thirties stated, "the Kinsey report does reflect a certain truth in that women are more biologically sexual than traditionally portrayed. All the females here enjoy the sexual act as much as the men."

His short, balding male friend lit up another cigarette.

"Well, I can't argue with his statistics either. Married men cannot resist extra-marital sex. Seventy five percent of the males in this room have spouses. I just don't think we're biologically designed to copulate with one woman all our lives."

"Or one man," the dark haired man added. "I know there are three closet homosexuals here today, all with wives and children. This is the only place they discover any freedom of expression. Morally, I still question it, however, just for the record."

Paul began to wonder exactly what kind of people he was surrounded by. Max noticed him standing around in bewilderment and steered him over to a very talkative young woman called Elizabeth, who rapidly attained dominion over the conversation. She proceeded to tell Paul all about her new secretarial job; she was one of few women who actually earned her own money. Elizabeth was young, perhaps early twenties and was naturally pretty with blonde hair, blue eyes albeit rather plump thighs and ample breasts. She smoked heavily and Paul listened intently as she chain smoked, he was actually relieved there was no pressure to contribute to the conversation.

"So," she changed tack, "what do you do?"

Paul was taken aback momentarily but thought, what the hell and relaxed a little more, but just a little.

"I'm involved in research."

"Research? That sounds very... intellectual."

"My background is science, it's my current love," he spoke it more as a truth than a joke.

Elizabeth's eyes lit up. "So, you're not married?"

Paul felt slightly uncomfortable. "Well, no, I was due to marry several years ago now but... my fiancée died in a blitz." For some reason it sounded like a clichéd story.

"And, there hasn't been anyone since?" Elizabeth pressed.

"No one special."

Elizabeth decided to glue herself, although not literally to Paul's side. He glanced over to see Max idly chatting with the three women he had first introduced and as the night progressed, everyone became suitably intoxicated. Wine and champagne released inhibitions, even Paul began to feel more relaxed and opened up socially. In this circle it was quite acceptable to pop pills and Paul was surprised to see Max indulge too, in addition to copious amounts of champagne. He realised then that he had been admitted to Max's inner circle, quite an established one by the looks of it and he knew he'd never see him in the same light ever again.

It became clear that Elizabeth wasn't budging for the remainder of the night and if anything, she became more flirtatious. Paul realised it had been a good few years since he had received any female attention, discounting a few of the research volunteers who noted the lack of wedding band. Max was with Roslyn and Eve, who noticeably led him upstairs and he looked over at Paul, giving a sly wink. Elizabeth smiled and looked him straight in the eye, in a fashion that telepathically suggested they do the same. She held out her hand and Paul took it, such a delicate little thing it was. He was led up the stairs and Elizabeth looked for an available bedroom, opening two doors and finding the rooms occupied. The main bedroom was occupied by Max and the two women, Eve was reclined on an armchair in nothing but stockings, an idle voyeur as Rosalyn's head bobbed up and down enthusiastically over Max's crotch. The next room contained two men and two women engaged in straightforward sex so Eve had high hopes for the last bedroom, but unfortunately it too was engaged, this time by a man who had passed out due to an excess of alcohol. A disgruntled brunette left the room. Elizabeth was not to be deterred.

"Ever fucked in a bathroom, Paul?" she asked.

She pushed him so that he flopped onto the toilet, with the lid down of course and then kicked the door closed, without locking it. She slipped her dress off, revealing a lack of underwear and sat astride him, pushing her generous cleavage into his face. Paul couldn't help but feel aroused, it had been a good, correction, bad few years since he'd been physical with a woman and Elizabeth was not objectionable in the least.

"What's it going to be?" she said, in her best seductress voice, "a straight fuck, a blow job or would you like to put it between my tits?"

This was quite an unusual predicament for Paul but one he felt unable to refuse, opting for the straight fuck. There was no kissing involved, which was no big issue for Paul and instead he grabbed her buttocks as she rode up and down on him. The smell of her was intoxicating, sex was always divine after such a long abstinence; the hot feeling of being inside a woman, to be able to hold her tight and experience an intense climax, to bury his face in between her breasts and forget everything for a moment.

Max must have heard his finale as he opened the door of the bathroom just a few minutes after and stood in the doorway, semi-clothed, drink in hand.

He smiled. "Now that you've been broken in, why don't you and Elizabeth join me in the master bedroom? You're just getting warmed up and she needs a little girl on girl treat, I think."

Paul, still somewhat dazed led Elizabeth into Max's bedroom and found Roslyn and Eve there in a state of semi undress, for Max liked to see lingerie. Eve took Elizabeth by the hand and sat her down on what was a very ornate four-poster bed. She hinted at her to lie back and proceeded to bury her face in between her thighs while Roslyn gently pushed Paul into the chair, using her mouth to revive him. Max watched intently at the two scenes of sexual pleasure, taking a breather from the physical aspect of it. Paul relaxed in the chair and closed his eyes, so he could forget he was being watched and enjoy the sensations of an experienced mouth and tongue. It was not long before he heard Elizabeth climax and he opened his eyes briefly to find Max had slipped in behind Roslyn, she was now on all fours serving the both of them. Paul came first, followed by Roslyn and finally Max, who preferred to save the best until last.

Everyone fell quiet for a few minutes. Paul suddenly began to feel self conscious and started to get out of the chair but Max handed him a glass of champagne.

"Congratulations," he said, "you've just undergone your initiation."

Paul gulped at the champagne, looking over at Elizabeth who still lay on the bed. Max smiled and gave him a surreptitious wink.

Looking at Elizabeth, then Roslyn, then Eve he realised they showed no signs of getting dressed. Max slid open a small drawer and took out what looked like a tin of snuff and sat on the bed next to Elizabeth. He tipped out some of the contents and created a line of white powder from her breasts to her pubic bone, then took out a roll of paper money from another draw and peeled off one, in a large denomination. Paul watched as he formed the note into a roll and proceeded to snort part of the line of white powder. Max sat up, looking over at Paul with a smile.

"You could have some cocaine if you want to continue the action," he offered.

Roslyn took the roll of paper and snorted part of the line, followed by Eve. Paul had never had a penchant for drugs but he realised the night had just begun and without some stimulation, he wouldn't be able to keep up with them. He, against his better judgement, accepted a line of cocaine and the bedroom party kicked into gear again.

The morning after, Paul opened his eyes in one of the spare beds and immediately closed them on seeing the sunlight streaming through the window. His head was pounding and his body ached from the sheer amount of 'exercise' the night before. He couldn't quite believe he'd been involved in a night of such debauchery but it had really happened. It was one of those experiences that left you a changed person, when your perceptions of those and others around you would never be the same. Paul had no regrets, he wasn't hurting anyone and everyone was a willing participant.

He glanced at the clock on the wall and noticed that it was two o'clock in the afternoon! A wave of panic washed over him, shouldn't he be at work? Then he remembered Max had given him time off. Panic was succeeded by a breaker of relief, it made him realise how automated his life had become in respect of research and the goal of recognition.

Paul rolled over and was surprised, although almost shocked to find Elizabeth asleep next to him. He smiled to himself, this had not happened for a long time, to awaken finding a woman asleep by his side. She still looked pretty, not all women did first thing in the morning. While she slept, he watched her and felt decidedly content for a short time. She must have sensed his gaze for she opened her eyes and smiled when she saw him looking.

"Morning Mr. Lover Man."

"Correction," Paul said, softly, "afternoon."

She laughed; no work for her either on this day, then she pondered. "I just have to take this diaphragm out," she said, shifting around in bed. That was a conversation killer, somewhat.

"I was going to suggest a repeat performance," he shrugged, which was more of a suggestion.

At this point, Max knocked and entered, then sat on the armchair with a contented smile on his face.

"I hope you had a good time last night, Paul, I certainly did. I can't expect you to work and not enjoy yourself every once in a while." He sat with a confident repose and continued. "I was going to reserve your surprise until after your holiday but I've decided it can't wait. Be downstairs in the hallway in half an hour."

Paul sighed and conceded that there would have to be another time for Elizabeth.

"Are you still going to be around later?" he asked her.

"Maybe," she chided.

With that, Max left the room and Paul forced himself out of bed and into the clothes he'd worn last night. After a wash and shave, he found Max downstairs in the hallway and he was taken out to a car which was parked outside on the gravel. Paul was impressed by the dark green, open top two seated roadster with wire wheels and Max couldn't help but see the wistful feeling spread over his face.

"It's a Jaguar XK120," Max informed him, "fastest production car in the world with a top speed of a hundred and twenty miles per hour."

Max reached inside for the pull cord as there were no external door handles and Paul slid into the tan leather interior, with matching dash while Max jumped into the driving seat beside him. He started up the engine and the wheels spun on the gravel as he sped away from the coach house.

"Nought to sixty in ten seconds," Max continued, demonstrating its capabilities by pushing his foot down on the accelerator. "One hundred and sixty brake horse power, 3442cc engine and a fuel consumption of almost twenty miles per gallon. Jaguar's first post-war sports car and most definitely a procurer of the feminine parts, to put it politely," Max laughed.

Paul allowed himself to enjoy the high speed journey, placing his trust in Max who expertly handled the car around the bends in the country roads they drove down. He took them to a small village about twenty miles away and pulled up outside a small cottage covered in ivy. It looked very cosy nestling within a coven of trees and a crumbling stone wall.

Max turned off the engine and sat silently for a moment, with a vaguely wistful expression on his face. Then he relinquished any emotional attachments to the cottage and told Paul, "It's yours. I appreciate you've been trapped in a bubble for a few years now and I believe it's time you had a home of your own." He handed over the keys. "Go and take a look, I'm sure you'll adore it."

Paul wasn't expecting this and if anything, wondered why Max was being so generous. On entering, Paul found it to be pleasantly furnished and decorated. The sitting room had a beamed ceiling, inglenook fireplace and two Chesterfield style sofas and the kitchen was a reasonable size, with pans hanging from suspended racks. Upstairs were three bedrooms, the master bedroom having a comfortable double bed with a cast iron frame and a magnificent view out of the window. The bathroom had a Victorian bath with clawed feet. Max was right, he adored it. It was cosy and peaceful, with no immediate neighbours. Transport wouldn't be too much of a problem as he had sufficient funds to buy a fine vehicle. Yes, he was going to be happy here.

Max stood in the hallway as Paul descended the stairs, awaiting a decision. Paul had no choice but to accept the offer.

"I hope you're happier here than the previous occupants were," Max said, closing the door on their way out.

Without even thinking of the repercussions, I showed Elizabeth the cottage as I felt I just had to share the good luck. She also fell in love with it instantly and there was to be no prising her away. I would drive to the Establishment most mornings and drop Elizabeth off at her place of work, then collect her on the way home. A few months after acquiring the cottage, I had opted to purchase a cute little roadster, the MG TF in an elegant cream with a 1250cc engine, headlights fared into the fenders, long flowing wheel arches and a tall, sloping radiator grille. It wasn't as impressive as Max's phallic symbol on wheels but it had style without being too flash.

As the winter closed in we sat by the open fire, drank wine, and listened to the wireless, particularly Billie Holiday although I never discussed work. We even managed to catch 'Singing in the Rain', plus a plethora of wonderful films such as 'From Here to Eternity', which brought out the romantic in Elizabeth; 'Shane', tense science fiction such as 'War of the Worlds' which caused Elizabeth to hide behind her hands and Hitchcock thrillers like 'Dial M for Murder' and 'Rear Window'. In those days, the feature would be accompanied by the Pathé News Reel, with the crowing cockerel, rousing theme tune and images of life in other parts of the world. The cinematic experience was a spectacle of feature film, B-movie, advertisements and the National Anthem would play at the end, to which the whole audience would stand up and sing. To me it felt like reintegration into the real world. There was also plenty of bedroom activity. I didn't feel as if I was in love but her companionship was as pleasurable as her body.

But from the night of the party, I was on the inside and not the outside of Max's personal circle. Parties were thrown perhaps once a month, or no less frequent than six weekly. At first I opted out, as I had Elizabeth and didn't have to work at securing sex but Max took offence to this refusal. Despite my insistence that I had a plentiful supply of sex, it was Max's belief that sex should not be confined to one woman. In the end, I relented and attended the second party, thinking I could pretend I had enjoyed sex with another woman but the expectation was to be part of a threesome, or foursome and feigning would be impossible. Elizabeth wasn't present that night but when I returned home, I felt guilty.

The parties were an ongoing feature of Max's life and there was a silent agreement that I was as much a part of it as Max. On the fourth party, I began to regard it as part of everyday life and felt less and less guilty. At times, I was curious about Max's sexuality as sometimes he would disappear upstairs with two women and an extra male, although I never personally witnessed Max have sex with anyone except women. I myself was approached by a man once, but I didn't feel inclined to stray into that territory.

Although Elizabeth and I still enjoyed such pleasures as meals at restaurants and nights at the theatre or cinema, the magic was not there by the milestone of six months. However, Elizabeth stayed, showing that security was more important than happiness. I began to wonder if I had been too rash in showing her the cottage but a year in, the matter was concluded by Elizabeth's unexpected appearance at one of the parties. She found me engaged in oral sex with Eve and took great offence, despite the fact that these parties brought us together in the first place and her appearance here suggested her own temptation to wander. A week later and I had the cottage to myself. Breaking up was not always hard to do.

It was back to the parties as my only source of female companionship, which made life much less complicated.

Research continued, this time into the effects of an electro-magnetic field on the human organism. Max supplied the volunteers, although I had no idea where he had recruited them, I had my suspicions as one volunteer referred to the fact that he was due to be hanged in six weeks time but he didn't feel I was in a position to question just exactly how ethical this study was. Given the choice between principles and the opportunity to discover something significant, there was little conflict of interests. Associating with Max had the effect of reducing my humanity somewhat. Later, I would regard this to be a nadir, a dark age.

This particular study, from conception to culmination lasted a few years, with other projects running concurrent and new projects created as offshoots. I applied both sub-sonic and high frequency electro-magnetic fields on humans and animals. Some of the low frequency fields had some deleterious side effects, which included incontinence and vomiting and in animals, a greater range of frequencies were used which resulted in cardiac arrest. Higher frequencies in humans caused disorientation and confusion, quite distressing to the volunteers and in many ways to me too. We also tested sub-sonic and high frequency EM fields on the human brain, to see if blasts of EM radiation could erase memories. The results were inconclusive but it also paved the way for further experiments on the use of EM fields for mind control; the manipulation of individual mental states and alteration of brain function. There was evidence to suggest that certain frequencies could create anxiety and influence mental susceptibility to psychosis, generally make the mind more pliable.

It was during this time that I lost a role model, a twentieth century icon. I would often have the bakelite radio on in the evening, an art deco beauty in teak from the 1930s with two dials, as it was my only real contact with the world outside of The Establishment and on the night of the 19th April 1955, there was a poignant broadcast.

"The imminent scientist and originator of the theory of relativity, Albert Einstein died yesterday in hospital in Princeton, New Jersey aged 76. He was admitted to hospital three days previously suffering with an internal complaint, but he refused surgery for a ruptured artery. In 1940, he became a US citizen after leaving Germany during the early years of the war. In a statement just released, US President Dwight Eisenhower paid tribute to the visionary and respected scientist."

The broadcast cut to the voice of the president.

"' No other man contributed so much to the vast expansion of the twentieth century knowledge. Yet no other man was more modest in the possession of the power that is knowledge, more sure that power without wisdom is deadly. To all who live in the nuclear age, Albert Einstein exemplified the mighty creative ability of the individual in a free society.'"

I also caught the broadcast on the television, which showed a black and white reel of Albert Einstein at various stages of his scientific life, a man who never shook his German accent or his desire for seclusion. It was truly a sad day for me, and for physics. Who would now complete his Unified Field Theory?

But life went on, as did the research. I also became involved in the British sibling of MK-ULTRA, a necessity in response to the allegations of Soviet, Chinese and North Korean mind control techniques on US prisoners of war in Korea. Much of the research conducted focused on the use of chemical substances to alter brain function, particularly LSD; attempts were made to increase the efficiency of perception and even induce psychic powers (I also tried the use of EM fields to stimulate psychic abilities but without success) and to use LSD and other substances to withstand torture and coercion during interrogation and brain washing. At The Establishment, experiments with LSD and other hallucinogens were conducted on volunteers, although I suspected tests were done elsewhere on members of the public without their knowledge or consent. I also oversaw some experiments using sensory deprivation tanks and their effect upon the mind.

It was during these years that I myself experimented with both LSD and sensory deprivation. The tanks were water tight and excluded both light and sound and the subject floated in a solution of salt water, which also removed any stimulus to the skin. I found it to be a peaceful experience, creating a state of mind where my mind was free to wander and solve problems but I knew that I could only withstand it for a certain amount of time. Enforced sensory deprivation for long periods of time caused disorientation and mental health problems, which my research found.

I also took LSD one day in June 1957, when it was still legal, at home, alone. I created a soft ambience and ingested a small dose of the drug, in an attempt to recreate Albert Hoffman's now famous 'Bicycle Day.' After a short while of riding a bike under the influence, my limbs soon became weak and my perspective of reality too distorted to pedal along safely.

I sat down in a field near The Establishment, first becoming aware of how complex the folds in my trousers were, I must have spent a while trying to fathom why they fell the way they did, appreciating their intricate beauty. The next thing of which I was aware was the oscillation of the things around me, particularly the spokes of the bicycle which now *lay on its side, they moved about, drawing together and separating in a rhythmic vibration. The flowers in the field shone with an inner light, shimmering as if they were breathing and I became fascinated with each and every breath.*

By now, the drug had reached its full strength and I found myself enjoying a trip that was rather intense but full of vibrant colours and sounds, strange visual effects. I closed my eyes to witness a scene of beautiful kaleidoscope colours, and when my eyes were open the sky was full of fireworks. When I moved my hand, it left trails so I spent a good hour or so moving my limbs around and watching the visual effects (not that I had any sense of time whatsoever).

Buying a pint of milk from the shop proved to be very difficult as people's faces were distorted, which made me laugh uncontrollably, much to the consternation of the other customers so I cycled back home, wobbling erratically as I tried to avoid the white lines in the road that had become writhing serpents. I found myself back in the study of my cottage, resting in my favourite armchair, listening to the layers of music coming from the gramophone. In turn, a particular instrument would become dominant, drowning my senses and then another instrument would receive my focus and go through the same process. The books on the shelves were trying to speak to me, shining with their inner light, wanting to fly towards me, pregnant with knowledge. Eventually, I drifted towards sleep and a lucid dream.

All in all, it had been a positive experience and one that I repeated several times, in different settings. It was truly a remarkable substance, although one that could easily drive someone insane, a view I shared with the author, Aldous Huxley.

Not everyone responded well to the drugs we administered, and we were dealing with stronger doses than I had been ingesting. Towards the latter years of the psychological experiments on willing, albeit sometimes regretful volunteers, I felt these tests were trying to turn me inhuman, dispassionate and uncaring and I asked for some of these tests to be carried out by my peers. Max realised the fact that I had found my limit. The studies attracted interest from many outside organisations and there were many meetings and exchange of monies. I had to concede, to my own conscience, that this was just a job. The nature of the work started to suggest military applications though and in the last year of the study, I felt very little enthusiasm for further discovery. Ultimately, there was a conflict of desire. Spiritual cravings began to take root and throughout this last year, I was beginning to feel like I would never get to investigate life's mysteries when Max announced something unexpected one day in late 1959. The fateful day was in the summer and the news was announced whilst Max and I were on horseback near the coach house.

"I have another project for you, I've noticed your enthusiasm has dwindled and your peers are experienced enough to complete the study. I'd like you to work at a sister facility called The Institute for a year, it's in London but quite accessible. You'll like this one, more up your street."

I was unsettled as to how the announcement threatened my sense of stability. Life so far had been all about The Establishment and Max, electro-magnetic fields and sonic frequencies, hallucinogenic drugs and deprivation tanks, with vague hints of the human soul. Did I really want to move on? And with that, whether I liked it or not, my reality was turned upside down again.

3
Key to the Door

Saturday 19th November 1988

The hallucination was followed by a crash, then a stifled shriek of despair. This was not the first time that particular hallucination had caught her off guard but it did have a habit of rearing its head at the most inopportune moment. Snakes; she often saw snakes, no specific species but it began with one, whom she found coiled on her bed about three months ago. A few weeks later (it must have bred cerebrally somehow), there were two, entwined together like a couple of lovers on her dinner plate. They made an appearance every fortnight, which seemed to coincide with the phases of the moon. Now as a scientist, she sought a rational explanation but so far it eluded her. The specific visions were beginning to affect everyday life in conjunction with the myriad of additional and generic hallucinations, which made even a tube journey an odyssey.

The stifled shriek of despair was caused by the fact that Ava Kavanagh had dropped the roast chicken on the floor, the chicken lovingly seasoned with thyme that was a feature of her 21st birthday party. The damn thing had been cooking for an eternity and the dinner guests were due to arrive any minute so there was no chance of putting another in the oven now. Out of character for her and partly because she didn't want to acknowledge what had happened, she picked it up from the floor and placed it back in the roasting tray where it had pride of place. It wasn't like the floor was dirty and a few stray bacteria strengthened the immune system anyway. Thankfully no one had witnessed her culinary travesty. She had all the vegetables sitting obediently in their serving dishes and the condiments awaiting utility with relish; they were all eager to be placed on the large dining table. Ava's guiltily concealed mishap would remain so she transferred the chicken to its platter and decorated it with additional sprigs of thyme and rosemary. What a glorious scent.

Her flatmates poked their head around the door, one male and one female both with hairstyles typical of the 1980s.

"Are you sure you don't want any help? It's *your* birthday!" Jason was the only male out of the flat trio, with blond, spiky hair reminiscent of Limahl and he sloped around in jeans despite the occasion. He often wore make-up but was cosmetically modest today as Ava's family were quite conservative. They would probably think he was homosexual, not accustomed to seeing such an androgynous human being.

"Ava, you're the only person I know who insists on cooking for everyone on her birthday." This speaker was female with blonde bobbed hair that had a spiked fringe, a little like Kim Wilde.

"Emma, I can't help being such a control freak." It was said with a sense of pride as opposed to embarrassment.

Jason and Emma assisted Ava in transferring the platters to the dining table, which was already laden with cutlery. At that moment the doorbell rang for the second time. This had to be the family, her closest friends aside from her flatmates were already here and drinking wine whilst lounging on the sofas. Ava ran downstairs (they resided on the second floor), walked coolly into the Victorian hallway and opened the extravagant main door to the building, with a big smile on her face.

A distinguished looking man in his late sixties and an elegant woman in her mid sixties stood in the doorway, each with a big smile. He was of average height with grey hair, and had an air of authority that was interlaced with good humour and a warm smile. For his age he gave the appearance of health as well as moderate wealth, one would think he took regular exercise and sunbathed. She was slim with grey flicked hair and a broad, hedonistic smile, as if she was a former flower power child of the 60s. Her personality was naturally effervescent yet mature. They each kissed Ava on the cheek and followed her up the stairs to her flat.

"That's a beautiful scarf you're wearing," her mother commented, "it looks so vintage."

The red silk scarf she wore was very conspicuous, with a slightly faded look suggesting it was indeed old. Ava wore it tied loosely around her neck.

"I found it recently," she explained.

Upstairs, Ava introduced them to the friends already in place, wine at the ready.

"This is David and Caroline Kavanagh, my parents." The occupants of the room all greeted the newcomers; some raising their wine glasses, by now only half full or virtually empty. "Mum, Dad, these are my flatmates Jason and Emma." Ava gestured to them. "And these are my friends from university; Sarah, Vicki, Rachel, Steve and Tom." The respective people were greeted by Ava's parents and all dinner attendees mingled very sociably. Emma took up the vacant post of dining table finalisations while Ava got her daily quota of exercise running up and down the stairs to answer the door.

Her oldest sister, Ginny, with her husband Harry were the next arrivals. She was around the age of 33 and was quite athletic, she looked like she probably threw javelins for a living or rode horses and she had flame coloured hair unlike the rest of the family. She was a modern day Boudicca while her husband had a Roman gladiator appearance; physically strong and tanned. They had a relationship akin to the Iceni and the Romans but they curtailed their altercations for Ava's benefit.

The remainder of the immediate family arrived last, as one unit. There was Jack, classic 80s yuppie complete with a Filofax, mobile phone as heavy as a house brick and a monotonous repertoire of conversation topics and jokes about his high-flying lifestyle. He was good looking and fancied himself as a playboy but unfortunately his demeanour was somewhat obnoxious. In descending order of age, next came Robert, who was in the army very much like his father had been. He was as yet unmarried but unconcerned about it. Then came Annette, who had her boyfriend Colin in tow; she was the epitome of what her mother was in suggestion, a free spirited individual. Annette was normally a brunette but currently sported a red henna rinse. She was due to spend six months in South America, as she loved to travel so always had something interesting to say. She was only three years older than Ava and as young children they had been very close. Now the whole family was reunited.

Everyone took a seat at the large dining table that the flat occupants had borrowed to add onto the table they already had, as they needed more seats and places. Now that had been an expedition, quite unlike Annette's travels but a mission nevertheless, ferrying a huge table strapped upside down on the roof rack of an Austin Maestro through the streets of Chiswick. It had been a further trial lugging it up the stairs. Furthermore, that had yet to be repeated in reverse. Ava gazed at the congregation, there were a few members missing however they had not been able to confirm their attendance. There was one she had wished to be present but that didn't seem possible now, she didn't want to feel disappointed so put that aside and gave her full attention to the people that were here.

"Well, this is cosy," said Caroline, realising how intimate it felt with over ten people sat at the table.

Ava stood at the head of the table and placed slices of meat onto plates, passing them around so the guests could help themselves to the vegetables. Aside from the chicken, there was also a large gammon round and a small nut roast for Annette and Colin, who were devout vegetarians. Once the vegetables had been doled out, she quickly removed the serving dishes so the table was less crammed. It was finally time to eat after an exhausting morning.

"So," Ginny began, as she picked up her knife and fork, "is there a special man in your life?"

Ava smiled surreptitiously, such a typical family question. "No. I split with Michael a few months ago." There was just a tinge of regret in her voice, as if it was inevitable but not necessarily welcomed. How could anyone understand her predicament, not even her family were aware what she had been going through.

Ginny was genuinely apologetic. "Sorry to hear that, you were such a promising couple."

"No harm in leading a single life," Jason interjected, "besides, you could have whoever you want, Ava. There's no rush, is there?"

Her mother changed the subject as Ginny was always obsessed about other people's relationships. "When you've finished your degree in genetics, what do you intend to do next?" The admiration in her voice was clear.

"Look for a job!" she laughed. "I'm going to contact the labs on my list. But first, I've to focus on the last year of study, a dissertation won't write itself."

Robert, the youngest son interjected. "What is your dissertation about?" He was genuinely interested.

"Telomeres, and their role in the aging process," Ava answered. "I think they have a big future."

"Telomeres?" he queried.

"The bits on the ends of chromosomes," she answered, realising it hadn't enlightened him any more.

He nodded appreciatively, accepting that he hadn't a clue what she was talking about. "You've always seemed to have your finger on the pulse of the future."

David, the head of the family was already engaged in discussion with Jack, his eldest son and Ginny's husband, Harry, subject; the new mobile phone technology. He showed them the brick he was extremely proud of, complete with chunky antenna, elaborating on the merits of being able to call someone while walking down the street.

"Of course," Jack stated, "not everyone will have one in the future, nice to be part of an elite. I mean, why would anyone want to call someone while on the move, unless you were a businessman?"

Ava switched off and began serving food while Jack began to boast eloquently of his last financial conquest. Robert was not as materially minded as his brother and made vain attempts at changing the subject but to no avail. Fortunately, if you looked at it that way, the door bell rang and Ava saw this as an opportunity to escape the inane onslaught of finance. However, it was Robert that stood up to answer it, indicating Ava had every right to sit and enjoy her meal seeing as it was her birthday. As he left the room, she wondered who was at the door. Three more people had been invited who were currently not in the room and there was one whom she very much wanted to be here. It was not that she didn't want to see the other two, in fact she did, they were all special people in her life. She heard two sets of footsteps coming up the stairs, so only one out of three were attending, then.

The door opened and Robert led a young man into the room. He was not the one she desperately wanted to see but still, Ava smiled affectionately and he returned the gaze, which he held for longer that what would be usual custom. Many of the room's occupants recognised him and were, in fact, pleased to see him. He was quite an unusual looking youth, insanely beautiful in an almost androgynous way with strong features, intensely blue eyes, ebony hair in a contemporary style, aquiline nose and slim build. His dress was not too formal, black shirt and jeans with a deliberate frayed tear at the knee, studded bracelet typical of the 80s. He looked vaguely like a rock god in formation. Emma's eyes lit up which caused Ava to smile, if only she knew, he had only just turned sixteen although he looked quite mature for his age.

But he didn't notice Emma, instead he appeared to be fixated on Ava which did not go unnoticed by Caroline, her mother.

"This is Sam," Robert announced, as Sam took an empty chair, "he's my cousin."

Caroline looked concerned. "Is your father not here?"

That was a moot point for Sam and he shrugged, bitterly. "Work comes first." The words were said with a degree of vehemence.

Ava smiled sympathetically at Sam, who tried to hide his feelings and she hid her own disappointment well, for she too had wished to see her uncle, who had guided her throughout her life. Sam took an empty plate and helped himself to the food, then quietly began to eat. Numerous times he glanced over at Ava, who returned his gaze with some fondness. She remembered him as a young boy, a boy who had had a difficult time growing up without a mother and had suffered the emptiness of a frequently absent father. As much as she adored her uncle, she didn't agree with the way he had nurtured Sam. She had thus taken it upon herself to look out for Sam, not quite as a mother but perhaps like a big sister would. Caroline too had always been there for him, for in his father's absence he had stayed with Ava's family many a time in his younger years. So it was not surprising that Sam had high regards for Ava and the rest of the clan.

"So," Robert said, always the one more interested in what others were doing as opposed to talking about himself, "what are you doing nowadays? Have you finished school yet?"

Sam spoke in soft, almost velvety tones that surprised many, for it had been a few years since he'd seen Ava, Robert, Annette or Jack and his voice was clearly much deeper.

"No, I have one more year."

"Oh, so that must mean you're ready to take your O levels."

"Well, actually they're called GCSEs now. So, I will be taking them next June, eight of them; all the usual ones but I chose music, art and German as opposed to taking additional sciences." He glanced over to Ava as if to say 'no offence'.

Jack interjected. "Where's the money in music and art? I can't say your father was too pleased."

Sam transposed from a placid manner to one that was decidedly cockier.

"Well, Michael Jackson's 'Thriller' was number one on the album chart for thirty seven weeks and it generated seven top ten singles, making him $125 million. U2's 'Joshua Tree' sold more than fourteen million copies worldwide and the tour grossed $40 million. I think that could be regarded as more substantial than mere pocket money. Would you like me to continue?"

Jack looked speechless at his snappy response. The conceit of his reply made everyone feel somewhat embarrassed and they all looked at their plates with sudden interest. A few cleared their throats. Jack was becoming annoyed at this teenager who seemed to think he knew everything. Caroline could see him flushing and decided to change the subject, more for Sam's sake as she knew how explosive Jack could become.

"You play a musical instrument, don't you?"

Sam smiled and stated proudly, "I play the piano and I've achieved my grade six, I play the guitar too, not like my father cares but I have my own path to follow. It's as valid as anyone else's."

Ava smiled at him. "You must play for me sometime, you will have improved enormously since the last time I saw you at the piano, which was probably about five years ago."

"Anytime," said Sam, "anytime." He held her gaze, making Caroline feel uncomfortable so she cut in with a suggestion of dessert.

Tiramisu brought the meal to a close quite successfully and Jason and Emma cleared the table between them while Ava circulated among the guests. This time around wasn't too much of an exercise in damage control. At her father's sixtieth birthday several years ago, Jack had been exceptionally patronising and

Sam had been particularly oppositional, counteracting Jack's supposed wisdom. Then, to further compound the issue Ginny and her husband contributed to the debate by one supporting Sam and the other siding with Jack. In comparison, today was somewhat more subdued.

A veritable feast of 80s music was played, with a slight disagreement between the flatmates as to what music to play. Emma was happy to indulge in some commercial pop straight from the playlist of Stock, Aitkin and Waterman while Jason insisted on the Smiths and the Sisters of Mercy, plus a little Bauhaus when no one was looking so Ava had to intervene, reminding Jason this was a birthday not a funeral. Sam had to agree with Jason in respect of music taste while Ava was happy to set her own values aside just for one afternoon to ensure there was peace.

"We have conservative guests today," she reminded them both.

The intermingling of different generations of culture was achieved, perhaps more due to Ava's ability to compromise than the actual personalities of the guests, who were akin to a mixture of dynamite and earthquakes. Ava skilfully circulated to ensure communication with each guest took place, first Jack which was not because he was the favourite but because he was the most obnoxious and it was better to get the dirty deeds out of the way to move onto more enjoyable conversation. He was discussing the merits of Kylie Minogue, star of the Australian soap 'Neighbours' with Colin, as she was just embarking on her pop career with a ditty entitled 'I Should Be So Lucky'.

"One hit wonder," Jack scoffed.

Colin was about to debate this when Ava weaved her way into the conversation. Jack smiled, commented on the high standard of the meal and predictably, quickly steered the discussion to work.

"If you don't find suitable work, you can always start as

my assistant. You'll soon work your way to the top," he declared, proudly.

Ava expressed her reluctance politely. "I'm sure I'll find something, there's an abundance of jobs in science."

Sam cut in, after eavesdropping. "I think my father is interested in recruiting you, when you've finished your degree of course. You know how he has a vested interest in science."

That would make a more viable proposition although she still preferred to carve her own profession independent of family assistance. She used Sam as a cue to exit Jack's company and his ensuing monotonous train of conversation concerning finance and accounts and they both encountered Ginny, who was just a few glasses of wine short of unconsciousness.

"What did happen between you and Michael? It's such a shame he didn't turn up today."

Ava did not like to be reminded of the separation and she had dearly hoped he would come today despite everything, just as a show of friendship if nothing else.

"I really don't know, it was very abrupt and I haven't seen him since. We were going to be leave for the States after I'd finished my degree but…"

Ginny tried to sound sympathetic but alcohol did not allow for the expression of tact. "Men are terrible for cold feet, never have the courage to say, they just stick their head in the sand and ignore you!"

Sam interjected. "I don't think she wants to talk about it."

"But of course she does, they were in love!"

Sam looked as uncomfortable as Ava and they both made their excuses, Ginny and alcohol were an unfortunate combination. They found Caroline, Ava's mother who gave both of them a hug, either due to a milestone birthday or long absence.

"I'm so proud of you both," she crooned, "the baby of the family will obtain a degree and Sammy is probably going to be a musician or an artist."

Sam found the recognition of his talent and intended direction surprising, he had become accustomed to his father's displeasure at his lifetime fascination with music and art and disinterest in science. Caroline made his effort seemed vindicated, it was a comfort to be valued and appreciated by another adult, apart from Ava who respected his wishes no matter. After a conversation with Caroline, Ava moved into the kitchen to draw on the wine reserves and Sam followed her. He watched her uncork a smooth red with the adulation of a teenager in love for the first time.

"You become more beautiful every day," he couldn't help but say.

Ava was taken aback by his words and stood looking at him with the bottle in her hand, unsure as to his intention. Prince began to sing 'When Doves Cry' in the background.

She replied with a compliment. "And you're turning into a handsome young man, I'm sure you'll have no shortage of girlfriends."

Sam fixed her with a more intense stare. "As long as they're like you and are as intelligent as you."

She found that comment more disturbing than the first and was at a loss for words. How could he think like that?

"Sam, I love you as a member of the family. I know I've played a huge role in your childhood, but, you're my cousin…."

His reply was unyielding. "Am I really?"

Ava didn't answer that, they were adopted cousins and that was a sensitive subject in the same way that Sam's father's absence was an issue. And that was not even broaching the topic of his mother.

Sam moved closer to her and placed one hand on her hip, she paused, bottle of wine still in her hand, unsure what to think. He placed her hand on his stomach and began to sing along with the music.

"Can you feel how my stomach trembles inside?" he asked

her, relating to the lyrics of the song.

Ava was momentarily confused by what Sam was doing. It was so direct and unexpected, as was his infatuation. He continued singing along and enjoyed the feel of her hand on his stomach. As he received no rebuttal, he began to move her hand further down his body and she was surprised how sexually exciting it was to touch him.

The situation was diffused by Annette bursting onto the scene, suitably but not excruciatingly drunk. At this point Sam pulled away, a little embarrassed and feeling his moment had fizzled and died like a firework. Ava was actually relieved; as much as she wanted Sam's company his unexpected romantic interest had disturbed her deeply and thrown up some confusing feelings. Annette provided a much needed distraction.

"Life has turned upside down this summer!" she declared.

Ava was fascinated by such drama and mystery. "Is this concerning your latest travels?"

Annette laughed. "Well, sort of."

"So, where have you been this time?"

The answer was unexpected. "To another fucking dimension! Seeing as it's the summer of love, I just had to experiment with acid."

In the background, the music changed to Bon Jovi, 'Living on a Prayer', to which Jason and Emma began to sing along to in their semi drunken state.

Ava was curious but shocked. "Acid? As in LSD?"

"Shhhh! Don't let mum hear, she'd have hysterics. Of course LSD, I wouldn't take hydrochloric acid or anything, would I?"

Ava lowered her voice. "Why would you do that?"

Annette rolled her eyes. "To free my mind, you really should try it. The colours are amazing and at the time, everything you know just makes sense, everything you think about is so profound, and the hallucinations really are out of this world. I was sat in someone's house after a party and the carpet was just writhing with snakes."

"Snakes?" Warning sirens began to sound in Ava's head.

"Yeah, it was mad, the patterns in the carpet turned into snakes. Good job I like snakes, eh?"

Ava didn't hear Annette's last comment. All she could think about were the snake hallucinations. Annette took acid and saw snakes, Ava saw snakes and experienced hallucinations, the similarity was striking. She made wild connections, or were they wild? Ava was convinced she was actually tripping, on a regular basis. Why?

4

The Institute

Paul arrived at The Institute which was an imposing Victorian house in Chelsea, London on December 8th 1959, five days before Max Richardson's 39th birthday. It was late afternoon and the sun was setting, casting a typical twilight glow over the city. Since the last time he had been in London, the air was less choking with no pea-soup smog to clog the lungs. However, in many ways it felt like nothing had changed. There was still little, if any traffic on the side streets and children were out playing before it got too dark and it was time to go in for tea. Boys played with hand-crafted guns made by whittling away a stick or lump of wood with a penknife and girls either pushed their dolls in prams or played hopscotch. Chimney sweeps with sooty faces were making their way home on their pushbikes; long-handled brushes, rods and dust sheet strapped on tight.

He stood on the doorstep after having tapped loudly with the brass knocker, not sure what to expect. It was an imposing front door; wide and dark green with a large stained glass effect window in it and an additional window high up above the door. No one answered so he tapped again. Looking around while he was waiting, he noticed a red Route Master Double Decker bus stopping on the adjacent main road and a few people jumped on the back, while a man chased after it as it pulled away.

Finally, a woman answered the door; she appeared to be late thirties or early forties by the first etchings of age in her face and the mature style of dress. She was slightly overweight and seemed somewhat stiff and awkward but when she saw him, she smiled, revealing a warmer side to her personality.

"You must be Dr. Paul Eldridge," she said, in a manner that suggested respect. "Mr Richardson informed me last week that you were coming to work with us for a while."

She introduced herself as Miss Tynedale and Paul stepped inside into the hallway. It felt incredibly different to The Establishment's warm interior. The walls were white and the floor was covered in chequered black and white tiles. There was an imposing Victorian staircase facing the door, it had very ornate spindles and newel posts also painted white. Miss Tynedale took Paul straight through to a fairly small office on the ground floor and closed the door. It was nothing like his or Max's office back at The Establishment; this room was a sterile one with rows and rows of books and several filing cabinets likely to be as full as the shelves. The furniture was simple and quite minimalistic; desk, chair and lamp aside from the cabinets and bookshelves. The walls were coloured a very pale green and the paint looked ancient. Paul's initial instincts made him feel somewhat uncomfortable and he became concerned that he would not want to work here.

"So," he began, hoping what she would tell him would allay his fears, "what am I here for?"

She smiled, straight to business; she liked that in a researcher.

"To work with some very special people. This is the more human side of Mr Richardson's business. He has a number of ….. investments he would like you to investigate."

She handed Paul an envelope and he took it tentatively, but did not open it straightaway.

"When do I meet these people?"

Miss Tynedale smiled. "Soon, very soon. It's getting late; we have prepared a room on the top floor for you. Tomorrow you will find out more but for now, please, rest and make yourself comfortable."

He was shown to the top of the house and on the way up, he got a glimpse of the upper floors. Pictures of scientists on the walls of the stairs impressed him but Miss Tynedale moved too quick for him to admire them. The Institute seemed almost medical as he progressed upwards, in juxtaposition to the period living style that The Establishment exemplified. There were more permanent people here it seemed and on the top floor it did provide some accommodation for a limited number of either staff or volunteers too.

He was led to another sterile room with an iron-framed single bed, blanket box, chest of drawers, wardrobe and spindly chair. Paul put his suitcase on the floor at the end of the bed and closed the fine drapes at the large dormer window. Miss Tynedale bid him a good night and arranged to meet in her office at 9am the next morning. He sat on the bed and felt deflated, this place was a world apart from what he was used to. What was he doing here; was he side-lined for his lack of enthusiasm for what he considered unethical studies or was Max actually doing him a favour, ensuring he wasn't wasted on a programme that his assistants were quite capable of running with no conscience?

His sleep was restless, it took time for him to adjust to a new bed and this one was not particularly comfortable. Initially he dozed, dreaming of his little cottage but it was a disjointed dream, tainted by sounds of the city that he was not accustomed to. Around 3am he woke and sat bolt upright in bed, disturbed by a presence in the room. He looked to the window and saw a feminine figure by the drapes, framed by moonlight which startled him, for there should be no one in the room. Had Miss Tynedale crept into his room, for some strange and almost perverted reason?

"Miss Tynedale?" he said.

The figure did not turn to meet his gaze or reply, which was deeply disconcerting.

"Excuse me, but this room is private. You shouldn't be in here."

Finally, the figure spoke. "Where am I?" She had a smooth, velvety voice.

Paul was rattled but attempted to hide the fact. "You're in my room, please leave."

"Where is your room?" she continued.

"You're in The Institute and I strongly believe you have no right to be in here." He tried to sound assertive.

"The Institute?" She seemed to recognise the name.

"Yes, and you must leave."

There was a pause, as if she was considering Paul's words then she made a decision.

"There is a better time and place for this," she declared, and promptly vanished before his eyes. There was a clatter, something had fallen to the floor.

Paul had to rub his eyes, he did not expect her to disappear into thin air, a feeling of coldness washed over him and he felt sick. The experience left an aura of surrealism and he began to question he was actually awake, lucid things could happen on the verge of consciousness. Even though he had subjected his mind to LSD in the preceding years, this appearance had a more disturbing aspect to it. Rather than worry about the event, he lay back in bed and shut it from his mind. It was not long before he was asleep again.

Sleep lasted until the morning and he awoke to the light of dawn, barely remembering the interlude from 3am. His rational mind had accepted the experience was part of the dream state. He rose and moved over to the window, to part the drapes and view his new environment for the first time. On doing so, he trod on something sharp. Wincing, he bent down to look, and found an ornate hair pin on the floor which he picked up and admired with some curiosity. It was certainly very beautiful, set with gems arranged into six numbers; 787878, which seemed odd for a hairpin. Someone must have loved it, for it looked well used. It could have been here a while unnoticed without piercing the foot of a visitor until now. Then he had a flashback of 3am, the figure had vanished with the sound of something clattering to the floor. No, his rational mind refused to make the connection; the figure didn't exist while the hair pin was a material object.

He took breakfast downstairs, which was kindly provided by part-time kitchen staff and he sat in the huge communal living area, which was somewhat more homely than the rest of the house. It had a delicately patterned 1940s wallpaper which was green and yellow and a slightly threadbare carpet that had a traditional pattern on it in green and brown. There were numerous old sofas in the room, a sideboard with a gramophone and Bakelite wireless on it and in the imposing bay window area of the room, there were three tables on which to dine. While drinking his tea, he handed the hair pin to Miss Tynedale and explained that a previous visitor must have dropped it. She turned it over in her hand.

"Hmmm, I don't recognise it and frankly, there have been no female visitors to that room for a number of years. I could ask the chambermaid though."

That had to be the answer, it belonged to the chambermaid. Fortunately, a distraction demanded his attention – the envelope given to him the night before, a message from Max. He slid his finger into the gap and ripped it open, finding a note inside. The message was succinct:

I realise I am wasting your talents back at The Establishment so have moved you to The Institute permanently now. I trust you will enjoy your time here, the people are most supportive and helpful. Your first research brief will arrive shortly but I have arranged for you to meet some rather special people in the next few days, they are investments of mine so take care of them. Don't worry, you haven't lost the cottage, it will always be there for you and at the weekends, you will be able to escape the city and return there if you wish. I will still see you from time to time, just not as often.

Best wishes
Max Richardson.

Paul folded up the note and put it down, feeling somewhat anxious at the prospect of being stationed here on a permanent basis. Miss Tynedale regarded the fact that he had read the note.

"I see you are aware of the proceedings. You will meet the first of the research subjects tomorrow, her name is Emilie. Today, you may take a wander around London, perhaps some sightseeing is in order."

She made her exit, leaving Paul to decide how to spend his settling in day. A day off was something new, all he had known was work, however, he felt no great desire to go sightseeing. He pulled a book out of his suitcase, a copy of H.G. Wells' 'Time Machine'. Here was an activity he didn't normally indulge in, reading fiction so he retired to his room, kicked off his shoes, lay on the bed and buried his head in the book for the rest of the day.

The following day dawned before he knew it and at breakfast, Miss Tynedale reminded him that Emilie was coming in today at 11am. Room 7 on the first floor would be prepared to receive them both, little was required of him, he just needed to meet her. She would be doing all the work. There were two hours to pass, so he wrote a letter to his family, people he saw so very little of and by the time he had finished it, there were only ten minutes until Emilie's arrival. He entered room 7 to find just two tables in the middle and a number of spare tables stacked at the side. This was not what he expected, it was more austere than the other rooms and quite likely it was not a room intended for sociable conversation.

Before long, there was a knock at the door and he answered it. A young woman stood there, it was Emilie; tall and elegant, with long, fair hair that was plaited and pulled back gently to reveal a fresh face, slightly freckled, with startling blue eyes, a short nose and a wide mouth. Her clothing was simple; a flowered dress to her knees and flat shoes. She gave an overall impression of shyness with a nuance of self confidence, an odd blend that gave her an allure that Paul found interesting. A thought crossed his mind albeit briefly, she was rather pretty, he found her attractive, could he date her? He gave her an approving smile.

"*Bonjour Monsieur,*" she said, revealing herself to be French.

"*Bonjour Mademoiselle,*" he replied.

He gestured to her to take a seat wherever she pleased and he sat opposite her, smiling. Emilie studied his face and looked thoughtful, then she smiled too.

"*Alors, Monsieur,*" she said, "*Je suis gêne, non, c'est flatteuse mais je suis une bonne fille!*"

Paul understood French reasonably well and lowered his eyes, he'd been mentally undressing her. For some reason she could sense what he was visualising.

"*Est-ce que vous pouvez lire mon esprit?*" He asked her if she could read his mind as a joke but was surprised at her reply.

"*Je peux lire beaucoup d'esprits,*" she said.

"*Qu'-est-ce que je réfléchis maintenant?*" he pressed.

She smiled. "You are thinking, how can I change this woman's mind?" She spoke beautiful English. "And how long can I continue speaking French fluently?"

Paul laughed. All that effort to speak his best French and she was fluent in English. Ah well. He looked her in the eye, delighting in the mischief, unable to resist flirtation.

"Where would I take you on a date?"

"Monsieur!" She took the question with good humour. "That is very romantic but I would most like to walk in the moonlight!"

Paul was fascinated, either she was an excellent magician or Max's 'investment' really could read minds. His rational mind demanded more and Emilie picked up on his cue. She diverted his attention to two pieces of paper and pens that she pulled from her handbag. She gave one set to him and proceeded to move to a seat two tables away.

"Draw a picture," she told him, "but do not allow me to see."

Paul took the paper and twiddled the pen before commencing to draw. He chose a diagram, the chemical structure of glucose, not very imaginative or passionate or creative but it was something of reasonable complexity that he hoped she would reproduce. When he had finished, he admired his scrawl and then put the pen down.

"Look at your picture, and see it in your mind," Emilie instructed.

He did so, just as she asked. Emilie concentrated, closing her eyes so that she could visualise what Paul had drawn and then she herself began to scribble. It took a few minutes, then she put down her pen, stood up and walked over to him.

"This is what you drew," she said, placing her picture on his table.

He pushed his picture towards hers and they compared. Paul was pleasantly surprised, close, pretty damn close. Her picture was a more artistic rendering of his glucose molecule. He was satisfied that she had indeed seen in her own mind the diagram he had drawn, in fact, he preferred hers. She had style.

Emilie smiled, quite coquettishly and made her way to the door.

"It is finished now," she said, "I hope to see you again soon."

Paul, on impulse got up and gently put his hand on the door. Standing close to her triggered a yearning and he realised it had been three months since one of Max's parties. Self-consciously, he tried to erase the thought of those parties from his mind and any notions of sexual encounters as she had sensed those previously. She paused then made no effort to escape.

"Please, let me take you out for a date. No obligation, I would simply like your company."

She looked him in the eye and decided he was trustworthy. "Okay, but you must behave!" she chided.

"Where can I find you?"

"I am here all day, it is a testing day."

"What are you doing tomorrow?"

She smiled and admired his enthusiasm. "There is testing in the morning but I am free in the afternoon."

"Then I'll come and find you after lunch."

The matter was decided and she had no problem with that. "Where are we going?"

Paul couldn't answer that. "We can decide tomorrow."

With the matter brought to a successful conclusion, satisfying both parties, she disappeared into another room, a clone of the room they were currently in except all the tables were set out and there were a number of men and women in there he had never seen before. He assumed they were carrying out research, perhaps much like what went on at The Establishment. He wondered if they were using electro-magnetic fields, LSD or mind control techniques with these people but Paul would know for certain soon enough, it was a taste of things to come.

Emilie appeared in the living and dining room after lunch and was dressed in a simple tailored neutral coloured dress that fitted her form snugly. Over the top she wore a classic black trench coat, coupled with high heels and her hair was swept up into a chignon. She wore just a little make up but could have gotten away with none with her clear complexion, luminous eyes and rose tinted lips.

"You look stunning," he said, sincerely. He felt honoured to take her out, somewhere, he hadn't decided yet; he rarely applied the laws of organisation to his private life. As he stood appreciating her elegant form, he wracked his brains for the ideal place to take her. Alas, he knew of no place, after all, they had just eaten lunch. So while he stepped out of the dining room to fetch his coat, he stood in the hallway pacing for a few moments. Tower of London? Too gruesome. A walk in Hyde Park? Maybe too droll. Perhaps she would enjoy an afternoon at the Natural History Museum? Maybe they could combine museum and walk. Whichever, it was a plan.

As they left, Miss Tynedale raised an eyebrow and seemed somewhat disapproving but Paul felt he was the golden boy and was safe in the knowledge that Max regarded all females as fair game. He was gentleman enough to hold open the door and led the way to the underground, allowing Emilie to dictate the walking pace. It was a relief to return to the normal world, even if it was the city and the most densely populated in England. It reminded him of his childhood, although the streets and environment had changed somewhat since the twenties and thirties.

"London is still an adventure to you," Emilie commented. "As it is to me, I have been here a year but have seen little of the outside world."

Paul smiled, maybe there could be advantages to dating a telepathic woman.

"Do you know where I plan to take you?" he mused.

"I can close my mind if I wish, because otherwise there would be no surprises. A life without surprises is dull, I do not want life to be written in advance."

Maybe then there could be disadvantages to the sixth sense, life could get predictable to the point of tedium but he guessed it was possible to prevent much of the heartache that often came a person's way. He then regretted that thought passing through his mind, for he noticed a concerned response from Emilie, although she remained silent, his inner sanctum had become briefly visible to her.

They took the underground and alighted at South Kensington, then proceeded along Exhibition Road to the museum. Two women walked by pushing perambulators and almost ran them over, they managed to dodge them at the last minute and a telegram boy in his navy blue uniform with red piping and pillbox cap passed by, bring news of a birth, marriage or death to some family on a nearby street. The museum came into view. Paul was impressed at the architectural splendour of the building, although Emilie did not pay as much attention. She was watching an old man, flat cap on his head, deep in thought whilst smoking a cigarette.

"Penny for his thoughts?" Paul queried.

Emilie smiled. "He is just worrying about his family, his son is sick."

They entered the museum and proceeded to view the dinosaurs and animals, which Emilie gazed at thoughtfully.

"Penny for their thoughts?" Paul joked.

She just gave an elusive smile and they proceeded to wander through cases upon cases of fossils. They talked intermittently, both trying to avoid the topic of what exactly she did at The Institute, it unnerved Paul slightly but Emilie did seem a willing participant so it was unlikely anything seriously unethical was going on. She seemed to be paid well for what she did do, for she was able to dress elegantly and Paul himself knew that Max had no shortage of funds. He wondered if Emilie had ever pierced Max's inner sanctum and pondered it quite intensely for that moment. She was aware of his interest.

"There are some things that we should not know," she declared, "and I do not wish to probe."

He admired her pretty face as a flicker of sadness glimmered transiently. Had she ever delved into Max's consciousness? Had she pierced Paul's own professional demeanour and what conclusion would she arrive at? Could she tell him about aspects of himself he did not understand? She was an intriguing woman and he was tempted to kiss her. He wanted to unclasp the pin that held her hair in an elegant chignon and allow her hair to fall around her shoulders. Paul stood behind her and put his arms around her waist, then, as he encountered no resistance, he kissed her neck. A family of four walked past, the mother tutting in disgust.

Emilie was still looking at the fossils, causing Paul to muse in jest, "Sometimes I feel like a fossil."

She laughed softly and cocked her head to one side, enjoying the feel of his lips. They continued to view the remainder of the displays in the museum and he held her hand, wishing to feel like a teenager again. They moved onto the Egyptian display area, where a selection of paintings were exhibited that depicted Gods and Goddesses. Emilie lingered over the images of the odd hybrid creatures; jackal, crocodile, ibis and hawk headed people.

Paul pointed out the names he could remember.

"This figure here with the dog-like head is Anubis, he presided over mummification and the afterlife. This is Sobek, with the head of a crocodile and I think this is Horus, with the small beak and this is probably Thoth, with the long beak, I believe he was the knowledge keeper."

"Where these Gods real people? What do you think?" Emilie asked him.

He shrugged.

"The Egyptians believed in the after life, and the other world which they called the Duat. Possibly they believed these Gods inhabited that world."

He said it without any religious prejudice, or scientific scorn for spiritual beliefs.

They didn't hover over the paintings for too long and wandered around the remainder of the museum. Towards the end of the visit, he requested permission to kiss her and she did not refuse, but as he kissed her, it did not feel right. He couldn't quite ascertain what he was feeling, then he realised what emotion it was, guilt.

His own conclusion was that she was too gentle and kind a soul to abuse in any way, he knew he could never give her any real affection, even though he was not deliberately unkind, he was naturally distant and his heart lay in his work. Could he change? Maybe not, it was too late for him. He was 38 and most men of his age had been married for several years with children. Still, he would scrutinise each woman he met but he was so locked in his bachelor life that settling down seemed an unlikely bet. Emilie caught his gaze and he noted the dismay that was briefly apparent in her eyes.

The next day was Wednesday and Miss Tynedale had planned meetings both in the morning and afternoon, stepping up the pace so all introductions were made, allowing Paul to progress to research much sooner. Room 7 was set aside again, and contained an identical layout to the previous day when he met Emilie. Whilst waiting, he recalled the pleasantries of that afternoon, how it had felt so relaxed with no pressure to fuck or perform. Yet it had not ended on a positive note. Fortunately, there were no recriminations and they both had realised they were going to work together.

There was a knock at the door and he answered it like before, this time finding two people, a man and a woman standing outside. The woman introduced herself as Beth and the man identified himself as Peter. Beth was a very pleasant woman in her late twenties with very long, dark, wavy hair. Her eyes were large and brown, her nose was somewhat large and her lips were full. She was slightly overweight. Peter was Swiss, tall, a little athletic and somewhat severe looking. His eyes were small and shrewd, his nose was disproportionately large and his mouth had a determined set. He was aged around thirty. They both sat quietly in front of Paul, who in turn was seated in silence, wondering when something would happen.

Beth was the first to speak, her eyes lighting up like a candle.

"You have a lot of people around you."

Paul would have been tempted to look round but he knew the room was empty apart from them.

"She speaks of those who departed," said Peter, with a subtle accent. "The spirits are strong with you."

This was the sort of thing that reminded Paul of Victorian parlour games but he was willing to hear them out.

"One spirit is very strong," Beth said. "Her name is Madeleine."

Paul's eyes opened wider at the sound of her name, both Peter and Beth were aware of his reaction.

"She is happy," Peter indicated, "at peace."

Beth paused, as if listening to someone speak then she spoke herself. "She is worried about you, and disappointed. You're such an intelligent man, so clever, so special but you haven't found happiness."

Paul felt strangely moved. Logic told him that she was gone but the memory of her still haunted him, he wanted these two people to truly be in contact with her but his scientific voice insisted on evidence.

"You could have done your research," Paul's rational mind spoke out, "how do I know it's really her?"

Beth smiled. "She understands." There was a pause while she supposedly listened to messages from beyond the grave. "When the bomb hit, she says it was instantaneous, 'I didn't suffer', she's telling me. The light came for me quickly."

Paul was still slightly unconvinced by these words, although her words had a ring of truth the nature of Madeleine's death had featured in the local paper at the time so if someone wanted to deceive him, all they had to do was go to the library and look at the microfilm. But then again, why go to all that trouble? This meeting challenged his beliefs, for it was not possible to contact the dead, he had not found any evidence of a human soul yet these two people insisted Madeleine was speaking to them. He wanted so much to believe in the existence of the human soul but there was no evidence whatsoever to prove there was an extension of life after death.

"W-where are you?" he asked, hoping he could scientifically relate to the answer.

Peter decided to continue the relaying of messages. "A beautiful place. It's everywhere, and it's nowhere. If you were to locate it, you'd discover somewhere which is of a different time and dimension to your reality, the thread of connection between my world and yours is very thin at certain times. If I was a scientist like you, I could explain it but this realm is beyond simple words."

"She wishes you could believe," Beth said it wistfully on Madeleine's behalf.

"There is something she wants to tell you, something she wishes she could have told you sooner," Peter continued.

"Okay." Paul was receptive, in the sense that his curiosity was aroused.

"'You don't have to be loyal to my memory', she's telling me. It's okay to move on and find happiness. When the chance presents itself, do not turn away because this is meant to be. I know you'll feel reluctant to take the plunge and I can't promise there won't be losses but if you don't, you'll remain an emotionless shell for the rest of your life. There is a woman who will show you great joy and great pain, love is as ever a double-edged sword but that should not prevent you from taking a wife."

Paul swallowed visibly. It was true, he hadn't moved on and was keeping his relationships deliberately shallow. His physical needs were being fulfilled but his emotional ones were being ignored, it was his safety blanket, it made life easy and risk free from heartbreak. Beth and Peter stood up, it was unnecessary to continue the connection, Paul needed to accept what he had been told. He sat quietly while they left the room and gestured to Miss Tynedale that he needed a minute. During that time, he regained his composure, swallowed down his emotions and mentally prepared himself to see who would enter the room next. The next meeting was after lunch.

After a satisfying omelette and a cup of tea, Paul again sat in room 7 and opened the door to his next special guest. Her name was Sakie, a petite girl from Japan with long dark straight hair, beautiful oriental eyes that could have melted Hitler's heart and compact little body. Sakie had the skin of a teenager, showing no signs of ageing or cellular degeneration. She sat down at his table, opposite to him but did not speak. Instead, she took a compass out of her pocket, placed it on the table, pulled up her chair closer to the table and suspended her hands above it.

Paul watched closely. Sakie moved her hands over the top of the compass, slowly at first then she gathered momentum, introducing bodily movements so that finally, the whole of her body performed a circular action. The needle of the compass first began to quiver in response to her hands. As her bodily movements increased in intensity, so did the needle, it responded by spinning around, initially in a sputtering fashion. At the peak of her movement, it spun wildly. When Sakie clocked that he had witnessed the result, she stopped and so did the needle.

A compass responded to the magnetic north pole by pointing towards it. For that needle to spin as it did, it must have been exposed to an aberrant electromagnetic field. Paul wished he had brought his equipment today to test her right there and then. As he hadn't he vowed Sakie would be the first to have her EM field measured, if that was what Max wanted him to do.

She peered at him and spoke. "Finish." Her voice was quiet forceful, a little staccato. She was a girl of few words.

"Thank you Sakie," said Paul, keeping it brief, assuming she knew little English.

Sakie picked up the compass and left, taking a bow before she disappeared out of the door. That was the shortest meeting ever, in and out in four point five minutes. He was speechless, and at a loss what to do for the next thirty minutes. There were three more people to meet, Miss Tynedale stated the best was yet to come. How could anyone top Sakie?

Tomorrow arrived quickly, after an evening of walking in Hyde Park and writing letters back in his room. He had been a guest here at The Institute for four nights now, including this one and it was only the first of these which had been in any way strange.

The visitor had not returned and he was relieved, for that had been a somewhat disturbing night time interlude that he did not wish to be repeated.

Two men entered room 7 at ten o'clock that morning, Oscar and George. George looked quite the gentlemen in his hat, which almost entirely covered his brown hair. He had the nose of an English lord and a wiry frame with it, looking older than his years but he was actually in his thirties. Oscar was black and thick set with dark, curly hair and velvety brown eyes. He was in his very early twenties and had arrived from the Caribbean quite recently at Max's request. They sat at Paul's table. What delights were they about to offer?

Oscar was the first to speak. "I think it best we set up a little experiment."

He pushed a piece of paper across the table towards Paul, along with a pen. This seemed to be a repeat of the task he completed with Emilie only a few days ago. He was about to start drawing on the paper when Oscar placed his hand upon the paper, halting the action of the pen. Paul questioned with his eyes.

"You must take the paper to another room in the house. There you will draw a picture," Oscar said, while George nodded in agreement. "Wait in the room for ten minutes after you have drawn the picture and come back. There will be a surprise waiting for you."

Paul disappeared from the room, slightly puzzled and due to only having knowledge of one more room in The Institute aside from the dining room, he made his way to the room in which he slept. There, he sat on his bed and racked his brain for something to draw. Looking outside, he saw a Morris Minor drive by so he drew a simple, almost child-like car on the paper. For ten minutes he sat as asked, then returned to the room, holding the picture.

When he re-entered room 7, George and Oscar had a piece of paper in front of them and Paul could make out a drawing. He walked over to them, curious and picked up the paper. On it was an image that coincidentally looked very much like the car he had drawn, too much like the car he had drawn. Surprised and convinced no cheating had taken place, he looked at the both of them in turn.

"It is like my eyes and my mind travel to another place, but my body is still here." Oscar pointed to his corresponding body parts and the chair he sat on. "I see distant places."

George seemed to be a man of few words and added nothing.

Paul reflected on what was said, the action of drawing the car seemed to be a result of a peculiar form of long sight which he had never witnessed before.

"Remote viewing," he mused.

There seemed less and less reason to think these people were magicians or charlatans and more reason to think that they were, in fact, psychic.

After lunch, Miss Tynedale brought the next visitor straight into room 7, where Paul sat yet again but for the last time. There was one more visitor and Paul had reason to believe he or she was special and a cut above the rest.

"This is Grace," Miss Tynedale said, gesturing to a sparkly eyed old woman in her seventies, "she's the longest serving resident here."

Grace looked quite withered for her years but there was still a glint of intelligence in her eyes. Her hair was white and wispy albeit long enough to tie into a bun which sat in the nape of her neck. She was small with rounded shoulders and she walked slowly, each step being carefully calculated for she was cursed with osteo-arthritis and a slight scoliosis of the spine. Paul warmed to her instantly, she was just like somebody's grandmother, the matriarch who would bake cakes and serve tea on a Sunday afternoon.

Grace took hold of his hands and the sparkle in her eyes

began to burn with a luminous intensity.

"You're wondering why you're here," she chortled. "Well," she continued, "you are meant to be here, to change your life. You see, you're here to find the answers, to challenge your own limited view of the world."

Paul looked her in the eye quite intently and she continued.

"I know you think you have already gained a certain view on life that elevates you above all the rest, but there's still plenty more to discover. Your journey will be rewarding but it will be painful too. You must learn to stay strong."

He found her words a little uncomfortable. "How do you arrive at this conclusion?"

She smiled, revealing a fine set of dentures. "I have always seen the truth about people."

He was intrigued. "What else do you know?"

"The future, of course," she said, as if it was unnecessary to ask, "that's why I'm here."

Paul decided to question her further, if at least for his own amusement. "Will I have a long life?" Not a very imaginative question, but one the majority of people would ask.

Grace scrutinised him and looked surprised. "Longer than you could believe!"

He wasn't impressed by her answer, it was too vague. Unconvinced, he questioned her further.

"Will I become famous for what I do?"

She paused to think, then answered. "In many years time, the world will know your name but not for the reason you expect. The Lord works in mysterious ways." Paul smiled at this remark, if only she knew. "Your work will be extremely important for mankind although you will not receive the recognition you deserve, but you will want it this way."

Paul found this hard to believe, he was driven towards recognition and often felt frustrated that his work was not published, if anything, given the choice, anonymity would his last choice. He still found her predictions vague and unconvincing.

"What else can you tell me about my future?" He decided to ask a somewhat inane question. "Will I get married and have kids?" This straightforward question was more of an in joke for Paul.

Grace seemed more interested in this question. "Oh yes, not for a little while but there'll be a very special woman in your life." Grace suddenly put her hand to her heart and looked distressed, but this passed. "Like I said, you will need to be strong, for yourself and your family. You will find solace." She paused and gave a big smile, which was followed by a look of abject confusion. "I do see children that are connected to you, lots of them, an awful lot of them actually."

Paul frowned. "Well, are they *all* mine?" It was too late in his life to be that busy.

Grace closed her eyes and opened them. "I believe so."

Her words were intriguing yet quite unbelievable, no one could substantiate them unfortunately and only time would tell. He himself didn't foresee a single child, it was too late a stage in his life for love and family now. As a scientist however he was eager for evidence so he couldn't resist asking another question.

"What's going to happen to me in the next week? Anything out of the ordinary?" He wished for a prediction that related to a particular event, that he could measure after it had happened.

Grace tried to focus in on the immediate future. She looked concerned. "There's a party this weekend, lots of wealthy people and girls looking for husbands and money. Don't leave Lucy alone in the bedroom."

Paul didn't know a Lucy but it was true that there was to be a party the coming weekend, another one of Max Richardson's extravaganzas. Well, he would find out if she was right soon.

"I'm not always right," Grace said, unexpectedly, "that's why you're here. I tell the truth according to what I see but not all my predictions come true. Max wants you to tell him why."

Paul felt a little exasperated, he thought he'd been brought here to uncover some of life's mysteries not investigate a clairvoyant. Surely the laws of chance dictate some predictions will be true and some false?

Grace stood up a little shakily and began to walk slowly towards the door, aided by Miss Tynedale. Before she left the room, she turned to Paul.

"It's not so bad, your life will be one in a million. You're just too impatient!"

Paul smiled, yes, he could be. Now that was a claim he could substantiate.

From that point onwards, I worked at The Institute while Max Richardson continued to develop upon my previous work back at The Establishment. Still today I don't know exactly what that continuation entailed but I was paid well throughout my time at The Establishment to not unduly worry about the exploitation of my findings. At least my work had not been in vain. Nothing was ever published, which was a disappointment to me and so far, I hadn't drawn any earth shattering conclusions, well, not since my doctoral research.

I did find I was able to apply some of my background knowledge of quantum mechanics to Grace's clairvoyance. A number of other so-called precognitives and modern day seers also came and went during my first year at The Institute, of which I became very sceptical. A few that claimed to have glimpsed the future gave some predictions that were largely incorrect, with the sort of accuracy that would be expected by chance. It's difficult to say whether some were simply attention seekers and some wanted to be prophetic because it 'ran in the family'. The seers, as I called them made much more dramatic predictions regarding the next forty years, which included the Third World War and the apocalypse. At that time, I couldn't have verified such long term prophecies, perhaps this was the reason they chose to make outlandish claims, because they knew they wouldn't be disproved in the near future. Many predictions were tainted by religious preconceptions of Armageddon and the coming climax of the millennium, something I called 'prejudicial interference'. For that reason I chose not to work with them.

However, Grace was different. She hadn't asked for this and in a way resented her life under scrutiny at The Institute. Her potential foreknowledge of the future, if heeded had the capacity to change events and the outcome of situations. She warned me not to leave a woman called Lucy in the bedroom alone. At that time I hadn't met anyone with this name so didn't give her words a second thought until Max's birthday party the following weekend. He introduced a new member to the circle whose name happened to be, fate would have it, Lucy. I became wary that night, a coincidence, or reality? Later that night, she took an accidental overdose of barbiturates after a session with Max in his bedroom, he left her in there while going to pursue another encounter. I had an intense foreboding and luckily for her, found her in time. A few years later, Marilyn Monroe wasn't as fortunate and sadly, Grace had made remarks concerning the blonde goddess who would be found dead in her bed, with the phone still in her hand. But who was in a position to change the future in this case? In Lucy's case, Grace was simultaneously right and wrong, her warning had been correct although in terms of a prediction, a death did not occur. I examined many of Grace's warnings and predictions and overall found a seventy five percent accuracy, in terms of key points made in the prediction that correctly matched the events that transpired. Her accuracy went way beyond what would be expected by chance.

How did she do it? There wasn't and still isn't any way of measuring her ability directly, it's hard to observe the unseen. All I could ever do was testify to her accuracy and hypothesise regarding the technique she used, the modus operandi. Does the future cast some sort of shadow that a few individuals can attune to? Is there an emotional, psychic shock wave that has the ability to travel backwards in time, like the tachyon or simply defy the laws of time completely? Time is not an absolute, it is only relative to the speed of the observer. More basically, the future can also be seen as a direct result of actions in the present, cause and effect so predictions become logical, as in when a person sees dark clouds in the sky they know with some certainty that soon it will rain. If a psychic could attune themselves to this natural flow, this pulse of the present moment, maybe someone shrewd and perceptive enough could deduce the future.

I never thought this latter interpretation could ever fully explain Grace's predictions. I think much came down to her ability to perceive another person's inner motivations, something akin to a shrewd, canny gypsy fortune teller but there were many specifics that she couldn't have known, for example, Lucy's name. Grace confessed that much of what she says is the result of a gut feeling, 'I have an instinct about people' but she also told me she sees words and pictures in her mind's eye, of disturbing events. There was a clear emotional connection with her predictions, for in the scientific, objective tests with the Zener cards, her accuracy wasn't significant but she was able to indicate if someone would suffer the loss of a loved one in the near future. I believe this fact alone will ensure there'll never be any definitive proof of psychic ability, despite the fact many of Grace's recipients have been deeply touched by her predictions. Throughout the study, I shied away from personal predictions because I had the impression there was something unpleasant in my future. Several times she tried to tell me but I declined on the grounds of objectivity. The truth was, I was too afraid of her accuracy even though I may have been able to change those events. Ultimately, after the events had transpired, I accepted them as inevitable cause and effect.

Finally, regarding Grace's accuracy, I drew the conclusion that the future is dependent upon quantum factors, namely indeterminacy. The outcome of a particular reaction can only be predicted in terms of probability, both at quantum and prophecy level. In the double slit experiment, one cannot predict which hole an electron will pass through, one can only state the outcome in terms of probability but until the process is observed, we cannot know for sure which hole it passed through. Quantumly speaking, that electron exists in a never-never land until it is observed. When we do not measure it, it displays both probabilities and when we observe it, it chooses a path, therefore we put the electron in a definite quantum state. Perhaps an analogy can be drawn here, Lucy was potentially both alive and dead until I discovered her and pushed her into a definite state of existence. Possibly in another parallel universe she died, *although such theories are hard to prove.*

Sakie was another matter entirely. I measured her EM field on the second day at The Institute and found it to be the most extraordinary spectacle I've ever seen. It was ten times more powerful than anything I've measured before and extended several feet from her skin. From then on, I termed this phenomenon the Biological Electromagnetic Field, or BEMF for short. She was able to drive a compass crazy and short-circuit electrical equipment, sometimes accidentally to her chagrin whilst listening to something beautiful on the radio, or watching a television programme. (In those days it was still very much a novelty, everything was black and white and there was only one BBC channel plus ATV, the commercial channel). After that, I saw little of her and I concluded that because of her abilities, she was regarded as a prize and contracted out for 'jobs'. I became wary when I heard of power cuts or plane crashes due to compass malfunctions. When I did ask her, she said very little about them and not just due to her poor English.

I did work extensively with, not only Grace but Emilie, Beth and Peter, as they didn't disappear from The Institute very often. With Emilie, I performed many experiments with her and volunteers, I wanted to be sure her answers weren't triggered by non-verbal clues and body language. Her accuracy was impressive, even when the volunteers' faces were obscured. At that time, I never reached any particular conclusion regarding how she did it but concurred that telepathy did indeed appear to be genuine, at least in Emilie's case. It was almost like the human brain transmitted some type of radio wave and Emilie had the ability to receive this transmission. When I was more established at The Institute, I learned that she was an interrogator's assistant who was contracted out when usual lines of questioning were not forthcoming. Beth and Peter claimed they could contact spirits and they were rigorously tested, again, accuracy was startling. Many facts could be checked, providing a good file of evidence. An explanation? Maybe there is a form of existence after death, death of the body but not of consciousness, not of the soul. Possibly consciousness then exists in another quantum state, another dimension even, I wasn't closed-minded towards that probability.

My work at The Institute was rewarding, spiritually although I got to spend little time at my own home. I stayed in London during the week and went home at the weekend, the only practical thing I could do at the time. That way, I felt my personal life and work were separate. I was also free of the pressure to attend Max Richardson's sex, drugs and alcohol parties, although I made infrequent attendances, after all, there was no special woman in my life. It was hard to believe but Grace insisted I would find love although in a way, I was relieved because the lack of it made my life less complicated.

During these studies, the Berlin Wall was erected which effectively divided the city and Europe into east and west with a high barrier topped with barbed wire. Even though World War II had ended, there was a new conflict of suspicion and mistrust. I also celebrated my 40th birthday quietly.

In 1962, however, Grace's health began to deteriorate rapidly.

It was so serious that Max Richardson dropped everything to rush to London, Paul had never seen such an immediate reaction. Max normally had a certain indifference where his protégés were concerned but Grace was special and perhaps there was more to it than being so gifted. On his arrival, Max gave the impression he had not slept all night and went straight to her bedroom, closing the door. There he found Grace in bed, her breathing strained and placed the flowers he'd brought with him into a spare vase. Gently, he drew up a chair and sat beside her.

Max was apologetic. "I'm so sorry I haven't been in touch recently, I've been too busy, I'm sorry."

Grace sighed. "I always accepted you have a life of your own. I know your work is important, it will be long after I'm gone."

He swallowed hard. "It'll happen soon, won't it?"

She smiled. "I'm not afraid, I will find peace."

Max didn't know what else to say but Grace broke the silence.

"When your time comes, you will find peace. I know that in your life, you will find it hard to be at peace because of the things you have done. God will forgive you. I forgive you."

He seemed grateful for her words, they did not come as a shock, he knew his demons and he fully expected to take several of them to the grave.

She continued. "But you should treat that child of yours better."

Max was now taken aback by her words. He had no intention of having children whatsoever.

"What child?"

Grace felt pained to talk about his offspring.

"Like you, your offspring will have demons, spending their entire life searching for peace within but you can still change this. Their aura will be very strong but it needs to be channelled in the right direction."

Max found this hard to believe. He had a long-standing casual lover but he never swore any commitment to her and couldn't foresee this changing.

"I don't want you to make a mistake that you will sincerely regret," Grace spoke with concern, for Max and his child. "But you will be very fortunate, you'll witness something, perhaps the single most important event in history. At first, you won't see it for what it is but you won't be blind to it either."

"What is this event?" Max was curious and wondered if he would indeed get a slice of the action.

"The Shining Lights," was her answer.

The first thing that came to Max's mind was the UFO phenomenon, it was the only explanation he could muster. However, surely he would see it for what it is, phenomenal!

"Will I play an important role in this event?" Max couldn't help desiring to share the glory.

"They will be very close to you, very close." She seemed uneasy and didn't want to say anymore on the matter. Instead she offered something else instead. "The Lights will cause conflict, because of what they stand for."

"War?" Max questioned, envisioning nuclear conflicts.

Grace hesitated. "Think of it as more of a revolution, which a lot of people will not welcome. These Lights will upset some very important people, although you will not see this happen. You will play a part in its genesis."

"Who are these people?" he continued to question.

She had one more thing to tell him.

"There will be a woman, a very special person who is a gift to the world, capable of having a great impact upon humanity. She must be protected at all costs as once the world discovers what she is, she won't be safe. Her secrets must not fall into the wrong hands."

"Who is she and how will I know I've found her?"

"Oh, you'll know from the moment you first meet her," Grace replied. "The research connected with her must also be protected, especially the primeval number. Many people will be interested in the power of this number."

"Is this my research?" Max pressed.

He wanted to pursue this further but Grace now declined, she needed to rest. Max stayed with her and remained at The Institute until her eventual death three days later. Paul saw him emerge from her bedroom after she had passed, surprisingly in a highly emotional state. Max was not normally emotional but Grace's death deeply affected him.

"I'm sorry too," Paul said, in sympathy.

Max turned to him. "Not as sorry as I am. She was my mother."

With that, he quietly and slowly retired to one of the bedrooms and wasn't seen for a few days. Miss Tynedale was the only one to enter and leave this room. During this time, his mother's words preyed on his mind. Meanwhile, Paul was shocked to hear the truth of Grace's identity. True, he had never seen her full name in print but he was amazed she had never mentioned it. Was she ashamed of him deep down, or had she not wanted to compromise the research? Furthermore, did Max have her gift? In retrospect, there was no evidence, although he did have a keen business savvy. Paul concluded he'd never know. All he did know was he'd neglected his own family and promptly telephoned, visiting very shortly after. No, he'd never take them for granted again.

So there were only six psychics now. Paul missed Grace, she was special but now she was no longer here. Beth and Peter claimed to have received messages from her but she was reluctant to be involved, The Institute had consumed much of her later years and she wasn't willing to be a part of it anymore. She was at peace, for now and if the necessity arose, she'd step in.

In Grace, Max had possessed a star, an outstanding psychic that offered England tactical advantages in the Cold War. Now she was gone. He had to find another star, someone special to replace not only the hole in his heart but put The Institute firmly back on the research map.

5
The Waking Dream

Saturday 3rd November 1990

Why does it always take so long to recover from a hangover? Ava thought, as she was finally able to stomach a meal.

The previous night, there had been a gathering for Sam's 18th birthday, and now that he had become an adult, a legal drinking session was in order. There had been a large group of college students, as he was in the second year of his A levels, plus Ava whom he could never leave out. She felt like the odd one out at first, as the group was considerably younger than her twenty two years but as the night had progressed, she had drunk sufficient alcohol to adapt to a younger mind set and by the end of the night, it became clear she would regret it in the morning. It had been good to see Sam again, and she couldn't help but notice what a polite yet intense young man he was becoming. After vowing to keep in regular contact with him, they had hugged and then she fell out of the taxi.

Life had moved on somewhat since the completion of her degree; it had commenced with repeated job searches, deliberation over whether to continue studies at a higher level and it had been tainted with financial stress. Emma, her flatmate had managed to find a job in a local fashion store, much to her dismay after studying for a degree in textile design and Jason, the former art student was still unemployed. Ava had finally secured a job at a small laboratory not too far away, although she did wonder sometimes what the prospects were for promotion. There had been a possibility of working in her uncle's lab, but she had wanted to make it independent of family help, although sometimes she'd wished she'd made a more formal enquiry.

Today, she had enjoyed a quiet day at the flat, an upgrade to the last dwelling but she had remained with her previous flatmates as they had such a good relationship. Instead of going to a local bar, which she would normally do on a Saturday night but didn't due to the previous night's intoxication, she decided to go to bed and read. While she had been a student, she had pored over text books about genetics, now she had finished she felt like indulging in something superficial and steamy. There was a Jackie Collins book sitting on her bedside table with a layer of dust on it so she dismissed the unwanted particles with a gust of breath.

She read until 1am then thought it best to sleep, to avoid wasting a perfectly good Sunday. She looked out of her bedroom window, finding a full moon staring down at her then closed her eyes, waiting for oblivion. For some reason it did not come. Insomnia was never her problem, although tonight it was. There was an odd tingle creeping across her skin, as if the air were filled with static electricity which was penetrating her body and pulsing through her nervous system. A moment later, she sensed a presence in the room. Reluctantly, she opened her eyes.

Someone was in her room, yet there was an inhuman and ethereal quality about this being. Light emanated from the person and they, although having a humanoid shape, in fact had no real features. Ava felt frozen in her bed, the situation felt surreal but as a scientist, she had to concede that it wasn't reality, it was impossible. Even more implausible was the existence of large wings, which the figure folded behind its back. Ava didn't know what to think, should she slap herself to wake up or allow the lucid dream to unfold?

The figure moved towards her but its presence was soothing despite its faceless features. All it possessed were eyes that glowed iridescently, moving through the hues of blue, purple and pink. As it neared her, however, the face began to take on form and transmuted into a young man with fair hair, whom Ava instantly recognised.

"Michael?"

The figure of a young man, albeit still with wings, no clothing or sexual organs sat on the end of her bed.

"I think it is essential you believe that to be," he said.

Ava realised that it was foolish to believe that Michael would suddenly appear in her bedroom with wings after a few years of silence, or even to appear with wings in any situation. The being in her room must have drawn a memory from her subconscious, one long suppressed, one that held a yearning for something no longer in her life.

"If you're not Michael, then who are you?"

The figure posing as Michael fell silent, as if in deep thought then answered, "I don't think you're ready for that knowledge yet."

She surveyed his face and found that the usual imperfections were absent, such as the slight kink in his nose where it had been previously broken and re-set, but the likeness was very convincing. It made her realise she still missed him, even after a few years had elapsed since his disappearance. The Michael figure smiled, conveying a sense of warmth.

"You must be wondering why your perception of the world around you seems distorted at times."

Ava felt reluctant to discuss the matter, how could she admit to anyone the psychological condition of her sister and her own leanings in that direction? She couldn't.

The Michael figure continued. "It is an essential process in your development and crucial to discover who you are and why you are here."

"Who I am?" Ava questioned. "Do you mean who my parents are?"

"Your creation will become a relevant matter one day. But for now you need to discover yourself, you are your own unique person and you need not tie your purpose to material relations.

You are currently resisting a natural process that must take place, it has been postponed for a number of years now."

Ava was interested in what the figure had to say, primarily because she had told no one of her psychological predicament and this entity appeared to be the only one with any answers.

"Why has this process you speak of been postponed?" she asked.

The figure pondered, apparently reluctant to give away the solution, much like a good teacher would encourage discovery in his students.

"The environment was unfortunate."

This answer was not helpful and Ava began to feel frustrated.

"Why can't I remember my parents?" she pried.

"Some things are simply too painful, especially for a young child attempting to understand her place in the world. You will remember, the truth will become known but you must examine this for yourself, in time. You are like a bookshop that has been closed for a long period of time, the knowledge has been abandoned, disorganised. Events will soon be set into motion which will enable you to begin reading these books again, and add new ones to the collection. There is a new job on the horizon, which you should be humble enough to accept. It is not charity, it is the beginning of the true path and yet, only the beginning. It is not your final destination."

Ava had to ask. "And what is my final destination?"

The Michael figure responded emphatically. "Something you cannot yet comprehend."

"But I believe in free will," she remonstrated, "you're suggesting that everything is preordained."

"Of course there is free will, you have already chosen your path, you just don't know it yet."

The figure started to fade subtly. Ava had one last question that had been sidelined, despite being a burning issue.

"Why did Michael disappear from my life?"

The fading continued, but, as if it were a sudden change of heart, the figure leaned forward and kissed her on the cheek. She felt a strange burning sensation, then nothing. The moon still shone through the window. It was 4am, which could be such a lonely time and the appearance of a figure who looked just like Michael exacerbated the emotional famine. Confusion about his absence returned and she wondered if the answer could ever be found. Her last memory of him was his pledge to take her to the States on the completion of her degree, he had already graduated at that time and as an engineer it was easy for him to secure work abroad, he had done so too. On their last day together, he had held her face in his hands, kissed her softly and told her with sincerity that their new life in the States was going to be wonderful. How could he just disappear after that? There was no answer since then on his phone and no one at his flat, in fact, there was a 'to let' board attached to the brickwork. Many of her friends had to conclude that he'd run out on her and had entered the States alone, without her. Did he ever mean what he had said? Michael had never lied to her, she could think of no instance when he had done so.

Her rational mind was in conflict; she found herself dealing with an old hurt but was also confused about the appearance of the figure in her bedroom. It must have all been a lucid dream. Absent mindedly, she touched her cheek and found it felt rough to the touch. Startled, she jumped up and examined her face in the bathroom mirror. A red mark stood out, as if it had been previously exposed to the sun. There was physical evidence to suggest that the lucid dream had been more real than she wanted to believe. But how could such a meeting ever have taken place and how could something imaginary leave physical evidence?

It called into question the other hallucinations she had experienced, did they have any basis in reality after all, no matter how absurd that reality? Recently she had begun to consider the possibility that somehow she was ingesting LSD, it seemed the only explanation for the similarity of her hallucinations to what Annette had experienced when intoxicated with psychoactive drugs. What was it Aldous Huxley wrote about? The doors of perception. Well, they were certainly opening, and refusing to close. But how could she be ingesting drugs? Could someone be contaminating food or drink with drugs? Then again, it would be necessary to isolate her food and drink and in the flat, many grocery items were shared. It led her back to the unfortunate conclusion; she was developing schizophrenia. Her sister Maria had been institutionalised for this and if Ava developed the same condition, it would ruin her career. Was it now time to seek help with the condition, or as the fire angel indicated, let the process take its course?

6

The New Recruit

Putting pen to paper is most unlike me, I'm not a writer and never have been a literary fanatic yet I feel I must tell someone my story. It's an incredible tale and for a long period in my life, I've been away and these writings are an attempt to fill in the gaps, but also to relate the story of where I came from and what I've experienced in my surreal life. In a sense I can regard myself as a traveller as I have been to places that no one could ever dream of or comprehend.

I was born in London on the 7th November, 1944. The time was ten minutes to eleven in the morning, Greenwich Mean Time and the day was cold and windy, the country was at war. My father is called Mohammed, like the prophet and he was born in Persia, although now it's called Iran, very early in the 20th century. He has a large family, three sisters and three brothers who still live in Iran although one brother lives in Saudi Arabia today. His grandmother was an Egyptian woman and I do believe that originally, my paternal line drifted to Persia from Turkey sometime in the 19th century. He came to London when he was eighteen to study at university and build a life for himself over here, believing that he could better provide for his future family in a place that produced more wealth than Persia.

My mother is a beautiful English woman called Elizabeth, her birth name was Brown and she came from a lower-middle class family who live in Scotland now. She knows very little of her bloodline. Therefore, I am an amalgamation of European, Persian, Egyptian and Turkish blood; I have my mother's features and long, dark hair with a tint of the Middle East in my complexion. Yet I have a fire that burns in my heart that is unlike both of my parents.

Elizabeth came to London to study history when she was 18 years old, that was in 1938, just before the war. My father was a lecturer at her university, he was a historian and she was his student. He fell in love with her because she was beautiful and intelligent, a perfect wife and mother but he could not be with her or marry her while she was a student. He wanted her to give up her studies but she wouldn't. When she completed her studies, she gave in to him and they married. Her parents were angry because she was marrying a man who came from Persia and they thought people from the Middle East were barbarians. I think her family were very racist. However, mother didn't listen and they got married in 1942.

Her parents refused to leave her money in their will but what truly hurt her was the wretched silence; they haven't spoken to her since. I think her sister, Hannah tried to keep contact, I met her a few times and found her to be a woman of great compassion but her brother, Donald's treatment of her was quite disgusting though. He would always refer to my father as 'that sand nigger', a term I was to hear much of during my childhood. My father continued to teach and mother stayed at home, which was in London. I think the fusion of two religions has been quite a challenge, although I think Islam provided the stronger influence due to father being the head of the household and in those days, responsible for all the decisions regarding his wife and future family.

I came along two years later. My birth was very difficult and because of this, mother couldn't have any more children. She tells me father was very upset that he would never have a son and she was afraid that he'd leave her and take me away. This didn't happen, I think he loved her too much to do such a thing. His family thought mother was no good because she couldn't have any more children and they gave her a hard time for something that wasn't her fault, something that was surely the will of Allah? She told me this was a very difficult time for her, I was only a baby but he was a good father and a good husband.

The first seven years of my childhood were spent in London, a place where it was generally tolerated if you had an alternative ethnic background so at first, the children would play with me and my childhood was no different to anyone else's on the surface.

You would play with someone of your own social class, so therefore *some children were 'too good' to play with and some were regarded as 'beneath you'. Gender roles were very clear; boys played war games and football, built go-karts and enjoyed train sets and being general scallywags while girls played hopscotch, skipping games and trundled their dolls prams around the streets. Even at a young age, I questioned these roles.*

"Why can't I play football with the boys?" I asked my parents, quite frequently.

"Because it's a boys' game," my mother told me. "It's too rough for girls."

"I don't mind rough," I replied.

This was a view entirely supported by my father, but I could never understand the reasoning. Suffice to say, I took no notice of their opinions and I would join in with the boys on another street so my parents couldn't see what I was doing. When I returned home with my dress torn and grazes on my knee, I would explain that I had been playing a chasing game and fallen over, enduring the sting of the medicinal iodine as I lied too convincingly.

I would enjoy playing handstands and cartwheels in the front garden with the other girls and we would delight in letting the boys view a flash of our navy blue knickers. However, if my father caught me he would drag me indoors and scold me severely with a slipper for my immodest behaviour, so much so that it was painful to sit down for the rest of the day. It didn't stop me though and father was so exasperated that he finally locked me in my room. I screamed and kicked at the door, hating the feeling of being trapped inside my room but no one would let me out, so I would climb out of the window, secretly play with my friends and then return to my room in time for supper before anyone realised I was missing.

"What am I going to do with you, Tahra?" father would say. "You don't listen to us and can't follow rules. You want to climb trees and play football with the boys and cannot restrain yourself as a girl should."

Mother tried to teach me dressmaking and home economics, as she repaired my clothes on a regular basis and hoped I would be enticed into cooking by baking some delicious cakes. However, I had other plans for my life.

"I want to do something really special with my life," I told her.

"What do you mean?" she questioned.

"Well, housework is so dull," I replied. "I want to do something outstanding, something magical, I don't know yet but there's more to life than being a mummy and a wife."

She frowned.

"But being a mother is magical, darling."

She failed to convince me.

"I'm capable of great things," I protested. "In my previous lives, I was talented and successful and this one shouldn't be any different."

"There's no such thing as previous lives," mother retorted, perhaps upset by my opinions.

I was aware then that I had lived before, even though I couldn't recall any specific facts and this disregard for my dreams and ambitions, and resentment at the limitations of my gender has helped lay the foundations for the path my life would take.

But my destiny took a different turn when we moved out of the city and into an area that was dominated by white middle class families. Because of the colour of my father's skin, people spoke to him differently and were naturally wary of him. The children didn't know what to think of me either and in my new school, I soon realised how cruel they could be. Because of my father's religion, we never celebrated Christmas which was never an issue for me previously, as you don't miss what you don't have but the other children on the street thought differently.

"Too poor for presents?" they would taunt, flashing their new go-karts, scooters or doll prams on the streets, while I had nothing to show.

I would try to explain our religion but they would continue their taunts, so much so that I got angry and threw a rock at one of them. That was my first beating at the hands of other children; two boys and a girl pinned me down on the ground and punched me in the stomach several times. It was then that I realised I didn't have the physical strength to fight back, even though I tried. I was too ashamed to tell my parents and too defiant to cry, they'd never see how they'd hurt me.

My life then comprised of bullying, taunts and a strong awareness of being different to everyone else.

"Go back to your own country," some would say, spitting at me.

"But I'm British," I would protest, although it fell on deaf ears.

The bullying continued no matter. I would get stones thrown at me, my clothes scattered around in the PE changing rooms, girls would pull my hair and tell me I was ugly because I wasn't white, boys would kick their footballs into my face; the list goes on. It was this aspect of my life that pushed me into discovering where my strengths lay.

I had a special friend called Annie who made those years bearable. We would always play together, games such as skipping elastics with a thick tree trunk as the third person or Knock-a-Door-Run after school, we were rarely caught out. One day, a boy called Edward threw a stone at me, which caught me on the side of my eye and it began to bleed immediately. Without thinking, Annie picked up the stone and hurled it back at him, which made his lip bleed and in response, he pushed her to the ground and she hit her head. I was so angry, not only that he'd hurt my friend but I also remembered every act of unkindness that I had suffered while at this new school. In my mind, I wanted to hurt Edward so bad that he'd cry and I pushed him hard at the wall, channelling all my emotions into that one act of bravado.

Then the strangest thing happened. He looked into my eyes, which were by now full of rage and his face crumpled. We locked eyes and something connected, burst out of me; a surge of emotion, a feeling of complete power, I had never experienced this before. Edward began to cry uncontrollably, it wasn't due to any physical pain as I had only pushed him against the wall, it was the energy, the power that I was communicating with my whole being. I could affect the emotions of others.

This made me realise that I could make people do things, sometimes things that would get them into trouble. In class, if children threw things at me, I could make them feel extremely angry and say swear words out loud, or insult the teacher and they would have to stand in the corner. Sometimes they would get the cane, which was even more satisfying. I *began to feel less afraid but I noticed the other children began to fear me because bad things happened to them when they upset me.*

Therefore, my childhood was not as happy as it could have been. It was very lonely and it's hard to explain how being ostracised over a long period of time makes you feel. I think sometimes the sense of powerlessness it can give you drives you a little crazy, so much so that you will grab any opportunity to regain that feeling of control. I hated myself for the dark thoughts I had and the impulses to hurt people in retaliation, and this only served to alienate me more. I think this affected my personality but I had one thing that other bullying victims didn't have; the hidden power to exact some kind of revenge that was undetectable and untraceable. In those days, bullying was not dealt with and I felt too humiliated to tell my parents, although they must have sensed I was unhappy but I had ways of dealing with it, without that power, I would never have developed any self confidence. This inner darkness excited and disgusted me at the same time, secretly it scared me though because once the feeling of revenge took over, it controlled me and it gave me pleasure. As I got older, I felt my power intensify. I began to wonder what would happen if one day, I got so angry and couldn't hold back, could I do something incredibly destructive that I could never forgive myself for?

I could also help others. If they were afraid to do something and wanted to be brave, I could make them feel courage. If they were sad and crying, I could make them feel happy again. Only people special to me, or who were kind deserved my help, I chose to punish those who wished to hurt me. This light within me gave me hope that I may not turn out to be evil. This is how I lived now; I could protect my loved ones and myself. I was comfortable.

I was able to focus on enjoying my life again, with this new found confidence. Very early in June of 1953, it was Queen Elizabeth's coronation and we crowded around our new television, a fine piece of technology in a wooden cabinet. It took a few minutes for it to warm up so the picture didn't come on straightaway and sometimes father had to move the aerial around the parlour to get a good signal. The picture wasn't very good but it was the first time anyone had ever seen royalty being crowned so we were entranced. This was followed by a wonderful street party and father helped the neighbours take out their tables and place them end to end in the road. There was bunting everywhere and party hats, sandwiches, cakes and crisps. I helped my mother tip the crisps into a large bowl and we twisted open the little packets of salt, sprinkling it all over to flavour them. That day forms happy memories for me.

Annie and I had a penchant for 'Journey Into Space' too, a wireless programme which scared children because of its creepy sound effects and spooky music. It was set in the future of 1965 and was all about man's conquest of the moon. We were enthralled by this half hour programme, which always ended with a cliff-hanger. The thought of exploring made me feel wistful and adventurous.

"One day, I want to go into space," I declared.

No one ever took me seriously.

But my happiness didn't last forever though. Annie and her family moved house, they went to live in a town much further west, far away from me. I could still write to her but it wasn't the same, I was overcome with loneliness and an emptiness in my heart.

It was then that I found a new ability. One night, I found myself staring back at my own body on the bed from the other side of the room. I realised I could move around my bedroom, completely free of my body and even watch my parents sleep in the next room without even being there. Maybe the desire to escape my sad and lonely life gave me some sort of incentive to master this skill as easy as learning to breathe, it seemed so natural and automatic. Then it occurred to me I could see my friend again.

I missed Annie so much that one afternoon, I suddenly found myself standing in front of her. She couldn't see me but I knew I was really there. Annie looked a little older and she wore her hair short and wavy now. Her bedroom was small and full of dolls and teddy bears. I could look out of the window and see rows and rows of houses, with children playing hopscotch or skipping games outside. After a while I came back home because I was tired. This happened again, many times I would visit Annie and each time she didn't know I was there. I began to think it wasn't real, how could it be but then in one letter, she sent some *photographs of her bedroom, her new friends and the street which she lived on. It all looked exactly like what I saw when I visited her, then I began to believe my travels were real.*

I could also escape my unhappiness at night as well as day. I travelled to many places, I don't know where but I found tranquil places in the mountains or on a beautiful beach with palm trees. To help me remember I would draw what I saw, my pictures were very vivid although I was not very artistic. Mother asked about them and I just told her they were special places. In secret I looked in my books about the world and found some of the places I drew. One drawing looked like a little village in the Alps and others looked like beaches in the Caribbean. I also found some temples in China and Malaysia. I had really been there! This was a fantastic way of going on holiday for free! But I couldn't share my travels with anyone, it was my secret.

The strange little talents I developed were kept hidden from my parents, my school, my community and society. However, I became too complacent and drew attention to myself. I used my talent to help me in my education and I was accused of cheating in my eleven plus exam. It was impossible to explain to the school why my answers were identical to those of other students, or why some answers were perfectly identical to those written on the answer paper. I remember sitting quietly, faced by my teacher and my parents, unable to tell them I was just different. Would they believe me? Would my parents embrace me because of my talents? I began to wonder if what was inside me was wicked and immoral, or whether there was a better way to use my talents. For many days my parents were upset with me but still I didn't explain. I thought about changing their feelings, giving out love and forgiveness but I questioned if this was right. Finally, I decided to tell all.

At first, they seemed shocked, what I was telling them didn't seem real. However, the more I told them, the more they believed me. I described my unhappiness here and the bullying I had endured, how it revealed what I was capable of, how I would visit Annie because I was lonely and I explained that when they felt despair, I would give them hope. I demonstrated my ability to let my mind travel to other places, describing some key places in Persia, which father confirmed were accurate. He told me I must use my talent for the good of others, which meant no more cheating in my tests, I must study hard and learn in the same way others do. It is not wise to show off, or to draw attention to that which people do not understand.

Did I heed his words? In parts I did but I couldn't give up my advantage. My ability was certainly useful in studying geography and in defending myself. As I neared puberty, I realised that my capacity to influence others now had the added advantage of attracting boys who were beginning to pay attention to girls. The attention I received was immensely satisfying and I found that despite my bloodline and background, I was starting to become popular with the opposite sex. Unfortunately, my father restricted me from associating with them and I resigned myself to climbing out of the window again, quite precocious rebellious behaviour for a twelve year old.

"How I can bring my Persian princess up to be a decent, modest and obedient young woman in this society?" my father despaired one night.

It was at this point where we abandoned our life in England and father took us to live in Tehran for the rest of our lives. The culture shock was beyond belief. I had become accustomed to tasting some degree of freedom despite the limitations of my gender, however, life for me now became unbearable. I realised how few rights I had as a woman and experienced a life now that quickly became intolerable. My education was an unhappy episode in my life again as I had an almost white face among a sea of bronzed, Middle Eastern skin. I couldn't grasp the language. I couldn't wear a dress that showed any part of my legs, or shoulders, or arms and I was faced with the prospect of marrying and becoming a mother at an early age. This move from England only served to cement my rebellion against authority. My hopes and dreams became a distant thought and I prayed every day for something to come along and remove me from this repressive life.

Then finally, on September 15th 1962, my prayers were answered. A man from England arrived to direct my destiny.

Someone knocked on the door of our house. My father answered the door and I didn't hear the conversation which took place, but I know it lasted for an hour before I was called downstairs. I tried to read while they talked but my mind drifted from the pages, attempting to listen to the discussion but their voices were subdued. To hear the conversation, I also put my ear to the floor and I almost used my special little talent to hear the conversation but eventually, I heard my name and a request to enter the living room.

As I walked downstairs I had no inkling, despite my sixth sense so to speak, of the fatalistic significance of the man seated on our best couch. He was a handsome man and I felt a peculiar feeling in my stomach when I saw him although to me he was not attractive in that I sensed a darkness in him that I could not understand. My first impression was that of a shiny, healthy fruit which was rotten at the core. He was well dressed, eloquent and probably rich, which impressed my parents but I was innately suspicious of him. The man certainly noticed me, for I saw a wistful gaze upon his face as I walked down the stairs, at my most graceful.

"Tahra," my father said, purposefully, "I would like you to meet Max Richardson."

He kissed my hand and I tried not to appear reluctant for him to do this.

"He has an offer for you."

Not a marriage request, I thought, disdainfully. I was at the age now where that was a distinct possibility but I think Mr Richardson sensed my trepidation for then he explained himself.

"It is an offer of business; your talents for my hospitality."

He fixed me with a firm stare but his words partially reassured me. I realised then that God, or Allah had bigger plans for me and that I would be a fool to disregard them.

In the summer of 1962, Paul was asked to return to The Establishment as it appeared his work was complete at The Institute. It seemed strange returning to his old research base and in fact, very little had changed in respect of the staff or the décor. The only thing that had changed was he himself, who had by now glimpsed the possibilities of the human mind. Where could he go from here? Studies at The Institute had not been conclusive but he believed in extra sensory perception and more importantly, was more and more certain of the human bio-electromagnetic field. What was unclear was the purpose of the field and its significance in quantum physics and perhaps, its mystical role if there was one. Paul sat down in his old office and decided he was going to draft a hypothesis, in the absence of any concrete instructions from Max.

Max himself was without cause and at a loss since the Grace's death. In August of 1962, and the day after the demise of Marilyn Monroe which was all over the news, he had to sort through the possessions of his most loved parent. It was symbolic; the world had lost a goddess in Monroe and Max himself had lost his own personal divine figure, his psychic mother. Both had had an impact on the world, Grace's significance albeit less public. Her room was as cluttered as Monroe's had been, even down to the containers of tablets on the bedside but Grace had been subject to time and age, whereas Monroe to the pressures of fame. In her time, Grace had been beautiful too, he mused as her gazed at the old photographs of her, taken at his childhood home. Photographs of his father were conspicuously absent.

It was this final act which gave him a much needed push in a new direction. Max found a note written by his mother, probably a few months before her death which she knew to be inevitable when her health deteriorated. One did not need to be psychic to see that coming.

He held the envelope in his hands for a long moment before opening it, an envelope which had his name clearly written on it, Grace's pet name for him as a boy. It was quite a short note.

My dear, and only son,

Please do not lose your way in your grief. There is a way to put The Institute back on the map and I want this as much as you. It has been my home for such a long time now and is important in God's holy plan for the world. Therefore, I am leaving you a clue, dear son. You must travel to Tehran in Persia, I know you have connections in the Middle East. You must find a young woman who is the daughter of a professor, she will not be hard to find because she has a white mother. Her name begins with the letter 'T', they are quite wealthy and can be located through your current connections. She needs a purpose in life and an outlet for her outstanding gifts, this is something you can offer her. Bring her to The Institute, for this is where she is meant to be.

After I am gone, she will be the shining light of The Institute and is capable of far more than I ever was.

I also ask of you to find your sister because you will need her in your life, you will realise much later why it is important to locate her and heal the wounds. I cannot ask you to forgive your father, as much as I believe in what Jesus taught us but please ensure a regular supply of flowers at Robert's grave, we must not forget.

I will love you always
Grace

Max swallowed hard, at the thought of his mother, now gone but also at the memories of his siblings and father. Yes, maybe he could heal the wounds with his sister but he had no idea where she was now, although for his father there would never be any forgiveness. That didn't matter now. He put the note in his pocket and did not hesitate to act upon the advice, where would he be now without her guidance?

On September 1st 1962 he was on a plane to Tehran, with a clear purpose; to find this young woman who would be his star. Locating her was challenging but not impossible and on the 15th

September, he plucked up the courage to approach the house where they lived and knock on the door.

It was answered by a distinguished looking Iranian man and in the background, he caught sight of a demure white woman, as predicted. Max had rehearsed much of what he intended to say.

"Greetings, Mr Mamoun. I realise this is rather presumptuous of me and that you have never met me before, but I am a businessman from England who may be able to assist you with something."

Mohammed Mamoun was sceptical at first and this was to be expected.

"How do you know of me and my family?" he asked, but not too gruffly.

"I believe we have an associate, Dr. Henry Rogers in common. It is he who imparted me with the information that brings me here." A little white lie but it was Henry that enabled him to find who he was looking for.

Mohammed nodded in recognition and decided to allow Max inside, generously offering him the best couch in the house. His wife offered some mint tea and Max graciously accepted. After a few sips, Max was asked of the purpose of his visit. Here goes, he thought.

"I understand that you have a, let's say, gifted daughter."

Mohammed smiled. "You are looking for a wife?" he said.

Max was caught off guard, then, without wishing to offend, debunked that assumption. "Actually, although I'm sure she is beautiful, it is more a case of I'm searching for special people, with talents. It is my line of business." He hoped the rejection of his daughter would not been taken in offence, maybe she was acceptably pretty and maybe not, but he had no interest in Middle Eastern women.

"Yes," said Mohammed, in admonition, "my Persian princess is a gifted child. She has produced some excellent results at school."

Max smiled, and looked him in the eye. "You and I both know that her talents go beyond mere academics." This was a make or break moment.

There was a pregnant pause and then Mohammed actually breathed a sigh of relief. "I do not know how you came by this knowledge, but yes, there are truths about my daughter that I have had to hide. Things that I do not truly understand, but maybe you do."

And from there it was plain sailing. The Mamouns needed a future for their daughter and Max Richardson could channel her gifts and use them for a greater good. He offered accommodation, security and the opportunity to study for a degree in whatever subject his daughter found interesting, at the end of those three years she would return to Tehran to be married. It was agreed between men of high status and then Mohammed called his daughter down. Max was excited at the prospect of meeting his new star, from what her father had told him, she had great potential – big business.

Tahra Mamoun walked down the stairs slowly, book in her hand. She was tall and elegant, of multi-racial origin which was unusual for the early 60's and was almost eighteen. Her hair was brown and very straight, draped over her shoulders and framing a face with quite prominent cheekbones. Her ethnicity appeared to be a mixture of Middle Eastern and Caucasian, she had her mother's looks with almond eyes that conveyed a sense of emotional power and intensity that was difficult to ascertain. Her skin was a milky chocolate colour, her nose straight and her lips naturally dark and full. She was quite feline, like a panther and she exuded an odd sensuality with the air of a dark, stealthy predator but she felt uncomfortable in the staid clothes she wore. Max didn't realise it but he was staring at her, wistfully. She looked puzzled on seeing Max.

"Good day" she said, in a smooth, velvety voice.

Max was surprised as to the intensity of lust he suddenly

felt. No woman had ever aroused him so much and he couldn't fathom why, the clothes she wore did her no justice. He then proceeded to move towards her.

"You must be Tahra," he said.

"That is me," she responded.

Max found a pair of dark, wild eyes gazing at him, not with timidity but with a passion and pride he found exciting. Such was the connection he felt on meeting her, Grace's prediction of a female who was a gift to the world crossed his mind. Was this the girl he had to protect at all costs?

Her father made the obligatory introductions and Max explained his reason for the visit. She sensed some apprehension about the changes that had been decided for her but he made a promise to himself, to her father, and Tahra that she would be well taken care of. Max surprised himself, normally he only liked English girls but this young woman was unusual and incredibly beautiful, so much so that it was a little intimidating. No woman had ever made him feel humble. As they cemented the business agreement, he knew he had to make her his, at any cost. For only the second time in his 42 years of life, he realised he was going to fall in love.

7
Forlorn Genius

There was nothing more Sam hated than coming home to an empty house, but it was often the case as he was an adult now. Yet he was still afraid of being alone, which angered him because he knew at the age of eighteen he should not fear solitude. The quietness of the house was disturbing, for in these silent moments the nightmares came, waking nightmares. They had plagued him all his life and he had never learned to deal with them, in fact, he never mentioned them to his father at all and he had no mother to confide in. Caroline, Ava's mother had been a strong, nurturing influence but he could not discuss his nightmares. The nearest thing to a confidante he had was Ava, she hadn't sent him back to his bed when he complained about monsters in his room, she had allowed him to be her teddy bear and gave him comfort. He missed her since she had become an adult and left home, he missed the feeling of family Caroline had given him as a child. All his father had offered was an empty house and an empty heart.

Sam's father's place was a large town house in the suburbs of north London. It was quintessentially Victorian with a double bay window at the front and dormer window at the top. He never used the front of the house and entered through the back so that he could put his skateboard straight into the utility area. Sam dropped his bag on the kitchen floor and opened the double doors between this room and the next, which created an open plan living area.

He soon realised that tonight, the house was not empty which was a relief. His father appeared to have a visitor, even though he himself was apparently absent. Many people came and went in his father's life; women, official looking men and friends so it was not unusual to find someone in the house. The visitor was male, middle aged with a full head of grey hair and he was dressed casually. He sat on the sofa which showed its back to the kitchen, so that only the top part of the man was visible. As Sam was ravenous (he had just been out skateboarding in the park), he began to prepare a sandwich – cheese and tomato.

"Hi," Sam said, nonchalantly, "you waiting for my dad?"

"I've been meaning to pop by for a while," the visitor replied.

Sam shrugged in an effort to appear indifferent although he appreciated the company. Because he was polite and believed in hospitality, he offered the visitor a drink and the man accepted a cup of tea so Sam put the kettle on.

"So," Sam attempted conversation, "are you here for business or pleasure?"

The man smiled. "A bit of both," he said warmly. "I'm Bill, by the way."

"Pleased to meet you," Sam replied. "I'm Sam."

"Oh yes, I know your name, you have been mentioned many a time, in a positive way of course."

This surprised Sam, he often felt non-existent and when his presence was acknowledged, there were complaints about what he chose to do with his time and his career prospects.

"So young man," Bill continued, "you're finishing college soon. What are you going to do after that?"

Sam found this a difficult question, as his interests were in juxtaposition to those of his father.

"I'd love to study music or art at university, to express my soul, to compose music for others to listen to."

"Well, I think that's wonderful."

"My dad doesn't." Sam appeared bitter. "He wants me to be like Ava and be a scientist because he thinks I'll make a lot of money from it."

"He could be right. Who's Ava anyway?"

"My cousin. Well, sort of my cousin, she was adopted." There was clear admiration is his voice when he spoke of her. "She has a scientific degree, but it's not for me, I could never feel passionate about examining and measuring things."

"I believe everyone has a role to play in life, I'm sure you'll find yours eventually."

"All I want to do is make music." Sam popped a teabag into an empty cup and poured on the boiling water. He stirred it with vigour. "Music is big business and as worthy a career as stock broking or science, not that anyone takes me seriously."

"I'm sure your instincts are correct, Sam, you'll find many of your gut feelings can be safely followed."

It was comforting to have his opinions respected. So much so that he picked up his guitar that was zipped up in its protective bag behind the sofa. It was a rarity for someone to be interested in his music, except Ava and Caroline who had shown him nothing but encouragement. With finesse, he tuned the guitar in a matter of a minute, put it to one side and returned to the brewing cup of tea. After pouring in a little milk, he took the cup into the main living area and picked up his guitar, walking around the sofa which showed its back. Bill smiled as Sam rounded the corner.

"Don't be too shocked," he said.

Sam was shocked, unfortunately and dropped the cup, spilling hot tea onto the carpet but that wasn't his first concern. Bill was sitting on the sofa but both his legs were missing below the knee and to make matters worse, the wounds appeared to be open. It was happening again, the visitors, they always looked so real but they weren't, they couldn't be. This one was particularly down to earth, except for the fresh wounds.

"Sorry to appear like this," Bill continued, "I needed to get your attention."

Sam closed his eyes like he always had done and breathed

deeply. Usually by blanking his mind then counting to ten, the visitors disappeared.

"You've shut us out for too long, Sam. You need to start accepting that we will always be around, to be seen, heard and felt. We mean no harm."

He opened his eyes to find Bill still sitting there, although he now showed complete legs.

"Industrial accident," he explained, "fatal, of course."

Sam shuddered and realised that Bill was here to stay. He set his guitar down in an admonition of defeat and grabbed a cloth from the kitchen to clean the tea stain on the floor. As Sam rubbed, venting his anger, Bill pursued the conversation.

"You didn't always ignore us, Sam."

Sam shrugged, with a surly expression on his face. "Well, times change, don't they?"

Bill gave him a benign smile, patient of the reluctance Sam was now showing.

"Who was your first, how shall I say, spirit visitor?"

Sam finished rubbing the stain and set the cloth to one side. "An old lady."

Bill nodded. "And she stayed with you for a while didn't she? Until you started shutting us all out, something you've done for the past eight years now, Sam."

Sam saw no problem with this, it had been essential for coping with the everyday world.

"Look, what do you want?" These visitors were as welcome as a boil on the face of a fashion model.

"To talk to you, Sam, you need a father figure. I mean, look at you, you're becoming a man and no male figure in sight to act as a role model. We don't want you going down the wrong path, do we?"

"I'm fine, really."

"No you're not, Sam. It doesn't make you weak to need others in your life."

He looked away, frustrated that he couldn't blank Bill out but he could still rebel by refusing to listen. Sam snatched up his guitar and furiously strummed acoustically, in the desire to drown out Bill's attempt at mentoring him.

Bill smiled, listening to the music emanating from Sam's anger, its raw power and energy and nodded in appreciation. "You have a gift, you know, your musical ability."

Sam paused, damping the vibration of the strings and remained silent for a moment before breathing slowly, deeply, then responding. "Thank you," he said softly. "That means something to me."

With the scarcity of praise in his life, for the first time in three years he played for another person, although it was difficult to quantify whether a dead person still counted as a legitimate audience. He played a softer, more delicate tune, including an arrangement of chords off the top of his head. As he played, picking the strings delicately he closed his eyes and visualised the landscape that was the tune. In his mind's eye it became a symphony of colour, vibration, an undulating horizon of sound and each new hill or feature on the landscape predicted the next chord or string to pick.`

Bill sighed. "Just beautiful."

Sam was now engrossed in the guitar so Bill decided to make an exit. At least there was a possibility of getting through to the boy. "Well, if you need us, we're always around, we'll respond."

The time wasn't quite right for Sam, Bill conceded, but it would happen soon, it had to, all the visitors knew that. Sam had his own path to follow, but in the war of the will of the soul and the will of the conscious, albeit angry mind, the latter could easily overpower the subtlety of spirit. There was always another day. Sam couldn't avoid who he was forever.

Part Two

Kismet

Man also possesses a power by which he may see his friends and the circumstances by which they are surrounded, although such persons may be a thousand miles away from him at that time.

Paracelsus (1493-1541)

8
The Nadir

While I worked at the Institute, a number of important things happened in the world. The early sixties were a whole new ball game and I would soon see the world become a very different place. Both the laser and the heart pacemaker were invented in 1960, hot on the heels of the microchip, and the Barbie doll. In 1962 the first TV broadcasts were transmitted in colour, not that I had spare time in which to watch it. Martin Luther King was changing the world and human rights. Cinema audiences were thrilled by 'The Magnificent Seven', 'Spartacus', 'The Time Machine', 'Breakfast at Tiffany's', 'West Side Story', 'Dr No', 'Lolita' and were frightened by 'Psycho'. Yet, considering the nature of my interests, there were a lot more pivotal things going on, the seeds of which were sown while I was still based at The Establishment. So let's rewind back to the late 1950s to begin the tale.

On October 4th 1957 Sputnik 1 was launched, the first ever man made satellite to go into orbit, Russian of course. Its mission was to study the Earth's atmosphere. Travelling at 18,000 mph, it completed an orbit of the Earth in around ninety six minutes and emitted a fast beep, beep, beep sound which was transmitted at twenty megahertz, very easy to pick up with a radio. I listened to the transmissions many a time during those twenty two days before the batteries died but at that time, it wasn't truly significant to me, merely a curiosity and a breakthrough to scientists who worked and researched in a very different sphere to my own. At that point in time, I was at The Establishment investigating the effects of electromagnetic fields on the brain and coming to comprehend the vulnerability of the human organism. I cannot remember which individual I was testing on that day because they all merged into one after a while, to the extent that they became faceless.

Sputnik 2 was also launched in 1957, hot on the trail of its predecessor and took mankind another step closer to space. This was the launch that took the dog Laika into orbit, who actually died due to stress from what I remember. It was at that point I took time to consider further the fragility of the biological organism. Could we ever survive space travel?

The United States, although one step behind and not set to overtake the Russians in the Space Race also launched a series of satellites, which did lead to the discovery of the Van Allen belts, funnily enough, named after a man with the same surname. It crossed my mind that in addition to the human bio-electromagnetic field, the Earth itself possessed one. If the BEMF of people constituted the human soul, did the Earth's EMF suggest a planetary spirit or consciousness? Maybe this was too unscientific, ridiculous even but possible, nothing is impossible and in the quantum world, nothing is rational. At the time though, I was unable to linger upon philosophical meanders into esoteric territories. I had a job to do, a paid job, where someone may take note of the results and acknowledge the conclusion.

On September 12th 1959, the Americans launched Luna 2 which soon after landed on the moon. This was a high point for the Space Race but a low point for me. The research into the effects of electromagnetic fields and psychoactive drugs on the human mind and body was dragging on inanely and I was wondering up until that moment in time if life had anything more to offer. But Max had taken me out on a horse ride and told me out of the blue that I was to be offered another contract at a sister facility in London. The 12th September was the night before Max told me about The Institute, so when Luna 2 landed on the moon, I had an inkling of what was in store for me.

I was fully engrossed in studying the residents of The Institute by the time Belka and Strelka successfully orbited and returned to Earth in 1960 (they were dogs, in case you were wondering). It paved the way for a biological entity to enter space and return via a plunge in the ocean, which did happen on the 12th April 1961 when the Soviet Yuri Gagarin became the first man in space. From what I remember, that particular day I was working with the wonderfully accurate Grace and the world was *brimming with possibilities, both in a mystical and scientific way and in a personal and global way. We could start dreaming of reaching the stars.*

On May 25th 1961, President John F. Kennedy delivered his man on the moon speech, declaring his intention to put humanity on the surface of the moon before the decade is out. The thought of humanity actually setting foot on the moon was mind boggling at that point in time, but certainly not impossible. While the Russians and Americans openly competed, forming a backdrop to my tireless research at the frontiers of belief, my own understanding of the world as a safe and organised institution was blown apart. How could I surpass this? How could I ever perceive life the same again?

Yet, in the summer of 1962, I returned to The Establishment to face an unexpected nadir in my life. Grace had died and Max had taken an introspective turn and in effect, had dismissed me from The Institute which had become the purpose of living. There were no new objectives in sight and instead of having to ponder the likelihood of being without research, of not undertaking anymore ground-breaking work, I sat down to form a hypothesis for the source of the human bio-electromagnetic field. What made the field emanating from psychics so much stronger, more vibrant and more extensive than the field from an ordinary member of the public? Was the field the source of their sensitivity, or did their talents intensify the field? But, more importantly, what produces the bio-electromagnetic field in the first place?

The first line of enquiry would have to be brain matter, since it thrives on electrical impulses but the real creator may be much more elusive, some unknown mystical force. Was there a line of upward causation from matter to energy, or downward causation from energy to matter? For want of a better term, I refer to this electromagnetic field as energy, which I believe to be more scientific than the term 'spirit'. The established mode of thinking implies that consciousness is a product of the brain and not a powerful entity in itself. I decided at this point, therefore, to focus my interest on consciousness and examine the relationship between consciousness and the bio-electromagnetic field. It was more philosophy than science in many ways but it was necessary to intellectually digest the findings of the last decade.

Maybe the Cartesian mode of thinking is largely correct; where mind and body are separate phenomena that interact. This concept states that the body works like a machine, having the properties of extension and motion and obeying the laws of physics while the mind, or soul is a non-material entity which is the complete opposite in its qualities. Yet what form does this mind, or soul take? Does it not take the form of some electromagnetic field? Is it, in fact the bio-electromagnetic field that I have been studying and measuring?

To gain some consistency and maybe some inspiration, I looked briefly into other religions of the world and quite clearly, there is reference to a soul or spirit of some kind that is separate from the body. In Hinduism, the soul is the 'Jivatman' but this term more specifically refers to this force as the Individual Self, which is related to Brahman, the Immensity. Therefore, it suggests soul and cosmos are part of the same fabric, or particles. Both share three qualities; being, consciousness and bliss, or love. We also find the concept of the soul in Sikhism, Islam, Buddhism and Taoism, to name a few; it is a fundamental belief common to the religions of the world.

Theosophy perceives the soul to be the field of our psychological activity yet only the middle dimension, as spirit is the highest form or the real self. Therefore, the soul links spirit and body and can be attracted to either, providing the classic battleground for good and evil. The body is a tool, or instrument that is used by the soul, or spirit in its ultimate purpose. However, we also find Reductionism totally rejects the non-corporeal but I believe I'm close to explaining the soul as an electromagnetic field, vindicating the faith of our world religions.

Trying to prove the existence of this field was frustrating though, to be honest. In order to achieve this, I needed to look towards science and provide some sort of verifiable evidence that this non-corporeal aspect of ourselves exists. There are tantalising anecdotes and studies relating to 'false limb syndrome' in which amputees claim to feel their severed appendage; for example, pain and itching in the area where the arm or leg would have been. How could this be the result of nerve endings that do not exist anymore? Could these sensations be due to the bio-electromagnetic field? Maybe the field will always be present even if the limb is not, possibly it's some kind of blueprint for the body to follow. DNA, from what I've read gives instructions to build proteins, but how do these proteins know what an arm, liver or ear is supposed to look like? This information could be contained within the field.

I was also very fortunate to discover some interesting research from the Soviet Union via my connections, many of which I owe to Max. In 1961, the year before Grace's death I was still closely involved with The Institute and during that time a Soviet named Semyon Kirlian published results of some research he'd carried out with his wife on photographing what they called auras. (Personally, I've always preferred Bio-Electromagnetic Field, it sounds more scientific). He was working as an electrical technician back in 1939 (the year I started my degree!) when he noticed that if he touched high voltage electronics in a darkened environment, there was a coloured glow emanating from his body. He continued to investigate this and achieved a kind of photography where high-voltage, high-frequency electricity was passed through a test object while it sat on photographic paper. The pictures show an extraordinary and beautiful field of energy.

This was just what I needed; clear visual evidence for the Bio-Electromagnetic Field. But rather than objects placed on photographic paper, I really wanted to develop a camera that could capture the field, show its splendour and its fluctuations. I began to look into this and played around with my measuring equipment, cine cameras and a pulsed electrical field to coax that photonic glow into a bank of evidence.

I had no idea what research was being carried out at The Institute at that time as I spent my time developing the camera and pondering the source of the bio-electromagnetic field and in my more productive moments, typing. In my spare moments, the thought of a man on the moon endeared me and I reflected upon the colossus undertaking to put a fragile organism into the icy vacuum of space. Initially, I had comprehended the vulnerability of the human organism, and at one point before the success of Yuri Gagarin, had come to accept the fragility of the human body but

I was reaching a point of wishing to go beyond the limitations of the human condition. My rationale for this desire was the knowledge that there was so much more to being human than a beating heart, pulmonary respiration and digestion.

My introspective moments often occurred while out horse riding, the fresh air had a habit of focusing my thoughts. However, developments took place in the physical as well as intellectual world whilst out horse riding. One time, I took a detour through some woods near the cottage and soon found myself riding alongside someone else, a woman, a woman who was appraising me. She looked quite athletic and had a mane of incredible, chestnut coloured hair. In synchronicity we rode silently, until the woman broke the mute spell.

"Do you ride here often?" she joked, an amusing ice breaker.

"Twice a week," I replied. "You?"

"Ditto."

"Beautiful horse you have there," I said in admiration, looking at her dappled equine wonder.

"Thank you," she replied. "I call her Laika."

I had to smile at that. "You've been following the space race."

"It's the ultimate travel destination," she mused.

"This is Hadron, a very proud stallion that I've just broken in."

"Hadron?" she queried.

"It's a new term applied to strongly interacting particles in quantum physics," I explained, although she didn't appear to understand. "I don't suppose you're interested in particle physics by any chance?" I added.

"Close," she said with a smile, "I studied chemistry."

"What do you do now?" I asked, becoming more interested in her by the minute.

"I work in a lab close by. You?"

"I think."

She laughed, and gave Laika a kick, spurring her into a canter. Intrigued, I copied and was soon alongside her again. We ran in reign and I followed her to a small cottage on the other side of my hill. She had been living close by all this time. The horses were tethered to a fence and they grazed happily as we stood, soaking up the chemistry and physics of sexual attraction. Five minutes later we stumbled into her sitting room, she attempting to kick off her riding boots as I fumbled with the fastenings on her jodhpurs. I was too much in a hurry to strip and was content to partially remove her jodhpurs before enveloping her in my arms and carrying her to the sofa. The sex was fast and furious but she liked it that way, she didn't care for dating first and had no qualms about welcoming a stranger into her vagina. I was fascinated, a liberated woman. The sex was over in five minutes and she climaxed just before I did, the brevity did not concern her, she expected seconds. I was not one to complain. The dessert was certainly sweet and it was savoured, as seconds should be. After it was over she lay on the sofa feeling as satisfied as I did, and lit a cigarette.

"*I'm Eleanor, by the way,*" *she said.*

"*Paul,*" *I replied.*

We shook hands.

Our alliance begun on the 15th September 1962, we were still together by that date in 1963. She tried to teach me about chemistry and I tried to convey my philosophical concepts about the physics of life and the bio-electromagnetic field. I don't think she was convinced, she was polite albeit supportive but she could still be persuaded. I surprised myself in that the relationship continued well into the next year and I saw no reason for it to end. Maybe I was finally ready to settle down, it felt so comfortable, so easy, I didn't feel tied down, I felt bolstered, loved and appreciated and in turn, I had the utmost respect for her. It was not an earth shattering romance but we fitted together, interlocking like an enzyme and its receptor.

During that time, Max was pushed further and further into the recesses of my conscious mind. After a while and many an hour hypothesising, I felt stale, very stagnant. While the everyday world was pleasant, my drive for success was not being fed so in the autumn of 1963 I took up a lecturing post again. This was as much for the intellectual challenge as well as the need to preserve my savings. I made a few investments along the way and built a nice fortune to boot, one day it would be useful. At that moment in time, my material needs were not foremost and consisted of food, sex, travel and horses.

In May of 1964, I received a visit from Max. It had been more than a year since previous contact and I had forgotten him to be quite frank. Why was he here? Why had he been so conspicuously absent in the first place? Initially the conversation was strained, as if some wrong had occurred but I knew that was not the case. He requested I formulate a hypothesis on how remote viewing could be blocked, which seemed a rather strange call, he was of the opinion that remote viewers could project their mind anywhere and that nothing would be safe. Why now? To be honest, I didn't even have any inclination at the time but I agreed, anything to get back on track, I was beginning to see the world through materialistic eyes again.

However, I gave my allotted task little thought, in our conversation he inspired me without realising it. It was a light bulb moment, the Eureka we all desire, how could I not have thought of this earlier? Everything I had being doing at The Institute was fitting together, cosmic synchronicity of chaos and order, the relationship of everything, it all happened for a reason. I had found the reason.

The second thing that occurred to me was Max's psychological state. He seemed very preoccupied and at that moment, I wished Emilie was at hand. Nothing had been the same since Grace died but I couldn't believe he was still grieving, Max was a cool businessman, there was too much at stake to spend his time moping. Something was bothering him, but I would never know…. unless I paid The Institute a visit. There was nothing to stop me, I had major justification in my task but also two driving factors – to build the foundations of my new vision and to discover the source of Max's trouble.

At this point, my life really did change.

9
The Golden Girl

I arrived in London on the 30th September 1962 in a state of apprehension, it had been such a long time since I had last been in London, or England even and the first thing I remember was the cold temperature. When you have been in Tehran for the last five years of your life, the desert temperatures are all you know and to be removed from that and thrown into a more temperate climate is a shock to the system.

Mr. Richardson was kind enough to meet me at the airport himself and for such a wealthy man he was very chivalrous and helped me with my possessions, tipping a porter generously to ensure all my luggage was transported quickly to his waiting car. It was a fine vehicle in dark green, he told me it was an Aston Martin DB4 whatever that meant and he reeled off a list of specifications that made as much sense to me as Chinese. All I remember that it was fast and I felt my back press into the seat as we pulled away. Suffice to say, it wouldn't take long to reach our destination.

That day, it was just Mr. Richardson and I and it was a little uncomfortable being in the car with him due to the way he looked at me. Despite his age, I believe at that time he was around 40, he was very handsome with no trace of grey in his dark hair but my previous intuitive opinion of him remained. His heart was hardened in some way, I couldn't figure out why and I felt then that dark secrets lurked behind his perfect gentleman persona. When I looked into his eyes, I saw glimpses of two personalities almost; a loving man and a controlling man. It was hard to say which aspect of him was dominant and quite possibly, Mr. Richardson could be any one of these at the drop of a hat and I decided to remain on friendly ground as I believed this man would mean a lot to my future in some way. He was a person who made things happen and I wanted to *bask in his powerful aura.*

He took me to a place called The Institute where I was to remain, both living and working in the same domicile. My first impression was that of austerity – how could I stay in this clinical place? The lady of the house, Miss Tynedale was quite cold too and it felt as if she didn't like me but Mr. Richardson ushered me up the stairs. I couldn't help but notice the paintings on the wall as he escorted me up the stairs, there were pictures of great scientists in chronological order beginning with Isaac Newton and finishing with Albert Einstein. He took me to a room on the second, or top floor and paused outside, hand on the door knob.

"I have a surprise for you," Mr. Richardson said.

When he opened the door, my face must have lit up for he smiled sincerely. My room was not cold and austere, it was warm and someone had taken the time to decorate it and furnish it Middle Eastern style. The dormer window was draped beautifully and there were cushions scattered over the bed, which had an iron frame. Some of the possessions I thought I must leave behind were there, like my favourite childhood toys. I didn't know what to say, I felt overwhelmed and stood in the middle of the floor.

Mr. Richardson walked up to me and paused, looking at me quite intently. He reached out and softly stroked my hair. I got the feeling that this was a rare moment for him and he was about to say something which would make him vulnerable, but then he drew back. I broke eye contact and he surveyed the room.

"I hope you like your new home, Tahra, I had the decorators in to make you feel comfortable."

It was a very thoughtful gesture. All I could say was 'thank you' but I said it with sincerity. Mr. Richardson knew that I appreciated it and that was enough for him, for a while at least. His generosity made me nervous but I couldn't help feeling pleased with his efforts. I felt accepted. I often feel like an odd jigsaw piece, maybe because of my gifts but also due to my ethnicity. Mr. Richardson accepted both of these qualities and I started to believe my time here would be a blessing. Maybe I would give him the benefit of the doubt.

Max sat quietly in his private study at home, watching the first burnished leaves fall from the trees in his garden. His new protégé, Tahra Mamoun had been living at The Institute for only a short time and he was disturbed by how preoccupied he was with her. He had spent much of his free time securing her university place, which unfortunately would begin next year as the academic year had already started. She had chosen to study psychology, because, as she stated with fervour, she loved the human mind, it was the most fascinating thing on Earth. With that finalised, he drew up a proposal for her part in the deal, a programme of research based upon her talents.

Very soon, the first demonstrations were due but Tahra was not worried. She did miss her parents though and wrote everyday at first, although now it was once a week. But Max had pulled out all the stops, something he had not done for Emilie when she arrived, or Beth, or Sakie. All this he had done and not yet asked for anything in return. Tahra was truly grateful, it was evident in her eyes so maybe there would be an end result that made it all worthwhile. He almost felt afraid to make a move as he had already invested so much, financially and emotionally, the latter of which was unusual for him.

The night before the first test, Max decided to take her to a restaurant for fine wine and luxurious food. She accepted graciously and at 7 o'clock that evening, he waited in the entrance hall of The Institute. Punctually, she glided elegantly down the stairs, wearing a deep red dress with paisley swirl that reached her knees and a black coat. During her time in London she had discovered make up and had accentuated her dark eyes with black eyeliner and mascara and her lips with a crimson shade of lipstick. She crossed the hall like a panther and stood before Max, presenting herself like a delicious buffet. Momentarily he was lost for words.

"I hope this is appropriate," she said, gesturing to her dress, "I've never been to a restaurant in London."

Max finally found his tongue. "It's perfect."

Tahra offered her arm and Max took it, leading the way to the taxi waiting outside. It whisked them straight to a restaurant in the West End and it pleased Max to see Tahra so happy. His previous dates were impervious to the wonders and freedoms London had to offer, whereas Tahra reacted as a child would in the toy department of Harrods. When she entered the restaurant, heads turned as she entered and eyes watched her as she strode over to their table. Max felt proud and honoured to be her date.

They perused the menu and reached a decision then awaited their meal over a glass of wine. Tahra's upbringing had been based around her father's Islamic beliefs so it was not deemed acceptable to drink alcohol but she enjoyed the taste and savoured the freedom of being able to drink it. In London she felt like a young woman, she felt protected but not smothered, it felt liberating. She realised she would never return to Tehran, there was no reason to with a salary to look forward to and soon a course of study at university, it seemed as if she really had the world in the palm of her hand.

Max pondered her presence here over his glass of wine. Anyone witnessing the scene would have clearly noticed his intentions towards her.

"You look very beautiful tonight," he said, with more humility than he would normally show.

Tahra smiled and lowered her eyes. Although by now she was used to his acts of kindness, she felt a little perturbed by his direct compliment and apparent physical intentions towards her. She wasn't sure if she could reciprocate his interest, for something still didn't sit quite right. Was it right to encourage him by accepting his invitation for what was intended to be a romantic meal? Or was she entitled to sample some freedom with a wealthy and handsome escort?

"I value your kindness, Mr Richardson, you've made me feel more than welcome."

"You can call me Max, you know," he said, dismissing formalities.

"I won't let you down," Tahra promised, "I will be worth your trouble." She may not deliver physically but she fully intended to impress everyone with her talents.

Max wasn't sure how to interpret this promise, was it personal or business? "I'm sure I won't regret bringing you here."

Their meals arrived and Max felt slightly unsettled to see how provocatively she managed to eat. His mind began to wander, thinking of sex which was unsettling in a public place. He watched her tongue lick her lips to catch a dribble of sauce and couldn't help but imagine it elsewhere, on his body. She caught his gaze but did not know how to respond. Persian men looked upon her as a potential wife and mother whereas it seemed Western men thought more of the physical aspects, she was unsure how to feel about that. She decided to divert his attention.

"I'm so happy about the test tomorrow," she declared, "I want to show you what I can do."

Max smiled. "I'm looking forward to it. I'm so confident that you can deliver that I'm skipping the initial tests."

Tahra was puzzled. "Why would you do this? You don't know me."

He paused then decided to be truthful. "Until recently, I had an advisor, a very trustworthy advisor who recommended I go to Tehran to headhunt you. I was informed that you had… superior abilities."

She was stunned. "Then it was no accident…. it did seem strange, you being in Tehran."

"So, you understand why I have invested so much time and money in you?"

Was he trying to distract her from his physical attraction which was nearing obsession in favour of his belief in her as his business protégé? Was he trying to convince himself? Did she believe him?

"Yes, I understand my responsibilities," she replied, wondering if there were any sexual obligations tied in with her role.

They ate silently for a few moments, Max aware of the mounting sexual tension on his behalf and Tahra coming to realise that maybe much more was expected of her. Finally, she decided to mellow the atmosphere.

"Why are you so interested in people with special talents?"

He was surprised at her question, but attempted to answer. "My mother… was an amazing woman, highly perceptive, wise and clairvoyant. It is she who told me where to find you, just before she died. It is my mother's gift that put me in the position I am in today." He paused to take a mouthful of wine and pondered his next point. "And I strongly believe it's people like my mother who have an important place within the context of the cosmos as a whole," he continued, "I don't really know the significance, I think my mother did but she never let anything slip."

Tahra was unsure, but offered, "Maybe their purpose is to keep us connected to God, or Allah."

Max had never thought of it like that, his subjects were functional, they produced results and they helped people.

He toyed with his glass, unsure whether he should continue with what he was about to say. Tahra looked at him, almost persuasively, as if she was aware there was something significant and formative of his personality to reveal.

"I also had a series of strange experiences when I was eighteen, lasting about a year." He was thoughtful for a moment. "I could never understand why they happened, or their purpose and they never occurred again. It never even happened to me as a child and children are supposed to be more sensitive. I waited for it to happen again but it never did." Max looked sad, something that weighed upon him and he didn't continue the conversation.

They ate their meal silently for a while as Max seemed retrospective but finally, they continued with friendly chatter. As the date progressed, Max could only feel more admiration for her and he got the impression that she at least developed a sense of respect for him. He paid the bill promptly and helped Tahra slip into her coat so that they could return to The Institute. She was aware of how close he stood to her as he helped her into her coat, feeling his warm breath on the back of her neck. At that moment, she wondered how it would feel if he put his arms around her, or what the consequences would be of an affair with her benefactor. Did she want him, or did she merely want him to desire her? There was clearly a difference.

Max walked her to her room, realising the time had come to declare his intentions. He was nervous, like a teenager waiting to ask his first crush for a kiss. She opened her door but didn't flick on the light, pausing in the doorway in realisation of the inevitable. Max saw the opportunity, she had left it open. He stood close to her, gently lifting her chin so she could meet his gaze.

"Tahra," he said, softly, "I would like to make love to you."

Her eyes widened in surprise and she was silent for a moment, then she told him something he did not expect. "Max, I'm a virgin. I've never been with a man before."

Jesus Christ, he thought. He hadn't seen that one coming. In fact, it only served to arouse him further, how long had it been since he had met a virgin? All his women were well experienced, too experienced and the thought of taking Tahra's virginity made him feel special.

"I promise to be gentle," he said.

She appearing to be contemplating it, then voiced her concerns.

"I don't want to be a mere conquest."

Max wondered what she knew of his past, but then acknowledged the fact that it wasn't possible to hide things from psychic people. Maybe he had the aura of a womaniser.

"That won't happen," he reassured her.

Tahra looked apologetic. "I will only give my virginity to my future husband."

He didn't expect that, she had principles. It wasn't the time to push for sex, so he asked for an alternative.

"Can I at least kiss you?"

Tahra smiled then nodded, allowing him to make the first move. Max was tempted to push for more but recognised that his actions now could dictate the final outcome so he tentatively gave her a soft kiss on her lips, awaiting her reaction. She did reciprocate therefore he pulled her close and kissed her, knowing it would the climax of the evening. Passively, she enjoyed his physical contact and was surprised at her own feelings of arousal. When it ended, she was sorry. He was sorry too, it looked like there would be no finale tonight.

For a moment, he was tempted to think she might submit and change her mind but she merely smiled, flicked on her bedroom light and closed the door. Max stood outside her door, not knowing what to think or do. No woman had ever turned him down before and he was speechless at being confronted with uncharted territory. Had he said or done something wrong? He stood there for a long moment and then finally made the journey downstairs to the waiting taxi, which was to take him home.

Back upstairs, Tahra had stood by the door inside her room, aware Max had stood there for a momentarily before going downstairs. Part of her wanted him to make love to her but the other part caused her to pull back, it wasn't good to be too easy and there was something amiss with Max. He was the perfect gentleman now, but what of the future? She ended the night in a state of inner turmoil.

Max arrived home an hour later, also in a state of inner turmoil. He had jumped into the fire. Here was a young woman who was the most sexually alluring female he'd ever met and she didn't believe in sex before marriage. What kind of twist of fate was this? Could he get her to change her mind or would he have to contemplate marrying her? That would be an extreme conclusion to the matter.

But what was his immediate concern was the sexual frustration, he wasn't accustomed to this. He paced the room several times, wondering how to deal with a rejection, a factor that only seemed to arouse him even more. The next party was two weeks away and tonight, an act of self abuse would be a poor conclusion. There was only one thing to do. He picked up the telephone and heard a familiar voice at the end of the line.

"I need a woman tonight," he told the person on the other end. In response to the query, he responded, "She needs to be about eighteen years old with long, dark hair." There was another set of questions and Max responded, decisively. "Nothing kinky, I just need some straightforward relief." He listened intently then decided, "She sounds perfect. Can she get over here within the next thirty minutes? Excellent!" He put down the phone and sat quietly for a moment.

In the next thirty minutes he showered and poured himself a glass of wine. He sat back in his favourite leather armchair, sipped his drink and waited for the door bell to ring. It wasn't a long wait and he answered the door himself, finding a tall woman standing there in a long coat. She looked as he had specified with long dark hair but she wasn't Tahra, acceptably close though. He gestured to the sitting room and removed his dressing gown, then returned to his favourite armchair.

"What would you like?" the woman asked.

Max was certain of his requirements for the night.

"You can start with a blow job," he said, in a matter of fact manner.

She strolled over and knelt before him, taking him into her mouth without hesitation. From his position, she was an acceptable impersonation of Tahra. He watched her head bobbing up and down and grasped her hair, pushing her head further down. After a few minutes, he closed his eyes and imagined it was Tahra, a fantasy that fuelled his level of sexual arousal. He allowed himself to come close to climax but then pulled her off. The woman posing as Tahra looked up at him, wondering if she'd done something wrong.

"Get down on your hands and knees," he told her.

She did as she was asked, after all, he was a good client who paid well and she didn't mind playing a more submissive role. He penetrated her quite roughly and grabbed her hips, using them to move her vigorously. As he climaxed, he dug his nails into her skin, oblivious to any discomfort she was experiencing. The relief was enormous although tainted with a sense of shame, it didn't agree with him having to pay for it but it was better than nothing. He didn't bother to offer the woman tissues, he merely got up, avoided meeting her gaze and disappeared into the bathroom. The money was already on a side table so she took it and left swiftly, finding her taxi already waiting outside. In the bathroom, Max stared at his reflection and didn't see a powerful, wealthy man, he saw a man who was afraid. He didn't like it, not one bit.

Max arrived early at The Institute the next day and sat in the dining area with a cup of tea and a newspaper. At times his mind wandered while reading it, partly due to the events last night but also because of the test that was due to commence in an hour. He kept asking Miss Tynedale if Tahra had awoken yet and if she had been down for breakfast. She just assumed it was because he was concerned about the test running smoothly and to schedule but he was aware of the underlying control freak in him that wanted to know what Tahra was doing now.

She came down for breakfast ten minutes later and was surprised to see Max sitting there. He ushered her over and she sat at the table with him, sensing something odd about him. Pushing the final events of last night to the back of his mind, he indulged in some light conversation as she ate breakfast. She appeared to be very relaxed about the upcoming test and his company this morning, laughing at his jokes which were intended to put her at ease.

"Is everything set up ready?" Max asked of Miss Tynedale.

Miss Tynedale smiled kindly at Max, not missing the look he gave Tahra. "Yes, we're using room 7 as normal."

The usual protocol was for Miss Tynedale to take the subject to be tested to the relevant room but Max insisted on escorting her upstairs. He opened the door to room 7 and Tahra found it to be minimally furnished with tables and chairs. Like the rest of The Institute, it was white and clinical but in this room, there was also a cine camera which was aimed at the table and chair in the centre of the room. On the table was a large, white envelope. Max asked her to sit down and a faceless technician set up the camera and started it rolling.

"In a moment, Tahra," Max instructed, "I want you to open the envelope. Inside, you'll find a photograph of a warehouse and a map. I would like to know what's inside the warehouse."

She nodded, unsure of what to expect. Max sat down near the cine camera, in a pondering pose, waiting to see what she would reveal. Slowly, she opened the envelope, aware of the eyes watching her intently and pulled out the photograph. It was indeed a warehouse, which appeared to be in the middle of a desert. She then looked at the map also supplied and found a red circle, indicating its location. Initially she paused then placed the resources back on the table. Tahra closed her eyes.

It began no different to when she projected her consciousness during childhood, when she would visit Annie. There was a drawing sensation and a subtle vibration then she felt her attention drift. In her mind's eye she saw the warehouse become clearer, it began as a shimmering mirage in the distance, finally becoming lucid in a matter of seconds. She moved towards the door, which was securely shut and reached out, feeling nothing then extruded through it with no effort at all. It was dark inside so it took a while for everything to come into focus, which it did slowly.

The warehouse was apparently empty, she couldn't even see any crates stacked up or signs of equipment used to move things around. Maybe this test would reveal nothing and she wondered why Max had asked her to look inside this warehouse. She moved her consciousness around and noticed there were a few offices at the back, so she decided to check them out. Surprisingly, in one office she found two men, chatting, smoking and laughing, nothing to report. Before she focused elsewhere, she happened to notice they possessed guns, rifles which were propped up against the wall. Now she understood the necessity of exploring this warehouse. What else would she find? She tried to listen in on the conversation but found it difficult, most of the time it was garbled as if the words were spoken underwater.

Giving up on listening, she shifted her consciousness to the other office and was taken aback by what she saw. There, on the floor, was a child. It was a young girl, who was bound and gagged. It then dawned on her that a kidnapping had occurred, the reason for it was not clear but she knew a crime had been committed. Distressed, she withdrew her consciousness and opened her eyes.

"There's a little girl in there!" she gasped, trying not to cry.

Max sat bolt upright. "What does she look like?"

Tahra composed herself and stated, "She has long, blonde hair."

"What is she wearing?" Max pushed.

"Blue trousers and a yellow blouse with flowers."

That was all he needed to know. "Miss Tynedale, can you ring Mr. Holmes immediately and tell him we have confirmation of his daughter's location."

"There are two men, they have rifles," Tahra said.

Max nodded his appreciation. "Don't worry, she'll be safe now."

He let Tahra rest and disappeared for a short while. In the

meantime, the technician removed the reel and took it to the viewing room, waiting for Max to reappear. Tahra was asked to return to her room, which she did, wondering if Max was going to come up and see her but first, once he had attended to urgent business, he met the technician and asked to see the recording. The viewing was to check they had evidence, but he was surprised to see something quite unexpected.

When Tahra had closed her eyes, a few seconds later there was a flash of light to the top right of her head. Max asked for it to be replayed and they both watched it again.

"What's that?" he asked.

"I would assume it's a ray of light reflecting off a surface behind her," the technician replied. "I've never seen this occur on previous tests with George and Oscar."

Max looked dubious. "There's nothing in there that would reflect light in that way."

The technician had no rational explanation other than what he had already offered.

"Let's see if it happens on the next test," Max said.

With that, he left the viewing room to visit Tahra. He found her lying on her bed, after knocking and entering. For a moment, he couldn't help but survey her slim and lithe body laid out like a sacrificial child for the gods.

"Did my talent please you?" she asked him.

Max sat down on the bed next to her and she looked up at him with the most outrageous bedroom eyes.

"You knocked me for six, Tahra."

"Will anyone rescue that little girl?" She was genuinely concerned.

"Don't worry," he reassured her, "the process is already underway. The perpetrators will be dealt with." There was a hint of ruthlessness in his voice as he said that.

Max kissed her on the forehead and stood up.

"You really are special," he said, then left the room.

She smiled as she'd performed something important and pleased her benefactor; the world was really her oyster.

Downstairs, Max spoke briefly to Miss Tynedale before leaving The Institute.

"In ten days it's Tahra's 18th birthday. I would like to make it a memorable one, pull out all the stops."

"Where will we hold the party?"

"Here," Max replied, "I want to make sure she gets to know everyone. Shortly after I will be away on business for six months and I don't wish her to be lonely."

Miss Tynedale nodded.

"And," Max added, "while I'm away, can you make sure that she doesn't get... involved with any men." Miss Tynedale raised an eyebrow. "Well, we don't want our new star to fall pregnant or lose her to some handsome young man, do we?"

Miss Tynedale watched him leave, concerned that the green monster of jealousy was raising its ugly head. She cared about Max and had the uncanny feeling that someone was going to get hurt but for once, it wasn't going to be the object of his affections; Max had found someone who willingly, or unwittingly was able to push the right buttons.

On the 7th November 1962, it was Tahra's 18th birthday. The Cuban Missile Crisis had flared up that autumn, when in October the USSR had established a nuclear missile site in Cuba. President Kennedy had ordered a naval blockade of the island and the disagreement had escalated to the point where nuclear war had seemed inevitable. The world had prayed for peace, members of CND had marched in London, fierce negotiations were the result and a peaceful conclusion was nigh. But Tahra wasn't particularly interested, she rarely read the news such was the extent to which she existed within a bubble and the only contact with the real world was via the wireless downstairs.

Max had called off all afternoon testing for the preparations and festivities and all The Institute's regulars were looking forward to socialising together as it so rarely happened. Most had not met Tahra either yet due to the fact that their tests did not coincide. Caterers came into The Institute for the first time, Miss Tynedale emerged in a chiffon dress, the main room was decorated with balloons and assorted paraphernalia and music was to be played, which it never was here albeit for occasional classical tunes playing in the background.

Tahra was instructed to stay in her room until called and she found this frustrating. For the first half hour she lay on her bed, on her front, on her back, on her side then she tried opening a book on psychology that her parents had bought for her – Freud, which failed to inspire her at that moment. She happened to notice her copy of the Qur'an on the bedside cabinet and felt guilty when she realised she had not picked it up to read since she arrived. For the next half hour she played records but she found them rather old hat, fifties rock and roll was all well and good but there was a new decade of music to explore.

For the final thirty minutes she showered and raided her wardrobe, which was still sparse as she had never been shopping alone and what she owned after coming to London had been purchased by Max and, unfortunately, already worn. She pulled out several outfits, tossed them on the bed and tried each one on, dancing to rock and roll in front of the mirror (well, there was no one watching). Although she loved the red paisley dress, she had worn it for her last date with Max, the black dress looked more appropriate for a funeral and the yellow, flower print dress required a summer day. She would have to improvise, opting for the black dress with a brightly coloured scarf tied around the waist. For added impact, she pinned her dark hair high upon her head and used black kohl around her eyes, along with an outrageous quantity of mascara. It was a different albeit very contemporary look and she decided she would have to stick with this.

Not long after, Miss Tynedale tapped on the door and asked

her to come down. She wasn't sure what to expect, Max would be there but she didn't really know anybody else. When she descended the stairs, she couldn't see into the dining room or communal area so was amazed to find a group of people waiting for her. The people there, all research subjects or workers of The Institute greeted Tahra with an expression of either surprise, curiosity or caution. She wasn't at all like they expected. George and Oscar, the established remote viewers were curious as they anticipated someone much older, not this lithe and sensual creature. Peter and Beth, the mediums were also curious as for some reason she was surrounded by an entourage of spirits, they also briefly sensed the presence of Grace, who had a vested interest in Tahra having made the initial recommendation. It was Emilie who was the most cautious, she found it especially difficult to tune into Tahra's thoughts and the way Max looked at her was unnerving. Strangely, there was a conspicuous absence – Paul. Most assumed it was due to the fact he was tied up elsewhere but Miss Tynedale wondered if there were other, underlying motives for his absence.

Max stood back to allow her to mingle, he knew he would be away on business for around six months and she needed to be able to socialise with the others. Neither did he want to draw too much attention to his feelings for her, although the trouble he had taken to organise this party was already beyond his normal level of involvement with research subjects.

A few of the technicians presided over the music and kick started the party with a chorus of party blowers. Tahra stood in the centre of it all, delighted in the effort made to celebrate her coming of age. Immediately after the introductory trumpeting, rock and roll music began to fill the room to the amusement of the party goers. Oscar responded first by grabbing Tahra by the hand and instigating the dancing. He moved well and twirled her around the floor, an act that caused the usually serious Max to laugh. Beth and Peter followed, while George and Emilie talked. Sakie watched, tapping her feet, wondering whether to join in.

As Oscar danced with Tahra, he took the opportunity to introduce himself properly.

"Pleased to meet you," she responded, "and my name is Tahra Mamoun."

"It's good to see new blood," Oscar commented, "and I've heard you're amazing."

She laughed, confidently. "I like to be the best I can be."

"I'm a remote viewer too," he told her.

She seemed genuinely surprised. "And you aren't worried by me being here?"

"There's enough work to keep us all busy," he shrugged.

"That's very gracious of you," she responded.

He smiled. "God brought you here for a reason, I'm sure it's part of his greater plan."

"Max came to find me, in Tehran. He believes in me."

Oscar looked her in the eyes. "Yes, yes he does. I've never seen him take such a personal interest in any of his.... subjects." Tahra met his gaze, knowing exactly what he meant. "Be careful," he warned her.

"Don't worry," she said, surprisingly confident, "I can handle Max."

Oscar gave her a quizzical look, shrugged and put his arm around her waist as they danced away.

Beth took a break and sidled over to Emilie, who was scrutinising Tahra closely. She wondered what was wrong, as Emilie was not normally so withdrawn.

"Why so quiet?" she asked of her.

Emilie didn't answer immediately, so Beth had to prompt her.

"I can see there's something wrong."

Emilie looked at her and asked her a question. "Have you noticed.... anything strange about our new recruit?"

Beth returned her gaze and Emilie wondered if she just assumed it was jealousy, but surprisingly, Beth answered.

"I know Grace is sometimes by her side."

Emilie didn't receive the answer she wanted, so decided to reveal all.

"I can't sense anything from her," she stated, "I've never known that to happen."

Beth looked quite concerned. "Do you know why?"

Emilie shrugged. "No, I do not." Her accent became thicker as she said that.

Beth decided to confide in her further. "She has more spirits around her than is usual, I find that quite odd."

The questioning was turned on Beth now. "Do you know why?"

"No," came the reply.

They both watched Max, whose eyes were solely upon Tahra.

"She seems blissfully unaware that Max actually has feelings for her," Beth said, almost wistfully. "I hope Grace knew what she was doing." Emilie gave her a questioning look. "Grace is the reason Tahra is here and Max hung on her every word."

Beth looked on with curiosity at this ingenuous and lithe figure, while Emilie viewed her with suspicion. It seemed to her that no female could be so oblivious to Max's obvious leanings towards her, which was a serious talking point in light of the many female admirers he'd had over the years and this made Emilie wonder whether Tahra cared, or bothered to care.

Another song graced the air, Chubby Checker singing 'The Twist', which motivated the majority of the partygoers. Max didn't normally dance but Oscar was stealing his fire so he had to cut in and dance with Tahra himself. She was delighted to see him loosen up and have fun. It seemed odd at first to see him dance but she was impressed by his ability to move his body in time to the music. He was actually rather good. It pleased him to dance with her and to see the enjoyment clearly written in her face. Oscar danced with Beth, and they both exchanged knowing glances watching the two of them together. Max's interest was obvious, although her intentions weren't so clear. For him, it was one of the happiest moments he'd experienced in a long while and it seemed such a shame he had to tell her about the business trip tomorrow.

My 18th birthday party had been a high point in my life, which up to now had been staid and unexciting but this was followed by an unexpected interruption the next day. Max told me that he was going to be away on business for around six months and to be honest, I did not receive the news well.

"But you can't be away for such a long time," I protested, "I'll get lonely."

Max was touched that I cared about his absence and I began to feel angry with myself for having become so dependent on him.

"I'm sure the others will look out for you while I'm away," Max tried to reassure me.

I sighed. "It's not the same."

I think at that moment I must have begun to cry as I remember him reaching out to my cheek and wiping something away, which, looking back I find a little embarrassing.

"I promise I'll write to you," he stated, "but please realise, I have to go away on business to ensure all my people here have work."

I shrugged, this was Max's life and I had depended on him too much. He placed his fingers under my chin, lifting it gently and kissed me, which I must admit felt good. The love and attention of a handsome, wealthy man is intoxicating, it is addictive and I don't know, at this moment, how I'll manage without it. For the first time since I saw him, I actually felt like I wanted him, so much so that I put my arms around his waist and laid my head on his chest. He was surprised by this, perhaps because I had reciprocated and hugged me in return. We stood like that briefly, it was a sincere moment and it wouldn't always be like this. He then stepped away from my arms and walked down the stairs, watching me fondly. When he was out of sight, I looked over the stair rail and noticed him speak quietly to Miss Tynedale then he picked up a briefcase and walked out of the door. Now I would have to make my own way in the world.

The first few days were tough, I spent most of the time in my room listening to music and reading. I had become so used to socialising and going on dates it all seemed very staid. The government had lifted the ban on 'Lady Chatterley's Lover' and I read it with fervour, finding the written dialect very difficult although the material was sexually explicit for its time. I began to wonder what making love was like; should I have given in to Max or was I right to hold out? Once I'd finished it, any excitement, even though literary escaped my life. After a few days though, there was a knock at my door and I opened it to find Oscar standing there, with a broad grin on his face.

"You lonely, girl?" he said.

I nodded.

"Well, I'm the answer to your prayers, step this way."

He offered his arm, I took it and we went for a walk around London, despite the cold and miserable winter day. I'd been absent from the place since 1955 and I was surprised at what had changed, so therefore it was a day trip of discovery for me. There were a few high rise blocks of flats that hadn't been there before and some characterless new housing had sprung up where there used to be run down old terraces. I also noticed there were a few factories in and around the housing and vans were pulling up outside people's houses delivering brand new washing machines or televisions. There were more cars on the road from what I remember and different types too, which Oscar identified for me; Cortinas, Morris Minors, Ford Anglias, Ford Consuls and my favourite, the Austin Mini.

But what intrigued me most was the change in the people. Gone were the flat caps and short back and sides on the men, now they were letting their hair grow to the top of their collar and the women...

"Skirts above the knee!" I commented. "This is more like it!"

Oscar smiled.

My father would be disgusted though, I thought, which made the fashion even more appealing.

I began to feel somewhat outdated and made a quick mental note of what the women were wearing now, not that I was a slave to fashion but it would help me develop my own individual style now that I was living in a place where I had freedom of expression.

We finally arrived in St. James Park, near Buckingham Palace after a long walk around the city. Oscar had put together some snacks and he pulled a few things out of his pockets, flavoured crisps! We delighted in the taste of cheese and onion crisps, such a novelty after years of plain crisps with the salt packet hiding down at the bottom and as we ate, we wandered by the pond and talked of our families.

I learned about Oscar's family in Barbados, who loved to fish and sing and I talked of my parents back in Tehran. We also discussed how we first discovered our ability to 'shift our consciousness', as Oscar put it and he was saddened to hear of my miserable childhood. I admitted that I had not always used all my gifts rightfully but he was very understanding and was curious what other gifts I possessed so I explained that I had emotional power of some kind, I could affect the way others feel and sometimes control the way they act. Oscar nodded quietly as I told him, realising that there was so much more to me than just shifting my consciousness.

"You are one unique woman," he said, "just don't go down the wrong path, I'd hate to see you angry." It was said in jest but he also meant it.

We sat on the grass and I didn't feel threatened by him, he just wanted to make sure I wasn't alone too much of the time and desired nothing more from me other than my company. I think he gets lonely too, so I closed my eyes and sent a feeling of warmth over to him, subtle though so he didn't know it was me. He sighed happily but did not make the connection. I didn't want my new friend to feel threatened by me.

"Let's go on a journey," he said.

I looked at him, wondering if we were both thinking the same thing.

"I want to see Barbados," I said.

Oscar took a photograph out of his pocket of his family and their home and gave it to me to focus on. We both lay back, closed our eyes and I let go, allowing my consciousness to pull itself to the location on the photograph. It came into focus slower than usual but then it became clear, I saw the house and some children running around. The sun was shining and the house was close to the beach. I followed the children into the sea and watched them splash around, wishing my physical body was there too because it looked like fun.

"My nieces and nephews," Oscar identified them.

We shifted our consciousnesses out to sea to look at the sailing boats and I got the impression Oscar started to get homesick. We pulled back and I suggested we take a trip out to Tehran. He agreed but unfortunately I did not have a photograph. I wondered if it was possible to 'hook' his consciousness and tow it along with me, I hadn't tried this before, or even thought of it. I asked him to hold his consciousness above his body and focus it into a ball of light if he could. I think this was very difficult for him and I held mine above our bodies with ease. To my surprise I saw a small orb floating above his head. With imaginary fingers I reached out and grabbed the orb, which caused Oscar to stiffen his body slightly.

"Just relax, trust me," I told him, in a soothing voice.

I visualised my hands cupping the orb and re-focused my consciousness, seeing my home in my mind's eye. Summoning enormous emotive power, using my loneliness and love of my new life I towed his consciousness.

"Are you still with me?" I asked.

Oscar was breathing rapidly, but managed to speak, I heard his answer to the affirmative. My home came into view and I saw my parents preparing their evening meal (Tehran is ahead of Greenwich Mean Time).

"Can you see them?" I asked Oscar.

"Yes, yes, you have a white mother and...."

The visit was cut short by a boy's football striking me in the stomach and we both jolted back into our bodies. I was quite cross, although the boy apologised as he retrieved his ball. Oscar lay on the grass, still and quiet. I was worried for a moment, I'd never tried towing a consciousness before and didn't know if there would be any ill effects. I shook him.

"Are you all right?" I said, concerned.

I was relieved when he began to chuckle.

"No one's ever done that before," he laughed, "boy, I can see why Max believes in you."

I gave him a more serious response. "He's only seen a warm up."

Oscar looked thoughtful. "All the more reason to stay on the right path."

Opportunities to socialise were few and far between, although it was comforting to know that at least someone cared. For a while I was angry that Max had not written to me and I didn't see a letter for a whole month. But before long, I was adjusting to life without him, I was used to the time I spent alone and I knew that I could always shift my consciousness elsewhere to relieve boredom. A few times I was tempted to find Max, to see what he was doing but I stopped short of letting my consciousness drift towards him. Maybe I was afraid of what I would find. I often suspected there were dark secrets where Max was concerned and that dark side was a key issue in deciding if I ever gave myself completely to him.

Oscar wasn't the only person to befriend me. Beth, ever curious finally decided to drink tea with me one morning. I was grateful for her company, for she was warm and friendly and I didn't intend to make enemies. It is inevitable that some people are wary of me but their fears are unfounded as it's not in my nature to intentionally harm anyone.

Beth stirred her tea thoughtfully then spoke.

"You really are quite the star, aren't you?" she said.

Her words were almost jealous but I don't think that was the intention.

"I am what I am," I replied, for I had nothing to be ashamed of.

Beth looked slightly sheepish. "You've certainly shook things up around here."

"As I said, I am what I am." I wasn't sure what she was getting at.

"Max likes you, I mean, really likes you," she said, raising an eyebrow as she said it.

I lowered my eyes, unsure if this should be common knowledge.

"Hey," Beth sensed she had embarrassed me, "I'm jealous, in a way, he's the most handsome man I've ever laid eyes on."

I laughed, aware of her light hearted although well meaning comment.

"Yes," I agreed, "I guess he is."

She seemed surprised by my almost indifferent remark, realised I didn't want it to become an open matter and changed the subject.

"You know," she continued, "I'm trying to figure something out. Maybe you can help me."

I was puzzled now.

"I, like Peter can sense spirits. Everyone I meet is surrounded by, or connected to at least 3 or 4 spirits. Some people have strong family bonds with someone to watch over them, others have a genuine spirit guide. But you, you have an awful lot of spirits attached to you."

Her words unnerved me, it made me feel like I was being watched.

"I wondered if you know the reason for this."

"No, I don't. Who are these spirits that have attached themselves to me?" I demanded.

"The only one I know is Grace. She was an amazing clairvoyant."

This spirit knew what God, or Allah had in store for me, most likely, I wished I did too.

"And what does Grace have to say about my future?"

"All I know is that her words brought you here, she's never told me anything about your future."

"Is she with me now?" I pressed.

Beth shook her head. "She says very little, just watches over you sometimes."

I hesitated, but then relented. "Well, if she ever shows up again, please ask her why I'm here. I know I'm here for a very special reason, but I don't know what my real purpose is. I was given these incredible gifts, I just don't know what He wants me to do with them."

For the first time, Beth gave me a friendly smile. "If she ever reveals that to me, I'll let you know."

From that point onwards, Beth and I became firm friends and she overcame her initial reservations. Now I have two friends here, I'm starting to feel more at home.

However, life was far from ideal. I only got the chance to explore beyond The Institute if I had a chaperone, which was Oscar and he wasn't always available. Miss Tynedale was very unyielding when it came to my requests for a little freedom so it was fortunate that she trusted Oscar to escort me. Sometimes it felt like there was little difference between this and my childhood, but I was made to realise how much had been invested in me and I was subdued with a guilt trip. Everyone else had their duties firmly cemented at The Institute too and I came to see that Max kept a tight rein on his investments.

Yet there were some truly happy times in that first six months at The Institute. In my life, I had never celebrated Christmas and that December, I finally came to be a part of the festivities. Everyone there found it hard to believe, that as a child I'd never received any presents, put up the decorations or a tree and engaged in the festivities. As a result of this, they made a point of each and every aspect of the celebrations.

Oscar accompanied me for the first ever Christmas shopping experience so that I could buy gifts for all the residents. Miss Tynedale gave me a lump sum to do this and it was my introduction to money management. I bought some fantastic gifts, as did Oscar and we both had to furtively choose gifts for each other so as not to ruin the surprise. There were so many different shops and market traders so it took all day to find gifts for all.

The week prior to the special day, we wrapped all our presents in decorative paper and set about putting up the tree. We had a genuine pine tree which was very tall, Max didn't believe in doing things by halves and it was Beth and I who placed all the baubles, tinsels and fairy lights on it, and Peter who topped the tree with an angel. It was Sakie and I who made paper chains out of crepe paper and George and Peter attached them to the ceiling with drawing pins. We created a snow scene in the window with cotton wool and glitter. The communal living area was transformed and I felt the same excitement as a child would.

On the day, we all helped prepare the huge turkey and the vegetables. Miss Tynedale was as much a part of the celebrations in as much as The Institute was very much a part of her life too. The living area was full of presents, arranged neatly around the tree; gifts from each other and some from Max, who was somewhere in America at that time. There was a huge parcel there and I was really quite shocked to discover it was for me, from Max. Everyone stared at me and I felt somewhat embarrassed, especially when I realised the others had, in comparison, much smaller gifts from him. No one begrudged it, except Emilie.

We opened our presents and I liked every gift. There were things like books, clothing and jewellery, while Oscar had given me a framed photograph of Barbados to remind us of that journey we took and a record.

"I know you love music and it's a new band that I think you'll love. It seems to be selling well," he explained.

I looked at the seven inch record, it was called 'Love Me Do' by a band called the Beatles. Looking around for the record player, I put it on straightaway and was infected with the sound and the melody, with the harmonica and simple lyrics.

Max's gift was opened last, as it was the biggest. It was full of beautiful clothes and jewellery from New York, no expense spared and I was amazed at how he'd chosen things that I loved. The colours and styles were perfect, very intuitive for a man and I reminded myself to write a long thank you note.

After our meal, we all sat around the aging television, a fine piece of furniture in a teak cabinet so that we could watch the Queen's speech, which was always on at 3 o'clock. The picture wasn't very compliant today but Peter had just the right touch and gave the cabinet a good smack on the top, which reset the picture. We found ourselves watching thirty year old repeats of Laurel and Hardy films and laughed hard over our glasses of sherry and port. All in all, it had been a day to remember *for me.*

However, January was bleak but the snow cheered me up. February was painful, in that I hated the long nights and the cold; summer was too far away. By the time March came, Max had been absent for four months and I had learned to live without him, but I was truly bored. I began to feel like I was imprisoned, a puppet to perform tests which were documented on film. My sole purpose revolved around tests and hoping to socialise with the others, although they were not around as much as I liked, especially Oscar.

I filled my time with music and television, immersing myself in British culture. I was partial to 'Ready Steady Go!' on a Friday evening, even though the picture was grainy and in black and white but I got a good education in pop music and fashion. Short broadcasts slipped in between the entertainment in those days, informing the general public what to do in a nuclear attack and I tried not to let myself become afraid of this happening. In my room, there was a small transistor radio and I would tune into Radio Luxembourg on two hundred and eight metres medium wave in the evening, fiddling with the knob to try and get a good reception. It played a good selection of hits.

On the rare days out with Oscar, I stocked up on records, at that time I recall it was six shillings and eight pence for a seven inch single and one pound, twelve shillings and three pence for a long player. I seem to recall buying the Beatles' next hit which was 'Please Please Me' and 'Big Girls Don't Cry' by The Four Seasons.

I was also able to buy clothes and adopted a more casual, youthful look than what I was used to. The fashion was for Levi jeans or short A line dresses, it was liberating to wear something with the hem above the knee.

Through the wireless and television, I did take some interest in the world around me and was intrigued by the Profumo affair and how the power of a woman, Christine Keeler caused so much trouble for an influential man. He tried to claim to the House of Commons that there had been no impropriety but I didn't believe that, she is a beautiful woman and he is just a man, no matter his position. Emilie, however begged to differ and reminded me that she was nothing more than a whore looking for fame. Whichever way, the story captivated me.

But I was still lonely and bored. Oscar had departed The Institute to take time off and see his family in Barbados so there was no one who was entrusted to take me out. There came a day late in March 1963 when enough was enough. There was no point asking Miss Tynedale any more for money or permission to go out alone as she always refused me. I'm an 18 year old woman who can make her own decisions and it was outrageous that I couldn't go out alone.

Therefore, I threw caution to the wind one night. I crept downstairs and hunted around the small office. Normally, I had a small salary paid into a bank account in my name but I didn't know how to access it. I hunted around until I found that account information and stole the evidence I needed. Next day, I put on a smart black and white dress, used a headband to keep my hair away from my face and plastered my face in make up, then popped on my coat. I waited until Miss Tynedale was out of sight and I crept up to the door, let myself out and closed the door behind me discreetly. Free at last!

Due to days out with Oscar, I knew where to go to access the shops. However, the first thing I needed to do was locate the bank, which was difficult. I had to ask a passerby but that made it all the more exciting, a real adventure. After a lengthy walk, I found the correct bank and entered, feeling somewhat bewildered by the adult world. Armed with the details of my bank account, I approached the desk and asked for assistance.

"I have some money in your bank, I don't know how much."

The man was taken aback at first but I sent him some positive feelings and he became helpful. He checked my account details on the evidence I provided and raised his eyebrows when he discovered how much money I had. My jaw dropped when he told me.

"Two thousand pounds?" I exclaimed. (It was a lot in those days, and for someone my age).

"Yes," he said, "that is correct."

"M-may I have some of it?"

"Yes, how much would you like?"

I was stumped then pulled a figure off the top of my head. "One hundred pounds?"

"Why, certainly," he agreed, and got me to sign some paperwork, then handed over the cash.

I walked out of the bank feeling fiercely independent. Thankfully, due to my previous day trips, I knew where to head for the best shops and boutiques, which was essentially King's Road in Chelsea and Carnaby Street, which is a small lane behind Regent Street. I managed to find the Underground but found the map difficult to understand so I had to ask a passerby. Eventually, after a jostled ride, I emerged from the Oxford Circus tube station.

For a while I just browsed, almost afraid to try anything on and in awe of the fashionable iconic shops such as Mary Quant, located on King's Road. However, after the fifth shop I plucked up the courage and tried on a dress, it was orange and brown with huge flowers and was perfect for me with my milk chocolate skin and dark hair. That was my first purchase, along with a plastic necklace comprised of large circles and a large floppy hat. I didn't stop there and in another shop I bought a simple black polo neck jumper and a pair of flared jeans. There was still money in my pocket but I didn't want to buy anything else so I sat down in a café and ordered some food and a drink.

Destiny must have intervened that day as I didn't go unnoticed. I had walked along oblivious to the outside world but someone had noticed me. A man with shoulder length, fair hair and flared trousers coupled with an outrageous belt entered the café, paused then walked straight over to me. This I didn't expect.

"I don't mean to startle you, but I was on my way home and....," he said, tentatively, "um, I've never done this before. Let me introduce myself, my name is Malcolm Greene, I'm a fashion photographer."

He stuck out his hand, I didn't know what to say so accepted his hand and shook it, cautiously.

"How are you?" he asked, a little flustered.

"I'm good," I said, "I've been shopping."

He laughed, nervously. "Mind if I sit down?"

I decided he was harmless. "Yes, would you like to drink tea with me?" I offered.

He took up my offer and we sat drinking tea. I introduced myself and talked a little of my background although I did not mention The Institute. It was then he explained himself further.

"I couldn't help but notice how striking your looks are." He had begun to relax. "You'd look fantastic on camera. I'd really like to photograph you."

"Me?" I found that hard to believe.

He laughed. "Of course, you. Have you never looked in the mirror?" he joked. "I know this sounds really forward but I have access to a studio nearby and I wondered if you'd come over and let me take you through a quick shoot."

I really didn't know what to say, so many things ran through my mind; was he a crazy man? What would The Institute think if they found out? Was this meant to be?

"Look," he admitted, "I know what you're thinking, you've just met me, I could be a nutcase, I know but I assure you, I have the best intentions and I have a girlfriend, she'll be there at the studio. My interest is purely professional."

I felt reassured by that and decided to trust my instincts, which suggested that this man was not crazy, he really did just want to take my photo. We finished our drinks and I accompanied him to the studio he mentioned, which was a twenty minute walk away. From the outside it looked like an old three-storey house, much like The Institute but when we entered, I could see it was very different. There was a reception on the ground floor where a woman with long, blonde hair sat behind a desk. The reception was warm and inviting with cream and brown walls and the woman recognised Malcolm, the photographer. She eyed me with a little suspicion though.

"Who's this?" she asked him.

"This is Tahra, I've brought her back for a quick shoot. Oh, Tahra, this is my girl, Carol."

That explained why she was a little suspicious. We shook hands and

I decided I liked Carol. She took me upstairs to the changing room while Malcolm prepared the camera. It was now starting to become somewhat nerve wracking. I decided to use my new clothes, beginning with the flared jeans and polo jumper accessorised with the circles necklace and floppy hat. Carol lent me a pair of shoes and led me into the studio. There were a number of huge lights, a big fan and a white backdrop. Nervously I walked in front of the backdrop. Malcolm asked me to remove the hat, which I did.

"*I'm just going to take some test shots,*" *he explained.*

I didn't know how to pose so he told me to relax. That didn't work so he asked me to think of something that made me happy. I thought about Christmas, which made me smile and Malcolm started shooting. He made comments such as 'great' and 'fantastic' and directed me to turn my head this way and that. I was photographed seated and lying down, then I changed into my new dress and Carol pinned up my hair. Malcolm took another series of photos then asked me to find a swimming costume from the box near the door. He put me through a variety of poses then finally asked me express a range of varied but simple emotions. After the shoot, I was ushered back to the reception.

"*How did you find that?*" *Carol asked.*

"*Well,*" *I began,* "*at first I felt clumsy, but then I started to enjoy it.*"

Malcolm came downstairs and sat next to me on the brown sofa.

"*The photos will be ready tomorrow. Can I give you a call then?*"

Now that would be a problem. Miss Tynedale would realise I'd been out and I would have a lot of explaining to do.

"*I... can't take phone calls at the place where I'm staying.*"

Malcolm looked puzzled but then changed his approach. He wrote down his number and said, "*Well, call me tomorrow then.*"

I grasped the note, realising that opportunity may be knocking on the door. Perhaps this was meant for me instead of The Institute, the world was opening up in ways I could never have dreamed of. Briefly, I thought of my parents, how would they react? But I pushed them to the back of my mind, they weren't here and I was old enough to make my own decisions.

"*What time shall I call?*" *I asked, with certainty.*
"*I'm free in the afternoon, the pictures will be ready by then.*"
"*Okay, I'll ring you in the afternoon.*"

I stood up, sensing it was time to leave and Malcolm shook my hand. He seemed sorry to see me go, perhaps unsure if I was going to call. I waved goodbye and began the journey back to The Institute, by Tube. As I drew closer to home, I began to feel a sense of trepidation, what would be waiting for me on the other side of the door? Miss Tynedale could have noticed I was gone, although there were no tests scheduled today. I hadn't been available for lunch so hopefully the alarm wasn't raised.

Then it occurred to me that I could easily discover what was waiting for me before I opened the door. I stood still, closed my eyes and allowed my consciousness to drift ahead of me. The hallway of The Institute came into focus, which was empty. I investigated Miss Tynedale's office and found she wasn't there, maybe she had run an errand. I made the most of this opportunity and hurried back, using the key I'd borrowed earlier to let myself in. I even managed to replace it in the office drawer (it was a spare, not the main key) and sneak up to my room. When I lay on my bed I was so relieved, I'd gotten away from The Institute and with no consequences! All I had to worry about now was making that phone call tomorrow.

I woke early, it was a big day and I still had to figure out how to get to the phone. Breakfast was served in the dining room like any other day, Beth breezed in just after me and Peter was already there. We sat at the same table, drank tea in a civilised manner and ate cereal. I found my appetite suppressed due to nerves and Beth noticed, giving me a look of concern as it was not like me to avoid breakfast. At that point it occurred to me to confide in her, so I quietly asked if I could speak to her in private. After breakfast, I went up to my room before her and ten minutes later, she tapped on my door. I let her in, hoping I wasn't arousing suspicion.

"*What's wrong, Tahra?*" *she asked.*

I sat on my bed and sighed. "*Promise not to tell Miss Tynedale?*"

Beth made an action of crossing her heart so I proceeded.

"Well, yesterday I went out on my own, to the bank. I took out some money, which involved finding my account details in Miss Tynedale's office and then I went shopping. Afterwards, I sat down in a café for a drink and some food and I was approached by a photographer. He shot some pictures of me in his studio and today I need to ring him."

Beth raised her eyebrows. "Okaaaay," was all she said.

"Have I done a bad thing?"

She sat on the bed next to me. "Tahra, you can't stay cooped up here like a chicken."

I smiled. "I was starting to go crazy."

"This photographer, he didn't try to take advantage, did he?" *It was said with a maternal-like concern.*

"Oh no, it was all very professional. I just have to get in touch with him today, I don't know how I can do this and get away with it. I'm lucky Miss Tynedale didn't catch me in the office."

"There is a telephone in the office," *she said,* "but she does receive an itemised bill so even if you managed to get in the office, she would investigate any unrecognised numbers on the bill."

"Shall I risk it?"

"You know, there is a phone box about five minutes away, at least then your call won't be traceable. Miss Tynedale will be in room 7 later today, between 2 and 3pm. I can let you back in again."

"You'd cover for me?"

Beth shrugged. "I can't sit back and watch you miss out on something like that. Your life is your own and your destiny is of your own choosing."

I breathed a sigh of relief, it felt so good to have a true friend. We arranged a time, 2pm when I would slip out with a pocket full of change and Beth would be in the dining area, reading a book from then until I returned. If I was longer than half an hour she would come out and look for me, but I assured her I could take care of myself. So it came to be that at 2pm I opened the door, closed it quietly behind me and headed for the bright red phone box. It contained a set of local telephone directories, neatly stacked but I didn't require these. My nerves were jangled with the excitement as I fed the telephone, dialled the number and waited for Carol to answer, which she did.

"Carol, it's me, Tahra."

"Oh, great, Malcolm's just here, I'll pass you over."

There was chatter in the background then Malcolm spoke. "Hey there, how you doing?"

"I'm good. Did you like my pictures?"

Malcolm was enthusiastic. "You look absolutely fantastic, so much so that I feel confident I could get you a modelling contract."

I was silent for a moment. Was this the real reason I had returned to England, with my abilities just the opportunity to be sponsored to come here? Yes, I did have commitments to The Institute, but surely I could fit in the modelling around that. It's not like I was being tested every day.

"Really? That's…. amazing!"

"I know there's a shoot coming up next week here in London, it's a general fashion shoot and there's a possibility I could get you on the catwalk within the year, if not sooner. I think we could get you noticed real quick."

I was almost stunned into silence. "What do I need to do?"

"Meet me here at the studio next Wednesday, I'll take you over. Ten am?"

Quickly I ran my testing schedule through my mind, thankfully there was no clash. "I'll be there."

The date was set, I just needed to get out of The Institute for a day without Miss Tynedale realising I was gone. Back in the dining room, I told Beth the good news, barely able to contain my excitement and luckily by then, Oscar would be back to help cover me. Sure enough, when he returned three days later, I told him all about what had happened and he agreed to help me out. He thought maybe if he asked Miss Tynedale to escort me to a museum or park, there would be no issues and no questions would be asked. Last time Oscar took me out, there was no problem and I figured a white lie was the only choice. Oscar said he would visit a friend who lived near Camden, so it wasn't a problem for him. In the meantime, *life at The Institute went on as normal.*

Wednesday arrived quickly and we put our plan to work. Oscar and myself parted company at the Tube station in Camden and I walked to the studio, still remembering the way. Carol greeted me and Malcolm grabbed some kit, then we all returned to the underground to make our way to the shoot location.

This time I was truly nervous but Malcolm calmed me by making me laugh, and he was so sure they'd love me. When I walked in, there were many eyes bearing down on me, I was the only girl with coloured skin in a vast sea of whiteness but I know that day I put them all to shame. The photographers were really impressed with me and I returned to The Institute floating on a cloud. Oscar was pleased for me and we walked in together at around 5pm, discreetly sharing the day's events with Beth who was eager to be kept updated. Miss Tynedale wondered how we had made a walk in the park last all day, but, well, that was our secret. She wasn't suspicious and was comfortable with my 'escort'. There were another two shoots in April, which went smoothly and without incident.

Then came the time when I was invited out to a restaurant one night late in April. Even though Oscar was a permitted escort, that didn't extend to nights out so I was unsure if I'd make it. What made it worse was the fact that I had a test the next day. But, I needed to go. Malcolm and Carol were my friends and there would be some influential people there so it would really benefit my career. The main issue was getting back in so late, Malcolm would order me a taxi but I just needed to get in the door at midnight. The solution was to borrow the front door key and get a copy made that I could keep for myself. I managed to replace it before anyone noticed.

The night of the event, I got ready in my room, quietly, choosing a demure cream dress that reached my ankles. I pinned up my hair and decided on heavy eyeliner and mascara, then came the crunch. Could I get out of the door without being noticed? Miss Tynedale hid in her office between 8 and 9pm, I'm not sure what she did, perhaps managerial things, therefore I managed to slip out of the door unseen. There was a taxi waiting for me at the bottom of the street (I didn't want to give out my full address, or draw attention inside The Institute) so I climbed into it and it took around half an hour to reach the restaurant. Malcolm and Carol were there plus two influential guests, both American men. They noticed me immediately and I warmed to them.

Malcolm introduced me to them and them to me, their names were Ben D'Arco and Ian Moore. The former was quite young with dark hair and the latter was much older and a little plump, I rather liked Ben who I suppose was a less formidable version of Max. I sat between Carol and Ben. The wine flowed profusely and I savoured a good few glasses of Chianti that night, along with a delicious meal while chatting to everyone at the table.

"So, Tahra, what brought you to London?" Ben asked me.

That was a difficult question to answer truthfully and I really didn't want to lie but how could I tell this crowd of people that I had brought over due to my abilities as a remote viewer? The Institute was not a place you discussed with ordinary people.

"I… was sponsored by a wealthy man, I'm going to study psychology at university in September."

Was that a convincing answer? Ben looked surprised.

"You must be really gifted, or something to attract sponsorship," he said.

I started to feel edgy about questions regarding my life.

"Yes, I was very successful at school, you could say I'm gifted." *Now that wasn't a lie.*

"Intelligent and beautiful," Ian laughed, "there's gotta be a catch!"

I felt my face glow somewhat red, hoping they would change the subject.

"So, who's this wealthy man, your sponsor?" Ben pressed (*and I dearly wished he wouldn't*).

"His name is Max Richardson," I said.

Ben and Ian pondered, then said nothing. Maybe they'd never heard of him.

"How would he feel if one of us were to sign you up as a model on our books, and fly you off to the States?" Ben ventured.

I think my jaw must have dropped and it's a wonder it didn't hit the plate.

"You're joking," I said.

"It would be a joke not to sign you up. I've seen your photos Tahra, rarely have I had the pleasure of finding someone with such an incredible photographic presence. Your eyes… such a …. mystical intensity, I could look at photos of you all day. How do you do it?" Ben was most enthused.

I lowered my eyes, unaccustomed to such compliments but also fearful due to my commitments at The Institute.

"I would love to work for you, I'm not sure how it would sit with my other commitments," I responded, not as enthusiastic as he'd hoped.

He tried not to look too downhearted. "These other commitments, you mean your study?"

I was momentarily lost for words, aware of keeping my true profession secret. Could I confess to being a psychic spy? In essence, this is what I was.

"Y-yes," I said.

"Is there something you're not telling me?" Ben asked, disconcertingly.

I was taken aback but quickly riposted, "No, I truly want to work for you. Could I model and study?"

"Girl, you may become so successful that you'll never need to study!"

And we drank to that, two more glasses of wine for me which was a lot and I began to feel somewhat drunk. The celebrations continued until midnight and by then I'd drunk another two glasses of wine so couldn't walk very straight. I don't remember giving away my real profession but I did give out my address, which in retrospect was not a wise thing to do. Ben put me in a taxi and I looked out of the back window to see him waving.

Half an hour later the taxi drew up outside The Institute (it was pre-paid by Ben) and I almost fell out of it. At the door I fumbled around in my purse for the key then let myself in, just avoiding tripping over the welcome mat. I closed the door, perhaps not so quietly (it's hard to remember) and tripped on my dress as I attempted to walk up the stairs to bed. I made quite a loud noise and my heart almost stopped. Lying very still on the stairs I hoped everyone was sleeping like a log, then took off my shoes and lifted my dress, finally ascending the stairs with a modicum of stealth. I made it to the bed and I think I passed out as soon as my body touched the covers.

In the morning, I awoke later than usual, still in my clothes to the sound of Miss Tynedale literally banging on the door. I sat up sharply and realised I had my first hangover.

"Sorry, I'm not feeling too well," I murmured, seriously regretting the wine the night before.

Miss Tynedale was silent for a moment then I heard her go back downstairs. I was glad of that, for a few minutes later I had to dash to the bathroom and throw up in the sink. Did anyone hear me? I don't know but I hoped no one noticed the fact I was still in the dress I wore last night. After dressing in some drab clothes, I attempted breakfast and when I ate very little, merely stated I was ill. Miss Tynedale gave me a stern look, which made me feel uncomfortable.

An hour later it was testing time, I sat in room 7 feeling terribly unfocused even though the camera and Miss Tynedale's eyes were upon me. Once given the task, I closed my eyes, half expecting my consciousness to re-focus at the given destination but this did not happen. When I closed my eyes the room spun but my consciousness stayed put. Even though I tried harder to concentrate, still it didn't happen. I failed the test, I failed The Institute.

"I'm sorry," I murmured, "I guess I'm too ill to perform."

The room was silent. Miss Tynedale glared at me. I expected her to shout but she didn't, she just disappeared downstairs. Embarrassed and feeling guilty, I stood up and returned to my room to sleep it off.

Miss Tynedale did not speak to me later that day, or the next day which was most disconcerting. To make matters worse, I couldn't remember if I was supposed to contact Malcolm or Ben, I checked my purse but couldn't find any contact details for Ben so I decided to find a suitable moment to *slip out, covered by Beth and ring Malcolm. He was glad I did, Ben was very keen to sign me up and Malcolm had another shoot planned for two days time. I gave him the affirmative that I would be there, I'd meet him at the studio at ten then he'd take me over like before. This new career was thrilling and it got better every day. Before Miss Tyndale realised I had gone, I would slip back inside, using my ability to look behind the door before I used the key.*

Thankfully, it didn't clash with any tests, there was one the day before the shoot and I made sure I performed to my best, no more alcohol! The day of the shoot I slipped out and met Malcolm at his studio and him made my way to the shoot. It was an interesting shoot for some very avant-garde clothing and the theme was rather space age. I was almost tempted to leave the make up on but I knew I was provoking fate so I cleaned it off and made my way home, arriving at about 5pm. As usual I checked behind the door before I walked in but that day, I should have looked further ahead.

When she entered her bedroom, she found Max sitting on her bed. Tahra's heart almost stopped and her stomach lurched, words frozen at brain level. For what seemed like an eternity they stared at each other. It was strange standing before him again and what made her feel so concerned was the fact that copies of her modelling photographs were strewn across the bed, plus, one of them was in his hand. Max felt a mixture of disappointment, anger, betrayal and jealousy, this was totally unexpected. He didn't know what to say and neither did she. To see him again aroused a mixture of feelings; a craving for his love and attention again, dread of what he would say and do, resentment that he had left her alone all that time and an admonition that she had actually coped very well without him.

Max broke the silence. "So, where have you been today? And," he waved the photograph in his hand at her, "what have you been up to?"

Tahra was ready to break her silence.

"I've been having a life," she stated, with surprising venom.

Max was a person who normally kept cool whatever the circumstances but she sensed today was going to break that rule.

"Having a life?" he questioned, incredulously. "And this is what you regard as 'a life'?" Again he waved the photograph.

At that point Tahra realised she had no reason to feel guilty, yes, it was what she would regard a life, her life.

"The world is opening up for me," she explained, "there are other options available for me."

Max was starting to grit his teeth. "No, there are no other options, Tahra. I've invested a lot of time and money in you, I've just spent nearly six months in the States creating business, work for you! I made a deal with your father to educate you in return for your talents! How dare you talk to me about other options!"

She swallowed hard, this was the first time she'd seen Max lose his cool and it wasn't pleasant. But she knew she had to stand up for herself.

"You disappeared out of my life for half a year, you hardly wrote to me, you never told me when you were coming back! What did you expect me to do, sit in my room alone? I was going crazy with loneliness! No one would allow me any freedom, this is not a prison, or is it? I just went out on my own one day and I was approached by a photographer, he shot some pictures and said I was amazing, amazing enough to get a modelling contract! This is a fantastic opportunity for me!"

It dawned on Max that he would never be Tahra's sole admirer and that others would instigate to draw her into their world. He had become complacent in his time abroad, assuming she would be there awaiting his return with baited breath but he was brought back to Earth with a crushing realisation for his ego.

Then he said, quieter, "You're too good for this."

He waved the photograph again and Tahra took it from him, it was a particularly provocative shot from the first shoot where Malcolm had asked her to express a range of emotions, this one being 'lust'. It was a stunning full body shot and she had lost all innocence here, giving the appearance of a sexually experienced woman.

"An agent wants me to go to the States, he wants to sign me."

That hit him hard, he looked crestfallen. It was below the belt, for Max personally and The Institute.

"You can't do that," he said, "you have commitments, to me, to The Institute. You have amazing talents, you're far too gifted to resort to parading your body, or using your looks to get ahead."

"I want this," she pushed.

Max wasn't happy. "You can't."

Now she began to feel angry. "Who are you to tell me what I can and can't do?"

His response came without warning. He stood up, grabbed her shoulders quite roughly and pushed her against the bedroom wall.

"Who am I? Your goddamn sponsor! Your reason for being here in the first place! You're an ungrateful little bitch!"

His fingers were digging into her shoulders, his face was close to hers, his eyes full of rage, heart pounding with heavy breathing. But she felt just as angry and outraged that he should act this way. They both stared at each other, eyes flashing with hatred and both breathing heavily.

"You don't own me!" she pointed out, angrily.

Max didn't return the verbal volley and for an awful moment she was convinced he was going to hit her. He didn't, his eyes continue to flash with rage and they continued to stand there, in a stalemate, breathing hard. It was the first time any emotions had erupted from either side.

"I forbid you to attend any more photo shoots," he said, still angry.

"You cannot forbid me to do anything, I am not a child, I can make my own decisions!"

"You relinquished your choices when you came here. Now,

you're going to ring this photographer and tell him that you won't attend any more shoots."

"I will not."

Max bit his lip then realised it was a stalemate, so a new strategy was required.

"Okay, if that's how you want to play it. I'll simply lock you in this room until you accept what I've asked you to do."

With that, he let go of her, walked out of the room, closed the door and turned the key. She couldn't believe it, this couldn't be happening. In frustration she kicked the door and pounded on it with her fists but at that moment he was already walking away. Realising he wasn't going to change his mind and open the door, she defiantly walked over to the window and opened it, then remembered with horror that her room was on the second floor. It was a long way to the ground and there was nothing to hang onto if she chose to attempt escape, so she closed it again with a sigh. Tahra now started to feel less empowered and instead felt angry and bitter, realising that her resolve would inevitably crumble.

Max sat quietly in The Institute's office and realised that his hands were shaking. He began to feel a sense of guilt as he had come so close to hitting her, something he'd never done, which was strike a woman. There had never been any need in the past, all his protégés and his women had done as they were told, but Tahra was different; she wasn't afraid of him, she wasn't besotted by him. With trepidation, he began to wonder what the hell he had got himself into. It was beginning to look as if he'd opened Pandora's Box.

The next day, there was a knock at Tahra's door, the key turned in the lock and Max entered. He looked a lot calmer and he found her feeling rather depressed.

"Have you made your decision?" he asked, with a cool and rather arrogant demeanour.

She gave him a stare of resentment. "Yes."

"Have you realised the futility of your interest in modelling?"

"I have realised the futility in thinking you care about what I want," she answered.

Max sighed. "Have I got to lock the door again?"

"No," she said, face deadpan, "I'll ring him."

He looked unsure as to whether he could trust her but nevertheless, she followed him downstairs to the office where he showed her to the phone. He sat in the chair while Tahra dialled Malcolm's number. Malcolm was surprised to hear from her and she felt sick with remorse as she told him the bad news.

"I'm sorry to tell you this but I can't model for you or Ben anymore."

He was truly shocked. "What do you mean by 'can't'?"

"I... have other commitments and responsibilities."

At that point she started to cry, despite her urge to suppress the tears and she sobbed into the phone. Max looked on nonchalantly.

"Baby," he said, "what's wrong? You've got me really worried now."

"I just don't have any choice at the moment, it's not my decision to make."

"Of course it's your decision, you're a grown woman." The concern in his voice was genuine, he knew there was something wrong as she was crying. "What's wrong?"

"I can't tell you," she sobbed.

"Tahra, hold on, I'm coming over."

"No, no, please…."

But he had already hung up. She didn't say anything to Max, they just stared at each other, she through tears and he with a sternness that disturbed her.

"Are you happy now that you've ruined my life?" she said, with scorn.

"I think the term is 'saved it'. As I said, you relinquished your choices when you came here."

Miss Tynedale entered the office at that point and offered a total lack of sympathy. In fact, it was she who alerted Max the day she walked in drunk. It turned out that the night she tripped up the stairs, Miss Tynedale awoke fearing a burglar and just caught sight of Tahra in her dress as she staggered into her room. She knew Tahra was hung over the next day and had phoned Max in the States, to which he had responded by flying back to London the next day.

"Tahra," Max said, "you're going to have to accept a few home truths. What you're doing here is vitally important, too significant to throw away on a modelling contract."

"Did it occur to you that I wanted to see the world?" She had stopped sobbing but was still wiping away the tears.

Max sighed. "A strange thing to escape the lips of a very talented remote viewer."

She sniffled, crestfallen. Then Tahra told Max exactly what she felt about him.

"I hate you."

The words were toxic to him, she saw him swallow hard and a look of panic briefly flickered across his face but then he brushed it aside. Silently he stood up and left the office. Tahra wandered into the communal living area, slumped in a chair and stared out of the window, wondering what could have been. Max remained in his office, shuffling papers and preparing to get back to business as usual.

Half an hour later, there was a knock at the door and because Max was in the hallway at that moment, he answered it. Tahra watched from behind the doorway of the living area.

"Hello, Tahra lives here, doesn't she?"

It was Malcolm, true to his word he had come over because he was concerned. Tahra was touched by this and stepped into the hallway.

"I'm here," she said.

He saw her, face still tearful and stepped inside, much to the chagrin of Max. After he saw her, he looked around the hallway of The Institute, wondering what on Earth this place was.

"You all right?" he asked, moving towards her.

She couldn't answer and he put his arms around her. Max stepped forward, anger rising again and asked Malcolm to leave.

"What have you done to her?" Malcolm demanded of Max.

Max contained his anger effectively. "Merely told her the truth."

Malcolm looked exasperated. "And what is this place?" he asked both Tahra and Max.

"I can't tell you," Tahra replied.

"Why? I don't understand," was his response.

He looked at her and found a tearful silence and then he looked at Max, accusingly.

"What are you running here, a brothel?"

Max became quite indignant. "The operations that run here are strictly confidential. You're intruding in an area where you are not welcome so I suggest you leave, now. You don't know what you're getting yourself involved in."

Malcolm looked really concerned. He looked at her and said, "Baby, I can't leave you in this awful place."

Tahra just wanted to hug him and Malcolm looked at her in a way that startled Max, who turned to him and asked him a question.

"Did you fuck her?"

Both she and Malcolm were shocked he had said that and Malcolm was incredulous.

"What do you mean, 'did I fuck her'?"

Tahra was embarrassed and looked down at the floor.

"It's a simple enough question," Max stated then repeated the question with vehemence. "Did you fuck her?"

Malcolm looked as if something had clicked within. He and Max stared at each other for a short while, Max trying to control his temper and Malcolm resisting the urge to punch Max. But he realised there was no winning here, he wouldn't be able to take her out of here because Max clearly would not let her go. With exasperation, he gave her a genuinely sorry and helpless look; sorry that he could not help her but sorry she would lose a fantastic opportunity. Admitting defeat, he walked towards the door and paused, giving Tahra a sincere apology with his eyes. Then he turned to Max.

"You know, your jealously will destroy her eventually."

And with that, he walked out of Tahra's life. Max closed the door, his victory written all over his face. With a vehement and icy stare, Tahra walked away from Max and returned to her room. There she sat dejectedly, trying to come to terms with what had happened and the dark shadow that lay within Max.

Max and Tahra didn't see each other for a few days but when he re-appeared at her door, he was troubled. Turning him away was not an option so she let him in and he sat on her bed, therefore she sat in the chair in the corner of the room. There was silence for a few minutes and like before, it was Max who broke the icy tension in the room.

"Do you really hate me?" he said.

She didn't answer immediately but eventually conceded, "Yes, I do."

He accepted the answer but then proceeded to defend his actions.

"I only want what is best for you, Tahra, as I said you're much too important to be wasted."

It did little to reverse her acrimonious feelings.

"What can I do to change your mind?" he asked.

"Let me go," she answered promptly.

"You know I can't do that, I have an agreement with your father."

She sighed. "Okay then," she figured she'd test him out,

"show me the world, show me the life you denied me."

He was silent for a moment, a long moment and she didn't expect a reply but he gave her the one she least anticipated.

"Okay."

Tahra was stunned. "What?"

"Okay," he repeated. "I have contacts in the States and I can find work for both of us. Visas can be quickly obtained. You want to see the world, I'll show it to you."

She couldn't believe it.

"Really?"

She began to thaw towards him.

"Yes." He was certain. "We can leave in a few weeks."

Tahra was lost for words, but nodded. How could she refuse? He must have felt some remorse and she realised that, in his own way, he must care enough to make this concession for her. She began to feel both a sense of trepidation and excitement.

"Thank you," she said, and meant it.

Max looked relieved and stood up, Tahra did so too. His expression was difficult to read, did he regret making the offer or was he getting something he wanted too? It looked like he had nothing more to say and went to open the door, obviously now there were plans to make but he paused before leaving.

"Did you... have sex with that photographer?" he asked softly.

She met his concerned gaze and replied, "No, I didn't."

He was satisfied with the answer and left. She sat on her bed, contemplating a new future. It compensated for the grievous past two days and gave her a sense of satisfaction too, although she wasn't sure how it would go. What did Max expect of her? Was she prepared to return his feelings? She was only just getting used to him being around again and for a while, it was going to be just the two of them, in the States. She swore she wouldn't allow herself to become dependent upon him again.

10
Blood

Friday 10th April 1992

Ava's world had changed considerably since the winter of 1990, especially since the appearance of an entity in her bedroom late one night. It had looked like Michael but had not offered any explanation of what happened to the person it chose to resemble. She wondered, in fact, if the visitation had been real but the one factor that continually swayed her judgement was the new job it had predicted actually came about. The entity had referred to it being the right path, and that it was not charity, it was necessary. Much of that made sense, for it was her uncle that offered her the job. Normally, she would have been too proud to accept but he made her such an enticing proposition that she couldn't refuse.

For about a year she had worked in a biological research lab, studying the genetic structure of a whole range of pernicious and destructive viruses such as Ebola, AIDS, SARS, high level security biological agents and potential weapons of terrorism. It necessitated full biohazard suits at times and security doors that could only be accessed by a code. However, due to the connections her uncle had, there was a potential long term contract on the horizon working on a new and ambitious initiative. The UK was involved with the US Department of Energy and the National Institutes of Health; the intention to embark on a fifteen year journey to identify all of the estimated twenty to twenty five thousand genes in human DNA and determine the sequences of the three billion chemical base pairs. It was known as the

Human Genome Project and had been running since 1990. As her degree had been in genetics, (a wise decision she had made there), her chances were high. She had completed a dissertation on telomeres, which are the chromosome ends and how they had been identified as having implications in human aging, plus her uncle's connections made a contract look highly likely.

The virus team, as they called themselves were a decent bunch of people who all lived near the research lab, which was in Cambridgeshire. As well as Ava, there was the team leader called Derek who was in his fifties, smoked like a chimney and ate too much fried food; Gary who was the newest member of the team, he liked classical music (the more dramatic the better) Indian food and growing his dark hair as long as possible; Damian, another colleague who was very business like and left long to do lists on the table every day; Camille who had long, copper coloured hair and had an ignorant, bigoted husband and finally Tom, who lived for rock music but kept his hair cut very short. They were a fine team who regularly socialised after work and had a dark sense of humour. Gary, as the newbie, had been the victim of a few practical jokes, as Ava had been in her first few months. It was the crew's way of extending their welcome. She was happy there.

It had soon become known that she was the boss's niece, something she had really wanted to hide. Derek, the team leader had shrugged it off, it made no difference to him although Camille had been somewhat perturbed as she had worked very hard to nail the job, whereas Ava had jumped the queue. Tom had chosen to flirt with her because he liked to get close to power, Damian had put forth suggestions to improve the efficiency of the lab to be forwarded to her uncle and Gary was very interested in the fact that she was related to the boss. He asked her quite a few questions about the relationship, but she kept her answers succinct. Family life needed to stay external to professional life. Considering the way some had reacted to her ease in securing this job, she didn't contemplate mentioning the up and coming

Human Genome Project.

Thankfully, the hallucinations had calmed down. The situation required attention and she had sorted it out, she just wanted a normal life. But for Ava, it would soon become clear that would never happen. This day changed that.

It was the end of the working week, 6pm on a Friday and most people had gone home, leaving Gary and Ava to clear away. Everywhere had to be to clean and tidy for when the team rolled in at 7.30am on Monday morning. The day had not been so productive, but as the last people on the job (as they were on flexi time and started late), they still had to see it through to the end. Normally, it was Gary and Damian who stayed late on a Friday as Ava and Tom usually began their shifts early but more recently, she'd been opting for the later shifts. As they tidied up, they discussed the virus and bacteria league table, which were the most destructive; the conversation eventually ended up here for all the new staff.

"Surely it must be AIDS," Ava said, "it doesn't kill you but lets everything else do its dirty work. AIDS leaves you completely helpless against even the common cold."

She keyed in the door code and they both entered the lobby area, where they put on their biohazard suits. At the end of the day, whoever was last on had to check refrigeration and storage of the viruses. They kitted up, including the head gear and the gloves, then keyed in the code for the storage room and entered. Once inside, they headed for the refrigerators and opened them up.

Gary begged to differ. "There is a little known disease called Creutzfeldt-Jakob Disease, originally linked to the consumption of brains. It's rare but it's fatal, dementia progresses very rapidly and there is no treatment."

"Well," Ava countered, "the only people who could become infected are cannibals, and I don't know many of those."

Gary laughed. "Unless you count the animal feeding

strategies in the farming industry currently. What are cattle really fed? If they consume brains in their feed and we eat the beef, there's nothing to stop us contracting the disease."

"True, however consider Black Death," Ava returned the volley, "a disease of squalor with the potential to decimate a population. Bubonic plague affects the lymph system causing swellings known as buboes. Eventually the infection overwhelms the nervous system causing neurological and psychological disorders. It has a fatality rate of 50-60%. The pneumonic form affects the lungs, causing sufferers to cough up blood, death is 95-100% certain. There's also a septicaemic form, attacking the bloodstream. It causes a rash within hours and death within a day. Remember the nursery rhyme *'ring o ring o roses, a pocket full of poesies, atishoo, atishoo, we all fall down'?* The ring of roses was a reference to the rash and the sneezing to some of the symptoms, *we all fall down,* well, that's obvious…"

"But, you need an infectious rodent population riddled with fleas, unless of course you want to unleash it as an act of terrorism. I think Ebola beats them all hands down," Gary declared with confidence, "it starts with a fever and joint and muscle aches, bit like the flu really but it clearly isn't flu, it's something far worse. Your throat gets sore, you feel weak, followed by diarrhoea, vomiting and stomach pains. Then your body starts to haemorrhage, you bleed out of the nose, mouth and even your anus, Ebola dissolves your organs, literally eating you from the inside out. Can you imagine the horror of bleeding out of your eyes because your brain was liquefying?"

Ava shuddered at the thought of it.

"Very prolific in Africa today," Gary added.

Gary took hold of a vial of Ebola from the fridge and looked at it with a mixture of awe and dread.

"Nasty little bastard, isn't it?" he said, keeping it in his hand. "There's no approved vaccine or treatment for this baby. Sure, we're experimenting, but we haven't got the antidote yet. So we wouldn't want this to get out, would we?" He gave the vial a little shake.

"But then," he continued, "we also have the plague." He selected another vial from a different part of the fridge. "Few survived this baby. They had to quarantine whole villages."

Gary replaced the vials and he was responsible for counting the vials of bubonic plague while Ava counted the Ebola, in fact, she counted twice.

"Aren't we supposed to have twenty one vials in this refrigerator?" she asked him, puzzled.

Gary smiled. "Yes, you're right. And aren't there twenty one in there?"

"I don't think so," Ava responded.

"Double check," he insisted.

She pulled the rack further forward and found one hadn't been replaced properly, it was lying down at the back, as if someone had been in a hurry. On checking the seal, she found there was no leakage and placed it securely in the rack.

"It's fine," she said, "we got twenty one."

They breathed a sigh of relief, closed up, de-suited and locked up the lab for the weekend. They slipped on their jackets, Ava still attached to wearing the red silk scarf she had mysteriously found a few years ago in her handbag and they headed for their respective cars, but then he seemed to change his mind and made his way over to her.

"Say," he began, slightly nervous, "do you fancy grabbing a bite to eat?"

Ava was surprised, was this a date or just a social invitation? She didn't find him attractive but did enjoy his company. What was the harm?

"Okay," she agreed, and they used his car to find a reasonably priced restaurant. As Gary liked Indian, that was his first suggestion and Ava was happy to go along with that, at least he had good taste. They found somewhere that wasn't too busy and chatted over a delicious tikka masala which was preceded by poppadoms and raita. Work was discussed and annoyingly, he raised the subject of her uncle again so she artfully deflected the topic of conversation to something less controversial. After the meal, she assumed they would go straight home but he surprised her again.

"Do you wanna pop back to mine for a coffee?" he suggested.

Ava seemed a little reticent.

"Just to be sociable," he added, "no pressure, like."

She agreed once he made it clear it was just a friendly offer. He reassured her that he lived close to the lab and would be able to return her to her vehicle so she could get home, this sealed the deal for her and she was glad of a social life outside of work.

Gary's flat was located on a high street, above a shop on the first floor and access was through a door around the back. Inside, it was furnished to a basic standard and it looked like he couldn't be bothered to settle in on a permanent basis, as there were a few boxes he had neglected to unpack. He didn't appear to have a lot of possessions to his name, except for a good quality sound system and piles of CDs. Music was important to him, exemplified by the fact that the first thing he did on entering the room was select a CD, twiddle the volume dial and check the sound was suitably loud. He put the kettle on and made conversation from the kitchen while she browsed his CD collection.

"Your music taste is very eclectic," she said, loud enough for him to hear.

He laughed.

"Yeah, I guess, I take a little something from all the different people I meet. Sugar?"

"No thanks," she called out.

Before long, he emerged from the kitchen with two mugs and they stood chatting next to the CD collection.

"My cousin adores music," she said, "he plays the guitar and piano. One day, I might find his work in your collection!"

Gary seemed interested.

"Cousin? Would that be your uncle's son?"

Ava was again perturbed by Gary's obsession with her uncle. However, something else was beginning to alarm her, she swayed suddenly on her feet, feeling quite dizzy. Gary fixed her with an unconcerned stare.

"I think I'm going to have to sit down," she said, stumbling towards the sofa.

"Oh don't worry," Gary said, "that'll just be the sedative I put in your coffee."

"What?" Ava mumbled, feeling afraid.

"To ensure that I can carry out what I'm going to do next," he added. "I need to incapacitate you."

Ava felt a wave of panic wash over her, what was he going to do, rape her?

He produced a syringe from a box near the CD collection and held it up, removing the stopper from the end of the needle. As he made his way towards her, she backed away but in her semi-drugged stupor, she fell over a box and landed on the floor, straight on her back which winded her. Gary stood over her.

"I've been planning this moment very carefully," he said.

Finally, Ava spoke.

"What's got into you? What have I ever done to you?" she asked him.

"Nothing," he replied, instantly, "but it's more a case of, what did your uncle do to my family? You see, I can't gain retribution by harming him, 'cause I can't get to him no matter how hard I try but I can get the next best thing. I know how precious you are to him, you're the favourite. I mean, he gave you a job, and a flat, and a car. Most people would have to fuck him to get those privileges. I came here to target your uncle, but then you came along... My plan finally started to fall into place."

"I'm... adopted," she said, not convinced it would alter the course of what would happen.

"It doesn't matter. What matters is the love he feels for you, above all others. Why are you so special, Ava?"

She didn't know, all she knew was that he had always been protective of her, right from the start, after she had lost her parents.

Ava backed away the best she could by turning over onto her hands and knees and starting to crawl towards the door, hoping she could either make it out or that he didn't have the guts to go through with it. It was clear he couldn't be persuaded to change his mind. Gary advanced towards her with the syringe and Ava found the front door, however, it wouldn't open, he had locked it. She was now backed into a corner. Her legs felt weak and she tried to plead with him but it did not deter him, if anything, he wanted to get the deed over and done with as much brevity as possible.

Realising he had to do it quickly or not at all, he held his hand at her throat, pushed the red silk scarf aside slightly and pushed the needle into her neck. Ava was pinned against the door with an expression of abject fear, she didn't know what he'd just introduced into her body but it couldn't be good.

Still holding her by the throat, he began to taunt her.

"Do you want to know what I've just given you?" he hissed in her face, teeth bared. "I'm going to tell you anyway, because I want you to feel fear, terror at what is going to happen to you next."

Ava tried to control her anxieties the best she could.

"My little gift to you is a shot of Ebola," he said, with an ugly expression of satisfaction on his face.

Ava began to cry then, realising the severity of the situation.

"Once it's got into your nasal membranes, or in your mouth, your blood, any contact with bodily secretions you're fucked, basically," he continued. "There's no surviving this one, my dear."

With that, he dropped the syringe on the floor and pulled her out of the way and she fell to the floor again. The room was spinning and she heard the door close as Gary made his escape.

He ran down the stairs, adrenaline pumping and sweat running off his brow, he needed to get out of here fast.

Ava lay on the floor of his flat, heart pounding in her chest, feeling a sense of mortality wash over her. There was no doubt, she was infected with something you never ever wanted to come into contact with. The empty syringe lay on the floor only a few yards from her and she could do nothing to stop the contamination from invading her body. She tried to collect her thoughts and focus on what she needed to do, she maybe had a few moments of consciousness remaining, how could she attract attention? The room was spinning so much that she couldn't identify a phone but she could see the window. Trying to keep a level head, she knew she couldn't pass out in here so staggered over to the window and opened it. The blast of cool air revitalised her slightly and she looked down at the street below. It was quiet out there but not dead. Time was not on her side so she placed one hand on the sill with the intention of climbing down but due to her weak muscles and onset of unconsciousness, she slipped and fell straight onto the concrete below.

The pain was quite excruciating and she lay there, sobbing. Ava just sensed the inevitable; death would soon be coming for her.

She remembered a whirlwind of activity, sirens, people jostling and bundling her into an ambulance, the lights of the hospital and doctors and nurses tending to her wounds. She heard one of them point out the puncture mark on her neck. X-rays were taken, blood samples were obtained. She still felt dizzy and her body hurt throughout. All eventually fell silent. The specialists and nurses had gone, the room was vacated and the door to the quarantine room was firmly shut, the lights were off. Light from a quarter moon was filtering through the blinds at the window and she could only hear the faintest of voices murmuring in the distant corridors. It was clear her room was empty, what was not clear was why she felt a presence in the room.

"Hello?" she asked, almost in a whisper.

There was no reply, but how could she expect one when the room was clearly empty? She wondered whether it was the angelic looking figure again, who had disguised itself as Michael.

"Your advice would be much appreciated at this time," she continued.

There was a slight shuffling and she swore she saw a faint shadow but there was no reply. Ava sighed and closed her eyes, hoping to sleep although she finally succumbed much later, only after running every worse case scenario through her mind.

In the morning, she was awakened by the specialists and nurses taking blood samples and conducting various tests on her. She felt much more aware of her body and was surprised to discover she was pain free, perhaps they had administered some excellent analgesic drugs. Plaster casts were conspicuously absent, she was relieved that she hadn't broken anything. Looking around the room, she realised the medical staff were wearing protective clothing. They were taking precautions after spotting the puncture mark and the police had broken into the flat she had fallen from, finding the empty syringe on the floor. They had bagged it and sent it for testing, then the alarm had been raised when they realised it was a biohazard.

For fourteen days, doctors and nurses entered the room, took blood samples and brought her food and drinks. Hospital meals weren't exactly haute cuisine but at least she didn't have to cook it herself. The sense of isolation was soul destroying at times, but often she felt that presence in the room which gave her an odd feeling of reassurance. Eventually, the tide turned.

There seemed to be a degree of excitement, not a sombre atmosphere at all. Her specialist, Dr Jeremy Da Silva entered the room, quite a young black man wearing minimal protection and he stood beside her with a smile on his face, revealing brilliant white teeth.

"How are you feeling?" he asked her.

Ava shrugged. "All right, I guess, although I'm bored out of my mind."

"Well, that's to be expected." There was a pause. "Have you noticed any fever, headache, joint or muscle aches?"

She stopped to think, albeit briefly then replied, "I'm okay at the moment." After a pregnant pause, she asked the toughest question she had ever had to pose. "Am I really infected with Ebola?"

Dr Da Silva flashed his teeth in a brilliant smile and said, "I'm glad you are feeling relatively all right, considering." Then he decided to break the news. "We've conducted a stringent screening programme with your blood sample, including the standard ELISA test but so far, we can find no evidence of contamination as yet."

Ava found that hard to believe, the content of the syringe had clearly been delivered into her bloodstream.

"I was attacked," she said, "it was no accident."

Dr Da Silva wasn't surprised but remained professional.

"The police are already dealing with the matter. Do you feel ready to be interviewed about what happened?"

She nodded.

"My attacker escaped… I don't know where they could find him though."

"Don't worry, I'm sure they'll locate him. We've already notified your next of kin, your lab has been extremely helpful, and concerned."

She was left alone again. In her boredom, she switched on the TV but found there was nothing on. Someone had, however, left her a newspaper so she picked it up and found the major story was the Los Angeles riots, which were caused by the acquittal of four Police Officers accused of beating a black motorist named Rodney King. A state of emergency had been declared due to shops and vehicles being set on fire, motorists being dragged from their cars and people being shot. She read the story carefully and then proceeded to pore over every detail of the rest of the paper; major and minor news articles, the agony aunt section and even the horoscopes.

A few hours later, the police arrived, a male and female detective in protective masks. She had to relate the story of the attack and give a detailed description of the assailant. They were concerned to hear of the incident, especially due to the nature of the biological agents involved and the attacker, but when they realised the identity of the attacker, they were suspicious.

"He matches the description of a dead body we found a week ago," the male officer said, "looks like someone got to him before we could."

Ava didn't know whether to feel shocked or reassured by that news. Had he died because of what he did to her?

She also realised that from now onwards there would have to be a security and recruitment review back at the lab. What had happened was deeply shocking and had ramifications for public safety.

Official visiting time came and went, for Ava was still quarantined and could only receive approved visitors. She really wanted to see her parents, or anyone who could offer some solace, something she couldn't get from the hospital staff or police.

Another batch of blood samples were taken from her later that evening. At this rate, she would need a transfusion to replace the blood taken in the last month. But each sample that tested negative gave her hope. Finally, a week later, she was allowed visitors as normal and her parents were the first in.

Caroline Kavanagh hugged her daughter with relief, she had been beside herself with worry all month and looked tired. She had many questions for Ava and, like the police, was deeply concerned over the attack.

"I can't understand why anyone would want to harm you,"

she said.

"It wasn't about me," Ava revealed, "he wanted to get at your brother, not me."

Caroline's brow furrowed.

"The way he lives his life should not affect you," she stated, in an oddly cold manner.

"I'm the boss's niece," she pointed out, "and the lab itself is a target, maybe this was just bound to happen one day."

"Ava," her mother said, in a soothing tone, "don't worry, I'm not going to let this go."

"What do you mean?"

"I'm going to tell him exactly what I think, I don't want you working at the lab anymore."

Ava shook her head.

"Mum, I like it there. This was just a unique occurrence, uncle would never put me in harm's way, not intentionally. Please, don't say anything. You know he'll freak."

Caroline was thin lipped, but she respected Ava's wishes.

"I can't help but blame him," she explained.

"I know mum," Ava said, softly, "but you've got to put the past behind you. He loves me and I'd rather be under his care than anyone else's."

Caroline sighed, she had to put her own issues aside.

"I'll see you tomorrow," Ava said, "I'm glad you came."

Sam followed her parents, relieved to see that she was okay.

"I knew you wouldn't die," he said, quite emotional.

He sat by her and held her hand as they chatted about various things. His visit raised her morale and she couldn't wait to see him again.

The next day, Tom arrived, one of her work colleagues. He'd been trying to get to see her all the time she had been hospitalised and it was only now the staff relented. He entered the room expecting to find a sick person but found someone who was astoundingly well.

"Bloody hell," was all he could say, "you had us worried, no one's been able to get any information."

"The only thing I'm dying of here is boredom," she said, "I can't wait to get back to work." Then she added, "How's work?"

"Well," Tom began, "the police have been all over the lab, and Gary's nowhere to be seen. Actually, he's dead, shot in the head. What the fuck happened?"

"He injected me with Ebola," she explained, almost matter of fact.

Tom was aghast. "And you're still here?"

"Well, yes," she said, unable to understand the reason.

"Jesus," he muttered, "what have they said to you?"

"Well, nothing," she replied, "but they haven't told me I'm going to die."

Tom looked at her with incredulity.

"You're a walking fucking miracle," he said.

"What do you mean? I'm lucky, but not a miracle."

"Well, your specialist doc, Da Silva told the lab you were fortunate because the contents of the syringe weren't live."

"I guess I am lucky then," she said, relieved but a little angry that she hadn't been told.

"Ava," he said, "I've worked in that lab 5 years and I've never come across a duff batch in all my time there. Plus, when he gave us the news, I tested the other samples, they're all live."

"What are you trying to tell me?" she asked him.

"I'm trying to tell you you're a fucking miracle. By now you should be seriously ill, bleeding out of every orifice in your body, dead even. You know that disease has a high fatality rate."

"Well I'm not so the sample must have been spoiled for some reason."

"Look, I eavesdropped the nurses who performed the blood tests. The test results *did* show evidence of infection, an enzyme conversion reaction took place indicating the infection got into your bloodstream. The tests they did yesterday show specific antibodies in your bloodstream, proving your body responded to the infection. It wasn't duff, your body fought off the disease."

Ava tried to digest what he was saying.

"You mean, I have a natural immunity to…?"

Tom looked at her, realising the significance.

"They found antibodies for Ebola, the *Zaire Strain.* It should have killed you inside of a week. Do you know what this means?"

Ava was finding it hard to accept the truth.

Tom continued, "Your blood contains the secret to fighting one of the deadliest diseases in the world today. We've got to research it, find out why, confirm your immunity."

Ava looked unsure, it was hard to believe. Could it really be true? And was it no accident that she had come to work at a biological research lab?

"Please, don't say anything to the others, not even my uncle."

Tom protested, "This is of major fucking importance."

"I know. We're not even sure yet, some people are lucky, Ebola doesn't kill everybody. We can't jump to conclusions. Our secret?"

He nodded reluctantly.

"Okay, our secret. We'll work on it together in our own time. You'll not regret this."

She hoped that would be true, because if there was something special about her blood, her whole life could be turned upside down.

11
Pandora's Box

We landed in New York on the 28th April 1963, not an eventful period in history but a key date for me, and Max too. The flight had been long and monotonous and I found Max a very quiet travelling companion; did he really want to go through with this? What was running through his mind? I did not know what to expect.

This sudden alteration of plans had a key impact upon my career and the agreement made between Max and my father, in that I now would not be starting university in September to do my degree in psychology. This was not a problem, I could put it off another year and I really did want to experience life in America, it was too good an opportunity to miss. I don't think Max has told my father of the change in plans, I know my father would be very displeased and would probably insist I return home to marry some man that I don't love. In many ways, I am a western woman; my mother is British and I have lived in London as an adult for about six months, long enough to appreciate how liberating it feels. The longer I can put off returning to Iran the better, life is good here and it could be even better in the States.

The landing was smooth and I found the airport was busy. I felt overwhelmed, all of a sudden I was thousands of miles away from The Institute and my friends and was now surrounded by a sea of American accents. Max steered me through, I could see he was an old hand at this. There was someone there to meet us, a woman called Marianne who had long auburn hair, huge eyelashes and wore a smart tweed trouser suit. She seemed to know Max very well, greeting him with a hug and a kiss and was delighted to meet me, she shook my hand vigorously.

"You must be Tahra," she said, in a throaty American drawl, "I've *heard so much about you."*

I looked over at Max, who gave nothing away and the three of us found a yellow taxi cab outside to transport ourselves and our luggage to the place where we were going to stay. Through the window of the cab, I got a glimpse of the skyscrapers of New York although none of the major landmarks like the Statue of Liberty or the Empire State Building. Max seemed nonchalant, he had probably seen it all before but to me it was fascinating.

Marianne had helped us locate an excellent apartment with a fantastic view over the city. The lounge was huge, as was the window providing the view and I immediately walked over to it, spotting the Empire State Building instantly. It was such a beautiful skyline, despite being a manmade panorama. The apartment, thankfully had two bedrooms, both large and it also had a luxurious bathroom, I was going to love living here. Marianne left us and said she would see us in a few days at a place called The Observatory. It sounded like a planetarium.

We simply flopped onto the king size bed in the master bedroom. Max was still in his suit although he did kick his shoes off and I wore my flared jeans and polo neck. We just lay in silence. Max looked over at me, as if to say 'well, we're here' and I returned his gaze as if to agree. It was a strange moment and I did actually feel quite close to him at that time, which was unusual for me. I lay my head on his chest, which surprised him and he put an arm around me and kissed my forehead. We fell asleep embraced like so, tired from the long journey.

Not every moment was idyllic. Only a few days later Max and I arrived at The Observatory and I discovered that Marianne was, in effect, the curator of this remote research centre. We had to drive at least a hundred miles out of New York towards the Appalachians, to this day I still couldn't pinpoint it on the map but it wasn't where I expected it to be, which was in the city. At first, I thought it housed a telescope for it had the characteristic dome but once we stepped inside, I realised it was not an astronomical centre at all. Aside from a number of offices, the former housing of the telescope was opened out into a grand hall that contained a number of partitions. Within each area were banks of typewriters and recording equipment, such as cameras, tape recorders and microphones.

I was steered to one such partition and two technicians conducted a number of tests which required me to separate my consciousness from my body and focus on a location designated on a map. The locations were in the Soviet Union and usually entailed looking inside of aircraft hangars, government offices and missile silos. You have to remember that the United States and the Soviet Union were in the midst of the Cold War and it was actually quite, quite normal to use remote viewers for espionage. Much of what I did at The Institute involved such work so my contributions to the United States were no different. In a way, it felt rather glamorous, being a spy. Since the Second World War, governments have become much more open minded about how they gather information. Reconnaissance was often used but remote viewers were excellent at penetrating areas of high security. So far, no one had discovered a method of detecting a wandering consciousness and probably no one will ever be able to. Nothing is sacred to a remote viewer, it's really down to your own morals and ethics. At the time, I believed in what I was doing in the name of international security and even today I do not take issue with it. Truth is, I liked my job.

I wouldn't say that I developed any close friendships, except with Marianne. Although she was the curator of The Observatory, she was the antithesis of Miss Tynedale; open, warm and friendly. I did get lonely out there in New York, Max was often not around. If it was testing day, he was the one who drove me there and supervised me but there were many occasions when he was absent, I always assumed it was just business. A few times I was tempted to remote view and search for him, but it felt too much of an invasion of privacy and to be honest, I was partly afraid of what I would find. Thankfully, on lonely evenings Marianne would draw me out and we'd drink at a bar or she'd take me to a party. We had a genuine rapport, she was not much older than I (unless she lied about her age, as women do) and we had similar taste in music. She made a number of attempts to match me with a handsome American guy and I did date a few but I was sticking to my principles, I didn't want to have sex with just anyone, which was a strange concept in the sixties. I was urged to take advantage of the new sexual freedom for women, but to me, it was a sacred experience to share with a true love.

My cultural interests developed somewhat and I became drawn to the music of Bob Dylan, with his lyrics intoning social change and voicing the new thoughts of the civil rights movement. He had the gall to walk out of rehearsals for the Ed Sullivan Show, something The Beatles would never have done. He was the idealist to their iconic pop flavoured tunes, but I accepted both in my life as different aspects of my taste.

The Space Race inspired me too, for Valentina Tereshkova became the first woman to orbit the Earth, following in the footsteps of Yuri Gagarin a few years earlier. She was a national pin up on her return and reinforced my belief that women could achieve something special and outstanding in their lives. I had always been quite fascinated with what lies beyond our planet and wondered what it would be like to visit space. However, it was very unlikely I would become a cosmonaut and being a psychic spy was almost as exciting.

Max was in and out of my life but he appreciated my company when he was around. There were free days when we would tour New York and he valued these times greatly. One particularly memorable day was in late October when we went right to the top of the Empire State building to appraise the city. It was windy but a beautiful day. He wrapped his arms around me as I surveyed the view and pressed his body close to me from behind. It was a little unexpected but I didn't push him away, it felt too reassuring. I lay my hands on his and we quietly looked upon the city. At that point, he told me he was taking me to a party tomorrow night, it was Marianne's birthday and there was a huge gathering at her apartment. How could I refuse?

The next day, we were back at The Observatory for a full day of remote viewing. Max watched coolly during the proceedings, his keen eye viewing his favourite protégé perform. I knew that during testing, he had his business head on and I had my research head on, I needed to tune out emotional distractions to be at my best. Today I was to explore a facility in the Soviet Union, I was given a suggested location and a photograph of the building, all I had to do was project my consciousness there. I went through the usual process and found myself inside a rather clinical building, which was very austere with an intimidating staircase straight in front of the main door. There were many rooms here and I had no map or blueprint of the building to guide me. When you remote view, buildings can be very confusing.

Many of the rooms were offices and I had been given no instructions on what to look for, I was a scout with a mission to discover the purpose of the facility. The offices revealed nothing so I pushed my consciousness up the stairs to find another set of rooms. I saw people, and technicians, and audio visual equipment... I realised what this place was and I should have noticed my first impressions. It was another Institute, or Observatory. They were doing exactly the same thing, testing remote viewers. I watched as they described locations in the United States and the technicians recorded the findings. After a short while I pulled back into my body.

"They have remote viewers too," I said, "That's what the place does."

Max didn't look as surprised as I expected, maybe this was his suspicion all along, he just nodded and then looked very thoughtful.

After that, we had time to go shopping. He bought me a new dress for the party and I took a lot of care over my hair and make up, finding it difficult to decide whether to pin it up or leave it down. Since leaving London, it had been cut slightly shorter and I had a fringe, with it high at the crown. I surveyed my reflection in the mirror, feeling unusually self conscious. While I stood there, Max walked up behind me and looked at my reflection with me.

"You look beautiful no matter," he said, kissing my neck softly. I closed my eyes and savoured the feel of his hot breath on my skin.

"But I have a little something for you, to go with the dress," he continued.

He opened a box and draped a necklace around my neck, still meeting my gaze in the mirror. I couldn't believe it, the gems looked like diamonds.

"They're genuine," he assured me, "only the best for my Tahra."

I didn't know what to say, so I turned round and kissed him quite sweetly on the lips. He smiled, it was the best thank you he could have received so he kissed me back. He was a damn good kisser and in my loneliness, I missed his affection but it was Max who put a halt to any further proceedings.

"We have to go," he said softly, "you don't want to miss the party do you?"

Marianne lived very close to us, a few blocks away so we walked the short distance. I felt like a million dollars and Max treated me like a movie star, holding open doors in a chivalrous manner and looking upon me with pride. Marianne lived on the 31st floor, we shared the lift with some other of her guests.

She had a sumptuous apartment with highly fashionable furniture, blending styles from different eras. There was a huge brown sofa, lots of large cushions and what looked like tapestries woven with a repeating leaf motif. It looked quite typical of a sixties apartment with some aspects of both the fifties and forties, evidence of furniture handed down from parents, perhaps. In the kitchen there was a huge bowl of punch, devastatingly alcoholic and several bottles of wine. There was an interesting buffet, which wouldn't last long as people were already helping themselves. Music from both the fifties and sixties emanated from twin record players, a friend of Marianne's took responsibility for selecting the tunes and he seemed very partial to Elvis Presley, Chuck Berry and early Motown. Everyone recognised Max, although not many knew me, I felt a little bit of an outsider but they did make me feel welcome.

"So, Max," said one man with a brown suit and collar length hair, "you've brought a date." It was said with some incredulity.

Max looked slightly disconcerted by the man's astonishment. "This is Tahra," he said simply, and steered me over towards Marianne.

Her eyes were drawn to the necklace then she gave Max a quizzical look. "Nice rocks," she said.

We mingled and helped ourselves to a glass of punch. The conversation varied from updates on family and friends; what they were doing, who had got married, who had passed away and who had given birth or something of a more political nature. I eavesdropped one such exchange.

"You know, Kennedy made a blooper in his 'Ich Bin Ein Berliner' speech," one verbose man in his thirties said.

"How come?" asked his date, a pretty woman with blonde hair and big teeth.

"Well," he began, puffing out his chest somewhat, "the indefinite article, and by that I mean the word 'ein' is omitted in the German language when speaking of a person's residence. Although he was trying to show solidarity with Berlin's citizens, they never actually call themselves Berliners. In fact, that term is used for a piece of confectionary, so in actual fact, Kennedy was telling Berlin 'I am a jelly-filled doughnut'."

His companion laughed and I smiled to myself, looking for the next conversation.

Once I became more comfortable with the crowd, I noticed people smoked a lot and sometimes shared cigarettes with a strange smell, later I understood it to be a joint. Max was offered some a few times but he simply said 'not tonight', looking over at me, wondering what I would think.

So we drank punch, although not too much. It was unusual to see Max drink alcohol to such a degree and we danced together to some recognisable tunes. He clutched me with a passion I rarely saw, which was frightening in a way because he normally had such a cool demeanour. But was it frightening because I feared giving in to him? Less time was spent in conversation with his friends, not that he ignored them but he regularly re-directed his attention towards me. We engaged in separate conversations to be sociable, discussing current affairs, family or music but both of us would make eye contact across the room. Sometimes I wasn't even concentrating on the conversation, I would be looking at Max in realisation that the inevitable was looming: I was attracted to him, I wanted him to touch me. Would I be able to retain my virginity as planned and save it for my husband-to-be? The feeling in my stomach and between my legs was intensely distracting and the sexual tension increased throughout the duration of the night. When we danced he looked into my eyes with an intensity I'd never seen before. By the time we walked back home, about an hour or so after midnight, there was an electric tension in the air. I squeezed his hand and he quickened his pace. When we reached the door of our apartment, I couldn't help but notice he fumbled a little with the key. Instead of letting me walk into the apartment, he suddenly picked me up.

"Max," I said, "what are you doing?"

He didn't answer verbally, just carried me into the main bedroom and placed me on the bed. I lay there, not knowing whether to halt what was about to come or to flow with it. I didn't stop him, despite my principles about sex. There was no doubt in my mind that was what he wanted. Did I want it? Yes, at that point I didn't want to resist anymore.

He threw off his jacket and unbuttoned his shirt, I could see his upper body was muscular and he had a light covering of hair on his chest. I kneeled up on the bed as I had to touch him and he enjoyed the feeling of my hands on his body, something he'd been denied for so long. We kissed, for a long time it seemed and I felt his hands on my breasts. Why had I stopped him before when it felt this good? Before long, he began to undress me which didn't take long, all I had on was a dress which he slipped over my head. As he surveyed my naked body, I felt both vulnerable and exhilarated. I lay on the bed and Max proceeded to stroke the skin on my stomach and I heard his breathing deepen. I found his touch hard to resist, no man as yet had touched me like that, or seen me naked. He kissed my breasts then worked his way down my stomach until he had buried his head in between my legs. Deep down I knew I should stop him but it was far too pleasurable, he used his lips and tongue in such a sensuous manner that I soon found myself in the throes of my first orgasm.

As I lay there contemplating what had happened, he threw himself on top of me and I could feel his hardness pressing against me. There was a yearning and a hungriness in his eyes that was irresistible, then I realised what was about to happen. I wasn't ready to give up my virginity, the orgasm I'd experienced had quietened my own hunger and because he had just given me something incredibly beautiful, I could not give him what he wanted, therefore I felt guilty.

"I'm sorry," I said, softly, "I can't, we're not married."

Max looked stunned. "What?"

"The time isn't right," I said. "I can't, not yet."

"Don't be afraid," he was surprisingly reassuring, "I won't hurt you."

He was practically begging me and I felt so selfish, what could I do?

He looked me in the eye and stroked my cheek, fondly. "Tahra, I'm on fire here, I've waited for this for so long."

What can you say to that? I wanted to please him, to return the pleasure he had given me, then I realised what I could give.

"Max, do you trust me?"

He looked at me, puzzled but nodded. I pushed him onto his back, which he didn't expect and lay on top of him. Hopeful of physical satisfaction, he gently tried to push me downwards in expectation of oral reciprocation but I shook my head. Disappointed but not giving up, he took hold of my hand and moved it down in the hope of a little relief.

"I don't need to touch you to make you feel the way I just did," I said.

He didn't say anything but decided to let whatever was going to happen, occur.

I focused my gaze on his and dug down into my memories. When I was younger, I could always affect the emotions of others, for better or worse. I knew I could find a way to pleasure Max in the same way. It's hard to explain how I do it but I always visualise intense feelings as flames, flames that have their origin in the belly or at the base of the spine. I visualised this fire rising, curling up the spine and sending out intense waves of pleasure out through the nervous system. Max seemed to be responding, his breathing was much deeper and as the process progressed, he began to look at me with an odd expression on his face.

"What are you doing?" he asked me.

"Awakening the fire within," I answered.

He looked puzzled, afraid and in retrospect, I don't blame him for I don't think he had ever experienced such an intensity of emotion before, or even experienced emotion before. Max clutched me tightly but didn't break eye contact with me, he stayed with me all the way. I intensified the fire within him and he began to tremble slightly, his breathing much harder, then his body stiffened and he cried out in an emotional climax. There was a quiet moment when he looked into my eyes, fully connecting with me for a brief moment and then he pulled away, walking over to the window. For what seemed like a long time, he just stared out of the window and didn't say a word.

Standing naked in front of the window, Max didn't worry about if anyone could see him from the streets below. He was wondering what the fuck had just happened. He'd buried his head between her legs and tasted her for the first time, and brought her to orgasm for the first time then she'd changed her mind at the last minute. Only half an hour before, he had been certain he would finally win her over but again, she'd refused to submit. Was she doing this on purpose? Did she know the extent to which she was fucking around with his head? Something had changed within her though, he could see that, for tonight she had clearly felt guilt about refusing him and had looked genuinely sorry.

The experience he'd just had with her though, had both disturbed and blown his mind. It was like having the most intense sexual experience you could think of, without touching anyone. The arousal he'd felt in his groin had been intensified and dragged up through his body, into his head and his very soul. It had taken him from a level of sexual frustration to the heights of ecstasy, with nothing physical actually occurring. He had begun confused, then felt alarmed, vulnerable but alive and satisfied in a completely new but strangely familiar way. It was better than any drug, she was better than any drug. While the feelings of vulnerability scared the hell out of him, he hungered to repeat the experience. For someone who avoided emotional involvement, he needed more of it, was this a good thing or was he unwittingly opening Pandora's Box? Tahra could teach him to feel again. She could also destroy him; there was the dilemma, the dichotomy. He knew now he could never let her get away, she was too unique.

Tahra got out of bed and walked over to him, pressing her naked body against him and wrapping her arms around him.

"Come back to bed," she said.

Silently they stood like that for a few minutes and neither of them spoke. In the end, he let her take his hand and lead him back to bed. They lay together quietly, he on his back and she with her head on his chest, unable to fall asleep, listening to the rhythmic beating of his heart. It was truly a perfect moment and nothing else mattered. Before too long, he spoke.

"Tahra," he said, softly, "you know what I'm thinking?"

She didn't answer but raised up onto one elbow and looked at him, wondering what he was going to say.

He turned to look at her and said something that was completely unexpected.

"I think I want you to marry me," he said.

In the morning, Max woke first and found her in the same position as she fell asleep – with her head on his chest. He felt strangely at peace, which was an exceptional experience, or one seldom felt. Here was this beautiful young woman, asleep in his arms; what more could a man want? He stroked her skin lightly and sleepily, she opened her eyes, meeting his gaze with a smile.

Max made her breakfast and they sat together at the table, making civilised conversation. It was strange considering what had occurred that night and both were skirting the important topic raised in the early hours of the morning. She didn't know whether to take his words seriously, the ones concerning marriage. Had he been sincere or was it said in the heat of the moment? Was it the only way he saw to get something that he wanted? Would she accept a proposal of marriage from him?

She didn't even know who he was, he shared very little of himself and his life, she didn't know what he was involved in while he was away and he very often was emotionally distant. However, he could show incredible kindness, he had done so much for her since she left her home, he never shied away from spending his money on her and he was capable of being a good provider. The key driving force was the growing physical magnetism, he was very handsome, she found him attractive, most women probably did (which was another worrying point) and she knew he was incredibly attracted to her.

Breakfast was finished and Max simply looked thoughtful, heavily preoccupied with something that was making him feel uncomfortable. There was silence and Tahra began to find it awkward.

"What's wrong?" she asked.

He shrugged and played with a spoon.

"Well, there must be something wrong, last night was wonderful, and now…"

"I'm just trying to think of a strategy," he gave as an explanation, "to address our adversary's remote viewers."

She smiled, but it was forced. "You can't control the consciousness of another person."

He gave her quite a wry look. "That I'm well aware of," he answered, almost sharply.

His response took her aback, his mood shift was unexpected. But she decided to ride it through and cut through to the core of the matter.

"Did you mean what you said, last night?" she asked him, directly.

He looked at her, unwilling to answer until she showed some sort of interest or commitment.

"Would you really marry me?" she pressed.

"Would *you* really marry *me?*" He turned the question back on her, which she did not anticipate.

The words wouldn't leave her lips, he was now putting her on the spot for an answer. It was a rather ungainly proposal.

"I think we need to consider it carefully." She realised she hadn't answered his question in the way he wanted. "You're away on business much of the time."

He didn't look very happy. "It's a necessity," he stated, bluntly.

"I – I don't know anything about you," she continued.

Max stood up from the table abruptly and disappeared into the bedroom. A moment later, she followed him in and found him lying on the bed, again thoughtful. She guessed she had hurt his feelings, for he had put himself on the line for nothing, or so he thought. She sat on the bed and held his hand, he didn't resist but didn't make eye contact either.

"This is a big decision for me, I'm still very young and it is something I will live with for the rest of my life," she explained.

He said nothing. She lay down next to him and put her head on his chest. This was at least something she was prepared to do everyday for the rest of her life.

The situation was difficult for another few days then Max was called away on business but not for long, just a few weeks. It gave Tahra some thinking space and the thoughts that ran through her mind were myriad; what were other men like? How would marriage benefit her, in light of the fact that Max was often absent on business? What did she really want? Was it better to have Max a part of her life or not? It was not possible to find an answer to these questions, the only way to know was to accept his offer but was she ready to do that? They hadn't really had a relationship, so in a way, it seemed strange that he should think of marrying her, or so she thought. But she missed him, she realised that she needed to be around him and while she was wary of giving in to him, she realised her attraction to him was urging her to do so. She needed his touch, his devotion. A part of her had already made the decision.

When he returned he was a different person, relaxed, confident and warm. He knew it was her birthday in a few days and had already booked a meal for two in a restaurant, that was one thing about him, she figured, he remembered key dates. She was glad to see him and the marriage situation wasn't an issue, they embraced and she kissed him warmly. The birthday meal was pleasant and Max was still more relaxed about everything, there was no pressure for sex or anything, they simply talked about general things. He didn't discuss the trip and when she queried how things had gone, he was dismissive and told her not to worry about it as it would only bore her anyway. It was then she came to realise that business and interpersonal relationships would always be two distinct entities. Maybe there was a reason for that and maybe it was for the best. What did Max offer? Financial security, undivided attention when he was actually here and pleasant experiences. He was stylish, had poise and charm, even though he was not always spontaneous or passionate.

It was now, or never.

"Max," she began, "I've been thinking, real hard."

He put his knife and fork down then looked at her hopefully.

"I know I said a lot of negative things a few weeks ago," she continued, "I just didn't expect you to say… anyway, marriage is a serious commitment."

Instead of his usual silence, he reached across the table and took her hand.

"I know, you've only just turned nineteen… I've come to realise though, that after so many years as a bachelor, I do want a wife. You're the woman I want to fulfil that role."

Tahra realised she couldn't refuse.

"Do you want to spend the rest of your life with me?" he continued.

She finally gave him an answer. "Yes, yes I would. We have all the time in the world to get to know each other better."

There was a flicker of worry on his face but it was soon replaced with relief and elation. They walked home arm in arm, slept in each other's arms and Max didn't pressure her for sex, it wouldn't be long now. Before falling asleep, they decided to marry in the spring, sufficient time to set up contracts and deal with clients to ensure financial security while he took time out for a long honeymoon. No one else knew of their plans, least of all her father.

November 1963 was a peaceful time for us, he disappeared a few times during November but didn't remain absent for long, I didn't ask where he went. We celebrated Thanksgiving with Marianne, who found it amusing that we arrived together. Marriage wasn't discussed in front of anyone else.

In terms of global affairs, it was an active time for on the 22nd November the president was shot in the head whilst sat in his motorcade. It was all over the news and made for fairly gruesome television but I wouldn't say we were so grieved, this was not truly our country and we were just visitors. Nevertheless, it was a shocking event, maybe someone back at The Institute foresaw it, maybe not.

On December 13th 1963 it was Max's 43rd birthday, he returned from his business trip in time to spend that day with me. He said it was only the second time in his life that he had shared his birthday with someone, but when I asked him about the first time he had spent it with someone special, he clammed up and didn't want to discuss it. Perhaps he had been hurt in the past, one day he may tell me about it but I think it was a long time ago. I had never seen any pictures of a previous lover, not even his mother come to think of it.

Christmas in New York was a charming experience, I enjoyed the festivities as I had done last year at The Institute. If anything, this Yule was even more special. I must admit, I did start to feel homesick for The Institute, even though in many ways it had been a prison but I sent gifts there for everyone to show that I remembered them. I hadn't written to Oscar as much as I promised so I bought him something extra to address my guilt. I spent the New Year with Max on an excursion to Philadelphia, where he met with an old business friend, someone called Thomas, that's all I knew. Thomas was married to a woman named Stephanie who made polite and stimulating conversation while the men talked business. Often my hearing strayed towards their discussion, as my prying mind was curious as to what business was conducted between my husband-to-be and Thomas. Little of it was meaningful, but I caught snippets of conversation that aroused suspicion, such as 'Don't worry, he'll be dealt with, like the others'. The words themselves were not threatening but the way he said it sent a chill down my spine.

The next few months were punctuated with Max being absent and arrangements being made for the wedding. I perused brochures with wedding dresses and found it so hard to make a decision, there were so many beautiful designs. In between the testing, I had to choose flowers too while Max located a surprise venue that would be memorable. Before long, it was February and the date drew nearer, in between all the planning and testing, I happened to catch an iconic broadcast on the TV on the 9th February 1964. The Beatles made their first appearance on the Ed Sullivan Show at 8pm that evening. They played 'All My Loving', 'She Loves You' and 'I Saw Her Standing There' and I was so glad to hear their songs again. These songs would later remind me of the time I made wedding plans with Max and exemplified the latter days of my time in New York.

It was all happening at such a dizzying pace that often I felt panicked as much as I felt excited. I was going to marry a wealthy and handsome man, what more should I want? I wanted to know who he really was; what kind of person was I marrying? There were a number of nights where Max appeared in my dreams; I watched him receive cash in suitcases, pass fat envelopes of information to dangerous looking people, oversee shipments of unknown goods and speak on the phone to faceless people, securing deals. Was it all real, was I unconsciously following him by remote viewing without realising it or were they simply dreams, fuelled by my suspicions? For so long I had avoided using my gift to see what he was doing but should I still put that off, considering I was about to spend the rest of my life with him? I was about to marry a man I knew so little about.

One night, when he had been absent all week and was due to return tomorrow, I decided to investigate who he really was. If I didn't do it now, there could be nasty surprises in store in the future, I needed to prepare myself for the nature of his business and be absolutely positive I wasn't making a mistake. I lay on my bed and closed my eyes, holding a clear picture of Max in my mind's eye. I then allowed my consciousness to drift and focused on his face, it brought me to an apartment not far away.

I recognised it, it was Marianne's apartment. What was he doing here? He wasn't alone with her though, there was a party, but it was a vastly different party to the one I had attended. The people were naked. Max was naked. I saw Marianne having sex with two men and then I noticed Max was with a woman with long, dark hair. He was seated in a chair while the woman was performing a sexual act on him with her mouth. I felt my heart sink and my stomach lurch, my Max with another woman. The sex didn't stop there, another woman came over to him and sat on his lap, having full intercourse with him. I couldn't bear to watch anymore and withdrew my consciousness.

At first I was stunned, I felt sick, and actually was sick in the bathroom. All this time he had been the perfect gentleman, sweet, affectionate... but he had most likely been doing this on a regular basis. Why? I couldn't believe it, but it was really happening and was probably still happening. I couldn't bear to think of him enjoying sex with other women. For the rest of the night, I sobbed, wishing I hadn't spied on him now. There was no going back, Max was not as honourable as I thought. How could I give myself to this man now?

Tahra didn't sleep well, the scene replayed in her mind in between the sobbing. He arrived at midday and breezed in looking relaxed and confident. She couldn't look at him, the sight of him disgusted her and she returned to her room as soon as he walked in the door. A moment later, he knocked on the bedroom door and she told him to go away. He didn't though, he entered and looked concerned.

"Tahra, what's the problem?"

She didn't want to speak to him, but he wasn't going to take no for an answer and sat on the bed next to her.

"There must be something wrong."

She wanted to maintain her distance and disgust with him,

instead she started crying. He was stunned.

"This is a bit… unexpected," he said, "has something happened?"

Tahra glared at him through her tears. "I can't marry you."

He was genuinely shocked, and a little angry.

"Why the hell not?"

What could she say? She had spied on him.

"I don't think you could be faithful to me."

He was puzzled. "What makes you think that?"

She just glared at him.

He started to suspect what was wrong. "You know something you're not telling me."

She sobbed even more. "How often has it happened?" she asked him.

He looked at her with an accusing, yet helpless stare.

"How often has what happened?" It was a poor attempt at innocence.

She finally became angry. "How often have you had sex with other women at parties?!" she shouted, through her tears.

He looked regretful; but was that because he had betrayed her or because she'd found out? Max swallowed hard, unsure what to say and knowing how it could affect the future. Instead, he treated it as an opportunity to clear the air.

"Tahra, this is what I used to be. My whole life revolved around easy sex, and lots of it. But do you really think I would continue this after we were married?"

It was an honest answer but she still found it hard to accept.

"But why were you still doing it, knowing we were to be married?"

Max realised he had no choice but to be truthful. "Tahra, you've point blank refused to have sex with me until we're married. I'm a man, do you know how fucking sexually frustrated I've felt ever since you walked into my life? You're the only woman I really want to fuck and yet you've refused it. Being celibate to respect your principles is impossible, sometimes Tahra, you're impossible."

She was taken aback, but still didn't understand.

"Couldn't you just… wait?"

Max sighed. "You need to live in the real world, Tahra. A man needs sex, physical sex, on a regular basis. I need sex. If you would have had sex with me, I wouldn't have been to any of those parties."

"So now it's my fault?"

Max was angry but didn't want to be, still, he couldn't contain his feelings.

"What would you rather had happened; me force myself on you, hurt you to gratify myself or me losing my frustration at a party? It was the only way I could respect your wishes, if that makes any sense."

She found it difficult to stop the flow of tears. "You're about to be married, and you've had sex with other women!"

Max began to look exasperated. "You're thinking like a woman. For a man, sex and… love are separate, men can fuck a woman but not have emotions, whereas women cannot separate the two. You're the woman I chose to marry, doesn't that mean anything to you? I don't want to party anymore, I want a wife. I want you."

She didn't know what to think, turning away and he sensed she wanted to be alone, so left her. As he was about to walk through the door, she said something impulsive that had been on her mind anyway.

"Max, I want to go back, to London, to The Institute."

She realised she was far too angry and upset to be around him. He didn't say anything. But late in February 1964, they arrived back in London.

12
The Egg

The arrival back in England was a blow to Max. In fact, the previous year had been a blur; a confusing, tumultuous blur spurred on by a desire to please a woman half his age. She had walked into his life under a research contract and he had been obliged to educate her and house her. The one thing he hadn't bargained for was an emotional connection with a strong minded female, one who insisted on no sex before marriage when she must understand fully the effect she has upon men. He knew he wasn't the only one who had shown interest, how could he be? She was provocative, but was it intentional? Was she a master manipulator or a hopeless romantic? Max wished he knew the answer, because she was influencing his decisions, taking his feelings on a rollercoaster ride and driving him insane. He wasn't eating well and had lost some weight, plus had acquired a leaning towards whiskey and gin.

He really started to believe that he had opened Pandora's Box by searching out Tahra. Had Grace known this would happen, or did she just see a talented psychic? He had spent about a year of his life away from home because Tahra wanted to see the world and he relented because he feared losing her and felt guilty about putting a stop to her modelling career. There had also been a proposal of marriage, along with a realisation that he wanted her beyond any doubt and a feeling of frustration when it came to gaining control in the relationship. Her ability to directly affect his emotions at will both repelled and fascinated him, for she could take him to the heights of euphoria and the depths of depression when she pleased. She had not intentionally caused him to feel low, but the collapse of his carefully laid plans was a result of her inability to accept what he had done.

Max now found himself back at square one. Here he sat in Miss Tynedale's office, getting a rundown of everything that had happened and where the research was heading at the moment. She had performed well in his absence and was a good manager, albeit not as attractive or liberal minded as Marianne. But where did he want to take it now? A new direction, an innovative impetus was required to take The Institute forward. Tahra may still be the key, but how? And did he still have a future with her? He really needed to know the answers at the moment. Max wished Grace was still here, because she always had the answers.

Then it occurred to him that there was a way to contact Grace. He had a facility full of psychics, two of which were capable of contacting the dead. The risk of airing his private worries with a research subject was the problem, there would have to be some protection of confidentiality through the use of a contract, a bit excessive maybe but, nevertheless, necessary.

It was with a contract and a heavy heart that Max requested a private consultation with Beth. She was surprised and a little offended by the contract but she understood that it was a confidential matter so put her signature on the typed document.

"You know, she may not want to talk to you," Beth warned.

"Well," Max countered, "when she realises it's me, she may make an exception."

Beth closed her eyes and took a deep breath, she was silent for a few minutes and Max began to get a little agitated. Would Grace come forward? She seemed in no hurry. He lightly drummed his fingers on the desk and reached over to flick through some paperwork, not used to waiting for anything. Finally, Beth spoke.

"She's here. She wants to know why you're so insecure."

Max felt uncomfortable at her remark but also felt overwhelmed at the thought of talking to his mother again, even if it was through a medium.

"Life has taken... an unexpected detour."

"Yes, yes it has rather," Beth relayed, "I see you managed to find Tahra."

Max felt a dichotomy; he wanted to talk about Tahra but then again, he didn't.

"Yes, she truly is gifted."

"You love her, don't you?"

The question took him by surprise, for it was abrupt and also very personal. Max was conscious of the fact that his mother was speaking through another, but it still felt like the words of his kin, therefore he found he was able to detach himself from the third party aspect of the situation.

"My... emotional involvement was something I didn't expect."

"Is that the reason you so desperately wanted to speak to me?"

"Yes," Max said, without thinking, then added, "And no. For what reason did you bring Tahra into my life?"

Beth was silent for a moment, as if she was listening to instructions then she summarised the internal conversation.

"To be the shining star of The Institute, there is a clear purpose for her on this Earth, and you and this facility are a large part of that."

"What is her purpose? And what is my role in all of this?"

"Max, you have your destiny to work through and your own karmic lessons to address but you'll find this will overlap with Tahra's purpose."

This didn't really answer anything. He felt exasperated, wanting a direct and simple answer.

"Where do I take The Institute?"

"You drew up a contract and pulled Beth aside to ask me that? You already know what the step is, once you take it, everything will fall into place."

There was something he'd been considering. He had

become aware of how much he'd neglected Paul, another gifted individual that belonged to the Richardson inventory, although he couldn't see how what he had in mind for Paul could possibly direct the future of The Institute. Tahra had to be the key to everything, otherwise he wouldn't have been asked to head hunt her. He did, however have another question, it had been simmering all through this meeting.

"Am I wasting my time with Tahra?" he asked, fearful of the answer.

Beth listened quietly, and relayed a summary.

"You are two highly individualistic people, it's very difficult to tell where two strong minds are concerned. She is the stronger one in many ways and you have to be able to live with that. Nothing is truly predestined, for we all have free will, you will do what you do and so will she. I'm sorry I do not have an answer for you."

Max sighed, he was none the wiser and felt she was being deliberately evasive. He had to draw a conclusion.

"So, you're telling me I have all the answers. Once I carry out the step I had in mind, the way forward will become clear. I'm assuming what I had in mind is going to be fruitful."

"Did you ever put a foot wrong, Max?"

Those final words were more like the voice of a mother, calm and reassuring. He felt a fool for doubting himself and setting up this consultation, he mustn't let anyone affect his confidence again. Max made a resolution to keep Tahra at arms length, something he had to do it for sanity's sake.

Tahra did not want to face Max on return to The Institute. Her anger turned inward and she entered a deep, albeit brief depression. Like Max, she didn't eat well and lost some weight. She listened to music and read books, finding that the Beatles served to remind her of opportunities lost and the whirlwind of an adventure she'd had in the States. 'All My Loving' took on a heartbreaking meaning in these romantically bleak times. She listened to their new release in March, ironically entitled 'Can't Buy Me Love' and reflected upon how much it reminded her of Max, a man who knew how to buy her things and spend money but was incapable of acknowledging the simplest things like trust and boundaries in a relationship.

For the first two weeks she couldn't face the others and they all wanted to hear about her adventure in the States, escorted by Max but didn't realise something had gone seriously awry. She found solace in books and her transistor radio, which was now able to pick up all the latest pop hits from The Beatles and The Rolling Stones via a new pirate station called Radio Caroline, which broadcasted from a ship off the south-east coast of England. Whereas Radio Luxembourg had only transmitted in the evenings, leaving her twiddling the dial in vain during times either side that, Radio Caroline broadcasted during the day. It filled her free time more than adequately.

By the time she emerged, they were quite concerned but found her strangely indifferent to the past year or so of her life. She had completed a mourning period, now she felt numb. Oscar was puzzled and felt that something had happened, for there was a darker edge to her personality that he couldn't put his finger on. Still, she was unwilling to discuss what had happened in the States, she had placed her feelings in a bottle and corked it indefinitely. Fortunately, Max did not schedule any tests for the first month after their return and he wasn't present at any of the ones in the second month. Nobody asked questions.

Much of the time, Max was able to avoid her as he wasn't required to be at The Institute on a regular basis, however, there were times when it was necessary to supervise some of the tests. He ensured he didn't oversee any of hers although he occasionally caught sight of her on the stairs or brushed past her in the hall. It was strange seeing her and he felt a pang of yearning yet also, a need to push her away. Tahra didn't want to face him either, she missed his presence in many ways but she didn't feel particularly forgiving or understanding. They would look at each other with a discordant mixture of apprehension and curiosity but didn't engage in any conversation. It was unclear at this stage who would crack first.

Max spent days contemplating the path The Institute should take and also his own future, as men in their forties often did. He realised he had reached the point where he needed to take a wife, although he was unsure about children, it was the only frontier he hadn't explored. It was also the only opportunity being denied him. However, there was little he could to repair the situation, which was the cause of his recent depression. Therefore, The Institute was the first priority and he deliberated for a while, until the 22nd May 1964 when he simply had to visit Paul. The procrastination was probably due to guilt, guilt because he had neglected Paul in favour of an emotional folly but there came a point when it was necessary to face up to the long period of silence.

Paul was not to be found at The Establishment, which was no surprise so Max drove to the cottage he had given him back in the 1950s, pulling up outside in his bright red E-Type Jaguar, declared to be 'the most beautiful car ever made' with its long sleek bonnet, good looks and high performance. He approached the front door with trepidation, wondering how Paul would greet him after such a long period of absence. After tapping on the door, which was delicately framed with ivy and clematis, the door was opened, surprisingly, by a woman. She had long, wavy chestnut brown hair and wore jodhpurs with a floral shirt, plus riding boots. Max thought she was somewhat pretty, in a mature kind of way but not as beautiful as Tahra. He wasn't sure what to say, but she alleviated the awkward silence by speaking first.

"Can I help you?" she said.

"I'm looking for Paul," Max answered.

She disappeared and a moment later, Paul emerged from

the sitting room, stunned to see Max stood on the doorstep. They were both silent for a moment then Max asked to come in and Paul nodded. He guided him to the cosy sitting room, where two leather armchairs awaited them. The room was well decorated with paintings of great pioneers but there were also loose newspaper clippings concerning key launches by NASA simply pinned to a piece of corkboard. The two men sat facing each other in the sitting room, appraising, wondering what each had been doing. The woman who had answered the door made herself scarce.

"So," Max began, "you found yourself an honest woman."

Paul smiled. "I've known Eleanor for a few years now, she stays over a lot. I met her while horse riding one day." The level of involvement seemed reasonably serious. "And you? Is there a woman in your life?"

Max shifted uncomfortably in his seat. "You know me, I'm a relationship dilettante." His answer was unconvincing and Paul got the feeling he was hiding something.

"Well," Paul needed to get to the inevitable questions, "what have you been up to all this time?"

Max didn't answer with the usual confidence and poise that Paul was accustomed to.

"I've spent most of the time in the States, there's a sister facility over there called The Observatory."

"Oh." Paul was wondering why he wasn't told of this before. "What do they do over there? Same as The Institute?"

Max nodded. "Parallel research, pretty much."

"How's The Institute?"

"Good, good." He didn't mention Tahra.

The conversation was dawdling, so Paul moved it on.

"So, what brings you here?"

Max was relieved, he could steer the conversation away from anything that required him to discuss Tahra.

"Some interesting facts were revealed whilst I was at The

Observatory, worrying facts," he explained. "We're not the only ones investigating the use of psychic individuals for application in the Cold War. In particular, there are remote viewers operating in the Soviet Union, mirroring the activities of George and Oscar." He didn't mention the star viewer, Tahra.

Paul sat back, amused at the irony.

"I presume they know we're doing the same," he commented.

Max didn't find it funny in the slightest.

"Is there some way that remote viewing can be… blocked?" he posited.

Paul considered the question carefully.

"Not that I'm aware of. To place restrictions on the movements of human consciousness is, well, somewhat elusive."

Max wasn't content with the answer. "I'm aware that alcohol, which we know dulls the senses has an inhibitory effect upon remote viewing. However, this is, obviously, impossible to use when you cannot gain physical access to the remote viewer. Have you any idea what form human consciousness takes?"

This was a question Paul could answer.

"I believe its basis lies in the bio-electromagnetic field."

Max used this information to persuade Paul into developing a theory.

"If consciousness is some kind of bio-electromagnetic field, is there some way this field, or energy source could be disrupted?"

Paul pressed his palms together as if in prayer and lightly touched his fingertips to his lips.

"Theoretically… yes, that's an interesting hypothesis."

"So, can I assume that you'll take this on as a new research project?"

Max wasn't going to take no for an answer and Paul remained silent as he considered the proposal.

"I must impress on you the seriousness of Soviet ability to see what we… and what I am doing in terms of the Cold War. Remember, remote viewers know no boundaries. They aren't limited by the restrictions imposed by the human, or physical body. Their consciousness can travel anywhere, unhindered, any distance, instantaneously. They have, in fact, a limitless capacity to explore. Do we want to grant that power to the Soviets?"

Paul was taken aback by what Max had said, but not for the reasons intended. He had just inspired him unintentionally. However, he had to put that moment aside temporarily.

"I understand the importance of this research. I'll see what I can come up with."

Max stood up, satisfied with the response for the time being. He nodded his appreciation and then turned to go. Paul showed him to the door and watched him trudge down the path towards his car, not his usual confident self. What was troubling him? Paul was now curious about what had transpired in his absence.

When Paul returned to his sitting room, his first thought was not the research project he had just been assigned. Something significant had happened within Paul, unbeknownst to Max, inspiration had struck. He reflected upon Max's words; 'remote viewers know no boundaries'; 'they aren't limited by the restrictions imposed by the physical body; 'they have a limitless capacity to explore'. He glanced over at his collection of clippings on the wall and wanted to sing. Paul Eldridge had now found his destiny.

The 1st June 1964 was no ordinary day. It was someone's birthday. In the dining room of The Institute the tables were set out for a meal and everyone was instructed to wear their best clothes. No one knew whose birthday it was, they all accounted for themselves, Beth's birthday was the 25th June but she was the nearest. At 7pm that evening, everyone involved in The Institute entered the drawing room. There was Miss Tynedale and the technical staff as well as the core people like Max, Beth and the other gifted individuals without which the facility would not be a success. Paul had not been invited, but no one thought to ask about him as he hadn't worked at The Institute for a few years now. Tahra arrived five minutes late and strolled into the dining room like a panther, wearing a low cut, black dress. Max faltered in his conversation and they exchanged a cursory glance then he resumed his discussion, wondering how to keep her at a distance.

After the customary conversation and social mingling, everyone was asked to take a seat. Max sat at the largest table along with Miss Tynedale and Oscar, but before Emilie could claim the last chair, Tahra took Max completely aback by striding over and sitting in it herself. They looked at each other; he in disbelief and she in contempt. He realised that it would look odd if he changed table now, so decided to put up with the situation even though he felt uncomfortable. She seemed determined to create a gauche and potentially inflammatory state of affairs. Emilie's reaction of disappointment and aggrieved feelings went unnoticed, she sat with Beth instead.

Max encouraged all to quieten down as he stood up and tapped a wine glass with a spoon.

"You must all be wondering why I've gathered you all together on this fine evening," he began. "I told you it was someone's birthday. Today, I'd like to commemorate the 10th birthday of The Institute and remember the birthday of my late mother, Grace Richardson."

Grace, of course had been there from the beginning and some of the others had been drawn into the cause only a few years later. There was much chatter amongst everyone about the matter. Max presented an open bottle of wine to each table and asked everyone to pour themselves a glass to raise in a toast.

"May we have another successful and fruitful ten years here at The Institute and also, in memory of my mother, who most of you will remember fondly."

Glasses chinked in a toast and the meal was begun. Tahra watched Max over the top of her glass as she drank, and he tried to avoid eye contact as much as possible, which she did not take kindly to. Why did he behave as though she meant nothing? She watched him engage in discussion with Oscar and Miss Tynedale but he did not say a word to Tahra. It didn't go unnoticed, if anything, Max seemed strangely indifferent towards her. Oscar smiled sympathetically and talked to her about the recent trip to Barbados to see his family.

But Tahra couldn't concentrate on what he was saying, all she could think about was Max, who was just across the table. She craved his attention again, his touch and those wonderful meals and trips together, she missed the feel of his arms around her.

Without thinking about the best way to resolve the situation, she decided to play devil's advocate instead. Slipping off her shoe, she moved her foot under the table towards Max, lifted her foot and slid it in between his legs. His reaction gave her a thrill, like a naughty child playing up her parents. He shifted awkwardly in his seat and briefly glanced at her with a big question mark on his face. It didn't thwart her. She proceeded to push her foot further and found what she was looking for, and rubbed it gently with her toes. Max wavered in his speech and tried hard to focus but he repeatedly lost the thread of his conversation. Miss Tynedale and Oscar looked puzzled. Tahra smiled, in a vain sort of triumph. She delighted in the feeling of him stiffen under her touch and she continued to stimulate him further in this manner. In a perverse way, she enjoyed it more than he. To some extent, he didn't want her to stop but it was raising some eyebrows at the table. The more she did it, the more he stumbled through the conversation. Emilie watched Max and Tahra, fully aware of what each other was thinking. Normally she couldn't read Tahra but the animosity was transparent. They both wanted each other but refused to admit it.

Not content with arousing him physically, she decided to raise the temperature somewhat by raising the fire within a little. Meeting his gaze, she pushed a wave of pleasure up his spine. Max dropped his fork and was speechless for a moment. Tahra smiled.

He met her gaze and gave her a warning look with his eyes, but the fear was showing, the fear of being vulnerable and abandoned in front of everyone. She repeated the action, causing Max to gasp slightly. He began to look quite helpless, which only excited her more so she did it again. This time, Max stood up abruptly and walked out of the room without a word. The whole room fell silent. Tahra smiled in a smug manner.

Out in the hallway, Max tried to regain his composure. How could he return to the table now? She wouldn't stop, she didn't care if she humiliated him. He stood with his back against the wall and listened to the conversation re-start. Someone came out into the hallway, Max froze, he really didn't want it to be Tahra but it wasn't, it was Emilie.

"Why do you let her treat you like that?" Emilie said, accusingly in her accented voice.

Max didn't want her interference.

"I don't know what you're talking about," he responded.

"You know exactly what I mean," she said. "That woman is driving you crazy and you let her."

A moment later, Miss Tynedale emerged showing motherly concerned but Max didn't want any sympathy or prep talk from anyone. Caught between a rock and a hard place, Max chose the sanctity of the office, where he regretted walking out but what else could he have done? The meal finished without him and Tahra hung around in the hope of seeing him, however there would be no opportunity, she would have to remain satisfied with a hollow victory. Meanwhile, Max realised one day, very soon, they would have to confront one another again.

The Institute was calling once more. Even though Max had not specifically requested his presence there, Paul needed to see George and Oscar and his secondary objective was to ascertain what had happened in Max's life recently, the suspense was killing him. It had been a few years since he had stood outside its door and he found himself in a position again where he was required to knock. As he stood there, he surveyed the street and surrounding area, noting what had changed. The people expressed themselves more through their less conservative dress sense; shorter skirts, Levi jeans and no more flat caps and mop tops for the men, page boy cuts for the women. Hem lines were becoming exceedingly short compared to what he had become accustomed to. Plus, there were certainly more cars on the road and of different types other than the Morris Minor. However, women stilled strolled with perambulators, people were still polite and the red Route Master buses still stopped at the end of the road.

Miss Tynedale didn't look too surprised to see him and he noticed she looked as stern as ever, time had given her no cause to mellow. Once again he sat at a table in the dining area, right beside the window overlooking the street. There was no evidence of the birthday meal two nights before. He was provided with a cup of Earl Grey tea and a scone, complete with butter and strawberry jam. George and Oscar appeared soon after and sat at the table with him. They were pleased to see him.

"We were beginning to think we'd never see you again," Oscar said, with a beaming smile of relief on his face.

Paul shrugged. "Me too," was all he said.

George decided to partake of the Earl Grey but Oscar chose a coffee instead.

"So," Oscar began, "what have you been up to recently?"

Paul was dismayed that he had little to excite them. "Well, I've been writing up some research mainly." Really he knew he had been filling time. "So, what's been happening here?"

Oscar sighed. "It's been all go here recently. I'm surprised you weren't at The Institute's tenth birthday party the other night."

Paul's face visibly dropped. Since when had he become an outsider, and why?

"Wow," he said, trying to be enthusiastic.

The situation began to feel somewhat uneasy and Paul had an agenda to follow so pushed the meeting onwards, quickly.

"I haven't seen a lot of Max just lately," Paul tried broaching the subject, "how is he?"

Oscar reacted as though he'd just asked the million dollar question.

"Woman trouble," was the reply.

"Woman trouble?" Paul was aghast then he laughed at the irony. "Max? Who's the lucky, or could I say unlucky lady?"

Oscar looked amused. "I stay out of it, they'll have to work it out on their own." He shrugged.

Paul found it hard to believe. Max, womaniser extraordinaire, having trouble with the female species? He became curious. Who was she? She had enough about her to cause Max to become so preoccupied, yet he never discussed her, at all. Maybe one day he'd meet her and discover what all the fuss was about.

Nobody really wanted to examine Max's relationship issues so Paul decided to achieve his primary objective. He was a man with a vision and hopefully the discussion today wouldn't shatter it. Paul tried to remain open minded.

"There was something I wanted to lay on the table," Paul revealed.

Both Oscar and George sat up in their chairs and were all ears.

"I have a potential project I was going to put to Max, but I needed to run it by you two first, as it would involve you."

They were eager to hear it so Paul continued.

"You may be aware of the fast developing space race between the US and Soviet Union." They both nodded. "Well, part of the problem is the human organism, our physical body and escaping the gravitational pull of the Earth, not to mention surviving in the harsh environment of space." He paused for effect. "My question is, why do we need our bodies to explore the cosmos? You have demonstrated that consciousness can separate from the body and observe remote locations. Well… why can't that be applied to space travel?"

Both Oscar and George were stunned. George spoke first this time.

"You know, I never thought of it. But, now you mention it, it could open up endless possibilities."

"I'm wondering though, how feasible is it? I mean, do you think you could project your consciousness into space? And report back the findings?" Paul really needed to know.

They were both thoughtful. "Well, I've never tried," they both said, simultaneously yet independently.

Oscar added, "I must admit though, I don't think I could muster enough psychic clout to get that far."

Paul felt his enthusiasm sink. "Why's that?" he enquired.

"Well," he tried to explain, "there's like a magnetic pull between the mind and body, I guess that's what binds it together or our minds would be floating all over the place. You need a lot of psychic strength to push against it, if you know what I mean. There often seems to be a limit, often I can feel the magnetism trying to pull me back."

George agreed. "You'd need a really powerful remote viewer to pull it off."

Paul's fervour sunk further like a lead balloon.

"And I bet they come along once in a blue moon, if you're lucky," he said in resignation.

He sat back in his chair, while Oscar and George exchanged knowing glances. Should they put him out of his misery?

"Let me put it this way," Oscar said, "you need to present this to Max as you may find he has someone to become this project."

Paul left The Institute feeling hopeful again. As he walked through the hallway, Tahra was standing at the top of the stairs watching as Paul opened the door and said goodbye to Oscar and George. Once the door closed, she instantly ran down the stairs, curiosity getting the better of her.

"Who was that?" she asked.

Oscar and George were certainly on familiar terms with him but she'd never seen him before.

Oscar looked at her, a knowing smile flickering across his face. "I think you're gonna find that out real soon."

13

To See the Truth

Sunday 31st October 1993

The call that he had been expecting still hadn't materialised. She was cutting it fine, a promise was a promise even though it was made three months ago. It had been so long since there had been any contact and Sam despaired, if there was anybody he wanted to see, it was her.

He was in his last year at university, studying a joint honours degree, spread between music and art as he couldn't decide which the primary love was. There was no other focus in life for Sam apart from music and art, he had already composed several pieces in classical style and specialised in piano and guitar. In his free time he painted and indulged in skateboarding, a little break-dance and going to the pub, all of which were typical hobbies for someone his age. His father still didn't approve of his career choice and had refused to provide him with a flat when he desperately wanted to leave home at sixteen. But once he had turned eighteen, he could access the account in which his father had built up a useful sum of money to assist with the initial hardship of independent living. He had found himself a reasonable, clean yet quirky one bedroom flat in Finsbury Park, just off Seven Sisters Road. Sam had taken to dealing cannabis to cover his additional living costs as London wasn't the cheapest place to live. He had grown up surrounded by financial security, it meant little to him and as long as he could be relatively comfortable, he was happy. He didn't care as long as he had music.

Sam walked along the road on his way home at dusk, having

visited a friend. On reaching his door, he took out his key and opened the door. His flat was on the ground floor, his own request as it made it easier to accommodate a piano. On entering, he placed his bag and portfolio by the door, put on the radio, searching for a classical station and jumped onto the sofa. He checked his answer phone to see if there were any messages and he was disappointed as there weren't. Maybe she'd call later. By force of habit, he pulled out some rizlas, a pouch of tobacco and a small lump of hash encased in cling film and proceeded to roll a joint. He lit it and lay back on the sofa, smoking thoughtfully and listening to the radio.

Smoking was effective at keeping the visitors away. Initially, he'd started drinking to keep them quiet and it did work but alcohol stunted his mental faculties, his ability to be creative and inspirational so he tried smoking a joint instead. Cannabis kept the visitors at bay but preserved his creativity. It had been a few years since he'd seen any of them. He was relieved, they were too intrusive and he didn't want their advice anyway.

After the joint, he sat at the piano and played a couple of his own compositions then the phone rang. He stopped, paused then answered it.

"Oh Sam, I'm glad you're in," the voice at the other end said, "I'm so sorry I didn't call earlier, I've been doing over time. I hardly get time to breathe."

"Don't worry," Sam replied, "I knew you wouldn't let me down."

"Well, happy birthday first of all. How's your day been?"

Sam shrugged. "Okay I guess, it's just another birthday."

"Just another birthday?" she queried, "It's your twenty first!"

"So it is," he laughed, softly.

"Have you planned a big night out, like the drinking extravaganza that was your eighteenth?"

She was surprised by the answer. "No, I'd rather do something quiet, I don't feel like partying."

"Well, as long as you're happy about it. I bet you'll spend it with your girlfriend."

"She's not my girlfriend," Sam said, quickly.

There was an awkward silence.

"So, are you going to sit in your flat alone or shall I come over, to force you to go out?" she asked him.

Sam laughed. "I think you're going to have to drag me out."

"Well, I did promise to visit. I'll see you in an hour."

"Looking forward to it," Sam said.

Everything was going to plan.

An hour later, he heard the door bell and he rushed out of the bedroom to answer it. He had just changed his clothes but fortunately was decent. Checking his reflection in the mirror first, he opened the door and flashed a welcoming smile.

"Happy birthday!" Ava said.

She looked different, more mature, more elegant but just as beautiful though. Her hair was straight now and layered, framing her face quite delicately. She wore a long coat over a pair of tight jeans and a lace bodice, plus her favourite red silk scarf was tied loosely around her neck.

Sam had changed substantially since the last time she'd spent any significant time with him, which was his last milestone birthday. They had spoken since, during the viral attack that she had miraculously survived although it had been a brief visit and she had seen him occasionally since then. He was tall, standing around six feet two inches and his glossy dark hair was longer, reaching his shoulders. His style hadn't changed; ripped jeans, loose black skirt, sweatbands and a few lethal looking rings but his physique differed greatly, he was a young man now. She wasn't used to seeing him look more adult and he noticed her looking him over.

She was so glad to see him and gave him a hug, he noticed how good she smelt.

"I'm ready," he said, rushing back to grab his money and keys.

They walked down the main road, chatting about his life at university, his music and his art. She was sincerely interested and told him he had to perform for her and show her his paintings, to which he agreed. Then he asked about what she was doing.

"Medicinal genetics, viruses, diseases... research into the genetic structure of them and developing ways to combat them. But I'm thinking of taking on a new contract in the near future, researching human DNA."

"It sounds very important," Sam said.

"Yeah, I guess it is. I didn't want to take the job at first, I never expected your father to feel responsible for my career but it's turned out to be a real turning point in my life. I'm seriously considering it. I wouldn't have gotten the opportunity to join the Human Genome Project if it wasn't for him."

That was an under-statement. Ava wanted to discuss the sideline research she and Tom were conducting but she had sworn him to non-disclosure. In many ways, the research was exciting and ground-breaking, the capacity to make a difference was enormous yet it also terrified her. She could never tell anyone, for she was genuinely unique and that was truly frightening. She had learned in the past year that there was clearly something unusual going on and she didn't want to believe that she was a freak of nature. More than ever she needed to know who she was and the reasons for someone observing or spying on her became more apparent and much more sinister. What would happen if the medical establishment knew about this? What would Sam's father do about it?

"I'm glad he's done something positive for somebody," he said, trying to hide his bitterness.

They found a nice local pub, quite traditional and it had a pool table so they placed a couple of coins on the table and it wasn't long before the table was free. Sam set up and took the break, sinking a red in the process. He strode around the table with confidence but refrained from showing off too much as he wanted Ava to enjoy the game as much as he.

A small group of young women watched Sam with appreciation and Ava smiled to herself but surprisingly, Sam did not pay them any attention. After the pub, they found a Chinese restaurant fairly close by and ate a meal, remaining seated to chat about the family and various things that had been happening. It finally got to the point where it was rather late. Ava realised she'd had a few glasses of wine too many and was concerned about driving home, Cambridge was quite a distance.

"You can stay at mine," Sam offered, "I don't have uni in the morning."

Ava shook her head. "I've got work in the morning…"

"Don't be silly, you're more than welcome. There's no way you can drive home tonight."

She relented in the knowledge that she was unfit to drive.

"There's nothing wrong with pulling the odd sicky," Sam laughed, softly.

The walk seemed quite long but there was no hurry. In fact, it was pleasant and humorous as it was Halloween and people were walking the streets, frequenting pubs and bars dressed up as witches, Frankenstein, Dracula or ghosts. The atmosphere was accentuated by the fact that it was dark and edging closer to midnight. It wasn't long before they discovered a young couple standing in the middle of the pavement, looking up at a second floor bay window which was slightly open. Rather than walk past, Sam and Ava stopped to ask if there was a problem.

"We've lost the keys to our flat," the man said, remorsefully.

"Don't tell me," Sam said, "you live on the top floor."

"Yeah," the man replied, sheepishly.

"No prob," Sam said.

Before anyone could say anything, Sam leapt over the wall, grabbed hold of the drain pipe and proceeded to climb up it with incredible agility. Ava was aplomb and the woman in the couple was concerned he'd fall while the man looked on, impressed. Sam reached the second floor window in no time, shimmying along the windowsill from the drain pipe without difficulty. Then he climbed through the open window, disappeared into the flat and reappeared a few moments later at the main door on the ground floor. The couple were extremely grateful.

"Most people don't give a shit," he said, "but thanks a million mate."

Sam shrugged.

"Don't mention it."

"You wanna pop in for a beer?" the man offered.

Sam looked at Ava, she seemed easy either way so he made the decision and declined the offer respectfully. They continued on their way, getting closer to Sam's flat which was just off the main street. There was an alleyway that cut through the buildings to the row where Sam's flat was, he used it a lot so they took this shortcut. Without warning, a man stepped out from the shadows. Sam and Ava stopped dead in their tracks as he brandished a knife.

"I'm not carrying any money," Sam said, firmly and simply, staring at the man hard.

Ava was surprised to find that it was the man who seemed intimidated instead of Sam.

"I will use this knife," he remonstrated.

Sam didn't flinch, not breaking eye contact with the would-be assailant.

"Like your mother did when she sliced her own wrists?" Sam said, without venom but with disdain. "She left you alone, with a younger brother to care for and a step-father who beat you both without mercy. Now your brother is a junkie and you're a drug dealer. You live in squalor, not caring for the future or whether the next day will be different. It's only a matter of months before you find your brother dead and you'll only outlast him by a year. I can hear the clock ticking for you already, the countdown has already begun, I think you should be careful who you buy from."

The man dropped his knife, looking terrified and ran off. Ava didn't know what to say, she looked at Sam with incredulity and some suspicion.

"Did you know that guy?" she asked him.

Sam shook his head.

"Well, you seemed to know so much about him," she added.

Sam shrugged. "I just see the truth, that's all."

She was still looking at him with a question mark on her face. The whole thing was just so peculiar; he had shown absolutely no fear even when confronted by a knife wielding junkie. If anything, Sam was almost nonchalant about the incident. He opened the door and stepped aside to allow Ava to enter first. After closing the main entry, he opened the door to his own flat and hung up their coats. He crashed on the sofa and gestured for her to sit beside him.

"This is all so weird," Ava said, a little reluctant.

Sam put his feet up and patted the empty space next to him. She kicked off her shoes and wandered over, then sat next to him, a little stiff.

"Just relax," Sam said, softly.

"Sorry," Ava said, "I just... never expected to be here."

He understood the awkwardness she felt, they had, after all, mainly known each other as children and now had to adapt to seeing each other as adults. There was a way to break the odd tension she felt, he jumped up and sat down at the piano, playing a composition of his own. Ava was able to lie back now and listen to the music. She hadn't heard him play for a long time. It was a slightly melancholic albeit meaningful melody that reminded one of lost opportunities, yet hope for the future. Sam had always been talented and she felt a sense of exasperation sometimes at the attitude of his father, who couldn't seem to recognise that fact. Thankfully, her mother and her family had given Sam a lot of support and had kept a piano at their house so that he could learn, away from the critical disdain of his father.

She wandered over and sat next to him on the piano bench, there was just enough room for two. He smiled and selected another tune, something familiar. The first few bars of John Lennon's 'Imagine' rang out and without prompting, Ava added the lyrics. She had a smooth yet smoky voice that was adequately in tune, an ideal accompaniment to Sam's beautiful and flawless piano style. She felt like Yoko Ono to his John Lennon, and gave a little sigh when he had finished.

"Better than 'Chopsticks', eh?" he queried with a laugh.

She smiled in return.

"Well, I certainly feel more relaxed now."

He continued to play further songs, some of them did not require lyrics such as Dvorak's New World Symphony and some did; he performed a surprisingly tender rendition of 'Nothing Compares To You' by Sinead O' Connor. It made the night very memorable. As Ava responded favourably to his voice and music, he continued to play well into the early hours of the morning. When it reached 2am, Sam sat back, feeling pretty exhausted. He pondered the piano playing marathon that had just reached its conclusion.

"I've got blisters on my fingers!" he joked.

Ava laughed and laid her head on his shoulder, she was tired too. Sam made a suggestion.

"There's a sofa over there that's reasonably comfortable, or there's a king size bed that's extremely comfortable."

She sat up, realising it was necessary to choose somewhere to sleep. Sam was looking at her expectantly and she lowered her eyes.

"It's not right," she replied.

"What's not right?" he asked her, softly.

"You're family, I can't share a bed..."

"We used to all the time, remember?" he countered.

Yes, she did. He was always afraid of sleeping alone so would snuggle next to Ava, where he would sleep soundly all night.

Many a night he had knocked on the door of her bedroom and had asked if he could lie next to her because of the monsters in his room. The visitors had started making an appearance at an early age, a disturbing experience for such a young child. She had never refused him, maybe she had felt scared or lonely herself too.

"But, that was different," she argued gently, "we were kids…."

"Ava, you're adopted first of all. We were childhood sweethearts weren't we? Besides, I'm just thinking of your comfort."

He stood up and walked to the bedroom, unbuttoning his shirt as he did so. Ava was rooted to the piano bench, no, she couldn't… Sam took off his shirt, threw it on the bed and walked back towards Ava. He stood in the doorway, hands lightly gripping the frame overhead.

"Which is it going to be?" he asked her.

She stood up and wandered over, standing before him. Ava felt disturbed by the fact that she found his body erotic; he was lean and muscular although it looked natural and not forced. Embarrassingly, she couldn't help but stare. Sam knew what she was thinking.

"Is there anything I could wear to sleep in?" she asked.

Sam paused, enjoying the effect he had upon her then searched his wardrobe for an old t shirt. He resisted the temptation to watch her change and slipped into a pair of jogging bottoms while she did so. Normally he would sleep naked but that wasn't appropriate tonight.

They lay on top of the covers, chatting and laughing. She was glad she had made the effort to see him. They remembered the times they would snuggle in the same bed as children, a comfort to each other in lonely or fearful times. He made her feel at ease as they lay there together but in the back of her mind, she was afraid of the truth. The truth was she was attracted to Sam and he was attracted to her. Was that so wrong?

14
OOBE's Birth

Since Paul made a passionate presentation to Max at the end of July 1964, he had been on tenterhooks. August, the height of summer, when he should have been holidaying with Eleanor was filled with stress and tension. The possibilities of space exploration via remote viewing overflowed his everyday thoughts so much so that he couldn't concentrate on the thesis he had spent the past few years writing up concerning his hypothesis for the origin of the bio-electromagnetic field and its possible connection to the concept of the soul.

Could he have envisioned something that would revolutionise space travel, even though it was just in its infancy? The current impetus was such an enormous undertaking, to expend so much fuel and dollars and subject the human body to such an extreme environment, that to only take the vital part of a person, their consciousness, the entire core of their sentiency was seemingly an obvious solution. In the future, possible worlds for exploration could be scouted first, before exploring physically. The scope of it was exciting, for maybe human consciousness could, indeed, know no boundaries.

The month of September was the turning point. On the evening of the 10th Paul was listening to the radio while attempting to type out his most recent thoughts and conjectures. Bob Dylan's 'The Times They Are a-Changin'' was playing in the background and he barely heeded the message of the song, so intent was he on voicing his hypothesis. A copy of a very recent physics paper was folded up beside him on the table in which he'd read an interesting article by a man named Peter Higgs, proposing a massive quantum particle called a boson which potentially gave atoms the invisible mass that equated with all that empty space, a topic discussed in one of his early lectures in which Max had first appeared in his life. He wasn't sure how this sat with his own work on the bio-electromagnetic field but it was certainly something he should ponder in the future, although his new project was taking up much of his thought processes at that moment.

The phone rang and Paul stopped typing. For some reason, he felt this was the call he'd been waiting for. Taking a deep breath, he picked up the phone and heard Max's voice on the other end of the line. Greetings were brief, Max wanted to get to the point.

"I've been giving your proposal a lot of thought," Max began, "and have come to a decision."

This was the crux, the moment of truth. If Max refused to pursue this, there was no place to turn to for he needed Max to gain access to remote viewers of high calibre and provide the funding.

"What you propose is radical, challenging yet progressive. It has the capacity to stretch frontiers and expand our knowledge of the cosmos, yet, the results will be difficult to prove and substantiate."

Paul didn't know whether to interpret this as positive or negative feedback.

"It is unlikely conventional science will ever touch this, however, as we both know, the government uses reports by remote viewers for a variety of different purposes, many of which are of interest to national security."

Okay, it was looking 50/50 now.

"I have decided to proceed with this project on a trial basis, lasting a year initially."

Paul wanted to punch the air. Although it was only a twelve month trial, that was all he needed and it would prove whether the project had a long life or not.

"How does that appeal?" Max asked, on not receiving a verbal response.

"It sounds fantastic." That was an understatement.

"Of course you'll need a remote viewer who is capable of this kind of advanced work."

That had been the only barrier, aside from persuading Max.

"I have someone, here at The Institute who'll be perfect for this project. She's shown astounding potential so far and I believe if anyone can pull this off, she can. However, she does have study commitments and duties here at The Institute so I can only lease her to you once a week at the most, hence, the twelve month long trial. Is that a reasonable acceptance of your proposal?"

It was all falling into place quite nicely.

"I'm happy with that," Paul replied.

"But don't forget you have my project to work on too, we need a method of protection against other remote viewers. I'm depending on you for this."

"Don't worry," Paul reassured him. "When can I meet this new remote viewer?"

"I'll send her over in a few weeks time. Her name is Tahra."

Max hung up and Paul breathed a sigh of relief. Everything was finally going to plan, all he had to do was meet this remote viewer and see what she could do. He wondered what she was like and why nobody had mentioned her before.

The inevitable had to happen. A message was relayed to Tahra via Miss Tynedale regarding a new project, so she had to see Max. On hearing this, she nodded quietly but did not convey the tumultuous feelings churning around inside of her. They had barely said a word to each other since returning to England and Tahra wondered if he actually cared at all. At the birthday meal for The Institute, she had sat opposite him at the table and he had behaved indifferently. Her behaviour that day had been unusual, and now she couldn't figure out why she'd done what she did.

She had got a reaction but had not got what she wanted. Max had seemed more determined to alienate himself from her. Now they had to face each other.

She knocked, heard Max say 'come in' then opened the door to the office. Feeling awkward and slightly humble for a change, she entered the office and found Max sat at the desk with a pen in his hand. For a brief moment, she thought she saw something other than indifference on his face but his cool demeanour soon returned. She took a deep breath and decided to hold her head high.

"You can sit down," he said. There was a vague hint of weariness in his voice.

There was silence for a few minutes, both people in the room trying to push aside everything that had happened in the States earlier that year. Regrets were felt but not expressed, remorse was gestating but any kind of reconciliation was certainly not on the cards. Neither of them conceded it was the end of the road but for now, the journey was aborted.

"There's been an unexpected addition to the programme," Max began, "I know you're very busy at the moment with your study and the projects at The Institute, but there's something I can offer you that will be an amazing opportunity, a challenge. I believe, in fact, that you're the only one who can do it."

Tahra felt bolstered by his show of faith, if anything, he had always been confident in respect of her talents.

"In a few days, you'll be dropped off at the sister facility, The Establishment where you'll meet a long time colleague of mine whose name is Dr Paul Eldridge. You'll work with him, when you meet, he'll explain the project and what he wants from you."

She wondered if Dr Eldridge was the person she saw leaving with Oscar and George a few months ago, the man with shoulder length, fair hair. At the time, instincts had alerted her to the possibility that this man was significant in her future. Now she knew this was true. What was the project? And why could only she pull it off?

Max tapped his pen on the table and looked as if he wanted to say something. Tahra opened her mouth, as if something were about to escape her lips but neither of them said a word. Max resumed scribbling and Tahra sighed inwardly, the stalemate would resume. She returned to her room, realising that she was expectant of a relationship that deep down, she knew was bad for her. Max was not the complete push over that she thought either. In the office, Max scribbled without focus, he still couldn't help but think about her and whether he could turn the situation around. But inwardly, he knew they were both poison for each other too.

Life is certainly on the move. I finally started my course of study at university in the latter part of September 1964, this would be completed by the summer of 1967(and not the summer of 1966) which seemed a long way off. It was part of the agreement between Max and my father, what would happen after that, I don't know but I suspect my father would be setting up a marriage to be finalised on my return. I didn't want to return to Tehran, I didn't want to marry some wealthy Iranian I didn't love. Recently I had come so close to marriage and that would have secured my stay in England, but that was now unlikely.

For a while after returning to England I felt hurt and I wanted to wound Max in retribution. It brought back feelings of my childhood, of feeling degraded and betrayed and ignored. I must admit, I felt the darker side of my spirit dominate, so much so that on a few occasions, I did send Max some negative feelings. I wanted him to feel as despondent as I did, to feel the suffering and pain that I felt. My actions only served to drive him further away as I sensed he was trying his best to avoid me. It only saddened me more.

As spring progressed, my anger and disgust gave way to a more sentimental feeling, one of regret and of yearning. Now I was alone, with no one to put their arms around me or kiss me, no Max. Although I hardly saw him in the flesh, I knew I had my talent to fall back on. I could have gone anywhere in the world but I chose to go to his house. I would focus on the image of his face and my consciousness would be drawn to his house. Unseen, a few times I watched him sleep, sometimes in an armchair after wine and a cigar but mostly in his large, empty bed. I wished I could have the pleasure of resting my head on his chest again.

There was a celebratory meal for The Institute in the summer and I behaved completely out of character. Was I so desperate for his attention to play with him like some toy? I realised afterward that it would only prolong the agony of the situation. I felt such a fool; I really must get a grip.

Finally, a meeting with Max was called. Deep down, I hoped it would be possible to resolve the issues that had hung around in the background like a stale stench but it wasn't to be. The discussion did not touch upon the events in the States, but we were both aware of them. By now, much of the hurt had dissipated, although perhaps the matter had gone off the boil and bygones were bygones. It turned out I was going to be working with someone new on a project that seemed tailor made for me. My new colleague, I think, was the man I caught sight of recently at The Institute. I believe this new project is highly significant in my life's purpose.

So it was that at the end of September 1964, I was driven to the sister facility of The Institute by John Eames, a man who had served Max for many years now. The sister facility was called The Establishment and this was where Dr Paul Eldridge was based. What is he like? I thought as we drove through Surrey countryside, in fact, I was more interested in my internal conversation than the scenery outside the car. A tingle of excitement pulsed through my nervous system as I really wanted to meet him. He was a useful distraction from Max.

John showed me to Dr Eldridge's office, which was empty, he hadn't arrived so I was asked to wait there. That was no problem. John disappeared to carry out some errands and would return in an hour. I sat in the guest chair, a very comfortable armchair and twiddled my thumbs. Why was I so nervous? I paced the room, flicked through some of his books although they were about quantum physics and religion so may as well have been written in Chinese. Why was he taking so long?

But then I figured, well, I really should make a lasting impression. Throwing caution to the wind, I sat in Dr Eldridge's seat, his swivel chair and tried to arrange myself in a manner that would stop him dead in his tracks. Should I look elegant and cross my legs? Should I be leaning forward on his desk, ready for action? I decided that was all too tame and put my feet up on his desk, with a book in my hand. Was this going to be too outrageous? Well, I was going to find out.

The door opened and he walked in. He looked nervous too and slightly befuddled as he was running late. His fair hair was a little anarchistic and was curling down towards the top of his collar. His clothing was casual but not too fashionable. What I noticed were his eyes. They conveyed a mixture of wisdom and insatiable curiosity, with a mystical quality. He was different to Max, not as handsome but intriguing with a commanding presence. I decided I could work with this man.

On entering the room, he stood still, dead in his tracks and almost jumped when he saw me sitting in his chair. He didn't say anything and I was worried for a split second that he was going to be angry because I was sitting in his chair. I looked at him inquisitively and he did the same, surveying my legs, body and face. I wasn't what he expected, I could tell.

Finally, he spoke.

"You must be Tahra," he said, a little unsettled.

"Yes, my name is Tahra Mamoun. I'm a remote viewer and a very good one at that."

He stood before me, realising it was a historic meeting.

"I've never seen you at The Institute before."

"I came to England in September 1962, to study and work at The Institute," I replied, putting down the book I was pretending to read. I felt embarrassed when I realised I'd picked up a book on Quantum Electro-Dynamics.

"Oh," he said, "I completed some research there not long before you arrived."

He sat down in the guest chair, not asking me to move.

"Well," he began, "tell me about yourself."

I told him about England, Iran, returning to England and about some of the projects I'd been involved in, but I omitted the part where I had been to the States with Max. He nodded appreciatively and listened while I gave a synopsis of my life story. I asked him the same question about himself.

"Well," he began again, "I studied physics, I've always been passionate about science and then I completed my PhD in quantum physics. I was picked up by Max when he came to one of my lectures and since then, I've been a primary researcher for him. He wanted to find the human soul and I think I've made a major discovery of what I call the Bio-Electromagnetic Field. Psychic people have a much stronger field. I've also investigated psychic phenomena and the effects of electromagnetic fields on humans, nothing conventional."

I was impressed. He was intelligent, highly philosophical and very passionate about his subject. He was also willing to share that, which was something Max never did. I couldn't help but compare the two of them.

"So," I continued, "what is this project you wish me to participate in?"

Tahra was not at all what I expected. What did I expect? I don't know, I didn't have anything in mind but I didn't anticipate such a young girl. I entered my office to find her sat in my chair, my chair of all places, provocatively placed with her legs outstretched. She was certainly an exotic looking and very stunning girl, although not my type. A good comparison would be a panther with her lithe body, almost black hair and sensuous, passionate eyes. She seemed to warm to me, which was promising as we would be working together.

I sat in the guest chair, feeling a little uneasy as she did possess a strong aura about her, I really must measure her bio-electromagnetic field, it must be off the scale. We talked a bit about our backgrounds and she appeared to be genuinely interested in my research, which was a positive thing. Then she asked me about the project.

"I've been told you're a particularly excellent remote viewer," I began, "can I ask you, what's the furthest you've projected your consciousness?"

She pondered the question and replied, "I've travelled all around the world with my consciousness."

I nodded then continued. "Have you ever left Earth?"

She was surprised at the question.

"Well," she realised what was about to follow, "I've never tried. I mean, it's not that I'm not interested in what's out there, I just... never thought of projecting my consciousness that far."

"Out there," I said, "I believe there are many worlds waiting for us to explore, when we can escape the confines of the Earth's gravity."

She had a good inkling of what the project entailed but allowed me to continue nevertheless.

"Instead of spending millions of dollars on powerful rockets and to avoid the necessity of spacesuits, does it not seem reasonable to use remote viewing as a method of space exploration?"

"Now that you ask that question, I think that it would be very worthwhile."

"Can you project your consciousness that far?"

She was thoughtful. "Maybe, I don't know until I try." *It didn't sound too enthusiastic. "But I'm not afraid to try," she added, "I'll stop at nothing to achieve this goal. I think I've found my purpose in life."*

She seemed so sure, so committed, so passionate.

"Would you like me to give you a little taster of my ability?" she asked.

I nodded.

Tahra stood up, moved closer to me and sat on the edge of the desk. She closed her eyes and her breathing became slightly heavier, I watched her intently.

"Where do you live?" she asked me.

I gave her the address and she was silent for a moment. As she concentrated, I waited with baited breath. There was silence for a few minutes and then she opened her eyes.

"It's a cottage," she described, "with ivy around the front door. There are boots in the hallway, and riding crops, pictures of horses... In the sitting room I saw books placed by your favourite armchair, the one

on the top is by Ian Fleming. There is a writers' desk in the corner... and newspaper clippings. There is a small dining room off the lounge... with rows and rows of books. The walls are red and there is a large open fire."

"Anything else?" I enquired.

She closed her eyes again, letting her consciousness return to my dwelling and she was silent for a few minutes, then she opened her eyes with a look of embarrassment, or was it disappointment?

"Sorry," she said, "I... didn't realise you had a lady friend there."

I looked at her expression, it wasn't just mere embarrassment. Surely she wasn't interested in me?

"What does she look like?" I questioned, testing her out.

"Long hair, chestnut coloured, a few freckles... she's wearing jeans, a yellow and brown jumper and slippers on her feet."

She remained factual despite being somewhat disappointed. Tahra was also correct, down to the clothes I had seen Eleanor wearing about an hour ago when I left home.

"What do you think of my talent?" she asked.

"I'm impressed," I replied honestly, feeling a surprising wave of positivity towards her. "In fact, I'd like to get started as soon as possible, say, in a few weeks?"

"I'll have to clear it with Max, but I would like that," she confirmed.

All that needed to happen now was Tahra's magic.

I left with a feeling of renewed purpose. Paul was an easy going person who I knew I would enjoy working with. I admired his passion, his courage and the mystical persona he carried about him. Where Max was materialistic, Paul was idealistic, where Max was cool and thoughtful, Paul was courageous and passionate, and where Max was calculating and shrewd, Paul was still spontaneous, or so I believed. I think he liked me but I don't think he was attracted to me. Did this faze me? No, it excited me. He was down to earth enough to have sustained a stable relationship, where, for some odd and undefined reason, Max hadn't. Paul was a safe bet, while still being warm and interesting. Max possessed power and oozed charm and sex appeal, but deep down I thought he had problems *relating to women. Would I end up making a choice between two very different men? That would all depend on being able to win Paul's heart.*

Paul gave the project a code name 'OOBE', which stood for Out of Body Experiment and it was officially born on the 7th October 1964 when he typed up the first document belonging to it. He set out the aims and objectives of the project and outlined his findings so far on the phenomenon of remote viewing and the benefits.

Experiment 1 was scheduled for the 19th October and Paul had prepared in advance. He wanted to test Tahra's aerial capabilities and had arranged some stones on a hillside into a word. She arrived at 11am and he ushered her into the lab, for first he wished to take a measurement of her bio-electromagnetic field so he set up the equipment and urged her to relax. The result was no surprise, her field seemed to extend about seven feet from her body and was particularly vibrant, in that the magnetic reading was well above average, in fact, it was the highest he'd ever seen. Only Sakie's came close. Paul showed her the readings and Tahra was genuinely curious for she asked a lot of questions and Paul had to explain what he knew about bio-electromagnetic fields in straightforward terms. He showed her the imaging taken using Kirlian-inspired photography, as he had developed a fairly rudimentary camera. She saw her bio-EM field in hues of blue, purple, indigo and violet. It was huge and egg shaped, with the bulge of the egg around her head.

"It's beautiful," she said, "I wonder if it changes when I alter my emotions or move my consciousness."

With no prompt from Paul, she began to conduct her own experiment. She thought about something that made her angry or sad, Max namely and focused on making her field darker and redder. Nothing was said to Paul to indicate the mood she was attempting to muster or the colour she was aiming to produce.

"Is anything happening?" she asked him.

Paul was surprised.

"Why, yes... your field is pulsing, cycling through a small range of colours... crimson, with flashes of scarlet and blue. How are you doing that?"

He'd never seen this happen before. He'd also never asked anyone to change their emotional state whilst being measured.

"I'm concentrating my feelings into short bursts," she answered.

Paul watched the pulsing colours; it was almost like a kaleidoscopic display, rather psychedelic yet infinitely beautiful. Then something truly amazing happened. Without warning, a brilliant flash of white light appeared in front of her forehead and disappeared, causing Tahra's field to expand somewhat.

"What did you just do?" he asked her.

She didn't answer for a while and had her eyes closed, then after a few minutes she opened them.

"Why? What did you see? I projected my consciousness," she replied.

Paul wondered if he had just witnessed something quite spectacular.

"I think I just saw... your consciousness."

Tahra felt a surge of excitement course through her veins. It was happening, the first of their discoveries.

"And this is our first experiment," she stated with conviction, "just think what we can achieve together."

Paul realised he'd found the perfect partner. She was as curious and passionate as he and she was prepared to push the boundaries. Where had she been all this time?

"No wonder you came so highly recommended," he said.

Tahra felt alive, awakened from a stupor of repetitive and inane experiments. There was light at the end of the tunnel, spiritual light and she couldn't wait to stretch herself beyond the limits.

"What's next?" she asked, hungry for success.

Paul smiled. She was indeed the perfect research subject.

"I have a little aerial test, got to get you flying and reporting back accurately," he said. "You feel up to it?"

"I certainly do," she affirmed.

"I'm going to give you a map with a marked location," he began, "there's something in a field that I created with stones. I want you to tell me what it is." It sounded like the experiments she was used to. "But," he added, "I want you to focus on the journey as much as the outcome, concentrate on the experience of travelling out of body, survey the landscape, be able to describe it, feel it."

That was more like it, she was beginning to think it would be too similar to her work at The Institute, which was becoming monotonous. This experiment was much more qualitative, experiential and ground-breaking.

"Okay," she said, "I understand."

In her own time she disembodied her consciousness and instead of homing in on the target immediately, she focused on allowing it to drift. She envisioned herself as a bird, in particular an eagle and allowed herself to travel, she flew to the location on the map. The journey took her across the Surrey countryside and she could see it all clearly, rushing beneath her 'body'; fields separated by hedges, country roads and clusters of small towns and villages. She had a clear sense of speed and expediency but was also aware of her surroundings, the crisp autumn sunshine, the russet tones of the leaves, the rise and fall of the South Downs and the roads winding through the greenery. Her journey took her onwards through East Sussex, although she was not aware of which county she was travelling over and before long she had reached the coastline, where the land seemed to end abruptly in chalky cliffs, with the waves breaking below on a small, pebbly beach. She realised she had overshot and swung round like a bird turning in flight and headed back inland. The undulating cliffs looked spectacular viewed from out at sea and she wished she could remain here, out of body. Heading inland, she found the field where Paul had arranged some stones. At first it appeared to be a random pattern but as she circled her consciousness overhead, she realised the stones spelt out a word. The word wasn't clear, to pick up accurate detail she had to narrow her focus and tune out the landscape to some extent. Then the word came into focus.

"Cosmos," she said.

Paul was silent for a moment then sat back in his chair. He laughed. Tahra jolted back into her body, she was none too pleased.

"I would appreciate it if you didn't make sudden noises!"

Paul was too elated to consider his actions.

"You did it!" he exclaimed.

Tahra laughed in response to his enthusiasm.

"Well, I guess I did," she conceded. "But in future, let me ease back into my head. The sudden snap back is a bit like falling out of bed during a really good dream!"

Paul became more apologetic.

"Okay, I'll remember that for next time." Then he added. "I'm impressed that you were able to speak while still out of body. That will prove very useful."

"Yes, Max said this is something I need to develop."

Still, Tahra had proved her remote viewing capabilities and was also able to describe her journey and the landscape with avid detail. In fact, he almost felt jealous of her ability to travel like that out of body and he wished he knew how it felt to do such a thing, so he asked her.

"It feels... liberating," was her response.

Yes, it was, addictively so. She couldn't wait for Experiment 2.

Paul woke on the morning of the 1st November with an intense feeling of enthusiasm, despite the fact autumn was giving way to winter. His new project made his life feel like the first buds of spring and the thought of Tahra's imminent arrival that day spurred him from the bedroom to the kitchen. He filled the kettle, lit the flame on the hob and switched on the radio. Herman's Hermits sang *'Something tells me I'm into something good'* and he smiled, considering how appropriate the lyrics were.

He arrived at The Establishment bright and breezy, ready for Tahra's arrival. She turned up punctually, eager to embark on another journey. Life at The Institute was becoming rather staid and although university study broke up the monotony somewhat, she wanted to be at The Establishment with Paul.

"What are we doing today?" she asked him, "Or, should I say, where are we going?"

"I've planned some more aerial work," Paul replied, "but a little higher in altitude."

He got her to survey the country of Italy from a high altitude, as if she were a jet plane. Instead of map coordinates, she had to focus her consciousness upwards, as if she were an aeroplane taking off and climbing to cruising altitude, which was harder than she thought. Work at The Institute had conditioned her into a standardised method of remote viewing and it was a case of breaking a habit.

Closing her eyes she focused on an upward movement of her consciousness, through the clouds and towards the blue, unblemished sky of the stratosphere. She felt an exhilarating sensation as she left the ground behind and she felt as if there were no boundaries, no pull back to the Earth and to her body. It felt as if she had cleared the atmosphere almost completely and there was no sense of gravity, only a lucid stillness. Realising that she was over-reaching, she paused and looked back, wanting to exclaim out loud. Beneath her she saw the lie of the land, not Italy but Greece. The view was awe inspiring, it took one's breath away; the crystal clarity of the coastline, the turquoise of the sea, the technicolour landscape and the myriad of islands in the Aegean. At this altitude, she should not be able to breathe and should fall back to Earth under the influence of gravity but she felt reassured that it could not happen, for this was the unique benefit of an out of body experience. There were no physical limitations.

"I'm going to practice my aerial flight on a regular basis," Tahra announced.

In her time off at The Institute, instead of listening to the latest hits on Radio Caroline, she now lay in bed and allowed her consciousness to drift upward, up was the only direction now. The sensation of clearing the clouds was truly inspirational, very spiritual and extremely addictive. It made it harder to focus on the factual, reconnaissance tasks required of her at The Institute, the urge was so great to escape the Earth. In her own experiments, she would gain sufficient altitude to look down upon a whole country and marvel at its landscape; the mountains that look like textured bumps, crisp outlines of the coast and clusters of lights where that country lay in darkness. She was experiencing real time, as the further west she went, it was daylight. In fact, she managed a whole circuit of the Earth out of body, a timeless trip that seemed to take an eternity but actually was only half an hour in duration. Was time distorted, or was she travelling as a body of light, a cosmic ray?

Tahra's birthday arrived and the 7th November was a lonely day for the start of her 20th year on the planet. There were no tests scheduled, so The Institute was extremely quiet. She briefly suspected Max had done it on purpose, for he knew it was her birthday but she quickly dispelled that thought, he had simply given her birthday no thought at all. He didn't call to wish her well and in fact, he was oddly silent which aggrieved her more. She had gotten used to his absence though and out of sight also equalled out of mind. If anything, she gave more thought to the experiments with Paul.

On thinking of Paul, she realised he'd given her a contact number, in case there was a problem and she couldn't make it for experiments. She contemplated ringing him because she was lonely. Would he mind? Did he regard her as just a test subject? Or did he genuinely enjoy her company? There was only one way to find out.

The phone rang several times and she was about to give up, when Paul himself answered. She was relieved Eleanor hadn't picked up the phone.

"Tahra?" he said. "Well, this is a surprise. How are you?"

"I've been practising my aerial skills," she answered, a hint of melancholia in her voice.

Paul paused then asked, "Are you all right?"

"I'm… feeling quite lonely. It's my birthday today…"

"Oh, you should have mentioned it when we last met. How old, or should I not ask a woman that?" He laughed softly.

"I'm twenty," she replied, feeling a little tearful.

"Are you not doing anything special? A young woman shouldn't be all alone on her birthday."

"No, there's no one around."

"Hey, look, I'm not doing anything today and it's only early afternoon. Can you get out?"

"Yes, I think so."

She was relieved he cared.

"Well, get on the train and I'll meet you at Croydon. That okay?"

"Yes, yes," she replied, ecstatic.

"I hope you like horse riding," he said.

"I haven't been on a horse for about ten years or so," she answered, with a slight nervous laugh.

"Oh, I'll sort you out a suitable horse, we can just take it easy."

Paul had it all in hand and he was enthusiastic. She thought he wouldn't have wanted to spend his spare time with her but it turned out he was warm and welcoming.

The train ride was fairly quick, she travelled by a modern

diesel locomotive as opposed to the now old-fashioned steam powered locomotive and Paul picked her up in his car just outside the station. He was driving a Triumph Spitfire, another two seat sports convertible although he had purchased and fitted a hard top for the winter months.

She felt truly grateful that he had done this for her and he seemed pleased she had rung him. Eleanor didn't come into the conversation and Tahra didn't ask. He took her to his local stables and saddled up his own horse, then asked for one to be prepared for Tahra as well. She looked a little nervous but he helped her onto her horse and they set off at walking pace.

"How do I look?" she asked.

"In a riding hat and jodhpurs?" he assumed. "Like a beautiful lady of the countryside," he laughed.

She was surprised by his answer. "I did mean, do I look confident or awkward in the saddle?" She felt more of the latter.

Paul was not unhinged at his unexpected flattery. "More confident than awkward," he answered. "Shall we pick up the pace?"

They took it up to a trot and Tahra couldn't grasp the rhythm at first but Paul coached her through it and encouraged her to relax. After a short while, she found her rhythm and began to enjoy the ride much more. They laughed and joked like old friends and didn't discuss the experiments, instead they talked about friends at The Institute, the countryside, music and their dreams. It was such a release to talk openly with him in a relaxed manner and the intellectual interchange was not only stimulating but deepened their connection with each other.

As she seemed confident in the saddle, Paul suggested a canter through the wooded area and she agreed. She found it much more exhilarating, in a way like projecting her consciousness but this was more physical. Paul's horse was ahead and she watched him, the experienced rider that he was but then a creature shot out of the undergrowth and startled her horse. The next thing she knew, the world was turning upside down and she hit the ground. Her exclamation of shock and pain alerted Paul and he pulled up, turned his horse and rode to the spot where she lay on the ground. Her horse was distressed but the priority was Tahra, she didn't appear to be moving.

"Oh my God," he said, turning her over, thinking he had killed the star remote viewer.

Tahra was still breathing at least, the hat had obviously protected her from head injury but he was worried about fractures so checked her all over. He was relieved to see her smile.

"Nice to receive such prompt attention," she mused, "and to be frisked so sensually."

Paul felt a little embarrassed but was glad she wasn't complaining of pain. He offered his hand to help her up and she gripped it tightly, however she winced as she did so. On examination, he found her wrist to be somewhat swollen but there was no worrying deformity, it was probably sprained so he advised caution until they reached the stables. There, the staff also examined her wrist and also suspected that it was a mild sprain. They advised a trip to the hospital if it worsened.

Rather than end the day on such a note, Paul offered to take her to his local pub, where fine ales and an open fire awaited them. It made a change from the fine restaurants she had frequented with Max, so she accepted his offer. Heads turned as they entered the traditional country pub, for they had never seen the likes of such an exotic looking woman in their establishment. They were also used to Paul in partnership with Eleanor, so they wondered who this exotic looking female was. Paul shrugged off the stares and introduced her as his friend, announcing her birthday so the pub landlord granted her a free drink. She had a glass of red wine while Paul stuck with his favourite, a pint of Guinness. They sat near the open fire, free of riding gear.

"Well," he began, "I hope you've enjoyed it, despite the fall."

She smiled. "Of course I have, despite the fall."

Spotting a smear of mud on her face, he reached over and gently wiped it away with his fingers. He didn't like to see her beautiful face so blemished. Tahra looked thoughtful at his touch, and realised she genuinely liked everything about him. He had a warmth and naturalness about him that was welcoming but never over bearing. His invitation to a day out was free from conditions and expectations; he had sincerely not wanted her to be alone on her birthday. It was rare to find a man so unselfish and she truly appreciated that.

"Thank you for the wonderful day," she said, "I will remember it always."

Tahra reached over and kissed him softly on the cheek, quite close to his lips. He was still yet receptive, but did not attempt to draw her further into a more passionate kiss. Instead, he smiled kindly.

"Don't mention it, it was my pleasure," he said.

Part of her wanted to be more physical with him, but he seemed content to sit and talk. She had to remind herself that he was already in a relationship and the locals were staring enough as it was. Wishing things were different, she accepted the situation as it was and enjoyed a mellow evening with a drink and a crackling fire to create a warm and trusting atmosphere. It was a sad moment when the evening drew to a close and he dropped her off at the train station. He bid her farewell, looking forward to their next experiment. She bid him farewell, not wanting to think about him going home to Eleanor. Why were all the finest men already taken?

They didn't see each other until late November and Tahra told him all about her own experiments, the unofficial ones back at The Institute. Paul was surprised, for she had done this with no prompting from him and he was impressed, she was worthy of the accolade 'fringe scientist'. Judging by the fine tuning of her skills that had been taking place, she would find experiment three a walk in the park.

"How do you feel about going into orbit?" he asked her.

"Just splendid," was her affirmative answer.

"Well," he began, "there's a capsule in orbit at the moment, do you fancy paying it a visit and a round the world trip?"

"I'll peep through the window," she declared.

It was common practice for Tahra to be out of body now and her consciousness drifted in an instant to alight far above the Earth. Italy was below her in its lucid splendour, if consciousness had breath, it would have been taken away by the view. The capsule was nowhere in sight though but getting her bearings up here was no problem, she had more problems with directions in London and navigating through the Underground. Skimming the stratosphere with her consciousness, she eventually caught up with the capsule, feeling as if she was travelling faster than it. Over taking it, she re-focused and swooped round, circling the capsule. It looked so fragile, more vulnerable than her robust and unbreakable consciousness.

She couldn't resist peeping through the window. She really had to focus when operating in real time, like creating a narrow beam of light to observe details of things, something she had become more adept at during her research at The Institute. Quicker than usual, the interior of the capsule came into focus and she could see one of the astronauts inside, taking measurements. Tahra watched him, his body protected by a spacesuit and the capsule shielding him from the hostile environment of space. She pitied him and his powerlessness against the icy vacuum of space. Without warning, the astronaut looked out of the window and she felt as if she was coming face to face with him. He was looking at the Earth, a view that no one would want to avoid then his attention was distracted. For a moment, Tahra felt as if he was looking right at her, not through her but at her directly. That was impossible, wasn't it? Nevertheless, it made her feel uneasy and she withdrew her consciousness back into her body quickly.

She looked at Paul with a puzzled expression on her face and told him what had just happened.

Paul was stunned. "You must be mistaken, consciousness simply isn't visible."

No matter, she shook her head.

"No, really, he looked right at me."

"Tahra, there's nothing there for him to look at. If consciousness could be seen, remote viewers would have been spotted years ago. I can't see how he could have sighted you."

"I can't explain it," she said, "and it's never happened before but for some reason, he did see me."

Paul was thoughtful; there were ways and means of corroborating this.

Later that night, after Tahra had returned to The Institute, Paul rang Max, who was surprised to hear from him.

"You have results so soon? Or do you just like the sound of my voice?"

Paul laughed. "I know she's good, but not that good."

Max was clearly amused.

"How's it working out with her anyway?"

Paul considered the answer then replied, "Well, she's not shy is she? That I can vouch for."

To Paul's surprise, Max was strangely silent on the other end of the line. What should he read into Paul's statement, which seemed very off the cuff?

"Tahra is confident of her abilities," was his response.

"Certainly," Paul agreed, "she's also very sure someone saw her while in an out of body state."

Again Max was quiet. Paul wasn't sure if he was in a state of disbelief or whether he was worrying about the ramifications.

"That's impossible," Max replied.

"Well, she's adamant. She doesn't understand it herself but she claims an astronaut saw her through the window of his capsule."

"This is certainly an unforeseen development, isn't it?"

"It occurred to me that you have a lot of contacts in various research departments. Is there any way you can verify or counter her claim? Identify any reported anomalies from the flight?"

Max was silent while considering the request.

"Yes, I can do that. I'd like an answer too."

"Thanks, just let me know when you hear something."

"I will. Oh," Max added as an afterthought, "I'm having a party for New Year, a masquerade ball. You're invited."

Paul seemed oddly reticent.

"I'm strictly faithful to Eleanor, I don't want to get involved in…"

"It's just a fancy dress party. I can suggest a good costume shop for nightly hire. Oh, and you can bring Eleanor."

"I will," Paul said. Then he paused and made a further request. "Would you allow Tahra to go too?"

Max was quiet then he replied, "Yes, I don't see why not."

"Great. See you New Year's Eve."

After putting the phone down, it occurred to him that he had invited the two central women in his life to the same party. Why had he done that? In the end he shrugged. Tahra was just a friend and a young woman had the right to party. What was the problem?

Experiment 4 was due to take place in the middle of December but unfortunately, Tahra was ill at that time and then Christmas made its presence known so he postponed the moon shot until after the New Year. He telephoned her before Christmas to send season's greetings and to check that she wasn't going to be alone for the festive period. She was grateful for his concern and informed him that the usual custom was for the research subjects at The Institute to spend it together.

It was a pleasant but rather humdrum Christmas, although Max wasn't there. He was apparently away on business but would be back in time for New Year. Paul had informed her that she was going to the New Year ball at Max's house and it occurred to her she had never been there, despite what had happened between them. She never mentioned the relationship and engagement with Max to Paul, to her it was irrelevant and belonged in the past. The upcoming party was an exciting prospect and Paul had insisted on an invite for her too. She questioned, although not to Paul whether or not it was a date but in the back of her mind, she was aware of Eleanor, his partner.

Christmas was soon over and it didn't bother her that Max hadn't left her a present. There was nothing between them and they had had little contact. She hadn't had time to feel sad about it, what was the point?

Before long, it was New Year's Eve and the costumes arrived as expected. Tahra changed into her ball gown, a cream and gold dress that had a tight bodice and a full skirt, framed with lace. It pushed her breasts upward and flattered her milk chocolate skin. The finale was a gold mask, almost Egyptian in its design. Max had agreed to let John Eames, his personal assistant drive her from The Institute to his home in the Surrey countryside. She found it difficult to exit the vehicle with such an enormous costume but managed to push the hooped part of the skirt through the door of the car.

For a long moment, she stood appraising the exterior of the house; the general size, the pretty symmetry of it and the large garage, suggesting he owned multiple vehicles. She approached the imposing, oak front door which was already open and she could hear the guests and music already.

This was the first time she'd seen Max's home. It wasn't as ostentatious as she had pictured it, in fact, it was surprisingly traditional with oak furniture and antique pictures on the walls. No expense had been spared. So this is what could have been hers too. There was a tinge of regret but a relationship was about more than luxurious surroundings.

She wandered into the main living area through the large archway. His home was full of people, who were not recognisable due to their costumes and masks. The double doors to the dining room were wide open and at the far end of it (the table had been pushed aside), she couldn't mistake Max. He was dressed in green brocade and wore a dragon's mask and appeared to stop his conversation briefly to notice her. She was surprised to feel a pang of attraction for him and wondered if he still felt something for her.

Then she found Paul, dressed in red brocade with the mask of a lizard. She walked over to him and he placed his hand gently around her waist, guiding her to a group of his friends. She was introduced as a truly gifted friend and they struck up conversation as a group, then Paul split off to tend to Eleanor, who was dressed in a dark blue ball gown. A wave of jealousy washed over her and she tried to swallow it the best she could. She hoped he couldn't see her watching them.

At the other end of the room was Max and to her surprise, he was watching her discreetly from behind his dragon mask. She met his gaze and was aware of it all throughout the evening as she danced with a large number of the male guests. She found it hard to gain Paul's attention, as he flitted between Eleanor and his friends which were part of Max's circle too. Paul eventually became aware of her attention and ensured he graced her with his presence frequently. She couldn't help but want him all to herself. Was this wrong, considering that he had been with Eleanor for a few years now?

Tahra began to feel uncomfortable as Paul danced with Eleanor, so she made her excuses and left the dining room to find the buffet in the kitchen. There was an adjoining corridor between these two rooms and she was surprised to find Max coming in the opposite direction. In juxtaposition to the indifference he had shown her all year, he now put his hand against the wall, creating a barrier between her and the kitchen. Tahra was taken aback and didn't make eye contact at first.

"Tonight has made me realise that I need you in my life again," he said.

In the past, that would have meant something to her but now, its impact was confusing. Why now, after all this time?

"Do you need me in your life again?" he asked her.

She wasn't sure if it was the alcohol talking or whether it was the long absence, but he seemed more ardent than usual. His intentions hadn't really changed, but what about her feelings? Tahra stopped avoiding his gaze and made eye contact, searching for that yearning in her stomach she had often felt before. Out of character and contrary to the balance of power in the past, she placed her hand around the back of his neck and kissed him. He reciprocated without persuasion and she felt his sexual desire awaken as it had done before on so many occasions. Her body responded more intensely than before, like a drug addict succumbing to their worst vice. But it was like old times and somewhere down the line something would surface to drive them apart again. That couldn't happen, maybe it was really time to move on, for both their benefit. She realised then that this wasn't a kiss to resurrect a relationship, it was a goodbye kiss.

Tahra broke away, lowered her gaze and walked away, into the kitchen. Max didn't know whether to follow or not, but luckily for Tahra, a group of people made their way down the adjoining corridor so he returned to the dining room. Realising he was in a situation again where he didn't know where he stood, he tried to put what had just happened out of his mind. In the kitchen, Tahra came to a definite conclusion: Max wasn't the right choice, she wanted someone else.

Decisively, she returned to the dining room and was relieved to find Paul dancing with a middle aged lady, who was the wife of an old friend. Politely, she asked if the lady didn't mind her cutting in and she found the lady compliant. Paul didn't complain and readily took hold of Tahra's waist and hand. She found his grip steady but not too intimate.

"I thought I'd never get to dance with you," she said, boldly.

"I thought the same too," he agreed.

"Why didn't you ask me?" she queried, although not in a demanding tone.

He shrugged. "I wasn't sure what was expected in terms of the researcher and subject relationship…"

"That didn't stop you on my birthday," she responded, curtly.

No explanation was necessary. He enjoyed the sensation of holding her and dancing. After a short while, she realised she had something important to tell him so she asked if she could speak to him in private. They wandered onto the patio area at the back of the house and sat on a wall. Tahra removed her mask and without thinking, Paul did the same.

"Is there a problem with the project?" he asked her.

She didn't answer straightaway and appeared to be taking a deep breath.

"Well, kind of," she began, "it's just that… I think I'm falling in love with you."

Paul felt a wrench in his gut and was unable to respond. Normally he would have been simply flattered by the attention of a young woman but for some reason, Tahra's words meant something. She looked at him expectantly for a reply but Paul didn't know what to say.

"What are you thinking?" she asked him, eager to know.

Paul opened his mouth to speak, but he didn't know what to say.

"I can't pretend I don't," she added. "Please tell me you feel the same."

Finally, he responded. "Tahra, I'm with Eleanor, in a relationship, a happy one."

She felt her heart sink at his response.

"So, you're happy with her?" she asked.

"Yes," he replied.

"Do you love her?" she pressed.

Paul felt unable to answer that question.

"Do you love her?" she repeated.

"What do you think?" he asked her, still unable to answer the question.

"I think that you're comfortable with her and you like her company, but you don't love her."

Paul was silent, it was as if someone had just unexpectedly punched him. He couldn't give a counter argument. Why did she have to ask that question? Tahra noted that her words had found the target and waited for his response. Unseen by the both of them, Eleanor moved away from the doorway to the patio and felt shaken. Realising she was beginning to cry, she abruptly left and returned to the dining room. Paul and Tahra still didn't notice her.

"Tahra," he said, "I can't get involved with you, I can't. We need to maintain a friendly but professional relationship. And besides, I'm twice your age. Wouldn't you rather find a nice guy your own age?"

She bit her lip and looked disappointed.

"I'm sorry I said anything."

With that, she stood up and went to find John Eames, asking if she could go home. He informed her it wasn't yet midnight but she insisted, claiming she didn't feel well so he conceded and drove her to The Institute. She saw the New Year in alone. A little while later, Max was dismayed to find she had left. Paul also felt unable to see the night through and Eleanor was in no mood to party, so they made their way home. They were both quiet throughout the journey home. Paul couldn't help but replay Tahra's words in his mind. He knew it was wrong to even consider her words, he didn't believe in being unfaithful but there was a first time for everything.

Experiment 4 took place on the 13th January 1965 and Paul was nervous about seeing her again. Since the New Year ball, his relationship with Eleanor had become strained and he had found his mind drifting during sex. What would it be like to be inside of Tahra instead of Eleanor? He knew he shouldn't think such things but he couldn't help it. Today he was going to see Tahra again and he wondered if the situation would be awkward or not.

On seeing him, she looked a little sheepish and still showed signs of disappointment, but looked to him to see what response there would be. When he saw her, he didn't know what to say. Thankfully, she broke the ice.

"So, where are we going today?"

"Fancy a flight to the moon?" he replied.

Things were starting to get interesting and it was time for the real challenge. She had proved herself during orbital flights of consciousness, now could she do the same moving out of the Earth's sphere of influence? Getting comfortable in her chair, she focused her consciousness into the stratosphere and let go, soon finding her awareness suspended above the Earth. With the moon in her sights, she focused on the luminescent orb and tried to push herself closer to it. She tried to put thoughts of the distance involved to the back of her mind, such as, can her consciousness remain connected to her body over such a vast distance? There was only one way to find out. She willed herself closer to the moon but found something was deterring her. Was it the doubts in the back of her mind? Or was the mind and body connection simply being over-stretched? Should consciousness be pushed to the limits like so, or remain within the Earth's atmosphere? Tahra opened her eyes.

"I failed," she admitted, "I'm sorry."

Tahra looked genuinely dismayed.

"You can do it," Paul urged, "try again."

She did as he asked, encouraged by his positivity. Again she focused her mind through the clouds and toward the moon, it appeared larger and she could see craters, this was more than what any astronaut had seen. She saw a dry, dusty ball of rock, totally devoid of life yet amazing, amazing because it was somewhere other than Earth. Once she had cleared the atmosphere, the pull back towards her body seemed to diminish and she started to believe that consciousness could indeed know no bounds. For a long moment, she hovered her consciousness but a short distance from the moon in astronomical terms to contemplate what she had done, gone where no man or woman had ever gone before. She looked back at the Earth, finding it small, the size of a beach ball. So far away from home, so alone... A sense of panic overtook her and she found herself yanked back into her body. When she opened her eyes, she found Paul watching her intently.

"I did it," she whispered, "I almost touched the moon."

For some reason, Paul almost wanted to cry. Something amazing was happening, frontiers were being destroyed and it was all due to a project he had believed in and initiated. But it would have been nothing without Tahra. She was an amazing woman.

"Where do we go next?" she asked, hungry for more.

Paul realised it was time.

"We start to head for the stars," he said.

Tahra smiled. "For you, anything."

He reached over and kissed her on the forehead.

"What would I do without you?"

She left in high spirits, proud of her success. Paul returned home feeling incredibly optimistic, project OOBE had only just begun and it was already exceeding the achievements of NASA and the Soviet Union. There was no stopping them now. He'd not been in long when the phone rang. It was Max.

"We haven't found life on other planets, yet," Paul joked.

He heard a soft chuckle escape Max's lips.

"It's not the reason for my call," Max explained, "I've just received some feedback from one of my contacts about that encounter with the orbital capsule."

Paul had almost forgotten about that.

"It seems there may be something in Tahra's belief that she was seen by someone in the capsule." Paul was surprised. "It's in a top secret report, so we'll never see it become official, but the astronaut claims to have seen an orb of light outside the capsule. It's being regarded as a UFO encounter."

After hanging up the phone, Paul was thoughtful and amazed. How could Tahra's consciousness be visible, as it seemed to have been? This was too much of a coincidence. What amazed him was the form her consciousness appeared to take. Consciousness could very well be photonic and if it was indeed photonic, it had the potential to travel at the speed of light. They really could be heading for the stars.

Part Three

OOBE

The entire universe is this gigantic loaf with many other slices, potentially. So our universe could be one slice, and a different parallel universe could be living on a different slice.

Brian Greene

15
A Year's Work

Friday 12th November 1993

The day had arrived. A year had flown by since Daniel Costa had been given an unusual assignment by a man who wished to remain anonymous and who insisted on a non-disclosure before the contract was agreed. A year's worth of privately paid investigation revolved around ten names, the majority of which were children. He was required to summarise their life history to date and provide recent photographs, noting anything that was out of the ordinary. Daniel now held a large ring binder, full of information and photographs protected in plastic wallets. He reached the university, where he was told to report to the biology department.

He entered the building and smoothed back his wavy, dark, shoulder length hair. His appearance drew attention as he wasn't recognised as a lecturer or student and he was dressed casually in jeans and a purple shirt. He didn't look professional but when it came to his job, he was no amateur; he had a keen eye for detail and a stubborn tenacity for the truth which made him good at his job. His rate was also very reasonable, he wasn't high maintenance.

At the reception, he was somewhat embarrassed when asked who he was here to see and he had to explain that the man didn't give his name, but told him to come to room 304 in the biology department on the 12th November at 2pm. The receptionist took his name, rang the biology department who confirmed that Daniel Costa was expected so he was given a visitor's badge and instructions on how to get there.

Daniel found the room easily, knocked and entered when a male voice called out 'Come in!' He entered a room with oak panelled walls and a large oak table in the centre of the room. The man who had given him the assignment was seated at the far end of the table. Daniel felt a little intimidated and walked tentatively towards the table, clutching the ring binder tightly.

"I take it you have a year's work to show me," the man said, leaning forward in his seat.

"Yes," Daniel replied, "I have brought what you asked for."

"Good, then let's get started straightaway."

The man gestured towards a seat at the table adjacent to him and Daniel sat down, preparing his notes in front of him.

"When you're ready," the man said.

"Well," Daniel began, "I did wonder what the point of the investigation was at first, then as I got halfway I realised there was a lot of... common ground."

He looked to the man for some sort of response, a clue that would tie up the connections he found but he gave nothing away. If anything, he seemed to become impatient so Daniel passed him the first of the photographs.

"Laila Foster," he stated, "born on the 17th June 1979 to Michael and Lorraine Foster. They live in Cambridge, Michael is an engineer and Lorraine home schools Laila as she didn't feel the state school system was meeting her daughter's needs. She is an incredibly bright child and Lorraine tested her IQ, which is validated at 155. Although she should be halfway through her secondary education, Laila already sat four GCSEs in Maths, Biology, Chemistry and Physics at the tender age of twelve, attaining A★ grades in all, indicating a clear aptitude for science and number."

The man listened attentively and nodded appreciatively.

"She passed an additional six GCSEs last year and is now studying A Levels at the tender age of fourteen, so would probably make it to university a full two years ahead of her peers. Laila is an only child and her parents devote themselves to her upbringing, despite her genius she has many friends and enjoys a normal social life."

The man surveyed the photograph, looking at a young girl with long, blonde, wavy hair and intense blue eyes. She was holding a rabbit and no one could have guessed from that picture that she was an academic genius.

Daniel passed him the next photograph, one of a young boy with dark, curly hair and greenish eyes. The boy was playing a violin and appeared to be lost in thought.

"David Timms," he continued, "born 2nd March 1980 to Donald and Joanne Timms. They live in Southend, Donald is a broker and Joanne is a housewife. Academically, he is competent so far but excels musically, having achieved grade 7 at piano, grade 8 at clarinet and grade 6 at violin. David has already composed his own music. He has two younger sisters, Caitlin and Millie, neither of which display any prodigious tendencies."

He passed the man another picture, which was of a boy with strong features, dark eyes and dark hair, dressed in a scout's uniform.

"Liam McKay, born on the 15th July 1980 to William and Molly McKay, they now reside in Edinburgh where William works in a hospital, Molly helps on a local farm. Liam is quite a bright boy but doesn't seem to excel in any particular areas yet. However, he seems to have a peculiarly acute sense of direction and place, as evidenced from his scout troop and is uncannily accurate when predicting the weather. He adores animals, as can be seen from the picture taken on the farm where his mother works."

The man seemed surprised but continued to listen attentively.

"Next we have Thomas Hitchin, born on the 7th September 1980 to Terry and Michelle Hitchin. They live in Bromley,

Kent where Terry drives lorries for a living and Michelle is a receptionist. Thomas is also a very intelligent boy, with a particular leaning towards languages. He's incredibly articulate, speaks three other languages fluently; French, Spanish and German and wants to learn Japanese next year. He has a brother, Scott who is academically average in comparison."

The man looked at a photograph of Thomas, who had blonde, curly hair and freckles, a proud smile and fierce eyes. He was in the school play, taking on the lead role.

Daniel handed him the next photograph, one of a boy with dark, wavy hair and small, piercing eyes. He was holding a circuit board and a screwdriver.

"Sean Greene, born 30th January 1981 to Colin and Tina Greene. They live in Dunstable where Colin owns a warehouse and Tina is a homemaker. Sean is a bright and gifted child with a leaning towards science, electronics and computer technology. At only nine years old, he built his own circuit boards and has made a number of gadgets, he also disassembled a BBC computer and re-assembled an improved version in the same year and has now progressed onto personal computers. At the moment he is learning to programme in COBOL. He has a sister, Yvette who displays no prodigious abilities."

Daniel passed him a photograph of a girl next, with long, strawberry blonde hair and freckles. She was painting a picture.

"Hayley Bennett, born 2nd May 1981 to Thomas and Janine Bennett. They live in a small hamlet in Leicestershire, where Thomas is a builder and Janine works in a local shop. Hayley is a gifted child who is incredibly artistic, she could paint and draw like an adult at the tender age of seven and produces her own original work. She also has the voice of an angel. Her father has built her a studio at the bottom of the garden, where he keeps all her work. She has a sister, Holly who displays no prodigious abilities."

The next photograph was of another girl, this time of mixed

race origin. She had skin the colour of milk chocolate and braids in her hair, and was very pretty with huge, brown eyes. In the photograph, she was in a school play in a lead role.

"Aleisha Keane, born 10th August 1981 to Roger and Beatrice Keane. They currently live in Jamaica, where Beatrice was born. Aleisha is academically bright, a good all rounder but seems to excel at anything that involves leadership, with an enhanced capacity for organisation and initiative. She also enjoys acting, and is very good at that too."

The man didn't seem as impressed but looked thoughtful. Daniel handed him another photograph of a lonely and troubled looking boy with dark hair cut in a bowl style. His large, blue eyes were startling as they were sad.

"Anthony Preston, born 29th December 1981 to Roy and Colleen Preston. They live in Carlisle where Roy is a headmaster and Colleen was a teacher but now she devotes her time to Anthony. He says very little but has a keen mind, capable of advanced maths and problem solving. Anthony plays chess on a regular basis and has beaten everyone who plays him. His memory is incredible and he can remember the entire sequence of a deck of cards."

The man looked concerned at the boy's sadness and studied the picture of Anthony intensely. Daniel passed him the next photograph, which was of a girl with long, dark hair and a pretty face.

"Katie Wright, born on the 12th February 1982 to Keith and Anne Wright, who live in Kettering. Keith is an optician and Anne works part time alongside him. Katie is exceptionally bright and sociable, with an early leaning towards science. At the tender age of eleven, she had an advanced understanding of the universe and wants to be an astronaut. Her brother, Jamie shows no signs of prodigious abilities."

"And finally, Ava Kavanagh."

Daniel passed him a recent photograph, in which Ava was

leaving the lab where she worked. Her golden blonde hair was straight and layered and her co-worker, Tom was also in the picture with her. The man stared silently at the picture, deep in thought until Daniel gave a run through of his findings.

"She was born on the 19th November 1967 to unknown parents and adopted by David and Caroline Kavanagh at the age of three. There's no trace of her anywhere until that age, my guess is that she was out of the country, or the Outer Hebrides. At school she was clearly brighter than the rest of the kids and leaned towards the sciences at an early age. She achieved ten O Levels, seven of which were grade A and four A Levels in all three sciences, plus English. Ava has also achieved a first in her honours degree which was in genetics and since 1991, she has been working at her uncle's research lab. This is where it starts to get really strange."

The man was very attentive now.

"Last year there was… an incident. One of the workers had a grudge against her uncle and decided to take it out on her, by attacking her with a highly contagious and fatal virus. The strangest thing is, she survived, and not only did she survive, she developed no symptoms. The official line is that the virus wasn't live, but my informant assures me the rest of the batch wasn't 'duff', as he put it. Since then, she has been involved in illicit research with her co-worker, Thomas Fisher based on her anomalous immunity to the disease. Their results so far indicate an almost… superhuman immune system, for want of a better word."

The man did not seem surprised at any of the findings, it was Daniel who felt that he'd stepped into a science fiction book or conspiracy tale. He looked to his contractor for some sort of feedback but he said nothing.

"I hope the information is to your satisfaction," Daniel said.

"You have told me what I needed to know," was the reply.

"Did you know beforehand that virtually all of these people are prodigies?" Daniel asked. "It's certainly… a coincidence. I also noted one other factor that most of them share."

"And what is that?" the man asked.

"Well, all of the kids were conceived *in vitro,* if you know what I mean. Except Ava of course, she was born naturally, somewhere. Although I know for sure she is adopted, David and Caroline Kavanagh are registered as her parents but the birth certificate is dated 1971, which is very strange."

"That is not a problem," he replied, "and your observations are noted."

"Is that all?" Daniel asked.

"No, I have more research for you."

He slid two envelopes across the table, one contained the payment for his work and the other contained a piece of paper. Daniel looked at it, another list, an additional ten names of children all born in 1982 plus eleven more names of people born much earlier in the century, with no apparent connection to any of the youngsters he was to investigate. Who were these adults? He looked at the man, incredulously.

"You have a year again to bring me the results," was all the man said. "You may find some of the adults now reside abroad somewhere, just do your best. I'd like to find these people very much."

Daniel nodded and stood up to leave, but then the man asked him a question.

"This co-worker of Ava's, Thomas Fisher… can he be trusted?"

"Trusted?" Daniel wasn't sure what he meant.

"With the knowledge that he holds about her," the man continued.

Daniel gave him a wry look.

"Well, let's put it this way, he talked for a lot less money than I thought he would."

The man seemed concerned but didn't trouble him with it, instead, he just nodded thankfully and Daniel left the room.

Outside Daniel gave little thought to Ava's potentially precarious predicament and looked at the list of children's names. The dates were much closer together this time. How many more of them would there be? And was there a more sinister, underlying connection between them? Who were these adults and how were they connected, if they were at all? A story lay beneath this and he was determined to get to the bottom of it.

Back in the room, the man was still ever impatient for results. He picked up the phone and called his friend, an associate researcher at another university whom he'd recently asked a favour of. His friend answered, the number was a direct line to his lab.

"Hi Mike," said the man, "have you found that electromagnetic anomaly yet?"

"Hey, I'm doing fine, thanks for asking," Mike joked. "Yeah, I was going to give you a call, just confirming the data now. I've picked something up in a remote part of the Far East, Hokkaido Island."

That didn't surprise the man.

"I also noticed some weird shit on Long Island, United States," he added, "don't know if it's related. The Hokkaido anomaly is continuous, whereas the Long Island one switches on and off. Do you mind telling me what this is all about?"

The man considered his request but was adamant.

"You wouldn't believe me if I told you," he said.

Mike responded, "Try me."

"Another time," the man deliberated, "we'll discuss it another time."

The man put the phone down, satisfied that his plan was beginning to come together. He sat quietly in reflection with the photographs strewn in front of him, looking over them thoughtfully, particularly the one of Ava. The woman walking through the park was her after all, so he wasn't wrong, he hadn't been watching her to waste time. Now he had to decide his next move.

16
Satus

Experiment 5 was all set for launch on the 28th January 1965. As enthusiastic as Paul was, our nation was in mourning as the great wartime Prime Minister, Winston Churchill had died a few days ago. The television and radio was full of tributes and crowds had gathered outside his house. At The Institute, we paid our respects with a three minute silence on the day of his death, then life resumed as normal.

I arrived at The Establishment early and Paul was ready to push the boundaries even further. More than anything he needed to see how far I was willing to take it and whether or not I could succeed. He was excited by the possibility of consciousness taking a photon-like form and of the potential to travel across the far reaches of space. So far, the bond between consciousness and body had not been broken and he did wonder if there was a natural 'stretching point' for this connection, surely there must be an inbuilt safety mechanism?

I breezed in, happy to see him and ready to do whatever he asked of me.

"I've been perfecting my lunar orbit," I declared, enthusiastically.

Paul smiled, the space race was so behind the times.

"Where are we going today?" I asked.

"Well," Paul began, tentatively, "I thought we'd leave the safety of the Earth and start to push onward."

This did not faze me.

"I was wondering when we'd get past the warm up," I said, placing my bag down and flopping into the chair, or hot seat as it was known.

Paul couldn't help but admire my attitude.

He produced an illustration which indicated the next assignment. It was a picture of the solar system with an arrow pointing to the fourth *planet and some artists' representations of the planet Mars. It lay around 70 million kilometres from Earth at its closest point and had been observed through telescopes for years, so it was already known as the red planet. Paul told me as of 1965, no probe had landed on Mars, although Mariner 4 was launched on the 28th November 1964 and was due to fly past Mars in the summer of 1965, so therefore there was little new data for Mars. I studied the illustrations closely, trying to visualise the destination.*

"I assume you've never been to Mars in your spare time," he mused.

I laughed softly and shook my head.

"But this will be much harder, as I only have drawings to work from."

I closed my eyes and held an image in my mind of where I wished to push my consciousness. With little prompting I felt a psychological surge and was soon focused, poised above the earth. But the next part was not as straightforward as I hoped. Although I held an image in my mind of the destination, it did not come into focus at all, I merely remained in suspension above the Earth. I withdrew my consciousness in frustration and opened my eyes.

"What's wrong?" Paul asked, disappointed.

"I'm used to working from maps, or objects that are obvious, easy to find. I can reach the moon because I can see it in the sky and know where it is, but I can't find Mars as I do not know where to look for it."

Paul bit his lip in contemplation. He explained we were going to need some sort of mapping system or astronomical coordinates, perhaps a combination of the two using a star based system that would help me navigate. That wasn't going to happen today as he needed a week or so to put that together. So it was that Experiment 5 was re-scheduled for the 6th February.

He conducted some research to draw up a map that would help orientate me, including declinations and degrees of longitude, and astronomical and astrological data; information that in itself made no sense to me but enabled him to draw an accurate map. The constellations made a great backdrop and he used stickers to pinpoint the current location of a star or planet, which he could update for each experiment by simply moving the sticker. When I returned in early February for the second attempt, he was ready and showed me the star map. I agreed it contained sufficient information for me to find my way and focus my consciousness.

I drifted out of my body with no difficulty, aiming for the constellations of Virgo and Libra which provided the background position for Mars. Putting negative talk to the back of my mind was getting more difficult, as it was impossible to ignore the distance required to travel and the enormous degree of separation from my body.

A small, reddish-orange ball of light grew larger as I pushed myself towards it. The effort to reach it was greater than my previous journeys and I realised I was fast approaching my limit. There was a sensation of winding down, like a clockwork toy. Maybe with regular practice I could overcome this, but how long would that take? It could take years. With one last push, a reddish-orange globe lay beneath me. It was stunning because it was not home, but it lacked the vivid blues, greens, oranges and white hues of Earth. It truly felt alien. While I felt at peace in the orbit of Earth, Mars had a different 'aura', or vibration, which was a little unsettling. For a finale, I moved into the atmosphere, the ground getting closer. I found the surface to be a desolate place scattered with rusty red rocks strewn around the lifeless landscape. The sky was an odd colour, and it really did feel like no place on Earth. I returned to orbit and tried to find the Earth, unsuccessfully, the isolation of space becoming an abrupt reality. Unusually, I felt panicked as I couldn't see the way home, there was no star map to guide me back in so I decided to open my eyes and endure the unpleasant jolt back into my body, akin to falling out of bed with a thud.

"This is the most ground breaking OOBE so far," Paul commented, awaiting my response, "what do you think?"

"It was lonely," was all I said, without the usual enthusiasm for my journeys.

"What did you see?"

I paused before answering. "Something so extraordinarily alien. The sense of desolation was unlike anything I've ever experienced."

"Was it beautiful?" he pressed.

"I don't think beautiful is the word," I replied, "but it was vivid, a very lucid experience, a little uncomfortable."

My inability to share it with Paul was saddening; maybe that's why I felt so flat, breaking new ground without anyone else seeing something so spectacular was a little disheartening.

Paul was lost for words. I was describing something no human eye had seen, and therefore it was impossible to substantiate. Eventually, a probe would land on Mars and my description would be corroborated, but for the time being he would send the recordings of my account to an artist to render an interpretation of the data. But still, he believed me without doubt. I had no reason to lie, in fact, I felt unexcited by my journey. I also felt noticeably tired, something that had not occurred before. Maybe it was a glitch; no one was a hundred percent all the time.

Experiment 6 took place on the 14th February 1965, ironically. The fact that it was Valentine's Day had not escaped Paul and it was tinged with a conflict of heart. It was also a Sunday, always regarded as a day of rest. He felt obliged to spend the day with Eleanor, yet he really wanted to work on his project with me. The process of discovery was addictive and he was in love with this more than Eleanor, or so it seemed to me and the project gave us both a higher purpose to serve and share, an ideal to pursue.

In the conflict of relationships and objectives, the project won.

He was grateful that I didn't mention the theme of the day, although he did decide a trip to Venus was in order. Everyone had preconceptions about the planet; Venus had always been synonymous with beauty yet no one had pierced the veil of dense cloud that covered the planet. The distance from Earth to Venus was less than Earth to Mars, 42 million kilometres from home to Venus when both planets were at their closest together and from home to Mars, 78 million kilometres at their closest, so it should be a little easier. It was also essential to check out the neighbours first before exploring the rest of the street, so to speak.

Not much was known about Venus, it was of similar mass to the Earth although closer to the Sun, which meant hotter surface temperatures and therefore, not a likely target for future colonisation. No probe had been sent there to land by either the Soviets or Americans as of 1965 although the American probe Mariner 2 made a flyby of Venus in December 1962, (that was my first winter in England in a long time) so it was now known that Venus had a baking hot surface and a dense, choking atmosphere, plus a day that was longer than its year.

I was still expecting to see a vision of magnificence, the ancients had regarded it as the planet of love and beauty due to it being the brightest planet in the sky, the 'morning star'. Some more ancient texts referred to it as Lucifer, light of the morning but this fact was little known and only by us as we'd researched it.

I closed my eyes, allowing my consciousness to drift as before and I hoped I would find no limitations. The previous night I had slept well, excited by the project and the prospect of Paul's company therefore there were no factors to hinder my progress. Paul had organised the longitude and declination and had plotted the position of Venus in the sky, nestling in Aquarius quite close to Mercury. I had my bearings and felt bolstered by Paul's faith in me.

The planet loomed into view, a vague colour lacking the vivid canvas that was Earth or the warm hue of Mars. Thankfully, I had enough psychic energy for the journey but I was aware of how draining these journeys were beginning to be. The descent was cloudy and eventually I emerged beneath, surprised to find a turbulent world behind the image of beauty. Winds howled above my head, I was aware of the sound but could not feel the force of it which was a very strange sensation, although I could see the clouds blowing quickly above me and this gave me an idea of it.

The landscape was bleak like the desolation of Mars but this was harsher, it felt very oppressive, if I were here in body I would be crushed by the atmospheric pressure. My initial impression was of the western world's concept of hell; oppression, intensity, turbulence, heat, volcanic environment, dark soil, quite mountainous in places topped by a virulent atmosphere. It truly was hell, without the demons and eternal damnation. I didn't like this world, and mankind would never land here. I gritted my teeth, opened my eyes and jolted back into my body.

Again, my descriptions were recorded. Paul showed me the drawings made from my previous account of the journey to Mars and I was delighted by their accurate representation of what I saw. The colours weren't quite true, but close and I recommended a browner tint to the surface. Paul stored them safely in a box until the whole collection of planets was complete and he would then seal and date them, ready for when NASA or the Soviets finally landed a probe on the surface.

I felt a little tired and, without thinking, Paul put his arms around me. I was surprised but didn't resist. No man had comforted me or given me affection since Max.

"I'm so proud of you and what you have achieved so far," Paul said.

Without realising what message he was sending out to me, he brushed my hair away from my face. Without thinking of the consequences, I leaned close and kissed him as a lover would do. Without resistance, he reciprocated. I broke away and looked at him, pondering whether or not to take the situation further. He had certainly mellowed to me, all the time we had spent together on a shared passion was bringing dividends, he must surely realise that the relationship was becoming more than professional and some serious thought was needed to the consequences. Would we regret it, or would it be a perfect match? And what about Eleanor? Yes, what about Eleanor?

I threw caution to the wind. It was clear to me that Paul and not Max was the man for me. Here was a man who was kind, warm and passionate about sharing his work, he didn't hide anything, not intentionally anyway and he was charismatic. It was now or never.

"I want you to make love to me," I declared.

Paul didn't know what to say. He realised then that he shouldn't have let me kiss him, he wasn't prepared for the consequences and the notion of taking it further. I placed my hands on his chest and looked into his eyes, still aiming to persuade.

"I want you to be my first lover," I continued, "I'm still a virgin, you know."

He told me that he couldn't, it was wrong and unfair on Eleanor.

With regret, he took hold of my hands and I was fleetingly hopeful that he was accepting the offer but he wasn't, he merely released my hands and stroked my face.

"I'm sorry, Tahra. It's not you, it's the situation. I can't do this to Eleanor."

My disappointment was clearly visible and Paul wished circumstances were different. I realised I had made an error of judgement, one of rashness. Instead of giving up hope, I decided next time I would just have to try harder and unleash my talents upon him. It was simply a matter of time before I got what I wanted.

Paul returned home wondering what it would have been like to accept her enticing offer, she was showing him a sensuality that Eleanor didn't possess. He was aware it would not be the last time this opportunity would arise and eventually, the inevitable would happen, which was a disconcerting thought. She was too good to be true, but she was true and he would never, ever find another woman like her. He entered his living room and found Eleanor waiting patiently. At first, he didn't meet her eyes and she immediately became a little suspicious. The fact that he was also somewhat indifferent to her affection was even more disturbing. She was losing him, the passion had gone and she could see it in his eyes. He knew that too, but the most disturbing fact was that he no longer cared that it had gone.

Tahra's next destination was Mercury and the date was 28th February 1965. Paul's 44th birthday came and went unnoticed by Tahra and he hadn't even spent it with Eleanor, not feeling inclined to tell anyone about it. He had shut himself away in his study with a typewriter and Billie Holliday playing in the background but other than that, no contact with the outside world. Eleanor was clearly upset when he emerged late that night and couldn't understand why he had wanted to spend his birthday alone. No explanation was offered. Tahra's company was a pleasant distraction from the difficulties in his relationship with Eleanor, despite the fact that Tahra was actually the cause of those problems.

They sat in the research room with the radio playing quietly in the background. The female vocalist of The Seekers sang '*I could search the whole world over until my life is through, but I know I'll never find another you*', causing Paul and Tahra to exchange a shy but knowing glance. He broke eye contact and fiddled around with the star maps he'd created.

As with Mars and Venus, there were no photographs of Mercury although scientists were well aware it was a small, rocky body baked by the sun on a daily basis. It was the closest planet to the sun and would make for a fantastic viewing. When Earth and Mercury were closest together, there was only a distance of 92 million kilometres between them. Paul had organised the longitude, declination and its position against the backdrop of constellations for the 28th February, Mercury was nestled in Pisces.

This was a magnificent spectacle to behold, the planet was dwarfed by the luminous orb dominating Tahra's vision. The sun was dazzling bright, with flames of light leaping from the surface only to arc back in again. It gave the impression of life, life that was teeming across its surface and exuding from within. It filled the whole of her vision so much so that she almost missed the tiny chunk of rock shadowed by this vast, nuclear giant. The planet itself was dull, a cratered rock but it was the mother of the whole solar system that made the journey so memorable. To be so bathed in light felt energising, she knew in private she would make this trip again.

The next trip wasn't until March 21st, coinciding with the Spring Equinox. Paul, as ever, wanted to push the boundaries and test my limits so decided a trip to Jupiter was in order. Again, there was little data and therefore knowledge of Jupiter was very basic. Although it had been seen through telescopes, no probe had as yet paid it a visit. At its closest to

Earth, it was 628 million kilometres away, the greatest distance as yet Paul had asked of me. He gave me the star chart, with the longitude and declination calculated and its location posited in Aries. I was apprehensive; each task was harder, the requirement of concentration superior to the previous, the distance more formidable and the worlds more alien.

My consciousness separated from my body with ease, which was not the problem, the difficulty lay in the distance. But was this just an issue of distance, or merely one of self belief?

A reddish-orange, striped orb came into view and I had been training my mind to remain focused, a high degree of mental tenacity was necessary now to complete these journeys. Over a period of time, I had been sharpening my external visual acuity, and that practice was now reaping dividends. The image before me was now lucid and clear, and also euphoric. Jupiter was the majestic giant of the solar system and filled my vision. The red spot loomed beneath me, a swirling mass that invited me to dive right in, it was almost like it was calling to me in some undecipherable and non-verbal language but the rational part of my mind decided against it. Surrounding me, as I drew closer, I realised the planet had a faint ring of dust encircling it which I thought peculiar as Saturn had rings, not Jupiter. Looking about me, I spotted a few of the moons not too far away but they were rather uninviting so I returned my focus to the planet itself. I was transfixed; it was calling me so I accepted the invitation and allowed my consciousness to drift further inwards to the core.

I passed through a series of gaseous clouds, which were turbulent but the sensations I felt that were penetrating my consciousness were not threatening, or intimidating, they were feelings of reassurance and an almost divine perception that there was more to life than what was currently offered on Earth. I knew there was a presence there with me, I knew it was trying to communicate with me but I couldn't comprehend the message. I allowed my consciousness to bathe in its presence and endorsed the eddies of gaseous cloud through and around me, not wanting to leave. Eventually, I would see the bigger picture, I just had to tune into what the planet was trying to tell me.

It seemed like an eternity before Paul's words penetrated the veil I had placed around me. His words sounded so distant but rang clearer and clearer like a bell travelling towards me, so that I was forcibly snapped back into my body. I was silent for a long moment.

"I thought I'd lost you there," Paul said, concerned, "it looked like, for a moment... you weren't coming back."

"Huh?" I responded, trying to focus my physical eyes.

"Your breathing... almost stopped." Paul was practically horrified.

"I was fine," I responded, in a daze.

He snapped his fingers in front of my face. I blinked and then seemed to return to reality.

"Are you sure you're all right?" he asked.

I nodded and then realised where I was. Slowly, I sat up in my chair, trying to digest what I had just experienced and then looked Paul in the eye, with an expression of childish amazement.

"It's alive," I whispered.

"What?" Paul responded, unsure what had just happened to me out there.

"The planet," I clarified, "it's alive. I can see it lucidly now, they're all alive. But Jupiter is the most magnanimous force of all, if only you could feel its power..."

Paul didn't know what to say. Part of him didn't believe me, or didn't want to believe me while the other half seemed envious of my ability to touch something so deeply that was beyond this world's confines.

"You're scaring me," he said.

"I need to go back," I declared.

Paul shook his head.

"You gave me a real scare," he admitted, "don't do that to me again."

I silently made a decision to revisit in my own time. Paul and I recorded more factual descriptions of the planet and I retired to The Institute, in a state of euphoria. No matter what Paul said, I had to go back no matter what he believed, the planet was alive and I wished to communicate with it. When I returned to my room, there was a message on my bed. Max wanted to see me first thing in the morning. Surprisingly, my stomach performed a somersault. But why would I feel that way?

And what did he want?

The next morning, Tahra sat in the dining room at The Institute feeling strangely nervous. Max wanted to see her at ten o'clock. It was eight thirty now, he was nowhere to be seen although the remainder of The Institute's 'inmates' were up and about, oblivious to the sense of trepidation she felt. Oscar joined her at breakfast and chatted merrily about the last visit to his family in Barbados. She was glad to see him, in fact, it took the nervous edge off her breakfast. Emilie lurked close by, still innately suspicious of her and Beth smiled warmly. Then eventually they all drifted upstairs for testing or relaxation, leaving Tahra alone with her thoughts.

Why, all of a sudden, out of the blue, did Max want to see her? Did he want to withdraw her from the OOBE project? Was there additional work for her? Or was it personal?

Before long, Miss Tynedale called her through and Tahra entered the office to find Max sat, pondering in his chair. He seemed visibly moved to see her again and couldn't help but notice the mini skirt and go-go boots she was wearing, revealing her firm thighs, so he quickly made eye contact. Tahra was disturbed to find her heart skipped a beat. Tentatively she sat down opposite him, their last encounter at the New Year party foremost in her mind again. Max was the first to speak.

"Well," he began, placing his fingers together, "you've been working on project OOBE for around six months now. How is it all going?"

Tahra felt slightly relieved that the topic was not going to be complicated.

"We've produced some pretty ground breaking results," she responded.

Max smiled. "You mean, you've produced some pretty ground breaking results. Make no bones about it, there would be no project without you."

Tahra blushed somewhat at his admiration.

"There would also be no project without Paul's initial idea," she countered.

Max felt slightly uncomfortable at the way she spoke about Paul.

"So," he continued, "which worlds have you remote viewed?"

She smiled enthusiastically. "The Moon, Mars… Venus, Jupiter…"

Max laughed softly. "Well, that's more than what humanity has achieved so far."

Tahra looked at him, surprised. "You believe me, without asking for proof?"

He gave her a direct stare. "I know what you're capable of. You get most of the work requests. You actually have a waiting list. Why would I question your results?"

His absolute and unquestionable faith seemed odd.

"Anyone else would ask for proof," she said, in wonderment.

He smiled, kindly. "I've been in this business long enough to know that there's more to life than this… material world in which we dwell. I've personally experienced an event..," he paused here, realising he was revealing something he wished to remain hidden, "I see miracles everyday. I'm surrounded by unimaginable talent on a daily basis." Then he added, "But you're the star here, by a long shot. You're truly unique."

Tahra found it difficult to know how to respond to his compliments and smiled awkwardly.

"God must have brought me into the world for this reason," was all she could say.

"You seem to be working productively with Paul," he commented. "It's a coincidence, my two outstanding talents working on the same project…."

She wondered whether or not he was looking for information about a possible relationship with Paul. But then she told herself that was just paranoia, there was no way Max could know of her intentions. Therefore, she needed to be careful about what she revealed, Max would probably not be happy to learn of her proposition to Paul.

Max leaned forward in his chair, looking at her intently.

"Why don't you come round to my house for a drink, tonight?" he propositioned.

Tahra was taken aback and couldn't answer.

"Pardon?" was all she could say.

Max shrugged. "You're the life and soul of The Institute and I don't appreciate that fact enough," he explained, "I'm extending a welcome to my home."

She experienced a conflict within her; part of her leapt for joy at the invitation, yet the other half was afraid. What if he pressured her into sex? What if she relented? Truth was, what did she fear the most? Why was it that she had put, or thought she had put her feelings to rest for him, and then out of the blue he had called a meeting and extended an invitation to his home? Why couldn't he have just let things lie? Was it because he feared losing her, or was it because he simply missed her company?

Without realising what she was doing, she accepted his invitation. Max smiled, broadly.

"John will pick you up at seven," he said.

Tahra then felt a sense of panic wash over her. What was she doing? She had chosen her path, even though Paul hadn't given in yet, so why was she accepting Max's invitation? Maybe, just maybe, she was meant to decide for once and for all.

The day passed by so quickly that she was sat in John's car before she knew it. She wore a maxi dress with a lace panel at the chest but had left her hair down, so she didn't look too dressy. The journey to Max's home took place just before sun set but the scenery wasn't familiar as the last time she rode this route, it was New Year and dark back then. Max's home was a little smaller than The Establishment, where she worked with Paul and was the old coach house to the main building. As the car drew up to the door, she was already having second thoughts. Max opened the door as soon as the car drew up and he walked over to them, opening the door for Tahra in a chivalrous manner. She swung her legs round and got out of the car elegantly then Max took her by the arm and led her inside.

It was much like she remembered it from New Year, albeit much quieter as it was not full of people. She noticed the hallway where she had kissed Max at the New Year party. The house had a different feel, it felt like a home with two armchairs by a crackling fire, soft lighting and 2 empty glasses on the coffee table, with a selection of wine bottles ready to be opened. She was invited to sit in the most comfortable seat and Max sat opposite her, asking politely which wine she preferred and then he poured two glasses of it.

At first, he noticed she looked awkward but after a glass of wine she mellowed and looked much more relaxed. Max appeared more comfortable in his own surroundings and after a glass of wine, he too appeared more relaxed, more human in fact.

They made polite conversation at first, then as the wine took hold, Max steered the discussion towards project OOBE as he wanted to hear the qualitative side of her experiences. Tahra was happy to share these experiences, Paul was the only one who was normally privy to the wondrous experiences she'd had. Max listened intently, pondering carefully everything she said. Then she reached the point at which she paid Jupiter a visit.

"You know something, and you probably won't believe me," she stated, "but I got a strong impression that it's alive."

She awaited the impact of her statement on Max and she expected an expression of incredulity, however, his response was in complete contrast to her expectations.

"Why do you think I won't believe you," he said, softly, "after what I've observed in experiments at The Institute?"

"Well," she began, "isn't it, a little crazy to think that a planet is alive?"

Max smiled. "I'm not a scientist, Tahra. My interests lie in furthering understanding and breaking boundaries, but I don't believe that everything must be measured. I'm aware that to really prove something, some degree of measurement is required but that should never obstruct the most fundamental cosmic truths, especially as the most amazing qualitative experiences will leave a deep impression on our consciousness."

Tahra was surprised such words of wisdom could leave Max's lips.

"You've had an experience," she said, absolutely convinced that something truly pivotal happened to Max that changed his whole perception of the world.

A strange expression came over Max's face, as if he was remembering something that stimulated a yearning, a craving for that experience to happen again.

"Please," Tahra continued, "tell me."

He opened his mouth but no words came out, then finally he said, "It's in the past, there's no point in discussing it."

Tahra realised that he was never going to share the most significant experience of his life with her. Would he, in fact, share it with anyone? It was frustrating for her, it held the key to what drove Max and what made him the man he was.

"Your experience is the reason for The Establishment and The Institute," she said, with certainty.

He smiled, not surprised by her shrewd observation. "I want to understand the secrets of the cosmos more than anyone but I have my life as a businessman, which is a necessity. None of this," he referred to not only his home but The Establishment and The Institute, "would be here if it weren't for that fact. Some things are a means to an end, things... I'm not proud of." At this point, he realised too much was already being revealed and he created a diversion by topping her glass up, and his.

But Tahra didn't want to let the topic go, or give up on the hope of finding out who Max really was now that the opportunity was presenting itself.

"What things are you not proud of?" she asked, directly.

He looked at her with a fleeting expression of terror then he shifted awkwardly in his seat.

"Things you should not concern yourself with," he said, not rudely but directly.

Tahra looked disappointed.

"I'm just trying to protect you," he responded.

"I want to understand you," she pushed.

Max looked concerned. "Are you sure you want to understand me? Would you like what you found out? Why can't you be content with what you can see?"

Tahra looked at him intently. "Because what I can see runs deep, I can see into the heart of a person and if I perceive darkness in a man's soul, then I need to understand it before I can accept it."

He didn't expect that answer and felt very disconcerted, so much so that he got up and disappeared into an adjoining room. Although she was not invited, she followed him and found him in a study with a large oak desk and shelves of books.

"What are you afraid of?" she asked him.

Max looked round, fear apparent in his eyes. The night was not turning out how he expected.

"Leave this subject," he said, with clear authority. It was an order not a request.

She bit her lip, feeling so near yet far from the truth.

"Then why did you bring me here?" she asked, directing the conversation towards answers designed to make him feel vulnerable.

He replied with disappointment, "To resurrect what we had," he answered, "to offer to share what I have in this world with you." He looked for her response, which was one of surprise. "This home… it could all be yours too," he continued, "you'd never want for anything. I'm a rich man, but I'm also a rich, single man."

Tahra realised he was laying his cards on the table. His offer was tempting, there was still some residual attraction which she had been repressing and he really did have a lot to offer. But was it right for her? Would it be a terrible mistake?

He took advantage of the fact she was caught off guard and walked over to her, standing before her. She didn't push him away so gently, he stroked her face with his hand. Tahra looked at him, now in the vulnerable position.

"So," he pushed, "what is it to be?"

She didn't have an answer and Max began to feel frustrated. It was difficult to remain patient after so many false starts.

"Love cannot be bought," she stated, simply.

Max sighed. "Any other woman would have married me long ago," he said, turning the responsibility for failure upon her.

She didn't respond well to this and replied, "In case you hadn't noticed, I'm not any woman."

Max found it hard to remain tolerant.

"What more do you want, Tahra?" he asked, clearly aggravated.

"No secrets," was her direct response. "I want a man who is not afraid to show who he really is."

Max bit his lip, realising there was a stalemate. He could offer her everything in the material world, but not this one thing. Sighing, he withdrew and sat on the desk, discouraged.

"Let me know when you change your mind," she said. "Now, I'd like to go home."

Without a word to her, Max called John, he arrived fifteen minutes later and Tahra left, with a steely resolve. She strode elegantly towards the door, opening and closing it without looking behind her. Max watched her go in silence, gripping his wine glass tightly then, when the door had closed, he hurled it at the wall.

The forays into the solar system continued, with a journey to Saturn on the 13th April 1965. I found it an inferior experiential trip in comparison with Jupiter, which I yearned to visit again as I felt there was something important it had to tell me. Saturn was easy to focus on due to its distinct rings and it was much like I expected it, yet it felt cold and authoritative, with an almost repellent vibration. Without thinking, I wistfully pictured Jupiter in my mind and suddenly found my consciousness drawn back to the gaseous giant. In little time at all, I was basking in its glow again, poised above the turbulent clouds. I wasn't aware of the change in my breathing, if anything, I felt more and more at peace. That same sense of reassurance was there again, almost divine, euphoric. It felt as if a presence penetrated my consciousness, like it had previously and this time, I felt closer to it and its message. Just as I thought that something was about to be revealed, Paul's words brought me back with a jolt.

"Tahra!"

I was none too pleased.

"What did you do that for?" *I asked indignantly.*

"You're scaring me again," *he said.*

"I'm fine," *I insisted.*

"I'm just looking out for you," *he said, a little offended,* "I'm responsible for your safety and well being during these experiments."

I smiled apologetically and explained myself.

"I... felt myself drawn back to Jupiter. When I was there last, I got the impression it had something to tell me. I just want to be allowed to hear the message."

Paul was sympathetic.

"It's just that... you seem to enter some strange... trance for want of a better word. Your breathing slows to a point where it's barely perceptible. I don't want to have a put an end to these experiments, but I will if I see persistent danger."

I gave him a concerned look.

"Anything of real value and discovery is risky. We can't let it get in the way of progress."

Paul knew I was right, but it wasn't worth death.

"But what if you... die? Surely you don't want that to happen?" Paul said, incredulously.

I was determined not to let anything stand in the way of something truly awe inspiring happening.

"If the worst comes to the worst, then resuscitate me," I said, almost ruthlessly.

He swallowed hard and I sensed his apprehension, reaching over to squeeze his hand.

"Let me try again," I insisted.

Paul wasn't sure. Could he actually resuscitate me if the necessity arose? Was it worth the risk? My eyes were pleading with him, and against his better judgement he agreed.

I closed my eyes and my consciousness slipped easily, in a moment I had returned to the previous location. I bathed in the planet's presence, waiting for that imminent contact. In my urgency to hear the message, I actually felt myself drifting away from the reassurance of its presence but rather than get frustrated, I realised that the link I had previously found with the resident entity was only accessible by letting go. I allowed it to penetrate my consciousness again, not thinking about any changes in my condition that Paul would have to deal with.

I felt my consciousness slide further into the planet, it was a peculiar feeling and I sensed the connection to my body loosen. Paul took hold of my wrist and checked for a pulse, his touch was barely perceptible yet it was reassuring. I reached a point of stillness, as if my consciousness had paused for breath and I looked all around me. The clouds had become more luminous and they swirled, making indiscriminate forms. Gradually, almost imperceptible at first, a message was coming through. Rather than eagerly ask for the message, I let go further and it began to become clearer. Then, it exploded in front of my eyes, causing me to laugh out loud; it was half spoken and half visual, burned into my consciousness like a cosmic branding iron. I wanted to scream, laugh and cry at the same time but nothing came out now. Instead, I accepted it. It was a word, one word. That one word was Satus.

17

The First Time

The word made little sense to Tahra yet it was full of meaning. It was a word she knew contained some special significance and it did seem familiar in some way, perhaps it could even be some ancient cosmic language. Paul wasn't much of a linguist although he was intrigued. When Tahra returned to The Institute, she perused a few foreign language dictionaries and eventually found the etymology and meaning of the word. It was Latin and the meaning was 'origin' or 'seed', an appropriate word as they were embarking on a new adventure. However, she wasn't sure what was to be inferred from that; was Jupiter the origin of something, or did 'satus' refer to the beginning of something else? And why had she heard Latin in particular?

She wrote the key word 'satus' in big letters on a piece of paper and scribbled the translations around it, then sellotaped it to the mirror. It was important, although at the moment, its real significance was unclear but one day, she knew it would all make sense.

Now, there came a point in May of 1965 where Tahra reached the edge of the solar system. She'd visited Uranus; an electric blue, luminous giant spinning on its side; giant Neptune as blue as the sea with a dark spot and skittish white clouds and tiny Pluto; rocky, icy and brown with its twin, Charon not too far away. The trips had been documented through the sketches of an artist and filed away, waiting verification from the future probes of NASA and the USSR. Paul knew that repeat journeys should be made to validate the previous descriptions and show some sort of reliability, yet he felt impatient to find some inhabited world to explore. The final planet, Pluto, had been viewed on the 7th May 1965 and had served as an anti-climax to the tour of the solar system. It hadn't been much to look at, a small rocky body in comparison with the four majestic giants previously viewed.

Paul sat in his study, perusing the entries he'd written in the journal, reflecting on what had been achieved so far and where he could possibly take the project from this point onward. Idly, he listened to the radio, his only contact with the outside world. The news of the day was the impending declaration of independence from the United Kingdom by Rhodesia, as white voters had overwhelmingly backed the Prime Minister Ian Smith's Rhodesian Front. The British Prime Minister, Harold Wilson's voice could be heard warning Mr. Smith of the consequences of *'defying Britain, the whole of the Commonwealth and nearly the whole of Africa and the United Nations.'*

He closed the journal, caring less and less for the outside world and realised that he didn't feel a sense of achievement, he felt empty. Paul shared this desire with Tahra on the phone. She was pleased to hear from him but wondered why he was calling out of the blue.

"Is everything all right?" she asked him, concerned.

He smiled, unseen. "No disasters," he said simply.

"Well, what do you want to talk to me about?" she asked, a little hopeful that he desired her company that night.

He paused, unsure how to begin.

"Tahra, do you think that the OOBE project isn't… fulfilling its potential?" he asked her.

She wasn't sure of his point.

"Are you not happy with my work?" she replied, concerned she wasn't pleasing him.

"Oh, yes of course, that's not the problem," he answered quickly, "no, you're wonderful, absolutely wonderful."

"Then you're not satisfied with the project," she said.

"I'm not," he admitted, "I need more, I need… other worlds

with alien beings, an undiscovered civilisation… contact with some other race in the cosmos, something outstanding."

She was silent for a long moment then spoke, quite softly.

"I don't know if I'm powerful enough," she responded.

Paul disagreed.

"You've already exceeded my expectations. This project would be nothing without you, I'm indebted to you for taking it so far already. It's just me, I never feel… satisfied. There's always more. I don't know if you understand where I'm coming from."

Tahra did know where he was coming from.

"There is always more, and I know I was put here on this Earth to do so much more. Maybe you are too. Maybe we're both meant to do that… together."

"This is the most important project I've ever been involved with, well, the most meaningful one to me anyway. I'm honoured that you've shared this journey with me and given it meaning," Paul said affectionately. "In fact, you have given my life meaning. We did this together."

Tahra was genuinely touched by his words.

"You know I'd do anything to make this project successful," she said, sincerely.

Paul valued her commitment.

"I take it you're willing to push the boundaries further."

"I want to know what's out there as much as you do. I remember as a child listening to 'Journey into Space' on the radio, wishing I could have adventures on the Moon and no one took me seriously when I wanted to be an astronaut. Now I can realise those aspirations."

"Then we'll take this a stage further. I couldn't do this without your encouragement… I couldn't do this without you."

"And you have given my life meaning too," she told him, "you believe in me and push me to being more than I am."

"I'll see you on the 25th then," he said. "I can't wait."

"Looking forward to it," she reassured him.

They placed their respective telephone receivers down and looked thoughtful. Was this actually possible, striving for the stars? What would they find? But this was what Paul had wanted for the project all along and it had been a huge relief to share that desire with her. She was a friend in addition to being the instrument of exploration and he valued her unshakeable belief in the project. He just wished she'd believe in her own abilities more. She was a truly gifted individual who had genuinely been put on Earth for a distinct reason and this was surely it. Now he just had to search the star charts for a destination.

While Paul remained lost in thought, Eleanor moved away from the door to his study at home. She felt sick to her stomach but she had known the truth all along, Paul had feelings for someone else. The way he spoke to the person on the other end of the line had the sort of affection that was normally only expressed to a love interest, or potential love interest. She wondered if it was the young woman he had been speaking to at the New Year party, as ever since then, Paul had become more and more distant. Their relationship was now at the point where they scarcely had any interaction. He had spent his birthday alone and it was quite a few months now since he'd shown any interest in sex. The project was consuming his time and his passion, and Eleanor knew she could never compete with this or share this with him. Obviously, the other person at the end of the line could. Eleanor knew what to do now.

In the background, 'You've Lost That Loving Feeling' drifted over the airwaves, unnoticed by Paul but Eleanor had not missed its significance.

The study door remained open yet he was engrossed in star charts. Potential destinations were the only thing he cared about and there were a number of stars relatively close by, in astronomical terms, for example Alpha Centauri was only 4 light years away and Sirius was about double that. It occurred to him that even light took several years to reach them, but consciousness seemed to possess a quality that superseded light, for it had taken Tahra little time at all to reach the planets. An explanation of this expediency eluded him at the moment, but the mechanics of it were not a matter of urgency, only the practicalities.

Three in the morning and he sat in his armchair, chin nodded to his chest and star maps on his lap. The lamp was still lit and the radio was off station. He never noticed the activity that was going on upstairs and didn't wake until late in the morning. The sun had already risen although the heavy curtains blotted out the full intensity of its rays, but it was the sound of the door closing that woke him. There was a strange silence in the house that he couldn't fathom and he sat for several minutes before moving the map with the intention of making a cup of tea.

As he walked through the sitting room, he realised there was something a little awry. Paul wandered into the kitchen then proceeded up the stairs. Entering the bedroom he was surprised, albeit not disappointed to see that Eleanor was not in the bedroom. She wasn't in the bathroom either. There were none of her clothes lying around and he also checked the wardrobe to find the things she normally kept in there were missing. He sat on the bed, trying to take in what had happened. It wasn't really a surprise, he had practically ignored her since New Year and had grown more distant as the weeks went by. If anything, he was almost relieved she had gone. What perturbed him was that he now had no reason to turn down Tahra's amorous requests; there was nothing to hide behind anymore. He was free to choose now with no restrictions. If he told Tahra about Eleanor, he knew she would make her move and he knew what he would do this time. Maybe he'd consider saying nothing, for his and her sake.

The next experiment was scheduled for the 21st May 1965 and I arrived tingling with excitement. Synonymous with the new impetus the project was taking, Paul had also adopted a new look. He asked my opinion on the sideburns he was cultivating and the length of his hair, which was *starting to curl past the collar of his shirt. I reassured him it was acceptably fashionable, although I didn't add 'for his age'.*

He was undoubtedly nervous about this journey of consciousness. I was nervous for him too and concerned that I wouldn't be able to pull it off. We looked at each other with an expression of 'we're about to do something really important here'. Taking the 'hot seat' was like taking a step into the unknown.

Paul showed me the star map and pinpointed the location of Sirius, not the nearest star to Earth but certainly the brightest and the one with connections to ancient Egypt. Out of all of them he deemed it the most worthy of a visit, he wasn't sure why he'd thought of ancient Egypt but it had appeared to him in a dream about me for some reason. He had carried out a little research on the importance of Sirius and found that the first night it was seen, or its rising marked the New Year, which coincided with the flooding of the Nile. Therefore, its marking of a new cycle was highly appropriate in terms of the next step taken in the OOBE project.

I didn't feel like my usual confident self and without thinking, Paul gave my hand a squeeze, I reciprocated with a return squeeze. Briefly, I detected a subtle change in the way he looked at me but now wasn't the time to ponder on its significance. I simply studied the star map, pictured the desired location in my mind and allowed my consciousness to drift.

The initial process flowed as smoothly as normal, hovering above the Earth happened instantaneously but it was difficult to focus on the new destination. The objective of the mission lay so far away that it was difficult to visualise and it did not come into focus at all. Usually I could picture the terminus of the journey and could 'snap' to it with relative ease but this wasn't happening today for some reason. Previously, there had been times when I'd struggled yet had overcome my doubts and used pure determination to conquer obstacles but this time around, the sheer distance made the target more elusive.

Paul urged me to try again and I focused intensely, pinpointing the target from the stellar background but it wasn't working. I felt too weak psychically to achieve the objective and my initial concern regarding not being powerful enough was not unfounded. Paul insisted that it was just because I didn't believe in myself but I tried to explain how I was travelling a certain distance and was running out of steam. The object was too unknown to be able to visualise clearly and I felt this was a large part of the problem. Another significant factor was the distance my consciousness was required to travel and the sheer magnitude of separation from my physical body. The last issue was picking out an object in the vastness of the cosmos. What was most frustrating was that I felt conquering these problems would take a lot of practice and time, lots of it, a lifetime maybe.

"I would have to train my mind on a daily basis for months, possibly even years," I explained, sadly.

Paul refused to accept this.

"Don't give up on me," he said, "I know you can do this."

"Everyone has their limits," I responded, "even me."

He sighed. "I can't force you, maybe we could try another day."

I had something else in mind.

"I don't want to spend months training the hard way. You're a scientist, I can see you build machines." I pointed to the camera he used to observe bio-electromagnetic fields. "Create something that will help me, speed up the process."

Paul was surprised, he hadn't considered this.

"It's certainly something I could think about."

It was definitely something he should think about.

"Call me when you've got an idea. Then we can make progress."

Paul was happy to surrender the day to move onto a bigger concept. He must have realised I was reaching my limits, yet was eager to move the boundaries and extend out of the comfort zone. I would do whatever necessary to make his project a success.

The new direction for the OOBE project was definitely something to think about, I didn't want to give Tahra the impression that I would certainly be able to construct something but I had a few ideas worth exploring based on my research from the 1950s conducted at The Establishment. In fact, it tied in to the project Max had assigned me concerning blocking remote viewing, the project that I had stalled in favour of OOBE and the one which Max would soon expect a progress report.

Much of my previous work had revolved around the effects of electromagnetic fields on people, particularly on their physiology as well as their mental state. It would be interesting to adapt the methodology and equipment to affect the bio-electromagnetic field itself, to intensify the field of Tahra which was already vibrant and powerful. However, for the more advanced task of stellar travel, it could be useful to amplify this field to increase Tahra's out of body potential. Another factor I could work with was the resonant frequency, using an oscillator. My previous research highlighted some destructive frequencies that had mild to powerful effects upon the physiology of people, there had to be a frequency that would yield more positive results and enhance the out of body experience.

Consequently, there also had to be a frequency that would disrupt the bio-electromagnetic field and hinder remote viewing. I was banking on finding both. I didn't want to risk permanently inhibiting Tahra's capabilities but it was a double edged sword, to find what I was truly looking for, I may have to put her through hell first.

By early June I had played around with the equipment and was ready to start testing a few resonant frequencies on Tahra, after a process of elimination from previous experiments. I knew which ones were harmful or undesired to the body's physiology so had a good starting point.

On the 3rd June, something strange and quite surreal transpired. It was the evening and I was in my office at The Establishment, reviewing the old research data from the experiments I had conducted here in the 1950s. I was watching the evening news on a small black and white television, in particular one news item that made me smile; American astronaut Ed White had performed a space walk, floating free of his capsule, Gemini IV for twenty one minutes. If only he knew, Tahra had succeeded at this with her consciousness long before. But then I had an unexpected visit from her. There was something about her I couldn't put my finger on and an odd intensity about her. I looked at her, not displeased, just surprised.

"How are you today?" I asked her.

She didn't answer this question and actually appeared to be concerned, so in a way she had responded, albeit non-verbally.

"What's troubling you?" I asked her.

Finally, after what seemed a long moment, she replied, "Do you realise what you're doing?"

I was taken aback, this was not the Tahra I knew.

"Of course," I answered, "have you got... cold feet?"

"You need to think of the consequences," she stated, oddly keeping her distance from me.

I could only look at her with a puzzled expression on my face. The new direction of the OOBE project was her own idea, she was the one pushing it further than I dared so why would she question the outcome?

"This is something you want as much as me," I said, softly, "the consequences can only be positive, we'll achieve our objective."

She shook her head, almost frustrated.

"No, no," she insisted, "you must think about the repercussions of pushing the boundaries too quickly. What happened when Pandora opened the box?"

"But if we stay in the comfort zone," I countered, "we'll never learn anything, or evolve."

Tahra breathed deeply to stay calm.

"It'll change everything," she said, sadly.

"Isn't that what we want? Don't worry," I reassured her, "don't forget that Pandora shut the box just before Hope escaped. It will all be worth it."

She realised my mind couldn't be swayed and changed her tactic.

"Don't go beyond sixty five," she cautioned, "sixty five is safe, but seventy five isn't. Remember this."

"I don't understand what you mean, Tahra."

I could see her fears were not allayed but rather than explain herself, she simply turned and left me sat there, still puzzled. I didn't hear a door slam but when I chased after her, she had already left the building.

It was a bizarre visit, so unlike her yet it clearly was her. I did have second thoughts about the next experiment but I decided to plough on regardless. Today was a blip. She would realise she was hasty in her anxiety.

Paul and Tahra finally met for another experiment on the 21st June 1965. It was a glorious day for the summer solstice and Paul sat in the back garden with a cup of tea and the newspaper. He perused it, skimming over reports of the US using B52 bombers to attack National Liberation Front guerrilla fighters in South Vietnam, a war fought thousands of miles from The Establishment and thousands of miles from project OOBE. After skipping the fashion section on Mary Quant and Vidal Sassoon's latest styles, he noticed Tahra had appeared out of the back door, relieved that she had found him. She appeared breezy and enthusiastic, eager to see the equipment that he had designed and the methods he would use. He seemed wary of her at first, puzzled by the swing in her mood yet again and she noticed his confused expression.

"What's wrong?" she asked him.

"I thought you wanted to be cautious with the OOBE project," he began.

"Why would you think that?" she questioned, mystified.

"Well, you came to see me, remember? You requested I think more about the consequences."

Her response was unexpected.

"I haven't seen you since the last experiment," she replied, confused.

Now Paul was confused.

"No, honestly, you paid me a visit a few weeks ago. You were adamant about the potential repercussions of what we're doing."

Tahra just looked at him blankly. He gave up.

"You must have been dreaming," she concluded, "they seem so real sometimes. Maybe it's your subconscious mind expressing your fears about the project. Conscious awareness is only the tip of the iceberg, the unconscious determines our behaviour just as much. The ego manages the id; takes our instinctive, primitive and even our psychic urges and expresses them in socially acceptable ways. It deals with reality, weighs the costs and benefits of an action. The image of me was a representation of the ego managing the fears contained within the id."

Paul shrugged; it had seemed real, very convincing in fact, as persuasive as her argument. But Tahra was no liar, her behaviour on arrival was totally unlike the mysterious visit a few weeks ago so he had to conclude he had, in fact, been dreaming and that the image of her had indeed simply been his unconscious mind trying to express some repressed fear about the project. There could be no other explanation.

"What have you created for me?" she asked, changing the subject because she was keen to hear the update.

"Well," Paul began, "I've been looking at harmonic frequencies using an oscillator."

Tahra laughed.

"In English, please."

"Vibration," he explained, "everything vibrates at a certain frequency; buildings, bridges, bodies… consciousness. Acoustic resonance was enough to bring down the walls of Jericho, its effects are underestimated. If I find the harmonic or resonant frequency of consciousness, I believe I can stimulate it, amplify it but not destroy it."

"It will make me more powerful?" she queried.

Paul shrugged.

"It's just a hypothesis, I can't guarantee anything."

"Will it be harmful?" she asked.

"I wouldn't do anything to hurt you. I'm aware of previous research highlighting destructive resonant frequencies but I haven't yet found the precise vibration for consciousness. It's just as likely I'll find the frequency that disrupts remote viewing, as well as the one that amplifies it."

"Would it permanently… disrupt my consciousness?" she asked, nervously.

Paul shook his head. "All of my experience with resonant frequencies shows that once the oscillator is turned off, the effect ceases. To bring down walls, the resonance needs to be persistent.

However, I think consciousness is more durable, like light."

"Your experience with resonant frequencies?" she questioned, raising an eyebrow.

Paul looked regretful.

"Something I'm not proud of," he said, clearly.

He sounded like another Max. But, unlike Max, would he share it with her?

"Did you hurt anyone?" she enquired, softly.

He lowered his eyes guiltily.

"Yes. At first, I was just testing for the existence of a field, looking for the soul initially but then it became a project to test the effects of electromagnetic fields on people, both their physiology and psychology. The testing gave way to an investigation into psychological warfare, we used electromagnetic fields and resonance on people to induce anxiety, mental illness, psychosis… you name it. We tried to wipe memories, we gave people hallucinogenic drugs… without their knowledge or consent, pretty nasty stuff really. It was a low point of my life, although I was finally removed from it to work at The Institute."

"You worked at The Institute?"

"Yes, the most rewarding experience I've had until now. I studied all the residents there. It made me feel closer to my goal."

"Your goal?"

"To find out what it's all about. Why are we here? Why was humanity created? What is the purpose of the universe? Is there a God?"

Tahra's heart skipped a beat. He was truly a man with a mission and he was a man capable of finding the answers. She was honoured he was sharing that with her.

"And you'll play a major part in that discovery," he continued. "Science thinks it has many answers, how it was all created but it can never answer the most fundamental and crucial question… why? There is a reason for everything. Biology tells us we are physical bodies with the sole purpose of reproducing.

Yet I know humanity goes way beyond the physical body and I know this because of what I've researched. But why maintain a species just simply to reproduce? It makes no sense. It serves no real purpose."

"We all have a real purpose in life," she agreed. "I know I have an important reason to be here on Earth. I just wish I knew what it is," she lamented.

"I think you're fulfilling that purpose right now," Paul answered, confidently. "You were made for this project."

He instilled such confidence in her it was addictive, much like the way Max's power and attention was addictive. She realised how much she missed the attention of a man, a good man. Reaching out with her fingertips, she touched Paul's arm and lightly stroked it, closing her eyes and visualising a wave of pleasure curling up his spine. She heard him gasp slightly, so she sent another wave of pleasure. Opening her eyes, she enjoyed his expression of pleasure, this time she knew he wouldn't push her away. It was a little unfair in a way, she had the advantage in that she possessed the ability to affect the emotions and energy of others, and the capacity to scout a situation and discover no one stood in her way anymore. Eleanor was gone so he had no morals to consider. Finally it was time to move in for the kill.

Paul had been trying to avoid the inevitable but she made him feel like that was not a bad thing. Finally relinquishing, he kissed her and pulled her over to his chair and she sat on his lap. It was the most intense kiss he had ever experienced, perhaps one they had both been waiting for. Her body was a pleasure to explore and he appreciated the contrast of her skin colour against his. He removed the flowery silk blouse she was wearing and she removed his shirt, slowly unbuttoning it before savouring his touch on her breasts and body. The feeling of the fresh morning air on their bodies was invigorating and conducive to nakedness.

Realising that they couldn't continue on the rickety garden chair, he placed his hands under her buttocks and carried her over to a smooth area of grass, which was a little more private from any prying eyes viewing the scene from a window. He hoped no one would see, although The Establishment was not busy at the moment. He suppressed her giggling with a rain of kisses, laying on top of her and he progressed to explore her body with his lips and teeth, removing her clothing with care. In many ways, it was like that moment in the States with Max; the anticipation, the pleasure of a man's lips on the most intimate part of her body… except Paul didn't allow her to climax, instead he lay on top of her again and spoke to her softly.

"Is this really going to be your first time?" he asked her.

She nodded.

He fully appreciated what she was giving him and kissed her with a passion he had not felt in a long time. For her first time, it was an intense experience and he was careful to keep a steady rhythm, as he wanted it to be a perfect introduction. Tahra coordinated her own body movements with his and they maintained eye contact throughout. Once she had become used to the feel of him inside of her, she focused on using her gift to send waves of energy coiling up his spine. Unlike Max, he didn't respond with fear, instead he embraced it, his breathing deepened and he opened himself to the experience. He wasn't selfish and focused on her pleasure too and only let himself climax once she had done so. When it was over, he lay quietly beside her, feeling completely drained by the whole experience.

She spoke softly into his ear.

"I've decided that I like sex," she declared, "we must do this every time we meet."

Paul laughed and hugged her.

"We'd never finish the project."

"Then we must meet more often."

Was that something he wanted? Laying next to her, he felt as content as she, she was his prize and he was the luckiest man in the world. Yes, it was something he wanted. But he wanted to complete the project too. He sat up, or otherwise he would fall asleep.

"We have work to do," he insisted.

She didn't disagree and remembered what they were supposed to be doing, so they both got dressed. He kissed her to conclude the intimacy of the session but then realised he wasn't ready to head to the research room, a wave of pleasure crept up his spine and he felt ready to repeat the whole experience. In retrospect, it now seemed foolish refusing her, if only he'd known how good it would be.

I don't know why that particular day I gave in, but I had no regrets. As a forty four year old man, a young woman just turned twenty is indeed a prize to cherish, especially one so beautiful and talented. Why did I not give in previously, when it was clear that I didn't love Eleanor? Maybe I didn't feel worthy, which is foolish. Maybe I felt guilty, assuming I would be exploiting such a young woman. It's hard not to become attached to someone you work closely with, when you know that the most significant piece of work you will produce in your life is directly related to their success or failure.

Any sense of guilt dissipated quickly, as she was the driving force behind this union. The age gap was difficult to get used to at first and she certainly saw the world with different eyes, but there were still some delightfully old fashioned values that she upheld. The project acted as common ground that connected us and transcended the twenty odd year age gap and, if anything, I needed that injection of young blood into my life.

I did start to see more of her from then. We socialised locally to get away from the intensity of the project, ironically frequenting the very pub I'd taken her to on a previous birthday. She became quite proficient at horse riding and we enjoyed outings to the cinema.

I also attempted to teach her to drive that summer, nerve wracking for me and an adventure for her, she refused to accept that she couldn't drive using remote viewing to check the road was clear ahead, or know which direction to take. I've never gripped a seat so hard in my entire life and feared for the life of my beloved Triumph Spitfire. Subsequently, I found reasons to avoid letting her behind the wheel.

The sex was an entirely different experience. I don't know whether it's the close proximity of her bio-electromagnetic field or whether it's something she deliberately does but my whole body surges with energy every time. The thought of sex with her had crossed my mind on numerous occasions prior to it happening but making it reality is another thing. Maybe I had believed the idea was more intriguing and that the reality would spoil it, I was wrong however, it was the other way round. She was a naturally sexual being and never let an opportunity slip by to enjoy her favourite activity, I always found it difficult to say no but I was comfortable with that. She was not afraid to experiment; maybe she was making up for lost time.

However, the OOBE project was the priority as well as being the cohesive force of our relationship. We fed each other's enthusiasm, almost daring the other to break all boundaries, a very sixties thing really without the drugs. The project took the place of drugs, and I felt no need to introduce her to LSD to induce a profound experience, because what we were doing was more real.

The project needed to move forward and for it to do that, I needed to understand more about the circumstances in which Tahra was able to project her consciousness. This was the key and at that point, I couldn't have imagined the profound nature of the events that followed.

In all my work with resonant frequencies, I had not found one in particular that equated with projection of the consciousness. That was mainly because my prior research with resonant frequencies had not focused on remote viewing and I had not met Oscar, George or Tahra. Before I was willing to play around with an oscillator, I connected Tahra to an EEG to measure her brainwave activity during her sessions. The results were very revealing. I found that Tahra could switch straight from beta wave activity, in the range of 14Hz to 30Hz at the drop a hat and quickly enter theta wave state in the range of 5Hz to 8Hz, without moving through a normal relaxed state known as alpha wave state, *between the frequencies of 9Hz to 14Hz. Beta wave state is a normal state of alertness which enables us to carry out day to day activities, at the higher range the brain engages in intense debate. Alpha wave state is relaxed, when we wind down in preparation for sleep or take a walk in the park. Theta wave state is interesting; it is equated with daydreaming and that time just after we awake, when the mind is at its most receptive and creative. When Tahra projected her consciousness, she was in theta. The precise frequency at which her consciousness left her body was 7.8Hz.*

I was no longer a virgin, the loss of which I had put off for a long time. Finding a worthy man had been a challenge and my access to worthy members of the opposite sex had been quite restricted to, basically, Max. Why did I insist on waiting until marriage and then give in to Paul, even though there had been no proposal or commitment even? I knew he was right for me and I knew he was a good man at heart. Max was extremely attractive and wealthy but he didn't share his life in the way that Paul was clearly capable.

I quickly came to the decision that I liked sex; it was physically pleasurable and I liked the sense of power it gave me over a man. I also liked to give pleasure, don't be mistaken, I am not a selfish person. I was fortunate to be able to control my fertility with a pill, something I would never be able to do in my home country. I wanted to enjoy sex for its own sake and was not ready to bring a child into the world. Being with someone totally was a new experience, and that had never happened with Max. Paul was much more open to the experience of what I called the awakening of the fire within whereas Max regarded it as something to be afraid of, that equated with a lack of trust and I knew Paul trusted me implicitly as he never questioned what I was doing.

Socially, we were active and he was a warm and pleasant companion, with the ability to laugh at himself and life in general, he wasn't stiff and uncomfortable like Max; he was easy going yet dynamic, relaxed yet authoritative if that makes any sense. I loved the way he could speak his mind, he never clammed up like Max, he was forthright and honest which was refreshing.

For a short while that summer, he took it upon himself to teach me to drive. I was grateful we didn't use the communal pale blue Ford Popular parked outside The Establishment, which was meant for staff to use in their duties there. Instead, he allowed me to slip behind the wheel of his Triumph Spitfire, a sleek and sporty number. At first, operating the clutch, accelerator and brake while trying to steer, and watch the road ahead was hard to grasp but I was determined to master it and Paul was a patient teacher. Once I had the basics, it occurred to me that I could become a more competent driver by using my remote viewing capabilities to see much further down the road ahead or check that directions were correct. I would never get lost!

"Tahra, that's cheating!" Paul objected.

"But why is that cheating?" I countered. "I'm not sitting an exam!"

"Because… that's not the way you drive," Paul insisted, weakly.

"If everyone else could use remote viewing to assist driving a car, they would," I told him.

"You need to keep your physical eyes on the road ahead at all times and look in your centre mirror," he insisted further.

"I'll just remote view in short bursts, when a panoramic view is required," I partially relented.

I pushed my consciousness up above the car so I could get a bird's eye view. I saw myself driving, and clearly noted the crossroads up ahead and a car approaching it so I switched back to a point in my skull so that I could make the right manoeuvres when I got to the junction.

"This is where remote viewing is very useful," I explained, "as I knew there was a car approaching the crossroads before I even got close to it."

On subsequent days, I was more confident behind the wheel and was prepared to take more risks with remote viewing and driving. Using a bird's eye view, I could see a straight stretch of road so put my foot down on the accelerator, seeing what the Spitfire could do. Paul began to look nervous as I could see he was gripping the seat tightly. I came up on a Morris Minor very quickly, and got frustrated as it was being driven much too slowly. Because we were on a country road, we encountered a series of s-bends, making it difficult to overtake. I pushed my consciousness far ahead, as if I was accelerating ahead of the car. I felt myself rushing at speed like a racing car around a series of bends and I could see there were no other cars coming in the opposite direction, so I put my foot down hard on the accelerator, pulled out and overtook.

"Tahra," Paul objected, "you can't overtake on a bend, you need to see that the road ahead is clear."

"But it is clear," I insisted, "I used remote viewing to check a mile down the road."

No matter, Paul gripped his seat tightly. I used a bird's eye view to check the road beyond and behind, I was still clear so I opened the engine up fully. It was exhilarating, and the car just handled the corners but it was a fight with the steering wheel, which made Paul all the more nervous. By the time I pulled into the drive back at The Establishment, he looked white. It was not surprising that there were no further offers to take me out for a driving lesson.

This was our only disagreement, however. We fitted together like a lock and key and became a cohesive force to be reckoned with. Working together on the project and socialising together made me realise that Paul made my destiny clear and was the missing link I had sought all along.

He wanted to increase my capabilities at a more rapid pace, he was as results driven as I, neither of us had the patience to wait for enlightenment. To discover the frequency at which my brain was operating, he placed electrodes on my head while I projected my consciousness and took measurements with an EEG machine. I was used to being monitored while I performed. He found that I enter a particular state of brain wave activity known as theta state and there is a specific frequency at which my consciousness leaves my body. I believe it's a very special number. That number is 7.8.

By July 14th 1965, the OOBE project was in a position to move onwards. They were both excited, as Paul was going to use an oscillator set to resonate at a frequency of 7.8Hz. He enclosed Tahra in a specially designed booth, complete with a comfortable seat, EEG hook up and visual monitor just to be on the safe side. Paul had also prepared a small control station, at which he could set and alter the frequency. Before the experiment began, he set the frequency to alpha wave state, a frequency of 10Hz to make the environment conducive and relaxing. Then Tahra was ready to pick up where she left off.

She closed her eyes and instantly felt relaxed. The tone of the frequency was subliminal and inaudible, yet it felt soothing. Paul noticed that within a few minutes, Tahra's brain wave pattern had synchronised with the output from the oscillator so he changed the output frequency to 7.8Hz after a short while. Within moments, her brain wave signature matched the output signal and Tahra, hopefully, was projecting her consciousness.

As expected, she focused her attention on the outermost limits of the solar system and the resonating signal seemed conducive to the process. Its effect was subtle but she did feel the projection was a little more directed from outside this time. She was gazing upon the bluish, ethereal planet of Neptune, a gas giant on the periphery of the solar system and felt peaceful in its presence, in touch with the rhythm of the universe. However, she experienced no push to go further and when she tried to leave the confines of the solar system, she encountered that same invisible barrier, which was frustrating. She also found that, because of the oscillator, returning to her body was difficult. Paul sensed her distress and changed the frequency, returning it to the alpha wave state.

A little concerned, he opened the door of the booth, trying to remain hopeful of the result the project needed. Tahra regained her composure and was relieved to be back in her body; the lack of control she had experienced had given her reason to panic, she was used to directing the movement of her consciousness from her body and back to it.

"Well," he asked her, "did it work?"

Her response was hesitant and Paul's hopes were crushed by

her lack of enthusiasm.

"I didn't travel any further," she stated, as disappointed as he, "leaving my body was easier, although getting back was hard. It was like being locked out of the house. I'm experiencing some degree of paralysis in my body, which is unusual compared to my usual remote viewing sessions, although I think I can still speak."

Paul smiled even though he was disappointed. Her down to earth similes for spiritual experiences were endearing. He kissed her softly and hugged her.

"We need to arrange a signal, when it's time to 'unlock' the door then," he decided.

"Preferably not my expression of distress, eh?" she joked.

Paul laughed softly, even though disappointed.

"Perhaps you could just raise your hand," he suggested.

"It's not as easy as you think," she responded, "This is not a normal remote viewing session. I could twitch a finger," she suggested in return.

"In that case, I can attach an electrode to your finger to pick up the signals relayed from the motor neurone."

Tahra gave him a puzzled look.

"In English please," she said.

"A sensor to detect any muscular twitches," he explained, "Because you can't lift a finger to help!"

Tahra laughed and kissed him.

"I love you, Mr Paul Eldridge."

It had been a while since a woman had spoken those words to him. It had been even longer since he himself had spoken those words, and meant it.

"I love you too, Tahra."

How could he ever regret this?

At the end of the day, time was allowed to unwind from the pressures of the project and they relaxed in Paul's old bedroom at The Establishment. He moved the small black and white television from the office and put it in a position where they could lay in bed together and watch it, he propped up on a pillow with Tahra resting her head on his chest.

There was nothing on the independent commercial channel but adverts, so they took a moment to kiss while the sound of Bach's Air on a G-String accompanied the voice over declaring that 'happiness is a cigar called Hamlet'. It was time to change channel, although he felt too comfortable to get up and do the dirty deed.

"I don't know about remote viewing," he said, "but we need a remote channel changer."

Tahra looked thoughtful, then picked up a shoe and threw it in the direction of the TV channel buttons. Surprisingly, it found its mark and they got BBC 2 instead.

"You could have broken the TV, you know," Paul objected.

"I'm sure we could have found something else to do," she mused, stroking his stomach lightly with her fingers.

It was a choice between an episode of 'The Likely Lads', in which the two characters Bob and Terry have to come up with ways of paying for their planned holiday, or make love. The sex won, with the sound of dialogue and canned laughter in the background.

The romantic element was a fortunate addition to the OOBE project, for without it he knew he would lose heart. For a whole month, they tried using the resonant frequency of 7.8Hz as an accelerator but to no avail. The 'release' system worked fine, the sensor detected muscular twitches when it was time to return yet the objective of leaving the solar system eluded them. Tahra was very supportive although she felt just as frustrated as Paul and she could offer no suggestions to achieve their objective, she was the vehicle for his idea as much as the inspiration.

She had spent less time at The Institute and had been able to do this as Max had been absent on business for the past six months. Miss Tynedale was led to believe that the reason for her extended periods of absence were due to the project with Paul and she had no intention of standing in the way of this. It didn't occur to her that she was in a relationship with Paul and Max had made no efforts to intrude on or enquire about her personal life before he had left. Was it because he no longer cared and that he had given up his pursuit? Did she care if he was now indifferent? She realised that Max was further and further away from her thoughts, his name never cropped up during conversations with Paul, it was an episode in her life that was finalised.

Paul wasn't motivated to work on Max's project, but he knew it wouldn't be difficult now to pinpoint a resonant frequency to disrupt the movement of consciousness. He would have to pay Oscar and George a visit soon, the risk of that experiment on Tahra was too costly.

She was spending many a weekend at the cottage as it was time away from the project and testing at The Institute and it was the only place that felt like home, The Institute had merely been a hotel, albeit a very clinical one. It was August 1965; people were rioting in Los Angeles and the Beatles were playing at the Shea Stadium to sheer pandemonium that drowned out their performance. The project was two months away from the review, which would determine whether or not it would continue and Paul was starting to feel the pressure. In many ways it could be called a success, as a number of experiments had been carried out and the results recorded, however, it wasn't enough for Paul. He needed something profound, like a meeting with a being from another world. Ironically, the Rolling Stones were singing '(I Can't Get No) Satisfaction' on the radio, he smiled sardonically. Tahra walked in from the kitchen, singing along and she danced over to him.

"Don't rub it in," Paul said, his face showing the frustration at their lack of breakthrough.

"It will happen," she insisted. "This is meant to be."

She popped a piece of fruit in his mouth and looked at him intently. He wasn't enthusiastic.

"I don't like to fail at anything," he begrudged.

Tahra gave him a stern look.

"You haven't failed," she stated, "this is just a setback."

He sighed. "I just want to find the answer, right this moment. I've never been very patient."

"It will come," she reassured him, "I know this project will succeed."

He smiled, she was always so positive no matter. She swung her leg over his knees and sat on his lap, idly stroking his chest.

"I can make you feel better," she declared.

Leaning forward she unbuttoned his shirt and he made no complaint as she delivered a little wave of pleasure up his spine, something he could never protest against. He grabbed her buttocks and she moved her body against his, creating the response she wanted. Paul tugged at her jeans, trying to get them undone and Tahra assisted, standing astride him and removing them as seductively as possible. She allowed him to confiscate her purple tunic and he discovered she wasn't wearing a bra. Tahra enjoyed his touch as he ran his hands over her body and used his mouth with incredible sensitivity. She stood astride him again and undressed him with finesse, then knelt in between his legs to perform his favourite act of foreplay. To conclude the sex, she sat astride him and teased him mercilessly before allowing him to climax.

They sat silently and contently in that position, satisfied for a while then both realised the bed would be a more comfortable option, so retired upstairs. Paul found it the most peaceful sleep he'd had in a long time, his earlier feelings of research frustration had not followed him to the bedroom. He soon closed his eyes and drifted into, what was in effect, a lucid dream. For the first time in his life he was actually aware of the fact that he was dreaming. He found himself in a partial desert, partially fertile plain with a river nearby, on which boats full of people floated. He contemplated walking over to meet these people, for he felt as if they had something important to say. They disembarked from the boats and came towards him, however, they couldn't see him. As they filed past, he decided to follow them and when he turned round, he was surprised by what loomed into view. The pyramids filled his vision, but they weren't the semi-ruins he expected, they were encased in polished limestone and reflected the light of the sun.

The people entered the pyramid through a hitherto unknown entrance and Paul followed them in his lucid dream state. To his surprise, the corridors were lit with some unidentifiable light source and they made their way to a chamber within the pyramid, where one person lay down. A brief ceremony ensued, which Paul did not understand and the person was left alone. A few moments later, he was aware of a steady hum, of such a low frequency that it was barely audible but it caused his body to tingle. The hum seemed to resonate throughout the chamber and elsewhere, it seemed to be channelled into the rock walls themselves.

The tingling seemed to draw him away somewhere, less of an actual shift but more of an adjustment of his vision. Shapes seem to move around the room, in the shadows and oozing out of the walls then they became more corporeal. He realised that many of them seemed to resemble Egyptian Gods, for they had human bodies and animal heads, while some were simply serpents, both winged and wingless varieties.

It occurred to him that the pyramid, in this lucid dream, was some sort of resonator. Paul longed to know the workings of this, it was not unlike his own research. Although he spoke no words, the beings, or Gods heard his thoughts and one serpent turned towards him.

"You want to understand the machine," it said.

Paul answered by thought.

"Yes, I think this is the answer to my problem."

"And what is your problem?" spoke the serpent.

"I'm using a resonant frequency of 7.8 to push consciousness towards the stars, but it isn't working," he answered.

The serpent seemed amused.

"Yes, you have found the ancient number. But life does not resonate at one frequency alone."

"I have to overlay another signal?" he proposed.

"Yes, you need to find the harmonics. 7.8 is always the base, but it is the harmonics that change the experience."

"And that will have the desired result?"

The serpent pondered the question but didn't affirm or contradict him.

"Look at the machine you find yourself in, you must understand its fundamentals and the results of these principles."

"And the results are?"

The serpent was patient.

"The use of the primeval number and the harmonics creates the field necessary to walk with us. You are looking at The First Time."

"The First Time Mankind walked with you and spoke with you?"

"Yes, this was always meant to be."

"What is the purpose of this contact?" Paul continued.

The serpent seemed glad he had asked this.

"Mankind contacts us to learn, but it does not just walk and speak with us, there are many other beings in the cosmos."

"What did Mankind learn from you?"

"Anything it desired, each form of life has its own knowledge and secrets; of the workings of the universe, the purpose of their existence or more practical matters such as medicine and technology. Mankind learned much in this way, although the consequences of the use of this knowledge are Mankind's only to experience. We do not discriminate, those who walk and speak with us are free to ask any question but Mankind has free will, we do not control whether the knowledge is used for good or evil, it is not our nature to intervene. It has always has been and always will be this way."

"Was there ever a Second Time?" Paul pressed.

The serpent moved closer to him.

"Not in your past, but in the life of the universe, there will be many times."

"I want to initiate the Second Time," Paul declared, eager to access this knowledge.

"Then you must build a machine."

"It's as simple as that?"

"It is simple to start something, it is not so simple to continue and accept the outcome of your actions," the serpent answered.

"I must do this," he insisted.

"Then you must build a machine," he was told.

"How?" Paul wanted all the answers.

"You must look at the machine. That is why you are here."

Then the serpent turned away and diffused into the walls, leaving Paul alone yet enthused. Although the serpent had gone, he was still here and he realised that the answers were here, he just needed to find them himself. Moving around the machine, he sought the source of the resonance and allowed his gut feeling to lead him there. He found an immensely tall gallery which was stacked floor to ceiling with columns and rows of bowls. Paul realised that the bowls were responsible for the resonance. It was difficult to pinpoint the actual source, but he knew an oscillator was capable of generating the required frequencies in modern society. The resonance was channelled into a small ante-chamber, which he surmised filtered the acoustics and directed them into the main chamber, where the participant lay. He also realised that the walls were full of quartz crystal, and that the crystal generated a magnetic field when the resonance was channelled from the gallery and the ante-chamber. The magnetic field gave strength to the signal, it helped 'tune' the consciousness to a different cosmic frequency. It released consciousness from its binding with the brain matter and allowed the mind to visit other worlds.

Paul knew what to do now.

He awoke with a fire in his heart. Reaching for a pen and paper, he started to draw. He was going to build a machine.

18
Long Way from Home

The schematics for the machine were close to the image and design portrayed in my dream, although I made a few major modifications. The dream was more an instigator, an initial piece of inspiration that would lead me to developing the tool that would take us to the stars. I stuck with the pyramid shape, for I felt sure the shape channelled energy in some way and plus, it looked good. The acoustic filtering wasn't necessary considering the technology I would be using. The original ancient design had used objects very much like Helmholtz Resonators in the grand gallery, which work on the same principle as blowing over the neck of an empty bottle and by altering the size and shape of the neck, different tones can be produced. However, I had the benefit of well calibrated oscillators which would be generating the resonance.

The quartz crystal was also not necessary. In the ancient machine, the quartz converted acoustic resonance into energy, more specifically, electro-magnetic energy. A magnetic field could be created quite easily with modern technology instead, which would rotate around the occupants of the machine and pulse at the frequency of 7.8 hertz, which I believe was the output of the quartz crystal. Oscillators would produce the harmonic frequencies that I was yet to discover. I hoped the solution to this mystery would not stall me too long but I had an inkling that they were based around multiples of 7.8, it seemed logical. Therefore, the harmonics would be 15.6, 23.4, 31.2, 39, 46.8, 54.6, 62.4 and so on. I would also experiment with 7.8 squared, which was 60.84.

As the resonance would have to be contained, I designed dampeners that would surround the pyramid without affecting the internal acoustics. As the chamber would be completely swathed, I would need to set up a cine camera system to monitor Tahra and an external control booth. I would also set up instrumentation to measure the magnetic field, especially during testing when I would use live animals to be sure the field was safe enough before putting Tahra in there. Furthermore, there would be both an Electro-Encephalogram (EEG) to measure brain wave output and an Electro-Cardiogram (ECG) to monitor her heart rate throughout.

The question of alignment was also a factor to consider, as the Giza pyramid was aligned with the compass. I decided to replicate this in my design; maybe it had something to do with an alliance of sorts with the Earth's magnetic field.

The last thing I would need was a building large enough to accommodate it and the funding to build and run it. This last factor was the most crucial and one where external assistance needed to be sought.

I enquired as to when Max would return and the answer was at the end of September, about three weeks away so during that time I researched and wrote an extensive proposal to take to Max personally. This was a big project and I felt confident that it would take OOBE to another world, literally, so hoped it wouldn't be too difficult to persuade Max and he was a man with finances at his disposal. I would be responsible for most of the technical labour, so it cut down on some of the expenses. The wait for his return was excruciating, I longed to start building today.

Tahra was very supportive, for it was as much about her as it was about OOBE and me. She was without trepidation, having been to the edge of the solar system she felt like there was nothing to be afraid of. The wait was as agonising for her as it was for me. We were one, whatever affected me affected Tahra also.

Time passed relatively quickly. In Max's absence I managed to source materials and potential buildings, but it wouldn't be set into momentum without him. I played around with the oscillators although I couldn't practise creating the necessary field. What the ancient machine had demonstrated was the application of both resonance and magnetic fields to drag consciousness from the body and propel it beyond current boundaries, so this is what I needed to focus on getting right.

Finally, Max returned from the States and I wasn't hesitant in setting up an appointment. There were a further two weeks in which to prepare for a presentation, and therefore two weeks to feel extremely nervous and worry like crazy. Tahra kept me sane, preventing self doubt which could have destroyed my enthusiasm.

The meeting was to take place at The Institute, where Oscar and George were pleased to see me and keen to hear about my project. They knew a little about project OOBE although it was just a little and I was careful to keep it zipped for the time being. I made polite conversation and then Max called me through.

He seemed quite relaxed and more at ease with himself this time, although he said nothing about his trip to the States. He rarely did though, perhaps he wanted to be an enigma. I placed a typed document before him and he picked it up, eyes lighting up when he read the title – 'Accelerating Remote Viewing Capabilities Through the Application of Harmonic Acoustic Resonance and Electro-Magnetic Fields'. He raised an eyebrow at me.

"I was inspired," was my explanation.

He read the proposal thoroughly and I felt incredibly nervous as he did so, wondering whether he would find the whole thing preposterous. I watched him nod occasionally, raise an eyebrow or scratch his chin then he placed my proposal down on the table.

"Looks like you've been busy lately," he commented.

I nodded. "Project OOBE has been successful so far, however, I believe it has the potential to go further."

Max considered my comment and proceeded to ask further questions.

"You have associated the resonant frequency of 7.8 with projection of consciousness?"

"Yes," I began enthusiastically, "I think it's highly significant in terms of what Tahra, Oscar and George can do. The frequency alone appears to enhance the process, although as yet, it hasn't enabled us to leave the solar system."

Max raised an eyebrow. "And leaving the solar system is your objective?"

"Absolutely," I answered, "I believe there is life out there and this *project may enable us to establish contact. Tahra has remote viewed most of the planets in our solar system, achieving far more than either the Americans or Soviets in the Space Race. The US only achieved their first space walk about three months ago and they're not even anywhere near ready to land on the Moon yet."*

"Although," Max countered, "your evidence is still subjective."

I nodded, reluctantly. "Yes. Tahra's experiences are the only evidence I have, as yet."

"You do realise," Max continued, "that for this to be of value, you need to show these results are valid and reliable with a range of participants."

"I planned on eventually extending the project to test the effects of the resonance and field on the other subjects at The Institute." It was more of a question, as I ended the statement with an inflection. Would he allow that?

Max smiled. "It would indeed be interesting to see if they would be able to remote view under these conditions. But," he continued, "I was thinking more of the application for people who have, in fact, no psychic or extraordinary abilities."

This is something I hadn't yet considered, would it even be possible?

"That would certainly make the project very... valuable to the scientific community," I agreed.

Max returned to perusing my proposal. There was a moment of silence as he was preparing another question.

"You wish to apply a combination of harmonic acoustic resonance and electromagnetic fields," he commented.

"Yes, I believe it 'fine tunes' consciousness, focuses it like a laser beam," I explained.

"You mean, it gives the remote viewer greater focus in their abilities, greater... power?" he postulated.

"This is what I believe," I said.

"And it could give an ordinary person the ability to do this too?" he pressed.

"That would be desirable," I stated with conviction, "I'll test it on myself if I have to."

"Will you test this new machine thoroughly before Tahra goes in?" he asked, on a more serious note.

I was surprised at his fatherly concern. "Yes, I give you my assurance that she will be well looked after." He seemed relieved, but then a little confused.

"Where is she anyway? She doesn't seem to be around and Miss Tynedale told me she has been conspicuously absent when not required at The Institute."

I wondered whether he was questioning me about any involvement with Tahra, or just simply wondering about her whereabouts. How would he react if I told him she was safe with me, in my cottage, in my bedroom…?

I shrugged. "She's a grown woman and as long as she turns up for testing, I don't ask what she does."

I hoped he couldn't see through my lie. I also hoped I was convincing, I wasn't sure how he'd react. He still looked perplexed and I began to feel uncomfortable.

"Be sure to encourage her to return to The Institute," he said, nervously, "this is her home."

"It's… a demanding project," I explained. "There's a lot of follow up."

He seemed a bit more at ease and so did I. It was disconcerting when he asked such questions, I've never regarded myself as a good liar.

Then he pondered his decision with great deliberation.

I got home shortly after and found Tahra waiting on tenterhooks. She stood up as I entered the sitting room, scanning my facial expression to predict the outcome of the meeting. I stood silently, keeping her guessing.

"Come on, tell me," she pleaded, "this is agonising!"

I grabbed her by the waist and picked her up, spinning her round.

"He gave us the go ahead!" I exclaimed.

"Really?"

"Really. Project culminates October 1967."

"Not long after I graduate," she commented.

"Something you will still definitely do," I added, ""I'm not going to interfere. You can study while I build and test."

"Okay," she agreed, a little sing song.

I put her down and asked her about something that was bugging me.

"Max is asking about you," I said.

She looked a little sheepish and I raised my eyebrows.

"I… haven't told him I'm here," she said, unsure.

"Neither did I," I responded, "and I didn't tell him about our relationship."

She looked at the floor. "Good," was all she said.

I became suspicious at her reaction.

"Is there something you're not telling me?" I asked, looking her in the eye.

She returned my gaze and looked hesitant, then smiled.

"No," she replied, simply.

I paused, unsure if she was telling me the truth or not. Sensing my scepticism, she kissed me reassuringly.

"He's my sponsor, I'm here because of Max and he feels very protective of me. He made a promise to my father to take only the best care of me, it's a promise he cannot break."

I nodded. Still, a gut feeling insisted I'd rather he didn't know about us.

I was both elated and worried when Paul returned. Elated because project OOBE was moving onto the next stage and this would satisfy my hunger for exploration and worried because Max was starting to suspect there was something going on as I was not at The Institute on a regular basis. I felt terrible lying to Paul, but I couldn't tell him about everything that had happened between me and Max. Neither could I allow Max to find out about my relationship with Paul, I knew the result would not be a pretty sight. Even though things were very much 'off', he would be *jealous and angry as I was his possession, that was clear in his mind. He wouldn't accept my decision to be with someone else. But was I foolish to think I could keep it from him? I decided to nip things in the bud and stay at The Institute a little more often. Max would surely stop asking questions then and I could study there when Paul did not need me for testing or moral support.*

It was strange being back there and at first, I tried to hide in my room to avoid Max as much as possible. This was mainly because when he saw me again, I could see that he still had intentions towards me and he didn't know things had changed, I was with Paul now. It pained me to have to keep this a secret, it wasn't fair, I had found the right man for me and I couldn't share that with the world. Sometimes, Max would brush past me on the stairs after breakfast, perhaps hoping for an opportunity to say something but choosing to maintain a professional air instead. At least I had my study and the new Beatles album to keep me occupied, although ironically, the song I played the most was 'You've Got To Hide Your Love Away'. It was especially poignant, and even Max looked pensive when he heard it. I was relieved to get back to the project with Paul.

Project OOBE was now becoming much bigger than either of us had envisioned and I think Paul found the pressure quite stressful. He had viewed some properties prior to Max's return and once he had the go ahead, paid a substantial deposit on a farmhouse in Wiltshire that came with a large barn and a few outbuildings. The funds promised by Max would cover the cost of refurbishing the barn to contain the machine and control centre, plus convert the outbuildings into basic living quarters when intensive testing began. The house itself was cosy and adequate and there was a train station quite close by so I could return to London easily for university or The Institute. Paul moved out of the cottage and it returned to Max for letting, so that he could concentrate full time on the machine.

Builders began the conversion of the barn on the 28th October 1965, which was ten days before my 21st birthday so I was not swept off my feet and taken to some romantic destination. I accepted an invitation to a restaurant, as Paul was not so ignorant to be completely absorbed by *the project to forget a milestone birthday.*

Afterwards, we relaxed on the sofa in front of the television, like an old married couple and he created a fine atmosphere with a crackling log fire, a bottle of wine and some candles. I appreciated the effort, however simple, in creating a romantic ambience. The television choices were limited (remember, this was the sixties) and thankfully we had missed 'Songs of Praise' due to our restaurant engagement. We had to settle for 'Sunday Night at the London Palladium' for a while, I am not a huge fan of variety shows for the masses so eventually we changed channel and found a documentary on the rise of protest culture across Britain and the United States.

The programme began with the 'ban the bomb' demonstration of 1958 in Trafalgar Square, where around sixty to a hundred thousand protesters brought counterculture to the world's attention. It gave an overview of the principles underlying the movement; the development of an aesthetic sense, a love of nature, independence and the distrust of governments, including their instruments of order such as the police. Sub-topics within the protest movement overall were covered, like racial segregation (the activist Martin Luther King), feminism and gay rights and it gave a good overview of the cultural components that enabled the movement to have gained momentum; such as the baby boomer era driven by young, affluent and disillusioned people; the use of psychedelic drugs; the creation of the contraceptive pill which heralded a new freedom and sexual revolution for women and the breaking away from the constraints of the fifties. TV, radio and the relaxing of censorship was a key component in people's awareness of what was changing in the world. The programme concluded with Bob Dylan singing 'The Times They Are a Changin'.

I think some of the principles raised struck a chord with me, in particular, feminism and I realised that I was in agreement with the growing school of independent thought in women. I had no intentions of having my life dictated by a man and abhorred the idea of domestic slavery. I was living the life I always secretly wanted, one of freedom and self expression and this project was cementing that ambition. The documentary exemplified the decade and culture in which I became an adult and in many ways, this era perhaps shaped my personality, emphasising the more rebellious, free spirited and spiritual aspects of my nature that would probably have remained more dormant if I had remained in the Middle East or was raised in the fifties. I felt vindicated, not the odd one out anymore.

The next day, it was back to work at The Institute while Paul acted as project manager and six weeks later, the barn had water and an electric supply, and the basic structure of the machine was in place. He worked with a technician for the next six weeks to create the machine itself and set up the control booth, the technical equipment and the 'pyramid', an enclosure in which to be exposed to the resonance and electromagnetic field. Paul explained to me the dampeners installed around the exterior to contain 'the field' and how I would be monitored throughout the experiments. It gave him great pleasure to see his vision come alive and I was proud to be a part of something so ground breaking.

While the building was going on, I divided my time between university, the farmhouse and The Institute, quite a juggling feat. At the time I felt I had to keep everyone happy; Paul, Max, the university and myself. It was useful to stay at The Institute as it made it easier to focus on the essays and exams but I missed Paul. I used the local phone box at first to stay in touch with him and hear the latest on the building work, but after a while, Max let me use the office telephone and was respectful enough not to listen in on the conversations. Afterwards, he would enquire as to the progress, and sometimes he glanced at me with a sad look in his eyes. I longed to see Paul to take my mind off these uncomfortable situations.

Then, before too long, the machine was finished. Paul couldn't wait to tell me when I arrived at the farmhouse one day in February 1966. I was as ecstatic as he, the time had arrived and he decided to run the machine without a participant to test the electrics and the field on his birthday, his 45th birthday. Luckily, this coincided with a day I was able to be there. I gave him a gift, which was a silk striped shirt (he loved it) a hug and allayed his fears about the emergence of grey hairs, telling him it was dignified and noble. He responded by admitting that his age *concerned him, particularly as I was so young and he didn't want to look as if he was my father, not my lover. He refused to spend time and money honing his appearance in the way Max did. In return, I admitted that I had always found the wisdom and security of an older man attractive, accepting that grey hair and a few crows feet went with the territory. It reassured him, and that was one of the few occasions he displayed any insecurities.*

He showed me to the completed barn which housed the machine (the guest rooms were to be completed in another six weeks). It was time to put all this hard work to the test, which was certainly nerve wracking and I hoped for Paul's sake that everything would run smoothly. With trepidation, he switched on the lights which flickered into life, revealing the machine and the control booth, which sat behind a screen of reinforced glass. The machine was beautiful, a pyramid finished in metallic shielding to contain the field. There were no windows, but it was lit within and equipped with cameras and apparatus to monitor heart rate and brain waves. The machine was large and inside were thirteen reclining seats set in a circle. Today there was some sensing equipment in the middle which Paul had set up to measure the field.

We sat in the control booth, full of rows of lights, buttons and dials. There were also machines to link up with the heart monitors and brain wave monitors when people were involved, plus a few screens so he could see what was going on.

Once he was satisfied the machine was closed up, he took a deep breath and powered it up. He activated the oscillators and it took a few minutes for them to come online and reach the correct intensity. There was a certain sequence for the frequencies to come online, beginning with the highest and finishing with the final and lowest, yet the most important – 7.8. Each frequency had a slider control and bank of lights. One at a time, the frequencies reached 50% of their full strength and Paul was happy to keep it that way. When he was satisfied, he activated the pulsed magnetic field but sustained it at 30%. The bank of controls gave him feedback about the field within the machine and the cine cameras allowed him to look inside. There appeared to be a slight vibration of the machine's shell. Paul nodded in appreciation.

"I've gotta say," he began, "the weather looks good in there."

I nodded in agreement, it did indeed. And one day, in the not too distant future, I would be in there.

The first operation of the machine was a relief, no electrical problems, no hassles, it was a pretty smooth process. The conditions inside the machine appeared to be conducive to my expectations. I tested the machine with no participants for ten days, progressively making the field stronger until by day ten, it was running at 65%. What surprised me was the vibration of the machine's shell but it presented no problem, it was simply a side effect.

After running it empty, I needed to begin testing the safety of the field on living organisms. I had a fair stock of laboratory animals and began with a plastic tank of mice. If Tahra had been here, she would have been horrified. With the mice inside, I ran the field at 30% and observed the mice closely, then, finding no obvious deleterious effects, I increased the field to 50%. I exposed them for five minutes and then powered down the machine. They were alive and apparently healthy, throughout the test run they had stopped running around but didn't appear distressed. For a week afterwards, I monitored the health of the mice and found no ill effects from exposure to the field. I tested two further batches of mice at field strengths of 60% and 65%, an intensity which caused them to stand still but yet, they did not appear distressed and on monitoring them post-test, they also appeared healthy. In fact, it seemed to make these subsequent batches a little smarter, more acute. Maybe I was imagining it. It was a shame they couldn't talk, I wondered what their experience was like.

At the end of March 1966, Max arrived to oversee one of the test runs. To compound matters, Tahra was also there and had arrived before him. It should not seem unusual for her to be there, after all, she was the first traveller, well, human traveller. Max had phoned me previously so I was aware of his visit and I was able to warn Tahra – no affection, just a show of a professional relationship. She was true to her promise and acted the role of test subject most competently. Max was strangely uncomfortable and he and Tahra said very little. I couldn't put my finger *on the atmosphere this created and it did raise my suspicions again, but, I knew there was little point in delving, Tahra loved me and I loved her unconditionally.*

The next test run was a step up from the mice; I had a chimpanzee as occupant, who was the test subject for this day. I called him Adam, somewhat biblical but he was the first sentient mammal in the machine I suppose, no offence to the mice. He was hooked up to the ECG and EEG and I watched him on the monitor before switching on the field. Tahra was on tenterhooks and Max stood, with finger on chin in a pondering pose. I wondered if he'd seen anything like this before, it was hard to say what his other projects entailed.

I initialised the field at 30%, bringing each of the harmonic frequencies online one at a time, beginning with the highest and culminating with 7.8. All the time, I watched Adam, who was so far responding well to exposure. The weather looked fine in there and once I was satisfied Adam was experiencing no distress, I increased the field intensity to 50%. Max wandered over from the spectator area to the control booth, wishing to observe the experiment from close quarters, Tahra followed. They could both see Adam was alert and healthy. I took the field up to 65%, adequate for the time being and constantly checked Adam's status. His ECG was acceptable, I expected an increase in heart rate but his EEG was fascinating, his brain waves had synchronised with the resonance, he was operating at 7.8. What was he experiencing? If only I could ask. Max appeared to be satisfied with the early test runs and Tahra was transfixed; these tests took her closer to her own, upcoming journeys.

After powering down, I cut the field completely and opened the hatch, releasing Adam. We all walked over to the entrance of the machine, awaiting a response. There was a pause and then Adam ran out, heading straight for Tahra for some reason. Max flinched as Adam jumped up to her, but she caught hold of him and was delighted when he put his arms around her. From that point on, Adam became very attached to Tahra.

Before he departed, Max gave everything the seal of approval. We chatted in the farmhouse and he commented on how extraordinary the whole thing was; the technical genius of the machine, the whole set up was very professional, or so he thought. I noticed him looking around the main living area of the farmhouse, as if he was looking for evidence of Tahra being more than professionally involved with me but I had carefully removed any intimate possessions of hers from the main house and had placed them in one of the bedroom conversions in the outhouses. It may seem a very deceptive thing to do but I didn't want to be put on trial or be asked to cease involvement with her. Tahra had no problem with this. It was best no one at The Institute knew, most of all Max.

Adam, and his sister, Eve were subjected to further testing for the next two weeks as I wanted to be certain there were no ill effects. They were both closely monitored and I found them to be continuously alert and happy, all their medicals checked out. If anything, they performed more efficiently in cognitive tests so I wondered if this was the shape of things to come, enhanced intelligence..?

The status of Adam and Eve meant one thing, Tahra was ready to go. It appeared that no harm would come to her although I would still be cautious when it came to her well being. Her first experience of the machine took place on the 7th May 1966.

Paul sat in the kitchen that morning, reading the newspaper with a pot of tea and several slices of toast and jam while waiting for her to arrive. The big story was the sentencing of Ian Brady and Myra Hindley, also known as the Moors Murderers to life in prison for the horrific killings of Edward Evans, Lesley Ann Downey and John Kilbride, which had shocked Britain since they had been arrested in October the previous year. He didn't get chance to read the whole story though, as Tahra arrived, ready to begin.

He greeted her with a kiss, enquired about her week at The Institute and asked if she was prepared to take the next step, she answered in the affirmative.

"Don't expect a lot for the first test though," Paul warned her, "I'm only running the field at 30% for five minutes."

Tahra sighed, like a child who realised she wasn't going to

get everything she wanted for Christmas.

"Why?" she queried, quite abruptly, "we know Adam and Eve are perfectly fine."

"Impatience is my vice," Paul replied, "not yours. You must respect my decision."

She relented and didn't press further. Yes, he should be responsible and he was the boss here. Tahra often assumed that because project OOBE currently revolved around her, she had authority whereas she didn't, she had consultative power only.

The hatch awaited her and she stepped inside, taking a seat and feeling a sense of awe at what was about to commence. Paul hooked her up to the ECG and EEG then gave her a kiss for luck. After the hatch had closed, she heard Paul's voice over the intercom, confirming that he could see and hear her. Inside the machine, it was silent, eerily so. This did not unnerve her.

"Okay, Tahra," Paul began, "I'm going to bring everything online, one frequency at a time and the field will run at thirty percent."

She nodded to indicate that she understood. After a few moments, she heard a hum emanating from the machine, then heard the harmonics come on line one at a time. The overall frequency became lower and lower, until she could no longer hear it. She was aware of the reverberation of the shell of the machine, although it did so softly. A peculiar vibration began to creep through her body, something she had not experienced before during any of the remote viewing sessions, however, she didn't resist it. The vibration pulsed through her body and she felt a sense of paralysis, which was alarming but she reminded herself that this would only last five minutes, so there was no need to panic. She wanted this more than anything.

In the control booth, Paul watched her intently, while she didn't appear to be totally relaxed, she was not in distress. Her heart rate was elevated but nowhere near maximal, her brain waves were synchronised with the resonance, operating smoothly at 7.8, so therefore, the weather in the machine was fine.

Tahra willed her consciousness to move and she felt an immense surge. The visuals were different to anything she'd previously experienced, she didn't find herself in Earth orbit or anywhere in the solar system, this was something else. There was a net in her field of vision, composed of shimmering hexagons, hundreds of them which were orange in colour. They appeared to hum, or was it just the machine? Before she could progress any further, they faded and she became aware of her body once more. The paralysis and vibration released her and dissolved, then she realised Paul had powered down the machine.

"Please confirm that you're all right," Paul said, over the intercom.

Tahra gave the all clear signal with a thumbs up. He popped the hatch and met her at the opening, finding her somewhat disappointed.

"That was the shortest trip ever," she complained, head hung a little low.

Paul lifted her chin and smiled, which encouraged her to return one of her own.

"You know we're dealing with something completely different here," he explained, "I need to be sure of your safety, as impatient as I am for results."

She nodded. "I know, I'm the really impatient one. I want more, we've come so far already."

"Soon," was all he said in response.

"Now I need to know what the grid is," she decided.

"The grid?"

She described the grid to him but could offer no opinion on what it was, Paul had no idea either. He found it intriguing and neither Oscar nor George had ever mentioned one. It would wait until another time. A medical followed the experiment, in which everything checked out so there was no reason to prevent further exposure in the machine. Forty eight hours elapsed before the next trip and during that time period, Paul made her stay over so he could observe her closely. She took advantage of this opportunity to share his bed and Paul discovered that in no way did exposure to the machine dull the sex drive.

The duration of this next trip was to last ten minutes this time at a field intensity of 40%, to give her a better chance of exploration. It was much like the previous one; the machine reverberated, she felt the same tingling vibration and lost awareness of her body and the grid appeared in her vision again. The hexagons shimmered and almost burnt an impression into her consciousness. Again there was a surge as she felt herself become detached from her body and she was rushing towards something, she didn't know what. Paul checked her ECG and EEG throughout, her heart rate was raised but within acceptable limits and her brain waves had synchronised with the base resonance of 7.8.

She seemed to hurtle beyond the grid and became aware of a point of light in the distance. This light was the focal point against a background of deepest black. She sensed a presence but could not ascertain its origin. Just as the point of light began to take meaning in an abstract kind of way, the field powered down and she returned to her body. This time, she hid her disappointment from Paul and discussed the point of light. Next time, she knew she would learn more.

Forty eight hours later, she was exposed to the field in the machine for the third time. So far there had been no side effects and all the medicals checked out. There was no reason to stall any longer.

"I want twenty minutes this time," she declared.

That was double the exposure in the previous trip, however Paul agreed. The question was, what percentage should he take her to? Fifty? Sixty?

"Sixty five," Tahra said, with conviction. "Adam and Eve took sixty five, therefore, so can I."

Paul considered her request. It was a big jump, forty to sixty five. They were getting results at forty and Paul was really tempted to offer her fifty percent only. But Tahra wouldn't accept fifty percent, he knew that and the only reason for his caution was the fact that he loved her and didn't want to endanger her. He told himself he wasn't being objective enough and realised that there was no evidence to suggest sixty five percent was unsafe. Therefore, Tahra would have her way.

She didn't admit to him that she was nervous although once she was connected to the ECG, it became apparent that her heart rate was elevated before they began.

"Are you sure you want to do this?" Paul asked her over the intercom.

She took a deep breath.

"I didn't come this far to chicken out," was her response.

There was a moment's silence in which Tahra dispelled any niggling doubts from her mind. She was aware of the different frequencies coming online one at a time and her body began to relax. The sound became deeper and lower, and then it was inaudible and from that point, the magnetic field was activated and powered up to sixty five percent in the space of two minutes.

She felt herself extracted forcibly from her body, as if a muscle bound man had physically thrown her. Briefly, she saw the grid again but burned through it in the space of seconds. The point of light came into view and she became aware of the presence but this time, it took hold of her and pulled her in. In the control booth, Paul noted she was approaching eighty percent maximal heart rate, the equivalent of a sprint but he waited in case it stabilised before he hit the kill switch.

If Tahra had wanted to resist, she wouldn't have been able to. She was committed all the way, until twenty minutes had elapsed. Normally, during remote viewing she was completely in control, that was one thing the machine took away and it was quite frightening. But without the machine, she was denied this experience. She was pulled through the point of light at infinite speed, or so it felt and she emerged in another location.

There was now land beneath her and stars above, a whole sky full of iridescent stars and each had presence, as if they were all alive. In the sky she could see other worlds, spheres of light and orbs like planets. There were white, blue and orange clouds very much like nebulae, giving her a feeling of connection to the cosmos. She realised that there was no turning back and now, her fears subsided to give way to a sense of awe. Hopefully, the machine wouldn't power down. It was as if the stars and planets were communicating with each other, but she couldn't tap into their consciousness.

She travelled above the land, flying like an eagle at a great height with great expedience. When she studied the land, she found it to be unlike anything on Earth. The water was iridescent like the stars and the land didn't appear to be composed of dense matter, it cycled through different colours and was conscious, that she was sure of. Before long, she felt a sensation of putting on the brakes and her consciousness was re-focused on a point at ground level.

The land felt stable under her feet but she was aware it was not solid like on Earth. The air around her shimmered, as if there were some field permanently powered up. On closer examination, it was almost like white noise and she could pick out what appeared to be molecules vibrating, or dancing. Within this sea of life, one of the molecules became aware of her and locked onto her consciousness. Because she was an outsider, the molecule took on a form to facilitate communication. A being came into focus before her in a humanoid shape. It had no real eyes, nose or mouth but where the eyes should have been, there was an impression which burned brightly. Its skin appeared white but again, was iridescent and cycled through different colours. Tahra also noticed it appeared to have wings which were folded up on its back. The image of it was vivid and she felt as if its eyes bored through her and could see into her soul.

"I've been waiting for you," it appeared to say, although no lips moved, "I knew you would come."

If Tahra had experienced this meeting in her physical body, she knew she'd be shaking.

"Who are you?" she questioned.

"You'll know everything that is required in good time," was the reply.

Not a good question. She tried another.

"You know me?" she asked. "You said you knew I would come."

The being seemed to peer at her and loomed closer, with those frightening eyes.

"I know everything about you, that's why I brought you here, there's a reason you were chosen."

Tahra was genuinely unnerved.

"Chose me for what?"

Did she really want to know?

"For everything," the being responded, without emotion.

"I don't understand," she said, afraid.

"Your life comes with a price. The possession of extraordinary gifts creates an imbalance that has to be addressed. In return, there is something you need to do."

She began to regret pushing forward so fast with the project.

"What will I have to do?" she asked, afraid of the answer.

"I'll tell you when it's time."

"When is that time?"

"Not yet," was the reply, which didn't reassure her, "I'll draw you here when that time arrives, just like I did here, to formally meet you for the first time."

"You set this meeting up?"

"Of course, it will take a long time to find this realm on your own," the being said.

"Where am I?" she said, realising it was somewhere significant.

"A long way from home," was the reply.

At that point, she saw the scene dissolve and realised the field was powering down, which was a relief. She became aware of her presence inside the machine again and before too long, she saw Paul's face as soon as the hatch popped open. He looked concerned, especially when he realised how shaken she looked. She was trembling. The first thing she did was hug him tightly and Paul returned the embrace, she needed it. For the remainder of the day, Tahra was strangely quiet, wondering only about the task that she would be requested to do.

19

Personal Experiences

She didn't want to share her experience for a few days and Paul realised that the first major journey in the machine threatened to be the last. He needed to record something in the OOBE diary and put something on film for posterity, to demonstrate that something was happening but he was also aware of Tahra's well being so it was doubly frustrating. In the end, he had to push the situation.

"We can't progress any further until you open up to me about what happened," he began.

She nodded. "I know, I'm sorry," she said, sincerely apologetic, "I can't explain why it has affected me so."

He switched on the cine camera set up on a tripod and attempted to extract the information from her. They began with a description of the world she had visited and then Paul proceeded to discuss the more personal aspects of the experience.

"Did you feel threatened in any way? You know I don't want any harm to come to you," he reassured her.

"Not really," was her reply, "but the experience touched me in a way I can't describe."

"It's good that you felt moved," Paul countered, "isn't that what we're striving for?"

"I encountered a strange being," she began, "made of energy but it could choose form if it wanted to. There were more of them hiding in the background too, I knew they were important beings and they knew I was important too. The being I communicated with told me that I was chosen, that it would ask me to do something."

Paul sat back in his chair and ran his hands through his hair. This was unexpected. Should he be taken aback because she'd interacted with a strange being or because it'd asked a favour?

"What does it want you to do?" he pressed, opting for curiosity.

"I don't know, but the being promised that time will come. What if I return there and it asks something of me that is evil, or beyond my strength and capabilities?"

Paul shrugged, almost helplessly.

"Do you think this being is evil?" he asked her.

Tahra thought hard about it.

"It was difficult to tell. The being had the most penetrating eyes, I felt like its eyes were burning right through me, but I can't be sure of its intentions."

"Well," Paul continued, fascinated, "what did it look like?"

"Sort of... like an... angel," she said, aware of how incredulous it sounded. Paul raised his eyebrows. "But not how they look in your bible," she stated, emphatically, "I know it wasn't human, it was more like a sea of energy, glistening, dancing... I felt like I could never hide anything from it. The scary thing was that it knew who I was, well, so it said anyway."

Paul realised that the experience had been a profound one and was taking some time to come to terms with. And why wouldn't it be? He also knew what he needed to do next.

"There are clearly far more powerful entities out there than us," he concluded, "but do you really want to lose the opportunity to find out what comes next?"

"No," Tahra conceded, "but I'm afraid."

Paul had to be the decisive one.

"Well, we'll be afraid together. We take the next trip as a team. It's got to work for non-psychics one day, so it may as well be now."

Tahra wasn't sure what to think. "But who will operate the machine and watch over us?"

"I'll programme it to run the sequence automatically for a

set duration," he explained, "I can't expect you to do something I wouldn't do myself."

He said it with courage and conviction, although inside he was as nervous as she.

June 3rd 1966 was the date of our joint machine trip and over breakfast, I reflected with amusement upon the progress made so far by the Americans and Soviets in the Space Race. It was a good outlet for Cold War rivalries, as it didn't involve firing anything at each other, only up into orbit. Mariner 4 had completed a fly by of Mars the previous year and I had managed to find an article which included a selection of the pictures sent back, the images of which correlated well with what Tahra had seen. Currently, the US was attempting orbital docking and just yesterday, Surveyor 1 had touched down in the Oceanus Procellarum on the Moon, however, astronauts were nowhere near it, the first space walks had only been achieved the previous year. I found it amusing the rigours astronauts were subjected to during training, Tahra had never had to endure freefall in a plane known as the 'Vomit Comet', or been spun around to simulate g-forces. The stress on the human body in our journeys was significantly less. It was a shame that our experiments would still be regarded as subjective and the findings would not be accepted scientifically until stringently proven.

I entered the machine with Tahra after having programmed the system to run on automatic for a set duration of twenty minutes. The EEGs and ECGs would still monitor us as normal and I could check the paper display later. The field would run at 65% and I tested the automatic system a few times to ensure it would power down as required. Everything seemed to be in order, although there was always an element of risk involved. I had installed an additional fail safe, triggered by maximal heart rate sustained for more than two minutes, indicating physiological and psychological distress. Therefore, I felt confident in my equipment, although a little less sure of my nerve in this experiment.

I placed electrodes on our temples and our chest then we made ourselves comfortable and held hands, it was unclear who was reassuring who. It was silent in the machine for a few moments after the hatch closed.

"Well, here we go," I said, somewhat nervously, "we'll soon see if non-psychics can make the journey too."

Tahra smiled graciously, my act of support was greatly appreciated. Most men would have remained an outsider I know, but my actions would ensure we could share the experience. It was the least I could do for her, although it didn't make her any less nervous and she squeezed my hand tightly.

I became aware of the hum within the machine as the frequencies, or series of signals overlaid upon each other were running through their sequence. My body responded by becoming more relaxed and I felt somewhat lucid, albeit slightly detached from my body. As the frequencies became inaudible, I became aware of much stronger sensations coursing through my body, quite powerful vibrations. They buzzed up and down my body, creating a progressive muscular paralysis which was rather disconcerting. I truly couldn't move, it was like incredibly intense pins and needles. I can't say it was a pleasant experience, being frozen in your body and powerless, however, I stayed with it and next became aware of some kind of movement. I could move again. As an act of relief, I put my hand to my forehead but was startled to find I could not feel my head when I touched it. It then occurred to me that maybe I was moving the bio-electromagnetic field version of my hand, for want of a better explanation.

At that point, the machine shell began to vibrate heavily and I realised the magnetic field was powering up and rotating around our heads, pulsing at the key frequency of 7.8 hertz. In a matter of seconds, I was ripped from my body and I felt my mind hurled into nothingness and sucked through a point of light. I didn't see the grid Tahra had spoken of, but it all happened so quickly I probably didn't notice. I found myself adrift inside the machine, unable to do anything but float above my body. It was the strangest thing looking down upon oneself, still and placid like a limpid pool of water, motionless as a rabbit caught in the glare of a car's headlights. The next thing I was aware of was a sensation of being scooped up, for want of a better word, as if my consciousness was being cradled like a baby. I was moved out of the machine and our world disappeared in a blur to be replaced by another which was coming into focus.

Colours began to come into the spotlight, very vivid colours which were unlike anything on Earth, it's hard to describe their brilliance. It was almost like a painting coming into view, with luminous watercolours depicting a forest of evergreen splendour, pearl-like streams and in the distance, serpentine tendrils and vines extending far up into the atmosphere. Instead of terminating at a point high in the sky, they curved inward and embraced, creating a warped perspective like a fish eye lens on a camera.

Looking closely at the foliage, I soon realised that the trees merely gave the impression of a forest and in fact, the trunks were actually shafts of energy and tendrils consisting of bead-like cells glistened and slithered up and down the central shafts. Not all trees were the same. Some consisted of a single tendril or vine whereas others were double stranded, some had triple strands and some even had seven tendrils.

The ground beneath my feet wasn't still; it appeared to be some kind of miniature labyrinth, full of mazes and spirals through which very small serpents slithered. It was a dizzying spectacle and one that I couldn't stare at for too long.

The scene actually reminded me of my experiences with LSD several years ago, in respect of the vibrant colours I was now faced with. However, the difference was that this was not a mere hallucination, the images weren't planted into my brain or field of vision, I was transplanted into the vision.

Initially I saw no signs of life. I began to wonder if Tahra was present here too or if she had been kidnapped so looked around to see if I could find her. Once I adjusted myself to functioning in this new realm, I recognised her presence and spotted a ball of light nearby. It wasn't necessary to speak as the communication was instant and natural. She told me that if I focused on a thought form of my image, I could materialise in human form. Tahra appeared beside me and when I pictured myself as I saw my body in a mirror, I too materialised beside her.

"Did you feel me carry you here?" she asked me, although her lips didn't move.

"Oh," I replied, a little surprised, "did you do that? I didn't realise."

"I can tow the consciousness of another person," she told me.

My eyes must have lit up. "That's a useful talent," I said.

Tahra looked around at the place we found ourselves in.

"This is not the place I visited before," she told me.

We began to move through the undergrowth, although not as you would with your corporeal body. As there were no legs to move, you had to focus your attention on your intended destination and let your mind draw you there, quite a strange sensation but fairly easy to master. I was so glad I had Tahra to teach me the ways of navigating without a body. We found ourselves by a stream which was populated by silvery fish shaped like the letters X and Y swimming in perfect rhythm and harmony, as if in time with a beat or pulse that flowed through the water itself.

"Do you think there's intelligent life elsewhere on this planet?" I asked her.

"I do feel the presence of sentient life," she responded, "in fact, I believe we're being watched."

We both stood still and looked around carefully, unsure what we were searching for. Then Tahra spotted something in the trees, I turned to where her 'finger' was pointing and found a host of serpents coiled around the trunks. There were long ones and short ones, two headed ones, winged serpents and some with very short legs and all of them were brilliant in colour; scarlet red, turquoise, jade green, yellow as the noon sun or orange as the sun set. It occurred to me that these were the serpent beings I had encountered in my lucid dream, the one in which they discussed the machine and The First Time with me. We moved over to their position and observed their movements. They were aware of our existence on their planet.

"You came here by virtue of the machine," one or more of them said, it was difficult to pick out an individual voice.

"Yes," I stated, "I built a machine to help consciousness reach the stars. Are you the ones who helped me do this?"

They flowed around the tree trunks like energy.

"Not us, but the serpents who helped you reside in this realm," they said.

"Can I find them here?" I asked, keen to tap them for any knowledge they possessed that could help me in my quest.

"If you so wish," they said.

"I seek knowledge, the wisdom of the Gods," I declared.

"Like many before you. Now you have the machine you can visit many realms," they responded.

"That is what I hope," I responded. "Are there many other worlds?"

"Yes, but they are all very, very different. The frequencies are the key," they told me.

I pondered what they were saying, how could the frequencies be the key to visiting many realms, as they put it? Then the answer became clear. Before I had time to respond to their hint, I felt myself being pulled back into my body, a sensation like releasing the tension on an elastic band. In less than a moment, I was back in the machine, opening my physical eyes as the field was powering down. I wished I'd set the machine to run another five minutes.

Tahra looked over at me, relieved the experience had been a positive one and we climbed out of the machine, moving over to the corner where the diary and camera were set up. I switched it on so as to record our thoughts on the experience.

"I'm on a high," I stated, looking directly into the lens of the camera, "all I can think about is the next trip. We achieved something so... profound today."

"The most important thing achieved today was the machine's ability to project Paul's consciousness," Tahra added. She turned to me and asked, "Do you realise what this means for OOBE?"

I'd almost over looked the obvious, the ramifications were enormous.

"It means anyone can do this," I stated, heart pounding. "7.8 hertz unties the binding of consciousness to the brain matter, to the physical form."

Tahra sighed.

"I feel obsolete," she said.

"We wouldn't have got OOBE off the ground if it wasn't for you," I said, forgetting we were on camera. "Plus, the machine extracted my consciousness from my body, I didn't know how to travel anywhere without you."

She shrugged.

"I guess so."

"This also means we're looking at non-psychic recruitment much earlier than I had anticipated," I said, on turning back to face the camera. "If I can do it, there's no reason why a group of people off the street couldn't do this. Of course, they wouldn't be ordinary people off the street, they'd need to be psychologically strong and grounded, and undergo rigorous testing."

"I can help," Tahra stated, "I can be their guide."

I squeezed her hand.

"We're in this together," I reassured her. "You need to tow them, like you did with me. Without you, they'd be bouncing around inside the machine."

Despite the new impetus in the project, all I could think about was our next journey in the machine and on meeting the serpents, I realised how to direct the outcome of the journey in terms of the destination. There was so much exploration to do and I realised how difficult it would be for me to stand aside and watch Tahra be the sole voyager. I had always felt envious of what she'd seen and done but now I didn't need to be, we could share the project in every way now.

Although I craved another journey, I allowed a forty eight hour break in which to get us both assessed medically. Everything checked out fine and if anything, I felt invigorated, cleansed and inspired. I thought of the next trip; do we pay the serpent world another visit or do we seek to create a travel guide for the worlds that we could reach with the machine? Tahra opted for the latter and I was inclined to agree, as I wanted to experiment with the combination of frequencies and their amplitude to propel consciousness further and further afield. I knew that, if I so desired, I could visit the serpent realm again, Tahra would be the necessary tow if I asked nicely.

Firstly, I made only a small adjustment to the frequencies, that is, I *replaced one of the harmonics to see what result this would produce. The system was set up on autopilot again, I attached us to the monitoring devices and we both sat inside the machine, hearing the vibrations as the field powered up. I wasn't nervous anymore, what was there to be afraid of? The paralysis of my physical body was expected and did not alarm me and I separated from my body within moments. I felt myself being drawn away from the machine towards another land as our world faded out and was replaced by another.*

We found ourselves in a very different land to the serpent realm. It seemed quite arid; there was a great expanse of semi-desert and a series of outcrops of rock reminiscent of Death Valley, in which there appeared to be a number of grand looking caves. These caves looked worth exploring at some point. The colours of this world were quite neutral; ochre and gold sand and rock with dark contrasts formed by the hardy plants that populated the landscape. The sky was taupe and somewhat insipid, cloudless yet with a pallid, subdued light, source unknown.

I focused my consciousness at a point in the distance and allowed myself to be drawn to it, while Tahra moved to a point a little further away, beside a huge, gnarled tree that looked as it were petrified wood. I found myself within a circle of very dry shrubs, the branches of which were spindly, curving around and twisting in on themselves. They were formed by an ebony shade of what looked like petrified wood, covered by some kind of shimmering substance. On closer inspection, I found the shimmering substance to be a swarm of silvery ants, oozing out of a small hole in the base of the shrubs.

I moved over to Tahra, who was transfixed by a strange looking creature. At first I thought it was a capuchin monkey, although it was slightly smaller and it appeared to have the tail of a rat and the fur of a yellow tinted polar bear. What was strangest of all was the face; it was a human visage on the body of a simian with startling blue eyes, a thin nose and lips yet ears high on the head. It was aware of our existence, even though we didn't present a physical body and screeched loudly, jumping off the tree then scuttling away into the distance. We watched it scurry across the floor of the desert.

It led our gaze towards the horizon, where we saw a most amazing sight. I focused my consciousness on a point nearer to them for a better view. There was a large herd of mammoth-like creatures, although, like our erstwhile simian friend, they were hybrids of animals from our world. They were not quite as hairy, their fur was darker and shorter but they bore tusks and a trunk much like our mammoths had done. Their body shape was a little like a triceratops, they bore an extra horn at the front and the tail was long like that of a stegosaurus, with a clump of spikes at the end. They were not interested in us and ambled on by minding their own business.

From our viewpoint, we could see a huge plain stretching out to what seemed like infinity. There were no mountains or valleys to break it up; it was flat like the East of England with the climate of Southern Spain. In the distance, we could see creatures that looked like golden gorillas crossed with the genes of a sloth and a sabre toothed tiger. They walked on their knuckles but had slimmer limbs than a gorilla and they had long, protruding fangs. Momentarily, they would stop to listen to something and then pound heavily on the ground before continuing on their way.

I began to wonder if there were any sentient beings here with which we could communicate then, at that point, something walked over to us, as if it had heard my thoughts. Tahra had already seen it, another bizarre hybrid comprising the head of an ibis and the body of a man. He was tall, standing over six feet at least, held a long staff in his hands and wore some kind of minimal padded armour. Tahra held his attention.

"Welcome traveller," he spoke, "it is good to greet human beings again."

"You know us?" Tahra said.

"There has been a long standing friendship between therianthropes and humans," he explained, "but there has also been a long absence. Welcome back."

"Where is the therianthrope's planet?" I asked, hoping for some direct answers in this realm. "What galaxy are we in?"

Our therianthrope friend looked thoughtful then answered.

"You have not travelled any distance in the physical sense," he corrected, "you have shifted your perspective, your reality. You are in the same locality, yet at a deeper level of creation. Both of you are beginning to perceive, to peel away the layers of the structure of the Monad."

This wasn't the answer I expected, I wasn't sure whether to feel disappointed as we hadn't travelled anywhere or curious as to what exactly we were exploring.

"What's the Monad?" Tahra asked, realising it was something significant.

He was respectful of her question.

"It cannot be explained," was the response, "it must be experienced to be comprehended, that understanding is the true quest of every sentient being. In time, we will share all our knowledge with humanity. For now, simply be and let us watch the light rise on the dawn of a new day."

He crouched on the arid ground, staking his staff in the sand-like substance and used it to support himself. We sat next to him, cross-legged and looked to the sky but quickly realised we were looking in the wrong place. An explosion of golden light projected from the ground, separate rays reached towards the pallid sky extending finger like beams that illuminated the heavens, turning everything a vibrant shade of yellow. It was intensely beautiful, as if the land was communicating with the sky. I didn't want to leave this place.

The therianthrope world faded as the field automatically powered down and the interior of the machine came into focus again. It took a few moments for our brains to recalibrate, so to speak and eventually, I moved over to the camera to record some comments for the visual diary.

"Well, I think that world deserves another visit. These journeys are addictive," I said.

"I'm so glad that I can share them with you," Tahra added.

I proceeded to give a description of the world we had just visited and added a final comment.

"I've just realised something though," I concluded. "He spoke of a shift in perception, in reality. We haven't travelled through space, we've discovered other dimensions of reality. We're not astronauts, we're… shamans."

Tahra returned to The Institute the next day, still feeling euphoric after the previous day's journey. She wondered how ever she'd be able to concentrate during the mundane tests and contracts that she had to fulfil there. Paul said he would follow not long after, as he wanted to catch up with Max to discuss the next stage of the project and he needed to see her fellow residents too. He was surging with positive energy; it gave the world around him a subtle glow.

Max was, luckily, in the office at The Institute and Paul caught him reading a newspaper with a cup of coffee at his side. He looked up as Paul tapped on the door and entered, pleasantly surprised to see him.

"To what do I owe the honour of your visit?" Max queried.

"An update and a request," Paul answered, directly.

Tahra appeared from behind Paul and he was puzzled to see a somewhat wistful expression flicker across Max's face. She stopped herself from putting an arm around Paul, holding Max's gaze while attempting to keep her own expression neutral. There was an odd tension in the air and it was Tahra who popped the membrane.

"We've made fantastic progress with the machine," she declared. "We've discovered two new worlds already."

Max folded his newspaper neatly and placed it on the desk.

"Have you documented these journeys for the record?" he asked.

"We're in the process of doing so," Paul interjected, "with a cine camera and a written journal."

"Do you want to know what worlds we discovered?" Tahra enquired.

Max found her enthusiasm infective.

"Yes, please tell me."

"The first place was the serpent realm, it was beautiful and vibrant, a world of forest and streams. Then the second place viewed was the therianthrope world, where the sun shines from within the ground and illuminates the sky, it was full of hybrid creatures and we met a bird headed man."

On hearing this Max looked thoughtful, as if her words had triggered a memory. Yet, he said nothing. Finally, he asked a question.

"We?" he questioned. "You said, 'we met…'. What do you mean by that?"

Tahra hadn't realised she'd used the personal plural, was she giving too much away?

"I went there too," Paul interjected. "My consciousness travelled too, she towed me and took me along for the ride."

"Towed you?" Max repeated.

"Tahra is a guide, provided your consciousness can detach from the body, she can take you with her."

Max looked thoughtful but worried about something too. There was something on his mind, a burning question yet he did not ask it.

"You do realise what this means, don't you?" Paul continued, unable to read his reaction. There was no response so he filled in the blanks. "It means non-remote viewers can use the machine successfully with the aid of a guide. This is what you wanted, to show viability of the project."

Max was still quiet and Paul began to feel a little irritated. Finally, he snapped out of it.

"And there's something else," Paul added. "Entities in both worlds have mentioned the acquisition of knowledge through making visits to these realms."

Max raised his eyebrows.

"What kind of knowledge?"

Paul shrugged, not a hundred percent sure but able to make a good guess.

"Medicine, technology… secrets of the universe, anything we need to know I guess."

Max appeared to be mentally chewing what Paul had just

said. Medicine, technology… all to the highest bidder….

"What do you want from me?" he asked, more and more intrigued by the OOBE project which was proving to be a real dark horse.

Paul was ready to lay his cards on the table.

"I want to incorporate the residents of The Institute into the programme," was his first request, "and I want an additional six non-psychic recruits, making a total of twelve travellers, excluding Tahra who will be their guide. The non-psychics need to be psychologically stable, with an open mind and a strong constitution."

Max smiled, admiring his directness but there was a silence while he considered the request.

"I can find you ordinary members of the public. Twenty people will be sent to you and you can select the six best candidates from them. I can arrange suitable remuneration for the successful candidates."

"And the residents of The Institute?"

Max sustained the suspense just a little longer.

"I'll call them down and you can put it to them. It's up to you to get them on your side and recruit them."

Paul made a little celebratory fist and nodded thanks to Max. He and Tahra temporarily took command of the sitting room, arranging the chairs in a semi circle. Ten minutes later, Emilie, Sakie, Oscar, George, Peter and Beth appeared. They looked a little older, several years on but not ravaged by time at all. Emilie looked more confident and her fair hair had been cut into a sleek bob in the style of Twiggy. She had abandoned the below the knee dresses in favour of wide leg jeans and a tunic, which accentuated her slim figure. Sakie was now in her twenties and was still petite, presenting a flattering bobbed hairstyle in the style of Mary Quant and sporting a mini dress with a block pattern in primary colours. Oscar, who had always been thick set had gained a little weight, making him appear quite jolly and his afro hair had grown up and out. George was still wiry, looking like the classic English gentleman as usual and neither had his dress sense changed either. Peter looked more athletic as if he were training for the Olympics and Beth had slimmed down somewhat, looking quite svelte with a sleek beehive, full skirt and jacket, with a mandarin collar, Nehru style. They were all happy to see Paul. Greetings and hugs were exchanged then the six of them sat down on the chairs that had been set out, looking at Paul and Tahra with expectant eyes. Max slipped in the doorway and stood by to watch over the proceedings. All Paul had to do now was pitch his idea.

He cleared his throat and began.

"It's great to see you all again, feels like old times, eh?"

There were a few chuckles from his audience, which helped him relax more and feel less nervous.

"Well, the reason I've brought you all together is to reveal exactly what I've – sorry, we've been working on," he looked over at Tahra, "to attempt to persuade you to join the programme."

He appeared to have grabbed their attention so proceeded.

"You're probably aware that Tahra has been drafted onto an experiment I simply call OOBE, which stands for Out of Body Experiment. My first intention was to use remote viewing as a form of space travel, to transcend the need for a physical body which is vulnerable to the extreme environment in space itself. I first proposed the idea to Oscar and George, then to Max and eventually OOBE was born."

This was not really news as word had spread about the basic objectives of the project.

"We concentrated on homing Tahra's remote viewing for detail skills then we worked our way through all the planets of the solar system. I transcribed Tahra's description of what she saw and an artist used this to create some impressions of the planets. There was a recent NASA flyby of Mars, and the images that have come back correlate extremely well with the artist's rendition and Tahra's descriptions of the planet. Before long, we reached the edge of the solar system and at that point, I realised we needed to take it further, even though our previous research had not been extensively validated."

Paul tried to gauge the level of interest in his audience and observed a few murmurs in response to his disclosure.

"Our first experiments beyond the solar system were not successful and Tahra asked if there was a way of giving her a psychic boost, so to speak. I took some measurements of Tahra's brain wave activity during remote viewing and I discovered there is a specific frequency at which consciousness detaches from the body, that frequency is 7.8 hertz, or cycles per second. We tried using this frequency amplified through an oscillator to no avail. Then one night, I had a vision, in a dream of what I needed to do and that was build a machine; a giant oscillator coupled with a powerful electromagnetic field to boost the human bio-electromagnetic field."

His audience really began to take notice now.

"We overlaid harmonics of 7.8 hertz onto the base frequency of 7.8 itself and achieved victory. The machine successfully pulls consciousness from the body and with the aid of a powerful and experienced remote viewer, Tahra, it is possible to visit different worlds. By adjusting the frequencies, harmonics and amplitude, a variety of worlds can be accessed.

"So far, we have visited two; one of which is populated by serpent-like creatures who reside in a technicolour forest and the other which is quite arid, inhabited by hybrid creatures, fusions of species like on our own planet. The really exciting bit is that you don't need to be a remote viewer to do this, although it is necessary for Tahra to act as a guide, you just float around inside the machine otherwise. What's more, we believe these worlds are not planets elsewhere in our galaxy; they're other dimensions, other realities which vibrate at different frequencies to our world. Think of it like a radio, there are many stations and when you move the dial, you can pick up another station.

"The reason I'm telling you this is that I want you to join the programme, I need to prove this project is viable for a range of people, psychics and non-psychics. I need to compare experiences to establish validity and reliability. I need to know if you're in or not."

Pitch over, Paul now waited for the response.

"Hell, I'm in," Oscar piped up.

"Me too," said George, the other remote viewer, "I need a vacation."

Well, that was two for a start.

"I will do it," Sakie spoke up, her English clearer and less accented.

"I'm intrigued," said Beth, "count me in."

"That means I'll have to come too," Peter added.

Emilie shrugged her shoulders and said, "Me too."

That was all of them on board. All that remained was the non-psychic recruitment.

As the residents of The Institute dispersed, Max touched Paul on the arm and took him to one side. Tahra made herself scarce, disappearing up to the room she hid away in. She had testing for the next few days so had to stay at The Institute, not her favourite place to be as it lacked the cosiness of the farmhouse in which she stayed while working on the OOBE project. When the room was quiet again, Max demonstrated why he had taken Paul to one side.

"Remember when I came to see you at the cottage a while ago now, with a new project," he began.

"Ummmm, yes," Paul said, realising what would come next.

"Well, the project I asked you to look at, what progress have you made with it?"

The true answer was none but Paul didn't think Max would be too pleased to hear that, so, he had no choice, he had to lie.

"Good progress, it should be ready sometime soon," Paul responded.

"Excellent. If you could have the results on my desk in

twenty eight days that would be much appreciated," Max said, delighted.

"Er…yes, that'll be no problem," Paul confirmed.

Max smiled and returned to his office, feeling satisfied with the potential of a new product or service to offer his clients. A remote viewing blocking device would fetch a good price with organisations that had something to hide. However, Paul felt like kicking himself. How could he come up with the goods within twenty eight days? He didn't have much of an idea how to build a remote viewing blocking device, what kind of technology would do that job? And how could he pull that in alongside the demands of project OOBE? Then he realised the answer may not be too far away. Thinking of project OOBE… the serpents and therianthropes had implied mankind used to communicate with them to obtain knowledge. Maybe one of them could help. In the next few days, he would have to go back in the machine.

Back at the farmhouse, he had some time alone so used the opportunity to conduct a little theoretical research into shamanism and begin to look for evidence of prior human contact with other dimensions of reality. He avoided the general literature such as encyclopaedias, favouring more specific and slightly offbeat narratives instead. There was a surprising amount of cultural and historical data on a hypothetical otherworld, so much so that he realised that what they were doing with the machine was a reflection of what had gone before. The more he read, the more he realised the significance of the project and its far reaching implications. He closed the text book, assimilating what he had just learned. It was so awe inspiring that he knew he would have to explain it to Tahra when she returned.

It was longer than a few days before she returned due to a backlog of work at The Institute and he found he was getting used to her company more and more, so much so that her absence seemed abnormal. Max wasn't a hindrance; he wanted OOBE to succeed as much as Paul did so requesting Tahra's services did not attract undue attention. She arrived to find him on edge and he told her about the deadline set by Max regarding the remote viewing blocker device, so they postponed finding a new world until they could solve this problem first. He was full of excitement about the texts documenting the culture and history of shamanism but that would have to wait. Within the hour, the autopilot had been set for thirty minutes this time with the same frequencies in respect of their amplitude and resonance. This trip would also show whether or not there was any reliability in their experiments, could the same results be produced under identical conditions?

Paul felt the same sensations as before, he was now accustomed to the buzzing and tingling which indicated consciousness was about to separate from the body and he couldn't help but think that these were good, positive vibrations. However, before he could dwell on the feeling, his consciousness was ripped from his body and he felt the comforting tow of Tahra's presence. They emerged in the same arid desert again to Paul's relief, so it seemed that the serpents were right, entrance to certain realms did hinge upon the combination, resonance and amplitude of the frequencies overlaid onto the base frequency of 7.8 hertz.

They didn't see the mammoth hybrids this time or the human headed capuchin monkeys although they did see a flock of the strangest birds, with lion heads and the wings of eagles. They swooped low, fascinated by the visitors and screeched a melodic cry as they flew gracefully around them. This seemed to attract the attention of the more sentient beings in this world, for a tribe of ibis headed men appeared beside them.

"Greetings," one of them said, possibly the same entity they had spoken to last time. "Do you seek knowledge, my brave traveller?"

"Yes, how did you know?" Paul replied.

"It is the purpose of all visits to the other realms," the entity responded.

"Well," he began, "I was hoping you could help me with a little problem. I've been asked to produce a device which will block the ability of a person's consciousness to travel freely and view whatever they desire."

There was silence for a moment but then the entity answered with a question.

"Why do you wish to prevent this from happening? The purpose is to find knowledge and merge with the Monad, why would you want to hinder this?"

There was that name again, the Monad, although he had more pressing concerns.

"In my world, it is not used to gain enlightenment, it is used to spy upon the enemy and to know his next move. We wish to defend ourselves from this intrusion."

The entity considered his request.

"It is not our choice how knowledge is used. Human free will dictates how it will be applied but if it is used in a negative way, then humanity must deal with the consequences, that is the way of karma and it has always been this way."

"So, you'll help me?" Paul pressed, without truly considering what had been said.

"Yes, we can answer your question. It is simply a case of changing the frequency and its amplitude; an electromagnetic field pulsed at 7.8 kilohertz will successfully halt the consciousness and prevent this spying that you speak of."

Paul nodded.

"Seventy eight thousand hertz, that's in the upper range of human hearing. I should be able to create such a device. Many thanks for your assistance."

"You are most welcome, it is an honour to help and share our knowledge. We have been teachers of humanity since the dawn of man and have witnessed the rise and fall of many civilisations, good use and misuse of knowledge. Use this knowledge as you will and use it wisely."

Paul was ready to part company with the entity but Tahra felt the need to question him further.

"Since the dawn of man?" she questioned.

"The very first contact was made by a few individuals who ingested a sacred plant. We taught them how to make fire and grow crops, how to write. But it was much later when contact was practised on a wider scale by humanity, in your years this began approximately twelve thousand years ago and there was a golden age ten thousand years long. We refer to this as the First Time, when the other realms were understood and incorporated into spiritual practice. Mankind as a whole understood the Monad."

"I told the serpents that I intend to initiate the Second Time," Paul pointed out. "I want to revive that understanding we had and rediscover that lost knowledge."

"The very first seed of the Second Time has already been sown, in the time period you refer to as the 1940s. However, you are the first teachers of the new cycle."

"Can we find teachers in the other realms too? I believe there are many more," she said.

"Yes," the entity replied, "but they are not all benefactors of humanity. You need to be very careful of toxic energies, evil does exist as it has to, there is no good without its antithesis; how could you quantify either without its opposite? You will need to know how to tell the difference between entities who want to help and those who wish to do harm, further their own agenda."

"Do you ever cross over to our world?" she queried.

"The concept of 'crossing over' is a misnomer. It is a question of shifting perspective, like I discussed before. Consciousness must vibrate at the primeval number of 7.8 to see us."

"Are all the worlds interlaced and superimposed upon each other?" Paul asked, remembering something that had been referred to on their previous visit.

"You are correct in many ways; they exist as one, having no physical location. Visible matter in the universe accounts for a small ratio, the rest is invisible to you at the moment. But what lies in the spaces between the visible matter? Is it not the apparent emptiness that is more fascinating and worthy of exploration? Here you will find many other realms, if only your eyes could see. The enlightened mind can see the truth of this and understand. Sit quietly, in tune with the primeval number every day and it will come."

At that point, the field began to power down and the world of the therianthropes faded from view. Visits to this realm were invaluable; there was much to learn from them, the original teachers of humanity. The machine came into view and they climbed out, Paul immediately hunting for a notebook and pen to scribble down the information imparted to him. It looked like he would be meeting the deadline after all.

The machine was as addictive as a drug minus the side effects, so it was within the week that we made another journey in the machine, to scout out another world. He tantalised me by informing me he had some really important information to impart and I begged him to divulge it, but he put it off until we had a long evening free, when he'd completed Max's project. He also wanted to press forward with exploring with the machine, so it would have to wait.

Paul kept the harmonics at the lower end of the range, noting the combination of frequencies and amplitude beforehand. The travel guide was building up nicely and we were giving the worlds points out of ten for friendliness, aesthetic value and potential for acquiring knowledge. So far, the therianthrope world scored high but we needed to expand the guide a little more. There was a new addition to the machine, a set of speakers wired to a record player on the outside. Paul had decided that we should listen to some music as our consciousnesses left our bodies, to add a little drama to the experience. He hooked us up to the EEG and ECG as the record began to play.

The field powered up to the sound of 'New World Symphony' by Dvorak and our bodies tingled and buzzed to the music. Our consciousnesses appeared in a world that looked very similar to our own this time. We found ourselves in a grand city with a very American skyline full of tall buildings, which were connected by thin walkways along which some kind of tram rode. No one bothered much with ground level. The sky was an odd shade of lilac, with whitish grey clouds and it was illuminated by a triple star system. In fact, even though it was daylight, galaxies and nebulae could be seen quite clearly, giving this place a really otherworld feel. Lifts ran up the sides of the buildings and across the walkways too, so it was possible to zip across the city quite easily.

It was difficult to see the beings that lived here so we focused our consciousnesses towards one of the walkways and were immediately drawn there. Our non-corporeal bodies stood on the walkway, with the lifts and trams whizzing past us. There was a stop nearby and we saw people get off just outside one of the tall buildings. Surprisingly, they looked very human but when I peered at them more closely, I realised their skin was somewhat translucent and it was possible to perceive their internal organs, such as the brain which had the appearance of iridescent watery milk. Their eyes were misty, as if they all had cataracts. Even stranger, each person had a faint neon like outline, as if someone had drawn around them with a brightly coloured pen. I also realised that they each had some kind of clip attached to their temples which had a blinking light on it. They moved about their daily business not really noticing each other, more focused on what was going on inside their own heads. I wondered whether the little clip was wired into their brain and this was how they communicated with each other, through some kind of mechanical telepathy. They didn't notice us either, maybe out of lack of interest or simply because they didn't know we were here. It was impossible to tell if they were good or evil, they seemed indifferent.

We pushed our consciousnesses through the buildings, observing people quietly working. At each desk there was something like a very flat television and next to it, a black box with blinking lights. On the far wall was a really large screen like you would see at the cinema, there was some kind of grid displayed on it and a vertical stack of lights that flickered on and off in a wave like sequence. Still, no one spoke.

Then something quite disturbing happened, I heard a very loud voice in my head and Paul did too because we looked at each other at the same time.

"What are you doing here?" it said loudly.

It was impossible to tell where the sound was coming from because no one looked up. Should we try and answer? But we didn't get chance.

"Get out!" it shouted, so loudly that we wanted to cover our ears. "Get out!!"

We realised we were not welcome so withdrew our consciousnesses back to the walkway, but apparently that wasn't enough for there was now more than one voice.

"Get out!!!" they cried in unison.

Where could we go? We pulled back to street level, hoping the machine would power down so we could make a fast exit but that didn't happen. More voices joined in, it was getting deafening.

"Get out!!!!"

Panicking, I pulled my consciousness upwards and Paul followed, so we were getting a bird's eye view, rising higher above the city. Looking down, I realised that the city was endless and repetitive, stacks and stacks of skyscrapers as far as the eye could see. This world was just pure city, there was no green land to be seen for miles. It made me wonder how they ate, did they not grow crops? Did they just make it in a factory?

"Get out!!!!!"

More voices were joining in, it was almost painful. Even though we pushed our consciousness upward, there was just city. Finally, this world began to fade, as did the noise and we opened our eyes to find ourselves back in the machine, hearing the field power down and the sound of the needle stuck at the end of the record.

We made our way over to the camera, ready to record our experiences. Paul gave a description of the world we had just visited and drew a conclusion.

"I think I can safely say we'll blacklist that world," Paul said, still a bit dazed.

"I second that," I replied, "so ignorant!"

Our next trip was scheduled for four days time and just as I thought we'd have time to discuss Paul's revelation, we had some surprise visitors. In fact, I was almost caught out as it was a morning call and I was still wandering about the farmhouse in my dressing gown. I opened the door to find Max standing there along with Oscar and George. My jaw must have dropped and he looked very puzzled to find me answering the door as if it was my home (which, actually, it was although he wasn't supposed to know that). It was a good thing that I'd showered, as I wouldn't imagine the smell of sex on my body would please him much.

"Is Paul there?" Max said, a little irritated.

I was perturbed but I didn't want him to see that so quickly, I scurried away to find Paul.

Quietly, under my breath I said, "Max's here, at the door, did you know he was coming?"

Mirroring my tone of voice he murmured, "No, not at all. This is a bit... uncomfortable."

He finished dressing, threw on a shirt and made his way to the front door. I followed but hung around in the background.

"This is a surprise," I heard Paul say.

"Why is Tahra here and not in the designated guest rooms?" he asked, very directly.

The annoyance was clear in his voice and I could imagine Paul felt very much put on the spot.

"Well, I felt guilty about leaving her alone out there so I offered her one of the spare rooms here in the farmhouse. It's easier to discuss the project."

I was impressed with his quick thinking, hopefully Max bought it. I dearly hoped he wouldn't ask to see the room in which I had supposedly slept. Max grunted a begrudged acceptance.

"Are you going to leave me standing in the doorway?" he said, impatiently.

Paul apologised and Max, plus the two other visitors, Oscar and George came in. They all sat in the kitchen as we had a large pine table in there. Paul made tea and I heard them in conversation for a while and as no one welcomed me over, I relaxed in the sitting room, reading one of my heavy and somewhat dry text books from university. It was getting harder to stay focused on the studying but the end drew nearer, it would only infuriate Max if he had to deliver bad news to my father. It suddenly occurred to me that I hadn't written to my family for months, in fact, I had barely thought about them. What would my father think about what I was doing at the moment, sleeping with a white man outside of marriage? To me, it didn't really matter, I was an adult, what could he do?

Finally, Paul popped his head round the door and announced that Oscar and George had asked to make a journey in the machine, so they'd be staying for a while in the guest rooms. Then he added that Max was going to oversee this test run so would also be staying, in the farmhouse. He shrugged, we'd have to go along with it. No sex for a little while, then.

We sat and ate lunch together at the table; Paul at the head of the table and Max sat right opposite me, which was awkward. Sometimes he would give me a rather disconcerting stare and it made the atmosphere at the table very weird, Paul didn't seem to notice though, was I just over-sensitive?

Afterwards, Paul showed Oscar and George the machine; how it was operated, an explanation of how it worked in layman's terms and he showed them the inside of the machine. They all sat inside it, Max included to get a feel for it before the trip the next day.

Later, we took a ride out to a restaurant in the nearest town and I must admit, it was a great evening. I had to refuse alcohol as it affected my remote viewing capabilities and Oscar and George were advised of the same. Paul and Max laughed together like old friends and thankfully, this distracted him so he wasn't giving me the eye all evening.

It was strange having to sleep in one of the spare rooms, which we hurriedly made up as if I had been staying there on a regular basis. Max was sleeping in the room next to me and it took me a while to get off to sleep as I was half expecting him to come knocking on the door, although that didn't happen. I encountered him in the morning coming out of the bathroom, hair wet, and semi naked and I lowered my eyes, embarrassed by the feelings of arousal that tingled through my body. He brushed past me, watching me intensely then he disappeared into his room. I felt so irritated, why couldn't he just go away? From then on, I made sure I didn't encounter him emerging from the bathroom again.

It was a very sociable experience having them stay over and I must admit, it made a change from nights in with Paul and I savoured the company although it meant his revelation was still pending.

Finally, the day of the next journey arrived and it was time to move into the barn where the machine was. Oscar and George were very nervous but both Paul and I reassured them. I wondered if I could successfully tow the both of them, although I would soon find out.

We climbed into the machine, the hatch closed and we all held hands, as it was now custom to do so. Max watched from the outside. The sound of 'New World Symphony' by Dvorak' came over the speakers this time and we heard the field power up, at this point, I gave their hands a squeeze. The buzzing and tingling overtook my body and after my consciousness had moved from my body, I waited inside the machine for the two orbs of light that would be Oscar and George. It wasn't too long before I saw them, now came the hard part. I visualised a net that extended from my consciousness, scooping them up like little silvery fish then I allowed the frequencies to take over me and draw us to the intended destination.

A world came into focus, again very different to the last one, (the ignorant city realm) and identifiable as contrary to our own world. It had a similar appearance to the serpent realm, in that the colours were so luminous. The overall hue was a deep indigo with violet and blue tones and the substance, or fabric of this world was very fluid; it reminded me of liquid mercury with rainbow ripples, like when you drop motor oil into water. The sky was deepest indigo with the texture of suede and there appeared to be no light source, in fact, everything in this world seemed to be self illuminated.

The foliage was a little like the serpent world; there were huge ferns that appeared to have some kind of inner light and like the ignorant city world, seemed to be outlined in ink. However, there were no humans *here, in fact, there were some strange entities that looked like the Indian Gods and Goddesses of the Mahabharata. There were female beings with multiple arms and people with elephant heads; maybe they had contact with humanity at some point in history.*

Looking up, we saw a train of what appeared to be bubbles in the sky and inside them sat entities, drifting silently through the deep indigo sky. As the bubbles moved, it was possible to see the ripples created in the fluid medium in which they propelled themselves. The bubbles converged on a point in the sky and disappeared into it, it was impossible to tell where they were going.

I gave guidance to Oscar and George on creating a visible body in another realm and after a short while, they created a rudimentary form of themselves. It was all so much easier in the machine. We spent a long moment taking it all in.

"I don't know what to say, it's... realer than real, so vivid," Oscar said.

"Are all the worlds so beautiful?" George asked.

"Most of them, but this one is especially beautiful," I replied.

We began to explore a little more and move through the foliage. There were creatures moving through the undergrowth, quite reptilian but not quite dinosaur. They had fluidity to them, as if liquid mercury were running through their veins and were coloured shades of blue, purple and sometimes pink, with the same iridescent outline as the larger entities. There were some quite large reptiles with pink pustules on them, they saw that we were happy to see them and pulsed, or cycled through a range of colours from pale pink to darkest blue. Other creatures like iguanas scuttled about. The happier we became, the more illuminated the world became so that the hues switched from dark indigo and violet to pale blue and lilac. We couldn't help but laugh with happiness; it was an interactive and surprising spectacle.

"Do you think we could communicate with them?" Oscar asked me.

I was thoughtful then replied, "I think we just did."

"But we didn't say anything," Oscar responded.

"We communicated with our emotions," I answered, "and they responded."

He began to understand now, not all communication involved words. It was hard to maintain sufficient emotional input to exact a response from them and the harder we forced it, the less feedback we got. The initial reaction we had previously was probably due to free flow of emotions.

Then the field powered down and the emotion realm faded from view, to be replaced by the interior of the machine. Paul opened the hatch, hopeful of results while I could see Max perusing the situation, keeping his thoughts to himself.

"Well, what happened?" Paul asked. "Let's get over to the camera."

Oscar and George were almost stunned into silence so I gave them a squeeze of my hand and led them over to the corner of the room designated for cine camera feedback.

"I... think that experience has just changed my life," Oscar said into the camera.

It would be true to say none of us would be the same ever again. I gave a description of the world we had just visited.

"I do believe we met Ganesh," Oscar added. As Paul looked puzzled he added, "You know, the Indian God thing with an elephant head."

"More references to ancient Gods," he pondered out loud, but not enough for Max to hear or to be recorded on film.

Max wandered over, arms still folded in some kind of display of authority.

"So, is this project viable?" he asked, as only a businessman would.

Paul looked satisfied and could barely contain his excitement.

"Send the rest of The Institute's residents over," was his emphatic response.

Max took Oscar and George back to The Institute, leaving the farmhouse quiet once more. Paul sat at the pine table in the kitchen while Tahra was upstairs having a bath. It was a good opportunity to return to the literature concerning mankind's encounters with supernatural beings, he needed to read more of the essays on the subject so that he could add to his notes and then share his revelation with Tahra. He was delighted when she emerged from upstairs, with damp hair and wearing her dressing gown.

"Sit down," he said, excited, "I've got a story to tell you."

She took little persuading and sat next to him on the sofa, nicely warmed by a roaring fire.

"I've been reading up on the history and culture of shamanism," he began, "and you'll be amazed at what I've discovered."

She was all ears so he began.

"The basis of shamanism is that there is a hypothetical otherworld that interpenetrates our own everyday world and it can't be seen by any normal means because it's invisible."

Tahra nodded.

"That's what the therianthropes told us, in essence," she confirmed.

"While we use the machine to access the invisible worlds, tribal shamans would travel to other realms by consuming sacred plants such as iboga and ayahuasca."

She considered what Paul had just said and then made a valid point.

"But did they access the same worlds as we did in the machine?" she queried. "Is there any frame of reference?"

"This is where it gets exciting," he began. "Typical 'visionary experiences' involved snakes or serpents, geometrical shapes, ladders, pulsing lights, *entities with men's bodies and crocodile heads...* Sound familiar?"

She really began to pay attention to what he was telling her now.

"What's amazing is the remarkable consistency of these visions, not only among the shaman tribes but with our experiments."

"Although we've encountered worlds and entities that

these visionary experiences haven't mentioned," she countered. "Is the chemical journey as valid as the ones in the machine? Psychologists tend to see psychoactive substances as short term 'model psychoses'," Tahra explained.

"Maybe psychedelic substances are tools. Let me elucidate," he began. "Since early history, the use of psychotropic plants has been well documented. The Eleusinian Mysteries of the Greeks were held for two thousand years, a practice that began in Eleusia in Greece but eventually it spread to Rome. Powerful personal experiences were undergone in the Hall of Initiation. On entry to the Hall, everyone was obliged to drink a special potion which induced visions and a feeling of oneness. Scholars believe the potion, named 'kykeon' was a concoction of barley and pennyroyal and it is interesting to note that the parasitic fungus, ergot grows on barley and that ergot was the substance from which LSD was synthesised.

"The initiation was believed to *unite the worshippers with the Gods and included promises of divine power and rewards* in the afterlife. It is likely many of the rites centred around a re-enactment of the Demeter/Persephone myth, in which Demeter's daughter was abducted to the Underworld, where her mother had to search for her. Along the way, she *teaches* the secrets of agriculture. Even though she was rescued, Persephone had to return to the Underworld for a season each year, during which no plants grew."

"Hmmm," Tahra's opinion on chemical tools to expand consciousness began to sway, "I can't help but wonder if the Underworld to where Persephone was taken was some other dimension. Interesting how there is reference to the sharing of knowledge and teaching; something both the serpents and therianthropes have referred to. Are there any descriptions of this Underworld in the Eleusinian Mysteries?"

"No," Paul said, sadly. "The practices were kept strictly secret, there's very little information what these visions involved."

"Maybe these mysteries are part of the First Time that the

therianthropes have referred to," Tahra pondered aloud.

"There's more," Paul continued. "Further references to psychoactive brews are found in the Vedas, many of which are devoted to a potion called 'soma'. It's referred to as plant, drink and God as one entity and it was believed to bestow divine qualities in the drinker. Listen to these quotes: 'I am huge, huge! Flying in the clouds. Have I not drunk soma?' Here's another one I wrote down: 'We have drunk the soma, we are become Immortals, we have arrived at the light, we have found the Gods'."

Tahra's eyes began to open wider, in many ways.

"I love the references to flying," she commented. "They remind me of my own experiences in the early stages of the OOBE project."

"Exactly," Paul reinforced. "But it gets better. Although there are no references to psychoactive brews being ingested, religious texts contain many visionary experiences and encounters with supernatural beings. Look at the seeds of Christianity: Moses saw a burning bush and accepted heavenly writings, St. Paul had a supernatural encounter on the road to Damascus and don't forget that Mary, mother of Christ was visited by angels."

"Now that you come to mention it," Tahra added, "the Prophet Muhammad had encounters with the Angel Gabriel, who gave him the text of the Qur'an."

Paul smiled. "And the Book of Mormon was presented by the Angel Moroni on golden plates that vanished into thin air."

They reflected on the examples discussed. It was Paul who drew the conclusion.

"The basis of our religions seem to revolve around Shamanism," he concluded. "They have a common frame of reference, and therefore a common bond of spirituality. Even Buddhism, which has no God, revolves around a personal journey of enlightenment. It's idiocy that religion causes wars, when its fundamental precepts come from the same place."

Tahra nodded, seeing the irony.

"The wars are about the validity of the messenger," she pointed out. "Each religion believes in one God, but they fight over whose God is true and whose teachings are right."

"We can blame the invention of monotheism for that," Paul commented. "Until Akhenaten changed everything, Egyptian religion revolved around a whole pantheon of Gods; the full spectrum of extra-dimensional entities. They believed in the Otherworld, which they referred to as the Duat. If you look at Paganism, the ancient nature based spiritual beliefs pre-dating Christianity, it too reflected deities and spirits synchronous with a creator entity. We've lost our awareness of these supernatural entities in favour of an all powerful God who controls the world. It's... sacrilegious," he said, almost in disgust.

Tahra was thoughtful.

"Definitely many of the world's religions recognise the other dimensions in the most simplistic sense, although it's reduced to a very monochromatic Heaven and Hell. I certainly haven't encountered anything akin to Hell yet," she said.

"Much of it does boil down to the ability of people to see these other realms," he pointed out. "It's possible that a few individuals were able to see these worlds and beings without the use of psychoactive plants. It was certainly seen as something natural and sacred, with great emphasis placed on these individuals as being special, gifted or holy."

"It's ironic that modern psychiatrists would see these same individuals as delusional or psychotic; *mentally ill.*"

Paul looked sad at that remark.

"How many gifted people reside in mental institutions for accessing the other dimensions? It will make my dream of initiating the Second Time a real battle."

"Well, there must be hope," Tahra said. "Are there not more modern anecdotes concerning contact with supernatural entities that don't involve insanity?"

Paul nodded. "Yes, both Joan of Arc and Bernadette of

Lourdes received visitations and encounters with a being referred to as 'our lady'. However, Joan was burned at the stake and wasn't as lucky as Bernadette. Such visions are not always confined to lone experiences either.

"A mass visionary experience culminated on 13th September 1917 when thirty thousand people witnessed a globe of light and the formation of a white cloud where previously three Catholic children had claimed to have seen the Virgin Mary. 'Petals' fell from the sky, although it was reported that the glistening globules grew smaller as they got nearer and melted away when people tried to touch them. It certainly sounds like some contact with the other dimensions, although there's no evidence of drug use. I'm stumped as to how thirty thousand people could see the same vision though."

Tahra added another revelation.

"What about the creatures of folklore such as elves, leprechauns and fairies, more anecdotes of the non-physical realms?"

"Quite possibly," he responded, "although we haven't encountered any."

"Our ancestors didn't have the machine though," Tahra pointed out, "we have a very powerful tool here."

"I'm not so sure about that," Paul pondered. "Before I built the machine, remember that dream I told you about?" Tahra nodded. "I believe the Egyptians used the Great Pyramid to commune with their Gods, these inter-dimensional entities. This was part of the First Time. What I don't understand is; *why did they stop using it?*"

Tahra shrugged.

"We must look to the future now. I believe, from my heart that we will initiate the Second Time."

Paul smiled, warmed by her faith and enthusiasm.

"Well, the therianthropes said the very first seed of this was planted in the 1940s."

"I remember," she agreed. "What do you think they were referring to?"

"I'm not sure, but there was some very interesting research carried out in that decade." Paul grabbed his notes to get his facts right. "In 1946, a psychoactive substance called Dimethyltryptamine, or DMT was isolated from a South American tree by a Hungarian chemist. He attempted to create an oral based solution but found it was inactive due to an enzyme in the intestines so eventually in 1956 he injected himself with it. After a successful but short trip, he injected thirty volunteers, who experienced visions of spirits, sunlit Gods and a sense of flight from their body. What's significant about DMT is that it's endogenous, in other words, it's a naturally occurring substance in our bodies." He paused then continued. "But I'm not sure it was this the therianthropes were referring to, maybe there's something... much bigger I'm missing."

They were both silent for a long moment.

"Maybe DMT is simply a mediator," he concluded. "I'm not sure how this is connected to the Second Time though. I believe my machine is the key."

"You must keep the faith in what you're doing," she reassured. "Our project really can change the world."

She laid her head on his shoulder and he hugged her. That thought was all that mattered.

Tahra returned to The Institute a few days later, while Paul wrote in his OOBE journal to record the experiences inside the machine. He liked to write detailed reflections and include technical information regarding the progress of the project. Tahra found The Institute less and less interesting and still tried to avoid Max, although he was regularly present during testing just lately. There was, as ever a waiting list for her special skills and he had several sessions lined up for her, so each time she returned, she had a backlog of work to clear. She was starting to think she was spending more time out of her body than in it.

It was strange not being in the machine to project her consciousness, but she knew the task didn't require technological help. It was easy, like playing with a pre-school toy. She was given some coordinates and a map, which she glanced over, then lay back and closed her eyes. The target was some kind of educational institution and an old, Victorian-like building came into view. It was very grand, probably very elitist and full of stuffy old professors. The strange thing was that this test felt much more vivid than her usual sessions at The Institute, in fact, it felt no different than if she'd walked up to it in her physical body.

She pushed her consciousness towards the heavy, studded oak door and it was so lucid she could clearly see the grain. Tahra moved through the door and felt herself glide down the corridors, it felt so free and liberating as she extruded effortlessly through the doors and walls. She passed by the people in the building who were making their way to classrooms or to the library and their faces were as clear as day; she could see their expressions as clearly as if she was standing right next to them. The words they spoke were much lucid and not as garbled as they usually were when remote viewing. For all intents and purposes, she was physically present in the building and the only reason she disbelieved that was because no one could see her.

But she didn't want to be here, it was mundane, not profound or spiritual like the other realms. A wistful feeling passed over her, making her yearn for the magical quality of the journeys in the machine. Then, probably due to her attention being diverted elsewhere, she suddenly wasn't in the educational institution anymore. A familiar face loomed in her vision and it was very vivid. The ibis headed entity from the therianthrope world spoke.

"Well done, my brave traveller. You have made it on your own."

Tahra opened her eyes. Was that a dream, a trick of the mind, or was she retaining the effects of the machine?

20
Now Recruiting

It was the beginning of September 1966; the excitement over a triumphant conclusion to the football World Cup in which England had been victorious had died down, although Paul had taken little notice of it. He was more concerned with taking project OOBE to the next level. Twenty people, a mixture of men and women arrived at The Establishment. They had been selected by Max for Paul to interview and recruit, although Paul had asked two of his favourite people to sit in on the interviews to give a second opinion. He needed to know Tahra would be able to work with them and he had asked Emilie to sit in to pick up any false pretences and hidden agendas that would be harmful to the project. It was a tense partnership between the two women, as Emilie had never really taken to Tahra but she thought highly of Paul and if he trusted Tahra, then she needed to as well.

He met them in the ostentatious hallway and the potential recruits marvelled at the high ceiling, the grand staircase and the oak panelling which gave The Establishment that stately home feel. As they stood around in awe, Paul quickly surveyed them; there was a black man and woman with the most outrageous afros, a petite copper haired girl, a Spanish looking woman, a fat man who looked grumpy and the rest looked like the average male or female from suburbia.

"This is really neat," said the black woman in between chewing gum, her accent revealed that she was American.

Paul ushered them to the communal sitting room, where Tahra and Emilie were waiting. Again, the potential recruits marvelled at the luxurious surroundings; there were beautiful green leather sofas to sit on, a magnificent inglenook fireplace and William Morris wallpaper adorning the walls. They looked Tahra and Emilie over, curious as to their role and they sat on the sofas when Paul asked them. As they were a bit short on seating, Paul and Tahra brought in some oak dining chairs from the adjacent room. He shushed the room of its excited chatter and introduced himself.

"Welcome to The Establishment," he began, "my name is Dr Paul Eldridge and this is Tahra Mamoun, my associate and Emilie Charron, an advisor."

He gestured to them and they were both faced with twenty pairs of curious eyes, momentarily.

"You are here because you've been short listed to take part in a project which will push you to the borders of incredibility, it will test your sense of reality and your nerve, so it is not for the fainthearted. You will need to be open minded and psychologically stable, so I stress to you now, if this is not for you, then I highly recommend you stand up and exit the room now."

Eyes widened in response to his honest and direct introduction, it provoked some chatter amongst the potential recruits but there was no way to ease them in gently, he needed to know they had the mental tenacity to handle it. There was an awkward moment, some shuffling of feet but thankfully, no one left the room.

"Well," piped up the black man with the mighty afro, "that's why we're all here! I don't dig reality anyway."

He was American too.

"Good. That means you're all motivated. I'm not going to explain the project yet, we're going to get to know each other first, as the six of you who are selected will need to be able to work together. It will give me, Tahra and Emilie an impression of your personality, your strengths and qualities and it will help you relax into the day."

He paused and then continued.

"Our schedule for today is mingling for the first forty five minutes, we will participate in some icebreakers and then go into a coffee break. After that, we'll administer some personality tests and questionnaires, take lunch which will be provided and the afternoon will focus on one to interviews. I have decided to interview ten of you, so you'll know after lunch whether you have been short listed or not. We'll make our decision tonight and you'll be notified by telephone tomorrow, with details of the dates and remuneration. Any questions about today's activities?"

Everyone thought the instructions were clear. The sofas and chairs were moved to one side and Paul set up some simple games that enabled everyone to get to know each other. Tahra got involved while Emilie was the objective observer, picking up on the undercurrents. She soon realised there was a relationship between Paul and Tahra, it stood out a mile and she sensed there was a great secrecy surrounding this, so for his sake, she would respect that. The two Americans were very conspicuous in terms of their honesty and transparency; they were people who had come here for reasons of personal development. Others had been enticed by the money and were in it for purely financial reasons, while some of these were also inquisitive and were keen to be involved to satisfy their curiosity. The Spanish lady was hiding something, the fat grumpy man felt as if he would rather be elsewhere and didn't have the social skills to mix with the others. She didn't like the way he eyed her up either.

They continued to mingle into the coffee break and then Paul took them upstairs in small groups of four to a research room, where he administered some personality tests. While he did this, Tahra and Emilie kept the others occupied by asking each person to give a short presentation about a favourite topic of theirs. Subjects ranged from The State of Tennessee, Spanish Cuisine, The Lost Library of Alexandria, Music of the 1960s, English Literature Classics, The Future of Robots, Renaissance

Art and Films of the 1920s. It was insightful as to what made these people tick, as individuals.

The morning passed quickly and it was soon lunch time. The presentation topics stimulated discussion over the delicious buffet that Max had ordered for them. Emilie gave Paul some initial feedback regarding who she believed were the most suitable potential candidates and Tahra fed into that too, his results largely reflected their gut feelings. So, by the end of lunch, he knew who had made it to the interview stage. He gathered them together, shushed the chatter and announced the lucky candidates.

"As you know, only ten of you will be interviewed this afternoon and we have come to a decision who these individuals will be."

He paused for effect.

"We will interview; Angelina Cortez, Tyrone Simpson, Nicholas Blair, Kevin Whitehouse, Samantha Thane, Sonya Marsh, Curtis Jacobs, Jane Berry, Dominique Benitez and Sally Harper. Those of you who didn't make it to interview, thank you very much for your time and effort and safe journey home. Transport has been arranged to take you back to the centre of London."

Half of the people in the room stood up, gathered their belongings and made their way to the entrance hall where three taxis awaited them. Some were sad that they hadn't made it, a few were nonchalant as it was, after all, just a job. The lucky ones still remaining in the sitting room were now wondering exactly what they'd let themselves in for.

He continued.

"You will be asked ten questions in the interview, some of them may seem quite strange and irrelevant to you, but all I ask is to answer them as honestly as possible, no matter how odd they may seem. You may be tempted to lie about some of these, thinking that I'm trying to catch you out but the questions that you may believe will eliminate you from the project will turn out to be the ones that will help me select you above the others. Best of luck with the afternoon."

Paul took them upstairs for interview one at a time. There were three crucial questions that would ultimately be the decider, he needed to know how open minded they were. He had already established that the ten remaining candidates were psychologically stable, with a strong mental constitution. Now he wanted to know what their beliefs were and what past experiences modelled them. There were clearly six people who stood out.

Angelina Cortez was the American woman with quite a flamboyant personality and honest manner. She was confident and warm, averagely attractive with full lips, large brown eyes and a huge afro, a front runner so far. Paul asked his final three questions in the interview.

"Have you ever taken hallucinogenic drugs or used marijuana?"

Angelina shifted uncomfortably in her seat and wasn't sure how to answer, realising this question could end her potential involvement in the project then she remembered what he had told them all.

"What the hell," she began, "I ain't gonna lie about myself. Yeah, I've taken hallucinogenic drugs and I smoke dope too."

Paul smiled.

"Do you enjoy them on a regular basis?" he added.

"I smoke dope every day, a few joints and I take acid about once a month, hey, I ain't the only one."

He continued with the next question.

"What is the most profound religious or spiritual experience you've ever had?"

Angelina took a moment to consider then answered with conviction, "My first trip."

"Why?" Paul probed.

She didn't hesitate with the response.

"It blew my mind," she replied. Then, out of sheer curiosity she added, "So, you tried it too?"

Paul admired her directness.

"Yes, I have," he answered, "but I've discovered something more mind blowing than acid."

Her eyes widened.

"Please tell me that you're gonna reveal all," she said.

"I think you're going to find out," he reassured her.

Then he went onto the final question.

"What are your reasons for wanting to join this project?"

She sat back in her chair, feeling much more relaxed and confident.

"I wanna open my mind," she responded, "nothing else to say really, my aim in life is to experiment, see everything there is to see, know everything there is to know, feel everything there is to feel. That's my goal."

Paul had already decided; she was in.

Tyrone Simpson was next, Angelina's partner. He looked quite similar with his large afro, full lips and big eyes. He wasn't as direct as her, although still a very straightforward kind of person; Angelina had more attitude but he had a greater wit. Tyrone gave almost identical answers to Angelina and Paul soon realised he couldn't have one without the other. It would be a pleasure to work with them.

He interviewed Nicholas Blair next, quite a tall man who had short, fair, curly hair and blue piercing eyes. His manner was eloquent, somewhat reserved yet he was perceptive and knowledgeable. He had given the presentation on the Lost Library of Alexandria.

On being asked if he had ever taken hallucinogenic drugs or marijuana, he answered,

"Once or twice, I wondered what I could learn from it."

"And did you learn anything from it?" Paul continued.

"I'm not sure... I mean, I didn't learn anything factual, I

analysed the experience although it's sometimes hard for my scientific brain to switch off. More than anything it opened my mind, made me aware that possibly there is something more to life."

Another solid contender, Paul questioned him further.

"Would you take LSD again?"

Nicholas considered the question carefully.

"Maybe another type of hallucinogen, I'd want a different experience."

When Paul queried his most profound moment, the answer was quite surprising.

"When I first read about the lost library of Alexandria, the idea of a vast collection of knowledge that has vanished forever, it inspired and saddened me at the same time. I always wonder what books it contained, what information…"

Paul smiled.

"And what are your reasons for wanting to join the project?"

"The potential for knowledge," he answered, "I want to learn something few people will get the chance to experience."

It seemed a reasonable motivation and Paul concluded he was a strong contender, depending on the other seven candidates.

Kevin Whitehouse was the next interviewee, a balding man in his forties who had travelled around the world and worked in quite a few different countries. He was not particularly interested in the drug experience, although his profound experience in Goa was his saving grace. His motivations for joining the project were quite straightforward; he had travelled around the world and needed to top the experience. Paul concluded that in some ways he was a suitable recruit, but he wasn't sure if he was open minded enough to withstand the very surreal nature of the journeys.

Samantha Thane had come across well in the psychometric testing but didn't interview well. She was very anti-drugs and had never really experienced anything that could be considered profound, with an almost indifferent response to the nature of her interest in the project, 'just curious' didn't cut it for Paul, he needed to see a spark ready to ignite.

However, Sonya Marsh was a different matter. She was petite with straight copper hair and freckles, green eyes and a slim build. Although she had never taken drugs, she was very open to the idea of trying to inspire herself musically. She played the cello and piano and was very devoted to classical composition and performance. Her most profound experience was hard to choose as there were so many on a daily basis when she wrote or played music. She wanted to join the project as her experiences would hopefully inspire her to write beautiful music. Paul decided she was another strong contender.

Curtis Jacobs also managed to impress Paul. He was young, still at university studying engineering and he hoped one day to build a robot. Averagely attractive, he had shoulder length brown hair and was of a slim build. Like many young people coming of age in the sixties, he had dabbled with hallucinogenic drugs and rated it as his most profound experience to date. As for his reason to get involved, he did confess to desperately needing the money but at the same time, he had come to realise, through taking drugs, that there was more to life; some spiritual reason for being here and not just to study engineering. His parents wanted him to study structural engineering whereas he was fascinated by robotics, 'they're the future', he stated. Paul considered him a recruit as he had a good feeling about him.

Jane Berry wasn't a likely candidate and neither was the last interviewee, Sally Harper, their views were too traditional and their concept of the world quite limited. That left Dominique Benitez as the last possibility. Something about her reminded him of Tahra. They didn't look particularly alike, Dominique's eyes were large with huge eyelashes, her nose narrow and her mouth wide, she had a fiery intensity about her expected from a Spanish woman, concealing a personal tragedy. It transpired she was seeking sanctuary from an abusive boyfriend and for that reason, he believed he had to rule her out but during the discussion afterwards, Tahra decided there and then Dominique was in.

"It will empower her, she's a strong woman and she can take the demands of the project."

"She'll be a wild card," Paul protested, "although her psychometric tests were sound, I'm worried about her."

"I'll look after her," Tahra insisted.

Paul had to concede, Dominique was in, along with Angelina, Tyrone, Nicholas, Sonya and Curtis. Now he had a complete team.

It was the morning of September 21st 1966, which so happened to be the autumn equinox and Tahra mentally prepared herself to begin guiding the residents of The Institute. She listened to the new Beatles L.P, 'Revolver', over a cup of tea and several slices of toast, wishing 'Eleanor Rigby' was a more cheerful tune. Shortly after, the six residents of The Institute arrived at the farmhouse ready to begin phase one of their involvement in the project. Oscar and George had already had a trip in the machine because they were accustomed to the out of body sensation but the others weren't, so Paul was going to minimise their exposure initially while they orientated themselves to the experience. He explained to Emilie, Sakie, Beth and Peter how he would ease them into the project, too much too soon would not be healthy for their state of mind.

The four of them sat inside the machine an hour later, wondering what to expect. It was quite a relaxing experience, Paul set the frequency of the electromagnetic field to 10 hertz, creating a subtle ambience and he even played some soothing music, Dvorak's New World Symphony, which was starting to look like the theme song for the machine, mainly due to a lack of any other contender. He then tuned it down to 7.8 hertz, which was also inaudible, announcing over the internal speaker that he was going to create an out of body sensation and that they mustn't be nervous. They responded well to the frequency, finding themselves floating peacefully inside the machine, free of their physical body. After five minutes, Paul tuned the frequency back up to 10 hertz for another few minutes then switched it off, opening the hatch with his heart pounding in his chest.

All four had a smile on their faces as it had been a good, albeit brief trip. Each person reported experiencing an out of body sensation and for these four, it was the first time it had happened. Paul sent them for a medical with Dr. Harrow, who was contracted to Max's facilities on a part-time basis and the preliminary results were good. They would be re-tested again after 48 hours and if everything checked out, he'd repeat the same experiment.

During that time, the residents of The Institute enjoyed staying with Paul and Tahra. It became known to the residents that they were in a relationship, which Tahra felt a little uneasy about but they all promised to keep it a secret. If anything, it was good to be part of their lives again, since Tahra had been absent frequently and Paul had only seen some of them briefly since 1962. They laughed and joked like old times, shared good food and fine wine while discussing the project.

Before long, they received another orientation in the machine, were checked out medically and all four confirmed they were ready for the next step. Tahra led two separate excursions into the serpent realm, as it was visually beautiful and the beings there were not hostile. First, she took Emilie and Sakie on a trip where they were exposed to the field and frequency for ten minutes, just so they could, essentially take a peek to see how they coped with seeing another world so completely alien to their own. Beth and Peter were taken on the next session 48 hours later. All four agreed it was a profound experience, that it felt realer than real and that it radically altered their view of reality and the universe. Tahra hadn't taken them beyond the previous level of exploration, so there was nothing new to present to the camera, just a report on the response of the participants.

"You know," Beth said, "I get the feeling we'll never be the same after this project."

Paul agreed. "It is life changing, you can't fail to be touched by the experience. It takes away the loneliness of existence."

He took statements from them, individually, concerning their experience. The reports were remarkably consistent, showing impressive reliability for the project so far and there was no question in Paul's mind that the frequencies did not give random results, but that each combination correlated with a different world, or dimension.

Over the next two weeks, they made a follow up visit to the serpent realm and a subsequent visit to the emotion world, again with Tahra guiding them two at a time. Again, she was careful to work within the confines of previous explorations, avoiding any unexpected encounters or nasty surprises. It came to pass that by the middle of October, they were addicted to the journeys in the machine and were ready to explore a new world. Paul warned them that not all realms were hospitable, indeed some could be very unfriendly but they understood the risks and knew the field would power down after twenty minutes and bring them home to their bodies. So it was that Sakie was chosen for the next trip.

On this occasion, Paul expressed a desire to go back in the machine so taught Oscar how to oversee the process, clearly instructing him on the sequence in which the frequencies and field needed to boot up. This allowed them to make a longer journey without fear of no supervision and Oscar himself felt honoured to operate the machine. The hatch closed, the field powered up to the sound of 'New World Symphony' and Paul, Tahra and Sakie found themselves hurled out of their bodies.

We emerged in a world vastly different again to anything we had seen before. The first thing we were aware of was the noise, it was almost deafening; an electronic screech that pierced the 'eardrums' and was disturbing in the fact that it was so relentless. It was difficult to pinpoint the source, in fact, it seemed to be generated by the very medium of space we found ourselves in. The screech did change pitch and modulation, but it never let up.

I looked over to find a likeness of Tahra and Sakie beside me, equally horrified by the horrendous noise we were confronted with. It felt as if it were trying to invade one's brain, attempting to penetrate the grey matter and communicate with the electrical impulses travelling along the neurons and across the synapses. After a while, we began to adjust to the intense environment and tried to focus on the visual aspects of this world.

The fabric of this world looked like the white noise you see on your television screen when it isn't tuned into a station, the individual points of light jiggled and danced in a kind of cosmic waltz, spinning each other round giddily. It was necessary to focus hard here, because at first glance there was nothing to see but once you accustomed your consciousness to its wavelength, you realised it was very busy.

In between the dancing points of light, we all soon realised there were other points of light that flashed on and off in miniature explosions, they were not dancing, they were jumping. These points of light were, perhaps, travelling through this fabric of white noise. But were these points of light some kind of craft or vehicle, and if so, were there any forms of life inside them?

"We need to find the entities that inhabit this place," I said, aware that the field would power down before long.

Tahra and Sakie agreed, but how to find them was another matter.

"I think we need to focus on a point of light and jump onto it before it pops up somewhere else," Tahra suggested.

"It would need to be the same point of light, we don't want to lose each other," I said.

"But we are too big," Sakie protested.

"Size has no relevance when in non-physical form," I reassured her.

"I'll choose a point and tow you," Tahra decided.

A moment later, Sakie and I felt ourselves being pulled, or more accurately, dragged at high speed. We hurtled towards a point of light and it was as if everything suddenly converted to quick time. Everything exploded across my field of vision so fast that I couldn't take it in and I found I had to re-focus my consciousness to adjust to this flow of time.

When I had done this, I began to realise there was no flow of time, flow being the incorrect world. There was a being inside the point of light, like a very small whitish-grey person with black beady eyes and no discernable sexual features. The strangest thing about this little person was that it appeared to jump through the fabric of time, very much like watching a reel of film not as a continuous movie, but sampling a bit here and a bit there from different points in the reel. It was truly weird, for one moment it was facing us, ready to communicate, then within the blink of an eye, it was doing something randomly different, like checking the controls on its ship of light. Was the entity subject to the bizarre rule of time here, or was it manipulating time as a means to an end?

"How do we communicate with it?" Tahra said.

"With great difficulty," I answered.

The entity acknowledged our presence and pondered our bewilderment. I realised we could attempt to initiate a conversation.

"Why does time flow in no logical order here?" Tahra asked.

The entity continued to appear at different points in the craft, but he inputted some sequence at the control panel and some semblance of logic seemed to settle in the interior of the craft.

"Time is not what it seems," the little being responded, "it does not flow in one direction, in fact, it has no direction at all. I have merely created an illusion inside this craft that time flows, so that you can have this conversation with me."

"Is there any meaning to the flow of time, or is it an illusion'?" I enquired, realising that he had done us a favour creating an artificial arrow of time.

"The future exists simultaneously with the past, and simultaneously with the present. All is one. The difference between past, present and future is an illusion."

"But why do we have time if it has no real meaning?" Tahra questioned.

"Time is what prevents everything from happening at once," it answered, "it is a construction of human artifice, a concept that belongs to the world of matter only."

"But why do we have time, and clocks, and seasons?" Sakie asked, in disbelief, finding the whole concept too mind boggling.

"Time is to tell you when to plant your crops and harvest them, when the sun will rise and set so that it will make your crops grow and to tell you to awaken and sleep, so that you may consume these crops to make your body of physical matter live and breathe and grow. Time only has meaning to you as you have constructed it; you require it to function in your world as you have made it, because you require a limited view of reality to survive. In the realm of energy alone, time has no meaning."

"But if everything happens at once..." Tahra began to protest. I think maybe she began to see the significance of the concept it was trying to explain.

"This conversation happens at once, with no beginning or end..." I realised. "Everything we do happens at once..."

"Are you, as human beings ready to see past, present and future as one?" the being was close to us now. "To understand the nature of time is to participate in it and direct it, to be at one with the Monad."

"Yes," I insisted. "I want to see the true nature of time."

"Then see," it said.

With that, it picked up what appeared to be a sword very similar to the ones used in fencing but it was more like a needle-thin laser. It moved towards us, holding it like a weapon and aimed straight for our eyes. We all flinched, yet felt powerless to move but luckily at that point, the field powered down and the white noise realm faded from sight. I looked over at Tahra and Sakie, who looked quite bewildered. We moved over to the cine camera and described the world.

"I feel like I'm going crazy," Tahra said, head in hands.

"I'm crazy too," Sakie agreed, her English much improved.

I commented, "We never got to see the true nature of time though, did we?"

"I'm not sure if I'm ready," Tahra admitted. "I feel as if I don't know what reality is anymore."

I considered what she said.

"You'll feel different in a few days time," I reassured her, "you need a chance to digest what you're seeing, that's all."

She looked at me, for once I detected that she didn't quite believe me and that did upset me. Was I right? But then I convinced myself that nothing ventured, nothing gained. Anything worth having did not come without difficulty, this project was so groundbreaking, so profound; we were dealing with realities so radically different from our own that it was going to shake our belief systems to the core. With that, we re-grouped with the rest of the team to relax and wind down. I would take their statements after a well-earned coffee break.

On the afternoon of 21st October 1966, the last six recruits arrived at the farmhouse looking enthusiastic and cheerful. It was an antidote to the sad news of the day; in the Welsh village of Aberfan, a slag heap had slithered onto a junior school, killing 150 people which were mainly children. It had happened at 9.30 that morning, precisely the moment Beth had spontaneously burst into tears as she had heard the voices of over a hundred dead children. Only later, had the news broadcast on the radio added clarity to the psychic distress she had witnessed. She was upset because she wished she could have prevented it, not sensed it; clairvoyance would have been more useful than hearing the already dead.

The residents of The Institute were all ready to meet and greet the final group of recruits and the sitting room was used as a communal area. The socialising helped Beth overcome her dark mood. Paul presided over the first introductions, going through the motions so that by the end of it, everyone knew each other's names well. They mingled over a small buffet with sandwiches, sausage rolls and cakes, something Paul had thrown together at the last minute as they didn't have the culinary organisation of Max this time. There was plenty of tea and coffee, and Tahra was happy to pose as a temporary waitress. She put the radio on in the background, to encourage a less formal atmosphere.

Once the mingling had begun, Paul was able to stand back as an objective observer and analyse the psychodynamics of this new group. Angelina and Tyrone were very dominant in the group although he was relieved to see this did not cause any resentment, they were naturally effervescent characters with a particular rapport with Oscar. This was not surprising as they both had a Caribbean ancestry. Nicholas was the erudite connoisseur of knowledge, he seemed to indulge in quite shallow conversation at first and Paul was worried he wouldn't cohere with the group but then he seemed to latch onto Emilie and become deeply involved in a discussion about something. There seemed to be a spark of attraction between the two.

"I see a romance brewing," Tahra sing-songed as she brushed by Paul.

Sonya flirted around the whole of the group and was a clever little chameleon; she really could be all things to all people. She enjoyed the attention as everyone was keen to hear about her fledgling musical career. Curtis seemed to prefer male company, spending equal amounts of time chatting to Tyrone, George, Oscar and Peter, so maybe he was very shy. Tahra made him nervous, although she tried her hardest not to intimidate him. Finally, Dominique was the opposite, she clearly preferred the company of women and spent much of her time talking to Beth and Sakie. Paul was a little worried about her; he hoped the wild card would turn up trumps in the end.

Tahra sidled up to him.

"I think we have a problem," she said.

"I thought the day was running too smoothly," Paul responded.

Tahra held up an empty milk bottle.

"And there's no more in the refrigerator," she revealed.

Paul was relieved it was no great disaster, it was a minor irritation.

"Keep them occupied while I drive down into the village," he said, quietly. "I'll be back before they know it."

He sloped off, picking up a bunch of keys from a hook near the front door. There was the communal Ford Popular borrowed from The Establishment parked on the gravel outside, so he took that and drove the few miles to the nearest village. There was a small grocery store and he parked outside, then dashed in, relieved it was still open.

"Good afternoon," said Albert, the middle aged shop keeper, in a cheerful tone.

"Afternoon," Paul mirrored. "I desperately need two pints of milk."

Albert obliged and put two on the counter, telling him the price. Paul dug into his pocket and pulled out a handful of shillings, thrupenny bits and farthings. He counted out the correct amount and handed it over to Albert, giving the shop keeper a pleasant smile as he did so. Then he paused, still holding the collection of spare coins in his hand.

Without warning, a series of vibrations pulsed through Paul's body, as if he were in the machine. He felt his body become semi-paralysed and for a brief moment, his perception was shifted to the other side of the counter, just behind the shop keeper. Surrounding Albert was a most peculiar rainbow effect, the bulk of which was around the crown of his head and beyond that, he saw himself standing as if captured on photographic film; still and motionless. It was a disturbing sensation to look at oneself, not in the mirror but in the flesh. After a jolt, he was looking at the shop keeper through his own eyes again.

"Are you all right?" Albert asked him, in a kindly and concerned way.

Paul nodded albeit not convincingly and put the spare coins back in his pocket. He looked back and thankfully, the rainbow had disappeared and he was still in his body. He grabbed the milk and made a fast exit, calling out a quick farewell as he left.

It disturbed him so much that he hurried back, dashed into the sitting room and headed straight to Tahra. She took the milk from him, finished a few cups of tea and then noticed the strange expression on his face. He pulled her to one side.

"Has anything weird happened to you just recently… while trying to carry out normal day to day activities?" he asked her.

She shifted uncomfortably on her feet.

"Actually, yes," she replied, "sorry I didn't mention it."

"What happened?" Paul continued.

"Well, I was undergoing a standard remote viewing test at The Institute, but it was different to all the others. It was more real, like I was actually there," her voice got quieter. "And then all of a sudden I was somewhere else. I saw the therianthrope world."

Paul digested what she had just said.

"So, it was like you were in the machine?" he queried.

"I guess so," she said.

"Well, I just… had an out of body experience in the local shop," Paul revealed, "which to say the least, was very vivid and quite disturbing. I also observed a rainbow halo effect around the shop keeper. I can't explain how or why this happened."

Tahra looked thoughtful now.

"Using the machine has side effects," she said.

But Paul was not fazed, in fact, his eyes lit up.

"This is exciting, it's changing us, taking us way beyond what we are!" he said, unable to contain his excitement.

"This is all very well," she said, "but what if we can't control it?"

"Don't be afraid," he reassured her, "this is a gift!"

He re-integrated with the recruits, leaving Tahra to top up the milk jug. It was as she did this that a song drifted over from the radio, one that she'd not heard before as it was a new release by the Beach Boys. She stopped to listen to it and once she heard the chorus, inspiration struck and she dragged Paul over. He listened too and realised why she had requested he listen to it.

"I think we've just found the signature tune for our journeys in the machine," he declared.

"What is that spooky musical instrument they're using?" she asked.

"I believe it's called a Theremin," Sonya interjected.

"I'm going to find a record shop tomorrow," Paul decided.

The song for the machine would therefore be 'Good Vibrations', it was all falling into place now.

He walked off towards the front of the room and tapped a spoon on the side of a cup to gain their attention. The group stopped chattering and gave him their undivided attention.

"Welcome back, my new friends. Now that you've all met each other, I'm going to explain the reason you've been recruited, I'm going to reveal to you what the project is all about, what will fill your life for the next sixteen weeks."

Paul looked over at Tahra and winked, consumed by the fervour and forward momentum of his experiment. She bit her lip, unable to quash the impending feeling of trepidation in her stomach.

The next morning, after the six new recruits had settled into their quarters, Paul called them through two at a time so they could receive their first orientation in the machine. Angelina and Tyrone were the first, he showed them the machine, explained what would happen and that both he and Tahra were on hand to support them throughout. They responded well to the out of body sensation and were keen to go ahead with the project still. Nicholas and Curtis followed, they also had a positive experience inside the machine then lastly, Sonya and Dominique took up the rear with the final slot inside the machine for the day. They had the greatest problems adjusting to the out of body concept but by no means were incapable of meeting the demands placed on them.

The basic orientations continued for another two weeks, with short duration sessions simply working with the base frequency of 7.8 run at forty eight hour intervals but by the end of that time, some were itching to move onto the next stage. Angelina and Tyrone were the first candidates and Tahra took them on their first excursion to the serpent world, a trusted initial destination. Paul was pleased to hear that the machine was just as reliable for non-psychics and was satisfied that the medical report didn't identify any problems. In the subsequent report for the journal, they described the same landscape, the feeling of the whole experience being 'super real' and expressed a desire to repeat the experience. They were a couple of people after Paul's heart, keen to break boundaries, no remonstrations. He couldn't believe Tahra was beginning to get cold feet, of all the people contemplating problems, she seemed the most unlikely.

Nicholas and Curtis were next, leaving their body to the sound of 'Good Vibrations', an appropriate signature tune with an otherworldly feel to it and Tahra towed them to the serpent realm again, as it delivered a good, reliable experience. Paul was satisfied with the follow up reports and was happy that the two men had experienced a positive outcome. They appeared to remain mentally stable after their encounters with the serpents and looking forward to another journey.

Sonya and Dominique fared better than Paul had envisioned, and in fact, it was these two women who seemed most eager for more. He realised it wouldn't be long before they were ready to explore new worlds too.

But the next step was to give Emilie, Beth and Peter an opportunity to accompany Tahra opening up another world, to add to their repertoire. He had been so focused on the new recruits and their initiation into the machines rites that he had almost forgotten The Institute's residents. They were still contracted at their normal research abode so it was necessary to ring through to Max so that Emilie, Beth and Peter could be sent over. Paul outlined the next objective to Tahra that evening as they relaxed on the sofa, she had just finished reading a chapter of a study book for the last year of study although she was, at times, distracted by the television.

"In forty eight hours we'll scout out a new world," he announced. "You can take Emilie with you."

Tahra looked at him, not wanting to scupper his enthusiasm but wishing he wouldn't be so impulsive.

"I was thinking of taking a break from the machine," she said, tentatively.

Paul looked disappointed.

"But I thought you wanted to push the boundaries..." he began.

She took hold of his hand.

"We've already done that, we've achieved so much already. I just think there must come a time to consolidate before we move on."

He looked at her with an expression that was almost pleading with her.

"We're so close here, I'm focused on an expedition with all twelve recruits with you as the guide by February next year. I need everyone to be an old hand at this by then."

Tahra squeezed his hand.

"It will happen, there's no hurry. We don't have to do everything so fast," she persuaded.

Paul sighed, realising it wasn't easy getting her to change her mind.

"I'm... just aware of the project's timescale, I need to show clear and definitive results. I've waited all my life to create a project like this, it could be the success of me... papers published and seminars all round the world, a whole new movement. I can't lose it now."

Tahra looked at the hunger in his eyes, this project was the culmination of his life's work so he would never let up, he would push it to its conclusion for better or worse.

"I love you," he said, "I would never do anything to harm you, you know that. Trust me."

She gave him a hug.

"Okay," she said. "For you, anything."

She turned her attention to the television so that she didn't have to think about the concession she had just made. An episode of 'The Twilight Zone' came on, and she looked at the opening sequence of a spinning door in space, wondering if it was trying to tell her something.

"…Beyond it is another dimension; a dimension of sound, a dimension of sight, a dimension of mind…" *If only they knew,* she thought. "You're moving into a land of both shadow and substance, of things and ideas…" Yes, she agreed, I have just crossed over into 'The Twilight Zone'.

So it was that on 30th November 1966, I acted as inter-dimensional guide (Paul's idea for the job title) for Emilie. Nicholas gave her a kiss for good luck and stayed outside to watch. We sat inside the machine, getting familiar with 'Good Vibrations' as Paul played it in the main house too, and we wondered what to expect this time. At this stage in the project, Paul was curious to see what results would be produced by shifting the harmonics to the higher end of the range so it was difficult to predict what kind of world we would be presented with.

I took hold of her hand and gave it a squeeze, she still seemed somewhat wary of me but I sensed she was beginning to see me as someone who can be trusted. Often I wondered why she had previously disliked me but this day, we were to put on a professional show and our differences aside, whatever they were.

It was easy to tow the consciousness of one person and we soon materialised in yet another world, but one that we soon regretted visiting. This world felt heavy, something akin to the 'pea soup' smogs of London in the fifties. It was as if your consciousness weighed more, if that makes any sense and it was actually quite depressing. It had a bleak and angry look about it; a dark landscape punctuated with pointed towers and large, stark trees of twisted metal, like a dimension based around an old junkyard. Large birds, very much like vultures dominated the sky, they had a huge wingspan and swooped down frequently to feed.

I looked at Emilie and noticed that she already seemed horrified at the awful place we found ourselves in.

"Well, I guess we should explore now we're here," I said.

"I'm not sure if I want to," she responded.

"I wonder if anyone lives in this world," I pondered aloud.

Emilie looked fearful.

"I think there are people here, I can hear their voices inside my head," she said, unhappily.

"What are they saying?" I couldn't help but ask.

She seemed reluctant to tell me.

"You don't want to know," she answered, "but they know we're here."

It took some courage but we focused on one of the towers and our consciousnesses were drawn there instantly. Moving inside, we found some of the entities who resided in this world; foul beings that were disfigured and grotesque, covered in pustules and wizened with age, then there were other quite amorphous creatures who were passive participants in the sick torturous practices we witnessed.

The disfigured creatures would take one of the passive participants, who would prostrate themselves on the floor, willingly I may add. Then the foul beings would press a foot into their back for leverage, take hold of their arms and rip them out of their sockets, listening to their wail of pain with a sense of sheer and utter delight. They would repeat the action with the legs and then proceed to mutilate what was left with a huge machete. There was no artistry involved; it was sheer brute force and butchery.

I pulled Emilie out of there, and I didn't want to see it either. We withdrew to a point on the bleak landscape and found a huge bonfire, which we thought may offer some kind of sanctuary but it was just another form of torture. Beings of different kinds were piled on the fire, still alive and they writhed in agony as they burned. It started to feel like *there was nowhere to turn to.*

Before we knew it, we had no control. We appeared beside one of the twisted metal trees, where we found some creatures bound to it in the most contorted way. Each were suspended by a branch of a tree, which projected through their torso but their limbs had been forced into a series of unnatural positions, and we could see broken bones protruding through their skin. The vulture-like birds would swoop down and pick the flesh from their grotesque wounds.

Near the twisted tree, we saw a metal edifice that stood tall and it had a wheel placed on top which was slowly rotating. Contorted bodies were woven into the spokes of the wheel, again, bones protruding through their skin, faces speared with the spokes of the wheel.

We were pulled away again against our will to see another despicable sight. Inside other towers were scenes of a more sexual nature; creatures were tied down with what looked like barbed wire while the disfigured, wizened creatures mutilated their genitals with broken pieces of glass. Other creatures were bent over while large, hideous objects with jagged edges were inserted into various orifices.

I felt like I could take no more and Emilie was becoming distressed.

One of the disfigured creatures shuffled over to us, he seemed to be a prominent figure in this world for he wore some kind of robe. He surveyed us intently, but this time I was not the focal point, Emilie was.

"Do you sense the pleasure?" it said.

She shook her head.

"Pain is pleasure, torture is ecstasy, and the ripping of flesh is the ultimate euphoria. We know your world and its liking for the pleasure of pain."

It had a horrible, rasping voice and leered at Emilie in a most despicable way.

"Our world is nothing like yours," I interjected.

The creature leered at me.

"Do your people not murder each other in the most hideously pleasurable ways? Do you not torture your own children with discipline and degrading sexual acts? Do leaders not find ways to exterminate the

undesired populations of your country and enjoy the sense of power that genocide brings? Does your church not rule with an iron rod of guilt and martyrdom, while it bleeds the population for money to feed its own power and gratifies its insatiable need for the sexual domination of young innocents?" It snarled with lust. "Our worlds are closer than you can imagine."

It refocused its attention on Emilie.

"The people of your world hear us, we're in their hearts. Some of you are sensitive enough to hear our voices and we can initiate them into the pleasure of pain. They think they're receiving instructions from God." It snarled the last word vehemently. "Our emissaries are increasing in number every day, and there's always room for one more." It stared lustfully at Emilie when speaking these words.

Emilie didn't like what he was inferring, because she could hear the voices of others. She was genuinely frightened and I was out of my comfort zone too, I had no control here, we were being bounced around as if we were attached to a piece of elastic. It seemed like an eternity waiting for the field to power down but finally it did and this monstrosity of a world faded from view.

"You'll return," we heard the rasping voice seethe.

I looked over at Emilie and her head was in her hands, so I grasped at her.

"Are you all right?" I asked.

"I can still hear them, they won't stop!" she responded, distressed.

I held her in my arms, realising we shouldn't have gone to that world.

"Shut them out," I suggested, although I really didn't feel like it was helping.

"They're in my head!" she almost screamed. "Make them stop!"

Nicholas rushed in and took hold of her hands, then made her look him in the eye. Once he did this, she began to calm down.

"You can make them stop," he said, calmly and lovingly. "Imagine a door closing."

"The voices..." she began.

"Are under your control," he added.

Nicholas, I then discovered, was a welcome recruit to the team. That day, he saved Emilie, he was her rock. Once I realised she was going to be all right, I moved over to the cine camera so that the journey could be evidenced.

"I think we just found Hell," I summarised.

I too began to feel like I was reaching my limits, although it came as no surprise to me that my concerns fell on deaf ears. Paul saw Emilie's predicament as a glitch and didn't realise how close she had come to pulling out of the project. He insisted I take Beth and Peter to a new world, as we needed to catalogue as many different realms as we could.

"I couldn't cope with finding another place like the one we just visited," I informed him.

"Yes, it sounded very sadistic and masochistic," he responded.

"Let's make that the last," I insisted, "stick with what we know. There are plenty of worlds worth exploring in more depth."

Paul considered my request.

"One more new world," he persuaded, "and I swear no more after that. For me?"

He kissed me on the lips and reluctantly, I agreed with him.

So a week later, I sat in the machine, holding hands with Beth and Peter. 'Good Vibrations' gave us a send off, and I hoped for a more positive experience.

I swept up the two orbs of light that were Beth and Peter's consciousness and we emerged into a dark and formidable world. The light quality was very artificial and the reason for this was a very odd luminous orb in the sky. It looked like a sun in some ways but it gave out a very eerie light that seemed manufactured. There was a host of machines around it, and either they were planet sized mechanical devices or the star itself was much, much closer than our sun is to planet Earth.

Looking over, I found Beth and Peter had taken a familiar form and they appeared to be bewildered by this world.

"Do you want to view the artificial star?" I asked them.

"Will we be safe up there?" Beth asked.

"Don't worry, you're with me. We need to give a good report on our return," I replied.

I scooped them up and focused my consciousness on the manufactured sun up there and within a moment, we were floating close to one of the machines. I was tempted by a distraction when I realised there were entities inside the machines but I decided instead to focus on the activities at the artificial star first. The machines were penetrating the surface of the sun, which was a kind of silvery liquid that gave off the eerie iridescent light. Inside the sun, explosions were going on, the sound waves of which were very low and booming, reverberating across the deep grey sky. Peter had an idea of what they might be doing.

"They could be mining it," he said, although not a hundred percent certain.

For a split second, I pushed my consciousness inside it to take a look and found an amazing spectacle. At the centre, there was a huge metallic globe with serpents of electricity running across it. It wasn't solid metal, it was liquid like the element inside a thermometer and when I looked closely, I could see it was spinning on itself like a tornado, or vortex. It began to swell and the electric serpents began to pulse faster and faster, it built up to an explosion and then it contracted again. I understood what was going on and returned to Beth and Peter, who were relieved to see me again.

"We thought you'd left us, got kidnapped or something," Beth said.

"I just wanted to confirm what they're doing," I explained, "they're not mining it, they're feeding it, they're operating the star."

Peter was fascinated.

"Such amazing technology!" he said with utter admiration in his voice, "What our governments would do to get their hands on this!"

A worrying thought flickered across my mind but I quelled it so not to spoil the visit.

"Let's scout the rest of this world before the field powers down," I suggested.

We turned away from the artificial sun to survey the mechanised world itself. Beneath us lay a world so completely artifice, it was stunningly *beautiful as well as being so utterly alien and inorganic. As far as the eye could see, there was a vast plain of metal skyscrapers and towers, each swarming with machines. At the top of some of the towers were vast spindles that projected outwards in a spiral and the machines would land and take off from the ends of these. Vast mechanical spiders crawled over the exterior of the buildings but I couldn't tell if they were the entities that lived here or some form of transport.*

Meanwhile, at ground level, there were signs of life of some kind. The street plan, for want of a better world looked like the circuit boards that you might find if you took apart a radio and small machines whizzed along the connecting lines between the different elements that stood proud.

The last thing that stood out lay in the distance, therefore it was something we didn't see immediately, it was a huge elevator. It rose majestically from the ground and projected quite a distance upwards, terminating at some kind of station where machines parked and departed. The shaft of the elevator was thick and contained about four separate lifts, or capsules.

"Let's take a look," I suggested, "see if we can find out what beings live here."

Beth and Peter agreed, feeling more comfortable in this world now.

We moved towards the station and observed some small people moving from the machines to the lift capsules. They were pale skinned, like a whitish grey and about the size of a seven year old child, wore no clothes but had nothing to cover up for there were no discernable sexual organs. I indicated to Beth and Peter that we would follow so I focused on two particular individuals and latched onto them.

The doors of the capsule sealed themselves shut, creating a seamless join and we found ourselves standing in the lift with the entities. It was possible to see them more clearly now; they had huge black eyes, small slits for the nose and barely perceivable ears, which had a sharp tip. Their head was quite broad at the crown and tapered to a point at the chin.

"They look like elves!" Beth exclaimed, in a whisper.

"Ugly ones too," Peter added.

I thought for a moment they were aware of our presence, as it seemed like one of the elves, for want of a better name, looked at us out of the corner of its eye but neither of them turned their head so I assumed we hadn't been detected. We watched as they interacted with a small console set into the wall of the lift capsule. A thick beam of whitish-blue light shot out of it and met a point on the entity's forehead, between where its eyebrows should be. After a few moments, the light beam retracted and the two entities looked at each other as if in silent communication.

Again, it seemed as if one of them was looking at us out of the corner of its eye. It was then that I felt an intense pain in my head, I had never known such agony and I was so consumed by it that I didn't notice whether or not Beth and Peter were affected too. I felt my consciousness sink, as if I were collapsing to the floor and the headache got worse, as there was an awful roaring sound building to a crescendo.

"Please stop," I heard myself beg, not knowing whom I was addressing it to.

I felt as if my head was about to explode and just as I couldn't take it anymore, this world began to fade and I was grateful for the machine powering down. As the interior of the machine came into view, I found myself holding my head in my hands. Paul must have noticed on the monitoring screen as he came rushing in, looking worried. I then realised that Beth and Peter were staring at me, and it was clear they were not in any pain.

"Tahra!" Paul said, urgently.

Slowly, I removed my hands from my head, as the pain was no longer there, just the memory of it. I looked at Paul and the concern in his eyes but I didn't want to worry him any more so I put on a brave smile.

"Are you all right?" he asked.

"Yes, I just met the machine elves," I responded, "and they're not very friendly."

He didn't understand what I meant although Beth did; she got up from her seat and put her arm around you.

"I think our guide here needs a stiff drink," she said, leading me away.

We moved into the main farmhouse and when we entered the

lounge, I was stunned to find Max seated on the sofa, drinking coffee over a newspaper. He began to smile when he saw me but when he noticed that Beth had her arm around me, his expression changed and he put his newspaper down then stood up.

"Everything all right?" he enquired.

"She needs a few minutes," Beth explained.

Max dismissed her with a little wave of his hand and we were both alone in the sitting room. Someone else tried to enter the room but Max insisted he have my undivided attention for the next ten minutes. The room was oddly quiet and I realised he was looking at me unsure if I was okay or not so I stood up straight, smiled politely and asked what he wanted to see me about.

He paused, then reached into his jacket and pulled out a letter.

"It was addressed to me," he began, "but you need to read it."

"Who's it from?" I asked.

"Your parents," he replied.

It suddenly dawned on me that I hadn't written to them all year and I started to feel very guilty, but when I read the letter, I realised I should have maintained contact.

"I failed to keep them updated too," he apologised.

The contents of the letter were not good. They were asking why I hadn't returned home to them because they believed I had finished my course of study and fulfilled the obligations of the agreement made between Max and my father back in September 1962. I held the letter, not knowing how to respond at first. I thought of how angry my father would be feeling and without warning, I found myself standing before my parents.

"Why hasn't Mr Richardson telephoned me?" I heard my father saying, irately, "He will have received the letter by now!"

"He's a busy man," my mother remonstrated, "I'm sure he'll contact you soon."

"It is not right!" he complained. "I have a husband here, ready to marry her on return. She knew what the deal was and Mr Richardson knows that. If I don't hear from him in the next two days, we are flying *out there!"*

I jumped back into my body and found Max clicking his fingers in front of my face.

"Tahra!"

I focused on his face and there was genuine concern there.

"You don't look good," he told me.

For some reason, tears began to roll down my cheeks. He reached out and wiped them away.

"You don't have to go back," he told her, "just say the words and I'll sort this out." Then he added, in a more subdued tone, "You're my best asset, I don't want to lose you."

"Am I just a business asset to you?" I asked, although I don't know why I said it.

He didn't answer affirmative or contradict it, his face was deadpan. Finally, he responded to my question.

"You don't have to go back," he repeated. "You're too valuable."

I gathered myself together and adamantly said, "I don't want to go back. I'm not my father's little Persian princess any more, I'm my mother's daughter, a free spirit; a free English spirit."

Max nodded.

"I'll have my lawyer draw up a legal and binding contract giving you indefinite stay in this country. Even though you were born here, you still need an income and a home to be independent of your family. Is that what you want?"

"Yes," I said with certainty, "this is my home now."

But still the tears didn't stop. He was more concerned now.

"What's wrong? I need to know, you're my responsibility."

Against my deepest principles, I couldn't help but spill the beans.

"The experiments are... challenging," I told him, "it's getting harder to focus, our reality seems less real and the other realities seem more than real. I'm not sure if I can tell which is the one I normally live in anymore. And not all the dimensions are friendly, I was attacked today... and Beth and Peter weren't..."

Max put his hand to my cheek and it felt strange to feel something *genuine from him again.*

"I don't like what I'm hearing, your safety and happiness are paramount. I'm giving you two weeks leave from the project, regardless of what Paul thinks. He's pushing you too hard."

"The project means too much to him…" I began to protest.

"Exactly. It means more to him than your safety. Grab your stuff, I'm taking you back to The Institute for some medical and psychological tests, and plenty of rest. I'll inform him of my decision while you do that."

I did what he asked, because I knew he was right. After five minutes, Max whisked me into his car and I looked out the window to see a helpless Paul punch the door of the barn where the machine was housed. The project would be stalled for two weeks; he couldn't do anything without me, except consolidate the statements and finances. I waved, and he waved back with a sad look in his eyes but it didn't console him. I began to wonder if this was the beginning of the collapse in respect of Paul and Max's friendship.

As we drove away, I saw the face of the machine elf that had attacked me; I saw it in my mind's eye very vividly as if it were stood in front of me. It smiled in a smug kind of way, whilst looking deep into me with those huge, almond black eyes. Why was it so satisfied?

It was strange being in the quiet of The Institute again, with an empty space next to me. On my bedside table, my copy of The Qur'an sat feeling neglected, covered with a thick layer of dust and without any feelings of guilt, I picked it up and placed it in the drawer underneath. I felt more connected to the divine through the machine, and in many ways, I almost felt divine myself.

As I brushed my hair, I looked into the mirror, feeling that my reflection held a deeper truth than the flesh and body I was sometimes trapped in. My eyes were drawn to the slip of paper I had sellotaped there a while back. In large letters I had written the word 'satus' plus its translation from Latin: seed, or origin. We had certainly started something, but would we finish what we had begun?

I fell asleep thinking of Paul, hoping he was all right what with the project being stalled for two weeks, it must have been so frustrating for him. But just because I had two weeks to consolidate what I'd been through in the machine, that didn't ensure a return to normality.

I opened my eyes in the morning to a strange and disturbing sight. At six a.m. it was still twilight, giving the room an otherworldly feel and the silence created a stranger ambience. Through the cast iron pattern at the foot of my bed frame, I could see a greyish figure crouching, its huge almond black eyes staring at me with a glimmer of satisfaction. All I could do was freeze in my bed, a cold chill ran through my veins as I remembered my one and only encounter with these beings.

Yet it did not remain at the foot of my bed. In its crouched position, it scuttled around the bed and began to move closer towards me, those huge black eyes bearing down on me, willing me to meet its gaze. I feared it was going to hurt me again and foolishly, I pulled the bedclothes over my head, as if it would offer some protection. My heart was pounding in my chest and after what seemed like an eternity, I eventually pulled the bedclothes away from my face.

There was no sign of the machine elf so far and I breathed a sigh of relief. These intrusions on my reality were not welcome; would this now be a regular thing? I wasn't sure I could cope if that was the case.

I dressed in some casual clothes and went downstairs to the communal dining area for breakfast. Max sat at a table, with a newspaper and cup of coffee but other than that, the room was empty. I helped myself to some toast and tea and sat down at the table with him.

"How are you feeling today?" he enquired, folding his newspaper and placing it on the table.

"Okay, I guess."

We sat drinking quietly, watching each other, unsure what to say. It was Max who broke the silence.

"So, tell me about the last world that you visited," he prompted.

I shrugged my shoulders.

"Well, it was a machine world populated by small grey people with big, black eyes. They weren't very friendly, I don't know what they did but

my head hurt so much it felt like it was going to explode."

"A machine world?" Max questioned.

"A world of machines and technology, they made an artificial sun and were feeding it energy, or something. There was a spinning orb at the centre of the sun which kept exploding. I'm not a scientist so I can't explain it very well."

"This technology sounds fascinating," Max said, looking very thoughtful.

"I guess. They certainly knew how to attack me without even touching me," I added.

Max was smiling, looking very satisfied.

"This world sounds worth another visit, doesn't it?" he proposed. "After all, this technology could be very useful for our world."

I looked at him, realising his business brain was working overtime.

"But they obviously don't like us, or they wouldn't have attacked me," I countered.

"Well, hopefully we can find ways of sending others in without putting you at risk. You are most certainly not expendable."

I smiled weakly, finished my toast and excused myself. His agenda made me feel uncomfortable. Max's suggestions could potentially change the driving force of the whole project. Would greed poke its grubby finger in the works from now on?

The two weeks passed slowly, interspersed with encounters with The Institute's residents, who were still required to fulfil contracts set up by Max. Each one I saw, I couldn't help but ask about Paul and how things were going in my absence and the responses were pretty much identical; 'he's frustrated', 'we're stuck in limbo until you get back' and 'Paul's not a happy man with the machine sitting idle'.

As I had too much time on my hands, I went shopping as I wasn't short of money. I had spotted a fantastic twenties style cloche hat on Twiggy in a magazine and vowed to find one exactly like that. I also found myself in Kensington that day and couldn't resist popping into the Biba boutique. What an amazing place. It had blacked out windows and a black and gold shop front. Inside it was dark and moody, very art nouveau and the clothes were so cheap. I walked away with two smocks and a skinny fit jumper.

But I couldn't go shopping every day. I was really bored so it was a relief to see everyone. Max realised I was at a loss what to do with my free time so when Emilie stayed over for a few nights, he gave us some money to go out and the use of a chauffeur for the night. Previously, we had not got along well but since the OOBE project involved everyone at The Institute, the relationship between us had developed into one of trust and camaraderie. It was a pleasant change to experience a night out with a woman, it felt liberating to laugh and joke about the shortcomings of men but also discuss the merits of finding one that is special.

"So," I began, tentatively, "is there something going on between you and Nicholas?"

She tried to keep her cool but then burst into a giggle, it was so refreshingly childlike.

"Maybe…" she inferred.

I lowered my voice so the chauffeur couldn't hear.

"Have you had sex with him yet?" I asked, I couldn't help but be inquisitive.

She was a little embarrassed at my directness.

Finally she answered, "I think it's on the cards soon."

I nudged her and gave her a big smile but then a more protective consideration came to mind.

"Make sure you take precautions," I whispered, "you can go on the pill now, you know. I don't think Max would be very pleased if you got pregnant."

At the sound of his name, she looked down at her lap and shifted awkwardly in her seat. I realised then that there was history there, was this the reason she had initially disliked me?

"Was there ever anything between you and Max?" I enquired, surprised that I had never noticed this before.

Emilie looked pained I had asked the question but she did answer, first with a nod.

"He… took me out to restaurants, bought me flowers just like a perfect gentleman, then I went to bed with him and after that… he ignored me," she told me.

The story sounded familiar, so much so it made me uncomfortable. That had so nearly been my tale too, I felt angry at Max and cross with myself for almost falling for it. I had been luckier than Emilie as I had not been another of his conquests. Part of me wanted to ask for further details about her experience of sex with him, I must admit, there was a pang of jealousy but it was overshadowed by the feeling of having had a lucky escape.

"It nearly happened to me too," I revealed, "but I said no, I didn't think he was a good man."

I gave her a hug and decided not to dwell on the subject as she had obviously fallen for him at that time and was hurt by the fact that he had used her, quite callously by the sound of it. Meeting Nicholas was a positive step for her, he seemed quite genuine and she probably wouldn't give herself so easily this time.

We went to the cinema, where we childishly flicked popcorn at the irritating people in front who couldn't keep quiet (I was the instigator of this retaliation). The film was called 'Alfie' and it starred Michael Caine, ironically it was about a man who had sex with lots of women. We concluded the character was like Max, except Alfie was kinder and more innocent. After this, we went to a small and friendly restaurant for a meal with wine (copious amounts) to finish the night. Then we were chauffeured back to The Institute, where we almost fell out of the car onto the street. I could see the curtain of the communal dining room twitch and we stumbled through the door, which was opened by Max.

"I take it you had a good evening, ladies," he said, amused by the sight of two normally serious and focused women now happily inebriated.

I gave Max a dirty look, which confused him (did it not occur to him that women compare notes?) and guided Emilie up the stairs to her room, she was less steady than me. Max watched us stumble upstairs sadly, he said nothing and retreated to another part of the house. Needless to say, I slept well.

In the morning, I was faced with Max in the dining room at breakfast while Emilie was being sick upstairs (I felt guilty about that, I obviously had a higher alcohol tolerance). He was a little out of joint after I had given him a dirty look last night but he said nothing about it. In retrospect, I realised that it had been a nice gesture to pay for us to go out and that I hadn't shown any appreciation.

"Thank you for the night out," I said.

He smiled and looked relieved.

"My pleasure," he responded.

I didn't linger, as soon as I finished breakfast I returned to my room, via a knock on Emilie's door to check she was okay. I spent most of my day reading or talking to Emilie, after she had recovered. By the evening, the alcohol had been metabolised from my body and my head was clearer. Laying on my bed, I counted down to my return to Paul, there were five days left and I missed him, I craved the excitement of the journeys in the machine. If anything, my two weeks leave had had the reverse effect, it made me realise what an important part of my life Paul and the project was.

Because I was thinking of him, I found my consciousness standing in the kitchen of the farmhouse. Paul was preparing his evening meal, alone and I could see a newspaper on the table, showing a completed crossword. He looked disenchanted with the whole two week leave thing, I could tell by the expression on his face. I stood very close to him and wished I could hug him, so with my consciousness I reached out and touched his cheek.

Strangely, he jumped a little and looked round, as if he expected someone to be there. I was stunned, was this just a coincidence? To test the theory, I placed my 'hand' on his back, gently stroking it and I was amazed to find Paul respond as if I'd done this with my physical body.

"Tahra?" *he asked, softly.*

I wished I could answer; this was a surprising development in my remote viewing capabilities. I had already found the remote viewing experience more vivid and now, in this moment, I also felt as if I was actually there in the kitchen. But this time, I had touched someone and made them aware of my presence, this was a new and empowering feeling.

Because I couldn't vocalise my thoughts, I retreated, knowing that I would be with him again in just under a week. As I pulled back, I passed through a chair and the strangest thing happened, it moved as if I had actually walked into it, making a scraping noise on the terracotta tiles. At this point, I stopped and looked at Paul's reaction, he was watching the chair intently. I wondered if I had imagined it, so I passed through the chair again and it responded in the same way, scraping along the floor. Paul almost dropped his glass of wine.

"Who's there?" he called out. "Is that you, Tahra?"

If only I could respond. I pulled myself back into my body and my eyes snapped open, a big smile on my face. I could remote view and affect the environment now. The side effects of the machine were starting to pay dividends. A sense of power and awe came over me, and I began to realise this was the beginning of something else.

21

Seventy Five

Tahra returned to the farmhouse in time for Christmas. The first thing she did was to hug Paul, unseen by Max's driver of course and he was just as happy to see her again. It also meant the project was up and running once more now that the missing link was back. To celebrate her return, he gathered all twelve recruits in the sitting room, where they were all delighted she was back. Tahra felt like the most popular person in the room.

For a while, everyone wanted a piece of her but when the fuss subsided, she was able to speak to Paul with openness and honesty.

"These two weeks have made me realise what's important," she declared.

Paul put his arm around her and kissed her on the forehead.

"Same here, you don't appreciate what you have until it's gone," he responded.

"This project is my reason for being, and you're a part of that reason too," she continued.

"I don't mean to put you in difficult situations," he began to explain, "but the nature of what we're doing is not without risks. I realise that you're right though, it is happening all too quick. It's easy for me, on the outside, harder for you to enter a different reality every few days. I can slow this down, just say so, you come first, not the project."

He kissed her on the lips this time.

"Earlier in the project, I had an encounter at Jupiter, remember?" He nodded so she continued. "I wrote the word 'satus' on a piece of paper and sellotaped it to my mirror at The

Institute. This truly is the beginning of an exciting journey, we can change the world. I came to realise that I just need courage to see this through, something important is about to happen and I'm not going to stand in the way. I'll do whatever's necessary."

Paul hugged her tightly.

"That means the world to me," he said.

With that, he released her and gathered all twelve recruits together, inviting them to take a seat. He hushed them and started to address them as a whole.

"I have an announcement to make," he declared. "Although the project has been on hiatus for two weeks, it is now very much ready to go again. I propose three major expeditions; one with all six of the residents of The Institute, another with all six new recruits and the third with all twelve together. On each of these expeditions, we will scout out a new world. We'll begin just after the New Year, culminating on the 21st February 1967."

Tahra nodded to agree and Paul smiled with delight. Project OOBE was back with a vengeance. He allowed them to discuss the next stage and while they did so, he pulled Tahra to one side as there was something he was dying to ask.

"About a week ago, I had a strange experience in the kitchen of the farmhouse," he began, looking to see what her response would be.

"And what experience was that?" she asked, touching his lips with her finger. "Did you actually cook something for once?"

Paul feigned indignity.

"No, my dear Tahra, I felt your presence, it was if you were touching me. Where you there, Tahra? Did you remote view me?"

There was a playful amusement in his tone of voice. She kissed him and smiled.

"Yes I did, because I missed you."

"How did you do it, make me feel as if you were touching me?" he asked, very curious. "It was so real."

Tahra was at a loss for an answer.

"I don't know," she whispered, "but since I've used the machine on a regular basis, I've changed, I'm... enhanced."

"Did you move the chair?" he continued to press.

"Yes, I believe I did."

"I've never known a remote viewer who could affect the environment," he said. "This really is something else, isn't it? It's the machine, I wonder if these are permanent changes. I need to take measurements of the bio-electromagnetic field..."

She interrupted him with a kiss.

"You were right," she declared, "it is exciting, it is a gift. Who can argue with that?"

The twelve recruits celebrated Christmas with Paul and Tahra and the dinner required 'one helluva turkey' as Tyrone put it. It was such a simple pleasure to sit around the huge farmhouse pine table (it was a little crowded) enjoying good food, wine and conversation. Opportunities to socialise outside of the project itself were rare and it was good to remember that they were all human beings with their own lives, foibles and social commentaries to discuss. Paul had bought a small gift for each of his recruits, commemorative cufflinks for the men with the number 7.8 created out of solid silver and similar hairpins for the ladies but with some pretty gemstones set into it, including one for Tahra too. They were a small token of gratitude.

"I'll wear this always," she said, "it will always remind me of what we achieved together."

"But it's not the only gift I have for you," he added, producing three more.

She opened them, beginning with the soft, floppy one, finding a beautiful red silk scarf inside.

"It reminded me of you," Paul explained, "your passion, your fire."

"And it will always remind me of the passion I feel, for my life, the project, for you..."

He tied it loosely around her neck and she proceeded to open the other two, which were boxes containing a delicate necklace and a ring. The necklace was nine carat gold and the ring was set with a ruby, Tahra loved them both and put them on immediately, then gave Paul a passionate kiss.

"I love all my gifts, thank you."

She then pulled out two gifts and passed them over to Paul, who opened them eagerly. There was a solid gold ring with an engraving of an Egyptian ankh on it and the other gift was a framed photograph of all twelve recruits, plus Paul and Tahra. He loved both presents and gave her a hug.

"This has got to be the most memorable Christmas I've had," he said.

New Year was also celebrated in much the same manner and with the same people. It had an intimacy about it, coupled with the feeling that 1967 was destined to be a special year indeed. Max was absent as he always hosted his own party every New Year and he never bothered to ask any members of the OOBE party, they'd formed their own clique now. They saw in the New Year with twelve bottles of wine, the chinking of glasses and some drunken foolery, which progressed from a pleasant merriness to something a little more raucous; it was allowed, they all deserved it.

Curtis took care of the music and he was happy to spend much of his time playing records, with some assistance from Sonya as she was into contemporary music as well as classical. They played music from earlier in the year, a little reminiscent of the summer such as 'Sunny Afternoon' by the Kinks and 'Summer in the City' by the Lovin' Spoonfuls. Most partygoers recognised the songs and as the night got underway, there was a whole line of them singing 'Reach Out, I'll Be There' by the Four Tops and many other hits. It wasn't long before requests were coming in and Paul's insistence was 'Good Vibrations'.

Nicholas and Emilie were becoming rather intimate to the

sounds of 'I'm Into Something Good' by Herman's Hermits, with a sing-a-long in the background. In his semi-drunken state, he felt inclined to join in too, placing his arms around her waist and moving in time to the music, somewhat.

"There is indeed something special on my mind," he agreed, touching her affectionately on the nose.

Emilie joined in for the last line of the chorus and they performed a duet.

"Somethin' tells me I'm into something' good!"

It wasn't the most tuneful rendition to have as a romantic come on, if anything, Nicholas and Emilie could only laugh. They kissed with passion, feeling less inhibited due to the inebriation.

"You've made me a very happy woman," Emilie told him.

Nicholas grasped her closer.

"You've made me a very happy man," he told her in return.

Paul watched with amusement, noticing how even the shyest of residents, such as Sakie were joining in. Tahra, Angelina and Tyrone were the most boisterous singers, with Oscar competing well and Dominique dancing seductively. Sonya joined them in the end, unable to take a back seat any longer.

Tahra sidled up to Paul, put her arms around his neck and her pelvis close to his, then she swayed in a semi-drunken come seductive manner. The soft dulcet tones of Nancy Sinatra singing 'These Boots Were Made for Walking' rang out, with accompaniment from the OOBE quintet and Tahra decided to get playful.

"Would you like my boots to walk all over you?" she asked, smiling and teasing as she sent a little shiver of energy up his spine.

"Mmmm," he murmured in her ear, "I hope you're not just going to be a cocktease."

Curtis noticed the sexual chemistry between Paul and Tahra, Nicholas and Emilie and Angelina and Tyrone and thought it appropriate to play The Kinks. At the sound of the tune, the three couples laughed as Curtis gave them a wink. Nicholas and Tyrone struck up their own individual accompaniment, although Paul stopped shy of singing; he simply moved his body in time with Tahra's.

"I'm inclined to agree with the lyrics," Paul said, running his hands up and down her body. "You certainly have got me going."

"And you really got me, too," Tahra laughed.

Tahra moved her body against Paul, brushing her lips against his but not giving anything away and then she pulled away and paused in the doorway. He laughed, realising he was supposed to chase her and relented. She paused at the bottom of the stairs, standing quite provocatively and he sauntered up to her.

"I hope you're not wearing your best underwear," he laughed, "because I'm going to rip them off."

Tahra allowed him to touch her then moved away, backing up the stairs one at a time. As she did so, she peeled off the smock she was wearing, looking at him all the time she was doing that. Paul laughed and began to follow her, also beginning to undress. She reached the bedroom and waited in the doorway and then as he approached, she allowed him to pick her up and throw her onto the bed.

The clothes came off in a hurry; Paul pulled off her underwear with his teeth and facilitated a quick, urgent entry. Elsewhere, in the guest barn, Nicholas had taken Emilie back to his room and Tyrone and Angelina had disappeared too. While Tahra cried out in a spontaneous finale, Emilie rode Nicholas to an ecstatic mutual orgasm while Angelina was crouched on all fours in the throes of a particularly intense climax. It was the perfect accompaniment to the twelve chimes of Big Ben coming over the radio.

Everyone felt rough the next day. Breakfast was not on the menu, glasses of water, alka seltzer and headache pills were instead. But by the evening, all agreed it was a much needed relief from the demands of the project and they settled down to an evening of quiet chatter, cups of tea and a small buffet of nibbles. It would be back to business soon.

And sure enough, when January 6th arrived, it was time to get down to business again. The previous night, everyone had congregated in the sitting room, ready to embark on the next major step. They had all watched the news together and had viewed in horror as Donald Campbell's attempt to beat his own water speed record of 276.33mph had ended in tragedy. As his turbojet hydroplane, 'Bluebird' approached 300mph on Coniston Water in Cumbria, the nose had lifted from the water and the hydroplane had performed a backward somersault, killing him.

Paul felt somewhat subdued.

"So much for wanting to push the boundaries," he said, quietly.

He hoped it was not an omen for project OOBE.

In the morning, it was time to climb back inside the machine again. The six residents of The Institute were first in line for a major step in the evolution of project OOBE. It would be a real challenge for Tahra, as so far she hadn't towed more than two consciousnesses so it would require some intense focusing and concentration.

All seven of them sat inside the machine; Tahra, George, Oscar, Sakie, Beth, Peter and Emilie, holding hands in a line and looking at the six empty chairs that would soon be filled. Emilie looked nervous, since her last journey in the machine had been a difficult one but Tahra had deliberately sat next to her and she gave her hand a reassuring squeeze. There was silence for a while then they heard the needle being placed onto a record, followed by the opening bars of 'Good Vibrations'. Tahra realised the song was beginning to get tiresome; why did he have to play it repeatedly around the house too?

The occupants of the machine felt the buzzing and tingling course through their nervous systems, the paralysis of their physical bodies and the separation of their consciousnesses then they were thrown headlong into the void. Tahra could clearly see six points of light and she visualised a net in which to scoop them up. But the world they found themselves in was strangely grey and featureless.

They emerged into a blank canvas, albeit one that felt charged with cerebral energy. All that could be seen was a likeness of each other, and each one of them looked beleaguered.

"Are we between worlds?" George asked. "This place is like limbo."

Tahra shrugged.

"Maybe we're meant to paint our own picture in this world," she guessed.

That turned out to be remarkably astute.

In the distance, or perhaps just the furthest most point of their vision as there was no way of gauging perspective, they could see a dot. It was reminiscent of the first impression made by an etch-a-sketch, a point that began to move towards them and which left a grey trail behind it. The point began to increase in size, becoming a fuzzy blur as it got closer.

"Do you all see that?" Peter queried.

They nodded and watched as it drew nearer and nearer, taking a more definite form the more they focused on it.

"It's… a samurai warrior," Sakie said, in disbelief.

The figure was clearly Japanese with ethnically correct eyes and a thin moustache typical of a samurai warrior, although there was something odd about his eyes as the irises were ebony black. He was clad in visually accurate armour, complete with helmet and he wielded a sword, raising it above his head. Sakie wasn't sure whether he would attack or not.

"I don't see that," Beth disagreed, "it looks like a crawling baby."

A small child, swathed in a nappy was crawling towards her but it was not a picture of innocence, its face was decidedly alien with greyish skin and huge black almond eyes set into a human facial shape. Rather than turn away, she found herself magnetically drawn to it, however repulsive it actually looked.

"Strange, it looks more like… a sexy Jamaican lady in a bikini," Oscar said, incredulously.

Indeed, there was a beautiful girl with the deepest brown skin, full sensuous lips and eyes which were ebony black. She wore a dark purple bikini and walked with a languorous gait, Oscar was entranced even though she didn't look completely human.

"No," Emilie interjected, "there are more people than one."

The original fuzzy haze they'd all seen separated. She saw a crowd of amorphous people, quite clone-like with identical features; greyish skin and black almond eyes and they walked around as if in some kind of daze. Each person had a little cloud attached to their head via a string, within it were displayed their thoughts, their internal conversations, their hopes and fears.

"I beg to differ again," George put in, "they're a platoon of soldiers."

He saw a multitude of people like Emilie did but he saw them as soldiers, complete with uniform, helmets and bayonets as if they were ready to leave their trenches for an assault over the top. But, like the other images as seen by the others, the soldiers had ebony black eyes which gave them an unearthly appearance.

"I see my dead mother," Peter added sadly.

She was a once sturdy woman who appeared to Peter at the age at which she had died, in her mid-fifties. Her grey hair was swept up into a chignon, she walked with the aid of a stick and again, she had ebony black eyes.

Tahra looked closely and found a recognisable figure. One she knew all too well.

"What do you see?" Peter asked her.

The figure was male, he looked angry and he was waving a copy of the Qur'an at her. Maybe this reflected the repressed guilt of placing the holy book into a drawer, to be out of sight and out of mind. She couldn't help but apply a simple Freudian analysis.

"I see my father," she said, awkwardly.

It was therefore established that they all perceived something different.

"We see what we want to see in this world," Peter pondered aloud.

"No," Tahra disagreed, "not what we want to see, what our subconscious is trying to tell us."

Sakie's samurai warrior progressed towards her with his sword and then stopped in front of her with it poised as if to strike. Beth's infant crawled up to her feet and raised a hand, willing her to pick it up while Oscar's femme fatale stood in front of him, untying her bikini. Emilie's thought bubble people began to amble towards her, George's soldiers formed a firing squad with guns at the ready and Peter's dead mother held out a piece of paper. Tahra tried not to look as her father thrust a copy of the Qur'an into her face.

It was at that point that the field powered down and the interior of the machine came into view again. Whatever their sub consciousnesses were trying to tell them would have to wait until another time.

Paul opened the hatch with an excited and expectant expression on his face.

"Well?" he asked.

Tahra nodded, hiding the guilty feeling that was a residue of her father's image.

"I can tow six consciousnesses," she declared.

Paul hugged her, clearly delighted. They moved over to the cine camera and Paul gave an introduction.

"The first major expedition of the OOBE project just came nearer to reality," he declared.

The 21st February drew closer, which was to be the day when Tahra would guide and tow all twelve recruits. In the meantime, Paul decided to focus on the six non-psychic recruits to ensure they were ready to press forward and consolidate their experiences so far. The date for their journey with Tahra was set for the 30th January so in the preceding week, he interviewed them one by one.

Angelina and Tyrone were coping very well, having been lucky with their experiences, as were Nicholas and Curtis who both appreciated the profound nature of what they were doing. Sonya and Dominique were surprisingly buoyant considering neither had ever taken any hallucinogenic drugs.

He asked each of them an important question.

"Since using the machine, have you had any unusual experiences in your day to day life?"

Angelina and Tyrone shrugged their shoulders, finding it odd he should ask that question.

"No," Tyrone responded on both their behalf, "if anything, everyday life is a little too dull in comparison."

Nicholas considered the same question carefully.

"No experiences as such," he responded, "but I feel honoured in my everyday life to be a part of this."

Curtis also reported a null effect.

"Nope," he said, "nothing outside of what I experience in the machine."

Sonya did feel some effect, however.

"Musically I feel more inspired," she declared, wondering if that was what he meant.

Dominique also reported positive feelings.

"I feel stronger as a person," she told Paul.

At the end of the interview day, he collated their statements and concluded that maybe they hadn't been exposed enough to the machine's field to feel any after effects, whereas Tahra was the most likely candidate to notice any changes as she was exposed to the field every time the machine was powered up. He himself had been exposed several times, which could explain the spontaneous out of body experience and odd hue he saw around the shopkeeper that day but since he had not been in the machine for a while, those side effects had subsided. To be sure of the conclusions he had reached, he also asked the same question to the residents of The Institute.

Oscar responded, "Well, I must admit, I do think my remote viewing skills have sharpened. I find it a lot easier and the visuals are clearer during tests at The Institute."

Paul nodded, so perhaps Tahra was right, the field enhanced their already existing skills.

George reported a similar effect.

"You know, now you're asking, my remote viewing tests are more lucid," he told Paul.

Sakie wasn't sure if anything had changed.

"Maybe," was all she said.

Emilie considered Paul's question carefully.

"When I hear people's thoughts, they are much clearer," she answered.

Beth and Peter, however, hadn't noticed anything out of the ordinary.

"Seems like business as usual to me," she said.

"Nothing to report," Peter told him.

There was more of an after effect with the residents of The Institute as opposed to the six non psychics, presumably because they were more sensitive. More importantly, there were no serious problems to be aware of; everybody was psychologically strong and happy with the project. A moderate exposure to the field seemed to have some temporary side effects, whereas frequent contact with the field appeared to have more far reaching effects.

With this information, Paul was happy to proceed with the next major journey.

The preceding night, the twelve recruits plus Paul and Tahra relaxed in the sitting room, chatting with the television on in the background. A piece of news came on regarding the space race, so Paul reached over and turned it up.

"Three NASA astronauts died today in a fire that swept through the Command and Service Module of Apollo 1. Ed White, Gus Grissom and Roger Chaffee boarded the capsule for a routine test, including a full launch rehearsal at 13:00 hours local time yesterday and a series of problems with the oxygen supply and communications halted the countdown throughout the day. At 18:31 hours, there was a call indicating there was a fire in the cockpit, but despite attempts to escape the capsule and efforts by the ground crew to open the hatch, the astronauts perished in the fire."

Paul watched with sadness as the news cut to a report from the United States, which concluded with a quote of Gus Grissom, who was interviewed three weeks previously.

"If we die, do not mourn for us. This is a risky business we're in and we accept those risks. The space programme is too valuable to this country to be halted for too long if a disaster should ever happen."

They all held a two minute silence as a mark of respect, not only for the dead but in recognition of the common mission they all shared; to break boundaries and explore what's out there. Paul only hoped it wasn't another omen for the OOBE project.

Seven of us sat in the machine on the 30th January; me, Sonya and Dominique on my right and left, plus Curtis, Nicholas, Tyrone and Angelina arranged in a semi circle around me. We heard the opening bars of 'Good Vibrations' and I decided there and then it would be the last time it would assault our eardrums. There were only so many times we could listen to the song. We held hands as it was the custom now and allowed the machine to release the bindings of our consciousness to the physical body.

We emerged into yet another new world and I began to wonder how many different realms there were out there. The predominant colours of this place were blue and red, but very vivid; the red glowed with a blood-like passion that seared with energy and conviction whereas the blue dazzled the senses with its electric coolness and luminosity. Red and blue corpuscles floating by, pulsing and rippling as if they were liquid electricity while a vast network of what appeared to be red and blue electrical cabling glowed and pulsed as if high voltage power ran through them.

Around us were the walls of what appeared to be some kind of tunnel, it was constructed of a fabric that was composed of tessellated hexagons, very much like the grid I had seen before. In the centre of each hexagon was a small jewel-like object, which glowed either red or blue.

In the background was a pervading yet reassuring noise, like a whooshing sound that had a steady rhythm and both the cabling and the corpuscles danced to the beat of this tune. There was a flow to the fabric of space we found ourselves in and it was easy to drift on this current, it felt safe and warm.

"It's so very beautiful," Dominique said, softly but we could all hear.

"That sound is like music," Sonya added, "it has a beat and tone to it."

"You know what?" Nicholas realised, "this is not so much a world, but a body. We're inside some kind of entity."

It occurred to me that he was correct; we were inside some vast body. The electrical cabling was the arterial and venous network and the corpuscles were the blood cells, it was all so clear now.

"Let's locate the rest of the organs then, or whatever body parts it has," I suggested.

They all agreed and I focused my consciousness on a point further ahead, where the arterial vessels seemed to converge. Where they converged, they formed a much larger vessel and this joined up with another set of vessels, creating a more complex network of arteries. I guided my six travellers towards a far point where there seemed to be a terminus, a final point of convergence in the arterial network. What we saw was heavenly.

In front of us was the heart of this entity, a glowing red hothouse of energy that filled our vision and our souls with its divine current. It had the appearance of silken meat draped with elegance like theatrical curtains and in places, stretched taut, displaying a radiant sheen. Intermeshed with the silken meat were what appeared to be gargoyle-like creatures or statues, their human-like bodies immersed within the tautness of the silken meat. They moved sinuously, engaged in some kind of euphoric rapture, making love at the heart of this being. On closer inspection, we could see vessels wrapped around the outside of this vast heart, entangled within the outermost parts of the silken meat and it was these vessels that carried flashes of light. Within and behind the silken meat folds, we could also see a tougher substance like the walls of the tunnel, composed of tessellated hexagons that glowed red and in between them, little glistening jewels.

"This would make a fantastic blueprint for a robot," Curtis commented, "a being made of electricity, circuits and a physical body. Maybe that's what this is."

"Whatever it is," Angelina added, "it sure is dynamite."

"Can we find the brain?" Curtis asked.

I saw no reason why not so I tried to picture a central thinking point in my mind, where the nervous system would terminate. We were drawn to a gangly white network of superfine threads, like angel hair but pulsing with flashes of light. The individual fibres were intertwined, wrapped around each other and there were some loose ends that trailed like a wispy fray. Again, there was some sort of rhythm or beat that the threads or nerves swayed to.

We followed the threads and they converged in an immense cavern, like the inside of a great sphere. In here, we felt like insignificant specks. There were great spinning discs that flashed with white light and from each of these discs tendrils stretched out like the branches of a tree, connecting each of these discs together into some kind of network. Further tendrils extended from the peripheral discs to the inner surface of the great cavern, the tips of which embedded themselves into the fabric itself. The tendrils were illuminated and flickered in pulses of light.

"This is amazing," Curtis commented, "I don't think humans could ever build something so vast and beautiful."

"Did anyone build this, though?" Nicholas questioned. "Or did it create itself?"

"I think we need to take a look at this entity from the outside," I decided.

I withdrew our consciousnesses out as far as I could, which took us through its vascular system and through subtle layers of energy akin to some kind of electrical skin. The entity came into view and she was truly divine.

Her lilac skin was iridescent and sparkled with tiny flashes of electricity while her face itself was heart shaped, with lips of deepest blue and the merest hint of a nose. She was human-like in many ways, particularly in the overall shape of her body and she was not clothed, so it was possible to perceive her breasts and something akin to sexual organs of energy between her legs. Her hair was white and dazzlingly so, it fanned out around her head as if she was underwater but the individual fibres reached out to the fabric of space around her, which on closer inspection, looked very much like the hexagonal tiling again. The ends of her hair embedded themselves into the hexagonal tiled grid, as if they had roots. At the moment, her eyes were closed, as if she was sleeping.

She was the only entity here in this dimension, and, perhaps, she was the entire dimension.

"That's one hot electric chick," Tyrone commented, in his inimitable style.

"Do you think she's dreaming?" Angelina wondered aloud.

At this point, she opened her eyes. I don't know if she saw us but she stared straight ahead and we could see that her eyes were deepest black. When I looked closer, I was stunned to see galaxies and stars within her eyes and I felt magnetically drawn to that cosmos within her.

"What the..." *I heard a few of us say.*

I felt compelled to let my consciousness be pulled into her eyes, that vast space within a vast entity, an immense goddess. Where would it take me?

But neither I, nor anyone else got to find out as the field powered down and we found ourselves staring at the interior of the machine. More than anything, I wanted to return and then it occurred to me, this was an ideal destination for the first major expedition with all twelve recruits. We would visit the goddess, we would find out what lay in her cosmos.

All the training and practice was due to culminate on the 21st February and as everyone had worked so hard, he gave everyone two weeks off. After the visit to the goddess, there was a period of consolidation where Paul went over the statements to begin preparing a final report and also to unanimously decide where the first major expedition would go, so the two week breather was useful to gather his thoughts. He and Tahra went over the previous destinations and ruled out the ones which had caused unpleasant experiences, although Tahra was keen to push the goddess realm as a front contender.

"I'm going to put it to a vote," he said, "between the goddess realm and the therianthrope realm, seeing as you've made several excursions each to the serpent world and emotion world."

Tahra nodded, that was fair, but she'd still fight to persuade the others on the merits of the goddess realm.

There was an interlude before the return of the recruits, and as it was Valentine's Day, the two of them took a break, making a journey to Scotland where they spent a few nights in the Glen Nevis area. They occupied their time walking and exploring, admiring waterfalls and eating fine food. Tahra thought the snow around Ben Nevis was pretty, although she didn't fancy trekking to the top.

Once back at the farmhouse, they assembled all the recruits together around the table. Paul stood at the foot of the table and introduced the proceedings.

"Welcome back from your break, I hope you feel refreshed and ready to continue," he began. "We are now at the threshold of a series of major expeditions involving all twelve of you as a team."

There were a few murmurs of excitement and Paul waited for them to subside before continuing.

"There are two possible destinations for the first of these expeditions," he continued, "the therianthrope world and the goddess world."

Tahra picked up the thread.

"Some of you may be familiar with the therianthrope world; it is a visually stunning world and very friendly, worthy of further exploration. However, there is an amazing realm inhabited by a vast goddess, she is incredibly beautiful, as some of you are aware of and she appears to be some kind of doorway to the cosmos, or another universe even. I believe we should visit this world first and foremost."

Paul interjected.

"Bear in mind that the therianthrope world has proven itself to be a vast storehouse of knowledge, which allows our findings to be put to some practical use. So, those of you who want to explore the therianthrope realm raise your hand."

Oscar and George raised their hand, but they were the only ones. It appeared to be a foregone conclusion.

"I assume the rest of you would like to visit the goddess, then," Paul said.

Ten heads nodded in unison. The goddess realm it would be.

The next day, Paul received a telephone call from Max, which was no surprise. After the initial pleasantries and enquiries concerning well being, it was down to business.

"If the upcoming voyage is successful," Max began, "there are a number of funding bodies very interested in taking this forward."

Paul sat up straight in his chair.

"What funding bodies?" he enquired.

"You don't need to know who these funding bodies are, just that they will ensure your project runs for another three years," Max pointed out.

Paul was torn; would his project be hijacked by some major corporation but would that be worth it to continue OOBE for another three years? Now the pressure was on.

"That would be excellent," Paul responded. "My deepest desire is to revive the knowledge and understanding of these other realities, bring them to the awareness of humanity again."

There was a pause on the other end of the line and then finally Max spoke.

"I would strongly advise against progressing down that route," Paul was advised.

"What?"

"The funding bodies in question will not want to share this knowledge and understanding. Their money buys exclusivity."

Paul was crestfallen, he sought to reveal the deeper truths of the cosmos, not line the pockets of the elite few. Maybe something could be negotiated as he needed the funding as much as the profound outcome.

"You need to give this some serious thought. These are the people I answer to, even if I do not deal with every one of them personally. They have followed this project every step of the way and will be looking at the results with anticipation."

Paul agreed to give it some thought and put the phone down, after Max had confirmed his arrival time to oversee the next trip in the machine. The outcome of this next voyage was crucial and he realised how badly he needed to impress Max.

Throughout the last week, Paul ran a series of maintenance checks on the machine, including the calibration for the oscillator and the rotating electromagnetic field. The field was operated at sixty five percent and then he ran it at full strength, just to be sure it was as robust as ever. He tested the monitors and the ECGs and EEGs and he checked the controls in the booth. Everything was working fine.

Before they knew it, the morning of the 20th February arrived, which was the day before the first major expedition with all twelve recruits. Paul awoke much earlier than he normally would, gave Tahra a kiss on the cheek and drove to the village shop to pick up a newspaper and more milk. He ate breakfast while reading and it took his mind off the major expedition the next day as he was jangling with nerves even though he had tested every single piece of equipment.

It was such a vitally important voyage and all he could do was worry. There was an inordinate amount of pressure on him to make this fruitful, both for the continued funding of the project but also to fulfil Max's expectations. Would a field strength of sixty five percent be enough to release the binding of thirteen consciousnesses from their bodies? It was clear the current setting for the field intensity was medically and psychologically safe, now he was giving serious consideration to increasing the percentage to seventy five. Surely it could do no harm and bolster the experience for the participants?

Upstairs, Tahra opened her eyes when the first rays of the sun breached the horizon, which was at five minutes past seven. The hazy early morning sun was not the only thing she noticed. She opened her eyes to a strange and disturbing sight. Sat on the end of her bed was one of the capuchin monkeys from the therianthrope realm, with a startlingly human face staring at her. Its green eyes watched her and she lay frozen in her bed, not knowing how to respond. As it did not move and it was disconcerting to be stared at constantly, she sat up, picked up her pillow and threw it at the monkey. It reacted to the pillow and jumped off the bed, screeching and disappearing through the doorway to the small ensuite bathroom.

Tahra sat still for a while, trying to comprehend the sudden reappearance of these other-worldly beings in her life. There had been a lull for a while, now they were back despite it being nearly three weeks since she last used the machine. Then she wondered whether the monkey was still in the bathroom, or whether it had disappeared back to its own realm.

She swung her legs round, got out of the bed and tentatively tiptoed into the bathroom, although why she trod so delicately, she didn't know. The door was half open and she pushed it wide, peering inside. There was no monkey to be seen but she still sensed the presence of something not of this world. She noticed the shower curtain was drawn and wondered if the monkey was hiding behind it, so she pulled it across, expecting to find the hybrid creature but there was nothing, just an empty cast iron bath with a lone rubber duck sitting near the plug. She breathed a sigh of relief.

While she was in the bathroom, she decided to take a shower so turned the faucets and a gush of water shot out. She drew the curtain and began to get undressed, hanging her silky nightdress on the brass hook by the door. Needing to check for signs of tiredness, she looked in the mirror and was startled to see another entity behind her in the reflection.

It was the ibis headed therianthrope, who looked totally out of place in the bathroom. He looked at her kindly, via her reflection and spoke.

"It is time," he simply said.

Tahra had a sinking feeling in the pit of her stomach.

"Time for what?" she questioned.

But he was gone.

She paused at the mirror, realising that there was something on the horizon, something out of her hands, something that had already been decided, something significant.

Tahra joined Paul at the table in the kitchen after her shower, with a towel still wrapped around her head. For some reason, she couldn't tell him about the visitation she had just received but he assumed her odd expression was just nerves before the first major expedition and he poured her a cup of coffee and set a few slices of toast in front of her. She smiled and nibbled the toast, finding no great appetite.

"Max is overseeing this expedition," Paul informed her.

Tahra shifted uncomfortably in her seat.

"He won't arrive until tomorrow morning though," he added, "so it won't disturb our… nocturnal activities."

She smiled, relieved he wasn't staying over as his presence here at the farmhouse still had the potential to rattle her somewhat.

"I'm considering a change to the operation of the machine too," he announced.

Tahra wasn't sure what to think.

"What are you proposing?" she asked.

"To compensate for having twelve bodies in there, plus you, I'd like to increase the intensity of the field to seventy five percent."

Tahra was surprised.

"Has the machine run at that level before?" she asked.

Paul nodded.

"I ran it at a hundred percent and although there was a lot of vibration, everything looked fine in there so it can take seventy five. That extra ten percent may act as a boost, be sure we impress Max and the funding bodies."

Tahra raised her eyebrows.

"Was this Max's idea really?" she asked.

"No," he answered, quickly. "I've been giving it some serious thought. It feels right but I wanted to run it by you first."

"I see no reason why not," she said.

"Good. We run at seventy five percent then."

The day was spent liaising with the recruits, testing the equipment again and generally trying to relax. But by early evening, Paul and Tahra were still quite highly strung. The outcome of this expedition would really cement the success of the OOBE project and Max's attendance signified that he was assessing its merits to date and its potential for a broader based programme of exploration. While the other recruits relaxed in their quarters, Paul and Tahra lay on the sofa in front of the television.

"I'm not really concentrating," Tahra said, "you may as well switch it off."

They lay together in a state of reflection and anticipation instead. Later, Paul popped his head round the door at the guest outbuildings to wish everyone good luck, before he and Tahra retired upstairs.

They lay under the covers, wide awake, unable to think of anything else but the next day's events.

"I can't sleep," Paul complained, "I keep wondering if something will go wrong, or whether the outcome will be mind blowing. The field will be powered for forty five minutes this time, the longest yet and if we impress Max, the project will be funded for another three years."

Tahra looked over at him and smiled.

"I know of something we can do to relax," she said, and reached over with her hand to arouse him.

He laughed, enjoying her touch and then quickly rolled on top of her.

"I'm the luckiest goddamn man on this planet," he declared, and using his lips, he worked his way down her body.

After he had buried his head between her legs, she inverted her body and reciprocated with her mouth, then sat astride him, riding him to a satisfying orgasm. They were then able to fall into a pleasant and deep sleep, ready for OOBE's first major expedition.

They both awoke the next morning with a tingle of anticipation; this was the day, this was the moment they had worked towards the instant Paul began building the machine. The test was due to begin at 13:00 hours and all recruits congregated in the kitchen for breakfast. Morale was high, no one wanted to back out and there was general excitement concerning a trip to the goddess realm.

Max arrived at 11:00, two hours clear of the start time as he wanted a debrief on the progress made so far and the schedule for the day. Tahra watched as they disappeared into the study, detecting an odd underlying tension in the air and she was left to keep the recruits motivated and confident in the meantime. The two men emerged an hour later, their expressions giving little away and Tahra couldn't help but wonder what they'd been discussing. Paul gave her a surreptitious wink while Max mustered a quick cursory glance in her direction, finding she had returned to her conversation with Emile and Nicholas.

Both Paul and Max ran some preliminary tests on the machine and the monitoring equipment, detecting no faults so Tahra and the recruits were sent for. They filtered into the machine room one at a time, having just finished a light lunch and Tahra arranged them in a circle before they climbed in.

"Let us take a moment to reflect how far we've come," she began, "consider the worlds we have seen, contemplate how these experiences have altered our perspective, our concept of reality. We stand at the threshold of a much deeper and greater programme of exploration, we will make further and much more meaningful contact with beings that inhabit these other worlds, we are treading where our ancestors walked on a regular basis. Maybe we will find worlds they have never encountered before. This is what I believe to be 'satus', the origin, the beginning of humanity's journey. Now let's go and visit the goddess."

Their heads were bowed slightly, showing respect and reverence for the beings of these worlds and the ancestors who walked with the Gods. They remained like this momentarily while Tahra spoke and when she had finished, they looked at each other, feeling fired up both emotionally and physically.

All twelve climbed into the machine, filling the seats in a clockwise direction and Tahra stood on the outside, looking over at Paul and Max who were stood in the control booth. She nodded that she was ready, took a deep breath and climbed inside, taking up the last empty seat. The recruits looked towards her and she smiled, taking hold of the hands of Beth and Peter, who sat on her right and left. The others followed suite and held hands, forming a tightly knit circle.

Paul entered the machine and hooked up the monitoring equipment, placing electrodes on their heads to measure their brain waves and also on their chest to ensure their heart rates were within accepted norms. He then retreated to the booth, where Max watched the proceedings, arms folded and finger on chin.

"Are you sure the visit to this world will yield the results I desire?" he asked.

"I'm positive the goddess will impart some knowledge," Paul answered.

"I was thinking of some useable technology, in particular," Max responded. "Only this will ensure the viability of the project in terms of sustained funding."

Paul nodded.

"I understand. But you need to give us time, this is only the beginning."

He turned his attention back to the people inside the machine.

"Are you ready?" Paul spoke into the microphone.

A chorus of 'yes' greeted him through the speakers. He hunted around for the machine's signature song, leaving the recruits wondering what the delay was. After a short while, he gave his apologies.

"Um, I can't find the record I usually play," he said. "Does anyone know where I last put 'Good Vibrations'?"

Tahra tried to look nonchalant but found it hard to suppress a giggle. The twelve recruits acknowledged her guilt and couldn't help but smile; who wasn't sick of 'Good Vibrations'?

"Just power up the field!" they called out.

Paul shrugged, a little nonplussed that the machine's theme song had mysteriously disappeared, especially on such an important day but he booted up the sequence of frequencies and powered up the field.

Looking at the incremental settings for the pulsed electromagnetic field, he set the intensity to seventy five percent as agreed with Tahra and also with Max. Both had given it the all clear and as Max had said, he was the project manager and was therefore responsible for such decisions.

Inside the machine, the occupants felt the customary buzzing and tingling throughout their bodies and the familiar feeling of paralysis. Tahra closed her eyes and immediately became aware of twelve manifestations of consciousness, but this time, there was something more substantial about them she couldn't put her finger on. She visualised scooping them up and focused on the destination the frequencies were opening up.

The transition between worlds was much more vivid this time. They found themselves, temporarily in some kind of nether world, the fabric of which consisted of bright orange outlines of tessellated hexagons. Tahra looked out at the twelve consciousnesses she was guiding and was astounded to find vibrant human energy forms staring back at her. They each had a body composed of pure energy, and there were concentrations of it around the brain and heart plus channels of electricity flowing like a vascular system of light. Each consciousness was a different colour; pure green or blue, or composites with pinks and lilacs, or yellows and orange together like semi-mixed luminous paint. She looked down at her own form, finding a composite of deep red and purple.

"What is this?" she thought, aloud.

"This ain't ever happened before," Angelina added.

But before the world of the goddess could come into view, Tahra felt herself being pulled away with a force too strong to resist. The last sight of the twelve recruits was of their energy forms scattering in different directions. She was losing them.

She tried to call out, but there was nothing she could do about it.

There was a blur and the hexagonal grid stretched and distorted before her eyes, then she found herself in a world that was familiar. She stood in a world where the sky was full of planets and radiant orbs, very much like suns but more rarefied. It was a world where the stars themselves seemed to communicate with each other, the land and water sparkled with an unknown iridescent substance and the air itself shimmered with a kind of white noise, full of dancing and vibrating molecules of energy. Tahra had been here before; it was the first dimension she had unwittingly visited. The memory of that encounter sparked a realisation.

One of the molecules of energy emerged from the background of noise and took a recognisable form. An entity stood before her in a blazing white effigy of iridescence, the molecules of which cycled through different colours. Again, there were no features on its face but burning impressions where the eyes should be and the appearance of something akin to wings were folded up on its back. It conveyed a sense of brilliance and power that was both awe inspiring and humbling.

"It is time," the angel-like entity spoke.

A feeling of dread came over Tahra, coupled with a feeling of helplessness, she was trapped here.

Meanwhile, back in the control booth, Paul quickly became aware something was wrong. The machine was behaving anomalously, displaying some unusual vibrations and behaviour. This had not happened during testing and he couldn't understand why there was a problem. He checked the readouts for the EEGs of the recruits and Tahra, finding them to be highly erratic and the heart rate tracings were also elevated.

"This has never happened before," Paul said, clearly confused.

Max was also deeply concerned as there were seven of his people in there, and his best people at that.

Paul looked at the dial and began to regret his impetuous decision. He'd never run the field at anything above sixty five percent with anyone in it. Why had he risked the unknown by increasing ten percent, on this day of all others? Why had he let money be the driving factor behind this particular voyage in the machine? Then he looked over at the monitor and his heart sank when all he could see on the screen was static.

"Visuals are down," he said, drawing Max's attention to the

monitoring screen. "I can't see what's happening."

It had all gone crazy in there and Paul was frustrated because he couldn't understand what was happening and why. What difference could that extra ten percent make? This hadn't happened in the tests during the past week and he had run the field at full strength.

"Cut the field," Max said, without hesitation.

"I'm going in to check on them myself," Paul said.

"Just cut the field," Max repeated.

Paul could only think of what was happening inside the machine. He rushed to the hatch and used the emergency release to pop it open and was stunned by what he saw. The field had produced a shimmering haze, Paul reached out to touch it and found it had a strong electro-static feel. He could barely see Tahra and the twelve recruits, something was happening to their bodies at a molecular level, it was causing a state of semi-invisibility. Max could see through the doorway from the control booth, he too saw the shimmering, electro-static field and its effects on the humans inside. All Paul could think about was Tahra, he stepped inside the machine against his better judgment and as soon as he had done so, he regretted it. He felt his consciousness dragged from his body, a sense of physical paralysis and complete and utter powerlessness. Paul could neither help himself or the others.

Meanwhile, Tahra was faced with the angel-like entity. She looked up at the worlds she could see, and noticed how silvery snakes wormed their way across the sky, how the stars flashed in a cyclical manner and how the multiple planets rotated slowly upon their axis. Then she looked to the iridescent landscape she found herself in.

"Where is this?" she asked, hoping for a clearer answer this time.

The entity spoke and again, no lips moved, its voice rang clear in her head.

"You have been brought to the quantum fire level," it

explained, "a place only a highly advanced traveller can find. You now exist at the most fundamental level of dark matter in the universe," it went on to explain.

"If it is so difficult to find, then why am I here?" she queried.

"Because I brought you here," the entity pointed out.

"Why?" she continued.

"Because it is time," the entity clarified.

"What is it time for?" Tahra pressed, realising the inevitable was approaching.

"Satus," came the reply.

"But we have already begun the journey," she pointed out.

The response was patient yet superior at the same time.

"You haven't yet tapped the full meaning of this word, for it is more than a word."

"Are you going to help me understand?" she asked.

"Yes, for there is something you need to do," it continued.

"What if I don't want to do it?" she countered.

"You have free will, I will not force you as it is not in my nature. But I believe that you will consent, and you will receive something in return to help you with this task."

Tahra felt more reassured by the fact she had free will.

"Tell me what this task is."

"I will show you," it said.

With that, it reached out with its arm and plunged its white fiery limb into her manifestation of consciousness, that dark red and purple powerhouse of energy. She looked down and found that she was glowing much brighter, but whatever the entity was doing was extremely painful, like being split in two. In her mind's eye, she saw a whole sequence of events, a clear plan, a purpose for her existence and on seeing it, she almost cried.

"Will you help?" the entity asked.

Tahra nodded. As soon as she had consented, the pain increased in intensity to the point where she couldn't bear it. She screamed, hoping this temporary distress would be compensated for by the task that she would carry out. The pain was so great that she lost sight of the world she stood in and all she could see was the grid, the tessellated hexagons, followed by blackness. The blackness was illuminated by a single point of light in the distance and in the background, she could sense a reassuring presence at least. But she had consented now, there was no turning back.

Back in the machine, Paul was as incapacitated as the others. At a molecular level, their physical forms were inconsistent and cycled through brief moments of solidity before they dissolved into a state of semi-invisibility again.

Then, without warning, the field powered down, the lights went out and the emergency lighting came on. Max had killed the power at the main switch, being the only person capable of decisive action. Paul found himself lain on the floor of the machine and was relieved to see that everyone had returned to a state of solidity again. He looked up at Tahra and found her staring back at him. All he could think about was the guilt at what he had just put her through and struggled to stand up. He succeeded and without thinking of the secrecy of their relationship, he took her in his arms and kissed her.

"I'm sorry, I'm sorry," was all he could say. "I made a mistake."

Tahra was breathing heavily and held onto him tightly. How could she explain to him what had just happened? She pulled away and looked him in the eye, tearful.

"I'm sorry too," she burst out, "I lost them, I'm so sorry, I lost them."

Paul looked puzzled, holding her face in his hands then he realised what she meant. He looked over at the twelve recruits and found, unlike Tahra, they had not come round. They were frozen, as if they were sleeping with their eyes open; it was a most disturbing sight. Paul was lost for words but finally he spoke.

"But why did you return while they didn't?" he had to ask.

"I was pulled to the quantum fire level, the world of the angels," she explained. "One of them set me a task."

Paul brushed her tears away.

"And what did it want you to do?" he asked.

She sobbed, unable to stop the flow of tears now.

"I can't remember, but all I do know is that I agreed to it," she replied.

Paul couldn't help but be afraid for her and without thinking, he kissed her again but more passionately this time and then rested his forehead on hers.

"I think I saw a whole chain of events," she explained, pulling back to speak to him again. "And even though I don't remember them consciously, I clearly recall feeling this sense of … awe, that there's a deeper truth to what the organised religions of this world have been telling us, something to do with the primeval number. It's… something beautiful, I wish I could remember."

She rose from her seat and couldn't help but notice Max stood in the doorway of the machine with his arms tightly folded, glaring at the both of them.

"Can I interrupt this tender little moment," he began, with a clear vehemence in his voice, "to ask what the *fuck* has happened to my people?"

Paul looked over at the twelve recruits guiltily, for they were still frozen and had not returned to their bodies. Tahra locked eyes with Max, realising that her relationship with Paul was in the open now and his accusing stare sent a chill through her blood.

"It's my fault," Tahra explained, "I lost them."

Max interjected, "No, lay the blame on the ineptitude of the project manager." He gestured to Paul. "He exposed you to a field strength of seventy five percent."

Paul simply lowered his eyes in an admonition of his mistake. Tahra looked over at the recruits.

"I've got to go back," she declared. "I've got to go back and find them."

Paul felt a sense of dread overtake him.

"Judging by the erratic readouts on their EEGs," he said,

"they could be anywhere."

"I don't care," she said, firmly, "they were my responsibility too. I've got to go back; I can't leave them in their... nightmares."

She moved over to the recruits, still shaken and touched each of their pairs of interlocked hands, wondering what world they were trapped in. Some of those worlds were very nasty indeed.

Paul stood up, facing Max's intolerance of his failure.

"You know," Max began, "I've seen something like this happen before."

"This project has been attempted before?" he queried, incredulously.

"No, not this exact same project," Max went on to explain. "There was an experiment conducted twenty three years ago, well into the Second World War. A powerful electromagnetic field was applied to a United States destroyer class ship in an attempt to make it radar invisible. The ship became invisible to the naked eye, and the subsequent reports suggested the ship had materialised briefly in another dimension."

"What was the project?" Paul asked, realising Max was jogging a memory, something from one of his lectures...

"It has generally been referred to as the Philadelphia Experiment," Max answered, the vehemence still apparent in his voice. "And do you know what became of the men that returned from that other dimension?"

Paul looked over at the frozen recruits, wondering if they'd ever return to their bodies and then looked back at Max, who was going to tell him the answer anyway.

Max took a step closer towards Paul and said succinctly, but clearly, "They went insane."

With that, Max stepped away from the doorway and disappeared from sight, leaving Paul to survey the mess he had made. Tahra put an arm around him and rested her head on his shoulder.

"Nobody ever said it was going to be easy," she concluded.

Bibliography

Berlitz, Charles (1979). *The Philadelphia Experiment*. Souvenir Press.
Blavatsky, H.P. (1888). *The Secret Doctrine: Vol I – Cosmogenesis*. The Theosophical Publishing Company.
Braden, Gregg (2007). *The Divine Matrix: Bridging Time, Space, Miracles, and Belief*. Hay House.
Capra, Fritjof (1975). *The Tao of Physics*. Fontana Paperbacks.
Chester-Lambert, Alison (2009). *Starry Messengers*. Midlands School of Astrology.
Dunn, Christopher (1988). *The Giza Power Plant: Technologies of Ancient Egypt*. Bear and Company.
Feeney, Paul (2009). *A 1950s Childhood: From Tin Baths to Bread and Dripping*. The History Press.
Feeney, Paul (2010). *A 1960s Childhood: From Thunderbirds to Beatlemania*. The History Press.
Goswami, Amit Ph.D. (2001). *Physics of the Soul: The Quantum Book of Living, Dying, Reincarnation and Immortality*. Hampton Roads.
Hancock, Graham (2005). *Supernatural*. Arrow Books.
Harrison, Ian (2005). *Where were you when... Remembering 180 extraordinary events*. Collins & Brown.
Huxley, Aldous (1954). *The Doors of Perception*. Vintage Classics, Random House.
Lemesurier, Peter (1981). *The Armageddon Script: The Power of Prophecy & The Secret Life of Jesus*. Element.
Lescott, James (2007). *The Forties in Pictures*. Parragon Books Ltd.
Lescott, James (2007). *The Fifties in Pictures*. Parragon Books Ltd.
Lescott, James (2007). *The Sixties in Pictures*. Parragon Books Ltd.
Strassman, Rick M.D. (2001). *DMT: The Spirit Molecule*. Park Street Press.
Talbot, Michael (1981). *Mysticism and the New Physics*. Penguin Group.

Plus a myriad of web sites that unfortunately I didn't keep track of, many thanks to all of them.

Made in the USA
Charleston, SC
10 August 2011